F.R.E.A.K.S.
FEDERAL RESPONSE ENFORCEMENT AGAINST KID SEX

FREQUENCY HUNTER IS NOT YOUR AVERAGE "JUST RELEASED FROM PRISON" EX CON. No, Hunter has patiently waited for the day he would be free to pursue and take down the rat who betrayed him.

Also a computer genius, there isn't anything Frequency Hunter can't make a computer do. And after he is released, he realizes that his money worm hack has gone astray and brought him a gift of undeniable sin. Forced to act when he uncovers an underground crime syndicate that thrives on the abuse of children, Hunter reunites with his tried and true comrades, each with their own unique talents, and begins the chase that will either save the lives of innocent children, or cost him and his team their own.

Read the exciting sci-fi thriller
by Ronnie "Ronn Ramm" Johnson
guaranteed to make you ask:

"What If?"

F.R.E.A.K.S. FEDERAL RESPONSE ENFORCEMENT AGAINST KID SEX

RONNIE D. JOHNSON

RONNIE D. JOHNSON

F.R.E.A.K.S.

Federal Response Enforcement
Against Kid Sex

Ronnie D. Johnson

F.R.E.A.K.S.

Extravagant Publishing, LLC is registered in the United States Patent and Trademark Office.

All **Extravagant Publication, LLC** Titles, Imprints and Distributed Lines are available at special quantity discounts for bulk purchases for sales promotions, premiums, fund-raising and educational or institutional use.

Imprint: *Extravagant Publishing, LLC*
www.Extravagantpublicationllc.com

ISBN 978-0-578-47701-5

I dedicate this book to my daughter and son,

Eboni and Ronnie Jr.

To the unconditional support of my mother Lillie M. and our entire

family, thank you.

Acknowledgments

I like to thank all of my families for being there for me. All the friends, who have waited so long for the book to be in print. I like to thank   Mr. Tony Peay and Mr. Rodney Kimble for sticking by me even in the tough times. And a special thanks to Case Management Inc- Memphis , ANH Narco and Nucor Steel Mill/Memphis for embracing me into their working family.

Without God none of this is possible, but now I will use this gift to educate others.

Georgia Thomas - editor

Table of Contents

Warning:

This book contains graphic language, explicit sexual acts, detailed violence against children, rape and murder.

Disclaimer:

The views expressed in this publication do not reflect the views of the author or Extravagant Publishing, LLC.

Chapter 1

The Gathering

Just like the start of any other day, Frequency Hunter sat up on his bed looking out a window wondering "What's next?" He had done this every day for the last 24 months. Being incarcerated had its ups and downs, but he made it through. Today was day 730, the end. He had had so many things in mind to do when this day came, but now, it was just about getting out. He had not planned to look for a job, because he knew that certain people owed him money that would facilitate his life for a while. He had come through the prison system untouched physically, but mentally scarred. He knew he had lost a whole lot of business. With this federal prison record hanging over him, he knew people would not want to hire him. But, that was not going to rain on his parade. He could put all of that on the back burner for now, and concentrate on picking up where he'd left off in life.

As he got up and took a stretch, he heard his number called overhead. "Prisoner # 453568-076 come to admin for release." Frequency Hunter is the name he was given by his father, but that didn't have anything to do with prison. Everybody is given a number in prison and that's what you are called as long as you're in the system.

As Frequency got up he was called by one of the cellmates named BDB. BDB was short for Big Dewayne Brown. BDB was serving a 12 year sentence for assault and attempted murder. He admitted to the judge that he would have killed his girl and the guy he caught her in bed with, if it wasn't for his children coming in the house when the fight started. He would have gotten a lesser sentence if he hadn't tried to attack the dude and his ex in the courtroom. To make matters worse he broke the bailiff's nose during the courthouse scuffle. BDB came and asked Frequency a question. He wanted to know if Freq, the nickname his cellmates started calling him, would help him get his lawn business started once he got out. Freq said, "Sure, you have my word." Freq got the journal that he'd started writing when he got to the prison camp. He put on a pair of warm-up pants and a white t-shirt. Then he headed to the administrative building for dismissal.

The building seemed to light up as Freq took his walk to freedom. He could hear the other cellmates screaming at him about how not to come back, but that had no bearing on the one thing that had kept him going. He had not touched a computer in two years. He had been put on notice by the head guard that he was not to touch any computers in the facility. Frequency Hunter's reputation as one of the best computer experts had gotten him banned from any contact with a computer of any kind. The withdrawal from this was what made his stay terrible. He could deal with the booty macks knocking off the weak boys. He could deal with the drug dealers and the junkies. But having to serve time without being able to touch a computer was just plain torture!

Now as he signed his papers to submit to one last urine test, he thought about how he had survived these years without any kind of computer. The countless computer magazines he had read. The numerous messages passed from one inmate to him about how his computer system was being tampered with by police officials.

They kept trying to find the lockout codes he'd used to freeze the police payroll system. They finally gave up and tried to cut all electrical systems going into his place. Freq laughed thinking about this now. Especially since he'd set up a solar powered backup system and put it into the foundation of his neighbor's house.

Thinking about that made him laugh again as he was told he could put on the   civilian clothes sent to him from outside. Freq then put on a starched pair of Old Navy khaki pants and then a light green short sleeve shirt. He put on a pair of George socks with a pair of Timberland boots that matched his shirt perfectly. And now for the jewelry, Freq put on his signature diamond encrusted pinky ring, his one-carat earrings, and his lizard skin belt. He felt great putting on clothes that made him feel as fresh as a newborn baby. Frequency promised himself that he was not coming back to this place as he stepped out into the waiting room. As soon as he stepped out he heard the sounds of "freedom."

The guard escorted him to the main exit and said "Hope not to see you later!" Freq laughed as he shook the guard's hand and said likewise. Frequency then stepped outside to the fresh smells and sounds of freedom.

He moved to the designated pickup area and looked at his watch. He programmed his computer system with the designated instructions and so far, everything he had planned was flawless. He had linked a private account to pay all of his bills while he was incarcerated. He'd even scheduled a limo service to pick him up on this day and, as he looked up from his watch, just down the street a limo was pulling up. Frequency laughed to himself as he thought of the worm program he set loose on the day he arrived at the prison. The program had been running for two years. How many saps had it hit for five dollars each? It was as simple as five times one million. Now it was time for him to cash in.

It took nothing less than sheer brilliance to make the program work. And the victims would never know! The program was written to find the elite of the American gene pool. The lawyers, doctors, CEOs, politicians, and judges were easy targets. He set it to bypass any person making under a six figure salary. Frequency did not want to touch any blue collar workers since he came from a blue collar family himself.

Frequency snapped back to reality when the limo driver called his name.

"Excuse me. Are you Frequency Hunter?" she asked.

"Yes, I am," he said.

She told him her name was Erica and she would be his driver. Frequency asked her if she received any instruction for this pickup. She said her contact was a computer generated message that scheduled the pickup and made the payment by phone with a credit card. Erica said she was supposed to take him to a post office box in Memphis. Then she handed Frequency the post office box key. She said there was champagne in the cooler and they should be leaving.

Frequency got into the limo and popped the bottle of champagne. He took a swallow and let out a yell. He turned on the TV and watched some HGTV. He was amazed at how clear the picture was. He asked Erica about it and was told that it was an LCD that was hooked up to mobile satellite. Frequency remembered reading about it in one of his magazines. Now he was experiencing it for the first time. Today would be a day full of firsts for him.

He would have asked for a computer but he knew he only needed to touch one: the one at his house that was making him proud. The limo then pulled up and parked at the post office. Frequency took the key and went inside. He went straight to the post office boxes and looked for box number 45. Frequency found the box and put the key in to open it. He looked inside and there were four envelopes.

He opened the first one and found his driver's license, social security card, and ATM card inside. The second one held the keys to his house and automobile. The third envelope had one thousand dollars in various bills. Frequency knew what he had to do so he opened the fourth envelope. It was empty. Now things were about to get ugly. He had been through hell just so he could be cheated out of his cut of a very big piece of cash.

He turned and found himself face to chest with one humongous dude. Frequency side stepped and said, "Excuse me."

The guy looked at him and asked, "You just open box 45?"

Frequency said "Yeah what's up?"

The dude said he had a message for him. Frequency stepped back just in case dude was going to try something stupid.

The dude said, "My name is James. I'm here to deliver a message from Mr. White. He needs for you to forget about the 4th envelope for right now.

He told Frequency that he should forget about the debt and go about enjoying being home from prison. And after James passed the message, he stepped to Frequency and made a threatening statement. He told Frequency that if he did not agree with Mr. White's plan he would be dealt with severely.

Frequency looked at James and said, "Look I have no beef with you or Mr. White. Tell him I've done my time like a true soldier and I'll deal with the loss in my own way.

James looked confused and asked, "What does that mean?"

Frequency answered, "I just want to go home and get a bath. I'll holler Latah." Frequency walked out of the post office and got back in the limo. Erica, the driver, asked Frequency if everything ok and he said everything was fine. Frequency already knew he had to put his guard up and be ready for anything. Mr. White had basically robbed him then dared him to try and get what was owed him.

Frequency knew he could not out power him. He had too much manpower and even more firepower. Frequency had to hit him where it hurt the most -- his bank account. Frequency already had the information he needed to knock his socks off, but he had to do it with finesse.

He was so deep in thought about his loss that something very vital had not crossed his mind. It had been a very, very long time since he'd gotten laid. All of a sudden the beautiful scent of Erica's perfume hit his nose. That's all his manhood needed to come to life. He had briefly looked at his driver earlier, but that was when he had money on his mind. Now that the business was taken care of, it was time to fulfill the rest.

Frequency turned down the TV and asked, "What's that perfume you're wearing?" "Eternity for Women," she said. That was some sweet smell and it had Frequency thinking some adventurous thoughts. He was just about to ask Erica another question when she pulled around a corner and threw him into his seat.

"Whoa!" Frequency hollered.

Erica said, "Sorry, but we're being followed.

Frequency sat down and then buckled up. Ericka might have been a small lady, but she knew how to handle that big limo. It was a Cadillac limo, but you would've thought it was a super charged imported sport scar the way she drove it.

"Hold on," she said, "I'm going to try something."

Frequency heard a screech of tires and then felt a hard jolt as she jumped the median strip, then turned down a side street. The maneuver worked. She lost them. Erica then headed to Frequency's home.

Now that they had arrived at their destination, Frequency was puzzled about the car chase. He had not done anything to anyone or left any unpaid debts. He decided to get rid of his company before starting to work on the worm program. Frequency invited Erica in for drinks. She declined since she was still on duty. She said that if it was okay she could come back after work. Frequency told her that would be cool and it would give him time to clean up. Erica got into the car and then pulled off.   Frequency pulled out the keys to his house and went inside. The house came to life with lights and sounds. The security system asked for deactivation codes. Frequency smiled and said, "Virago." The alarm shut off and the remote panel came into view from behind the wall. Frequency went to the panel and gave the voice command that brought his old system to life.

The house was dusty and old smelling. He could tell nobody has been inside since he'd left for prison. He went into every room looking to see if everything was still the way he'd left it. The security program worked flawlessly. He could not believe nobody had figured out how to access the system. The patent for it alone would make him millions.

He then went into the room that carried the most significance for him. The computer room was in the basement of his home. It was the most uninhabitable space in the house, but it had the best climate control. Freq touched the keyboard and the system came to life. It had "what is the password" on the keyboard screen. He put in 'freaky' and the room lit up with lights from the 32 inch CRT on the wall. It displayed Freq.'s favorite picture. Money with black leaders on the faces of the bills. Freq then went to work looking for the worm.

As soon as he typed in the 2048 bit encrypted commands a map of the world appeared on the screen. The worm was enrooted to an offshore account. This confused the hell out of Frequency. The program was only supposed to run locally. Something major had gone wrong, and it was too late to turn back. Freq went into action. He set up multiple dump sites for the worm. He could not bring him home 'because that would bring the Feds straight to him.

Freq then pulled up all his existing accounts so he could assess his financial status. As each account appeared on the screen, it gave Freq a new outlook on life. Out of the ten accounts he checked first, five had reported 50,000 dollars and counting. No looking for work. No worrying about where his next meal was coming from. Now it was time to get cleaned up. Freq set the computer into voice activation mode. The computer made the announcement, "CMAX is online. How may I help you?"

Freq said, "Start up the environmental system and run the cleaning program."

CMAX said, "Environmental system has been activated and the cleaning systems are GO."

Freq then told CMAX to run him some bath water. The bath program was initialized, and CMAX started to rundown the system status for Frequency. CMAX told him city power had been restored exactly one week ago, no intruder had been able to breach the house defense system, and the patents for the systems and five other packages had been sent to the patent office as ordered. Then CMAX informed him that it was bringing the security camera system online. Freq turned toward the 32 inch CRT and watched as all cameras around his home came to life. He watched as the robot vacuum and duster went to their jobs cleaning the house. The lawn mower was moving in the precise pattern as was written in the program. Frequency left CMAX in charge because he was going to relax in the tub. CMAX acknowledged and said voice command had been initiated throughout the house. If he needed anything all he had to do was ask.

Frequency just smiled and went to the bathroom to take that long awaited bath. As he stepped into the bathroom it was like he was in a spa retreat. Everything was clean and in place. The Jacuzzi was bubbling and the temperature was just the way he liked it. Frequency took off his clothes and immediately jumped into the tub. It had been years in the making but it was well worth it. The Jacuzzi jets were hitting the right spots and Frequency was starting to relax.

CMAX came online to let him know a car was approaching. Freq then remembered he told the limo driver to come back for drinks. Then CMAX said there was one man in the car. Freq told CMAX to activate the bathroom monitor. Freq had never seen this guy before.   As his visitor was getting out of his car Freq caught a glimpse of a badge. It was a stinging reminder that he was still on probation. His sentence was for two years with two years of probation.

Frequency told CMAX to let the guy in and instruct him to have a seat. Mack Master got out of his vehicle and readied himself for his initial visit with another parolee. He had no idea what type of person Frequency Hunter was, but his file made him out to be a high level computer geek. Mack grabbed his usual supplies -- urine cup, notepad and appointment papers. He looked around the house and noted that the lawn was cut and the house was neat. He stepped onto the porch and rang the doorbell.

CMAX asked, "Who is it?"

"Mack Master, US Probation Officer here to see Frequency Hunter." CMAX initiated the 'door open' command and announced Mr. Master was entering the premises. Mack Master was hesitant to enter but his curiosity got the best of him. CMAX then directed Mr. Master to have a seat as Mr. Hunter would be in shortly.

Frequency was now dressed and ready to discuss the criteria of his probationary obligation. Frequency walked out and introduced himself to Mr. Master. Mr. Master was taken aback by how Frequency looked. First of all, he did not look like the computer geek that his file made him out to be. Second, he dressed like the CEO of a dot.com company. Third, he had the build of a lightweight boxer. They shook hands and Mr. Master went into his usual spill.

He said, "Mr. Hunter you must provide a urine sample at least three times within the first 90 days of your probation. You'll be fine as long as the results come back negative. Anything after that is at my discretion."

Frequency indicated he was fine with that. Mr. Master then asked if Frequency drank, used drugs, had any weapons on the premises, or had already violated any rules of his probation. Of course Frequency said no.

"I do not drink, or use drugs. I have no use for any weapons and I have not left my home since I got out." Freq replied.

Mr. Master said he knew the answers to all the questions, but it was part of his script. Frequency asked if he needed any more information. Mr. Master said there was one last question: how long before Frequency started looking for a job?

"I will abide by the rules of my probation and get a job within the next 30 days. Frequency told him.

Mr. Master gave Frequency a 'yeah right' look. "Don't get your hopes up Mr. Hunter. You're an ex-felon now. A lot of potential employers look down upon that.

Frequency laughed and said, "Mr. Master I am quite sure you are aware of my expertise with computers."

Mr. Master said, "I have read of your many computer accomplishments."

Frequency added, "Here is a small demonstration of my abilities. Would you like something to drink?"

Mr. Master said, "You know I can't accept any gifts from parolees."

Frequency smiled and said, "How 'bout a bottle of water?

Mr. Master nodded ok.

So Frequency called to CMAX that Mr. Master would like bottle water. "One bottle water coming up," CMAX replied, and a little robot came out with a bottle of Ozark spring water. Mr. Master was amazed.

Frequency said, "CMAX has over a one million Artificial Intelligence commands written into its program."

Mr. Master then said, "Mr. Hunter I don't believe you will have any problem getting a job and being a productive citizen again."

Frequency said, "It's money in the bank."

Mr. Master told him he was leaving and that he would be popping in from time to time. Frequency made it clear that it would not be a problem. He would instruct CMAX to be as hospitable as possible. Mr. Master then headed for the door.

After he got into his car and drove away he thought to himself, "That was one extraordinary man. Maybe I won't have to be as tough as I would on my other parolees."

Frequency then commanded CMAX to give him the status on the WORM. CMAX replied that the worm had entered a state of immobility. It picked up some files that might be very informational. Frequency told CMAX to bring the information up on the bedroom LCD. CMAX acknowledged his command and it was done.

Frequency started going over the information. Most of it was a bunch of egotistical socialites in some kind of internet social club. All of the members had titles of wealth and status. They were Judges, lawyers, doctors, ministers, priests, CEOs, master level engineers. The initial membership fee alone was $50,000 dollars. Some were women, but most of them were men. They had moved the club around from state to state each time in an undisclosed location. They all had to go through connected people to get to the meeting place. Then there was a file that had a super encryption rate of 512bits. What was in this file that made such a high encryption rate necessary? Frequency told CMAX he was going to the basement to crack this file. CMAX reminded Frequency that the WORM had not yet stopped.

Frequency thought about it as he got to the basement computers' main keyboard. He touched the proximity reader, and then gave the command "FREAKY." The keyboard lit up and brought the file in question online. Frequency ordered CMAX to send the WORM to his new probation officer's computer. CMAX announced, "Command initiated."

Now Frequency could work on the problem at hand. The computer that the social club's file was on was good. As a matter of fact, it was one of the Rolls Royce's of computers. But that would not stop the Freq. Frequency started 20 different cracker programs and had CMAX initiate them at 20 second intervals for every millisecond that went by. No mortal man or woman could type that fast, but a computer like CMAX could with no problem. Once the program was initiated all Freq had to do was wait. And that didn't take long. The program made a cracking sound, like that of a board being broken, to alert Freq when the encryption had been cracked. Silly people will never learn to use more sophisticated passwords he thought. CMAX opened the file on screen and, just to play it safe, Freq copied it to a local banks' computer to be viewed later.

The file contained MAC addresses from various group members' computers. A MAC address is the hard coded file number on every computer component that connects to the internet. Inside each MAC address file were .bmp or mpeg files, basically pictures and videos saved on the computer. Freq then opened one of the files and was hit with a bombshell. The video was of a woman and a younger dude having sex. The woman looked to be about 34 and the dude was maybe all of 15 years old.

Frequency opened up another file and this had an old dude and a very young girl dressed up in a school uniform. Frequency closed that file and opened more. They all were the same. They showed was a bunch of rich perverted socialites raping kids. Who would've ever guessed that these rich, well connected professionals had formed a pedophile's social club?

Frequency closed the files, then shut down the cracker programs 'cause he had seen more than enough. He then set off a couple of trace route bombs to cover his exit. Frequency told CMAX to go into full security mode until he got back.

He grabbed his car keys and headed for the garage. He opened the door to the garage just as CMAX announced that there was someone at the door. Frequency told CMAX to activate the garage monitor. It was Erica, the limo driver. She came back after work like she said she would. Frequency had to make a quick decision. Stand her up and go to the computer store, or don't go to the computer store and risk getting caught for hacking that computer. He thought for a few seconds and decided, "As Deon Sanders would say, I'll do both."

Frequency went to the door and was hit with an eyeful. Erica had changed into something that would have made a dead man's nature rise! Frequency tried not to stare. She caught him and asked, "Should I have left my uniform on?"

Frequency shouted, "Hell no! But I need you to do me a favor."

Erica asked, "Are you going to let me in?"

Frequency replied, "Sure but I really need to go pick up some computer parts before the store closes."

Erica said, "Ok, is that all you need?"

Frequency could not help himself. He said, "That's all I need from the store, everything else you got already."

Erica laughed and said, "Come on man, let's go."

True to what he had experienced earlier this woman could drive. She drove a tricked out Honda Element with a bumping sound system. She turned the music up and headed to the nearest computer shop.

She said, "The best computer supply store in the city that has everything you could possibly need is about 20 minutes away."

"I didn't mind as long as I was riding and in good company."

Erica had on a mini skirt set that made a man wonder, if she also worked as an aerobics instructor. Her legs looked as if they were molded with just the right amount of muscle mass. Frequency was trying not to look, but that skirt made it impossible. And his manhood was reminding him that a woman hadn't been on the menu in two long years. Erica broke his train of thought by asking, "How long were you locked up?"

Frequency replied, "2 years and now I have 2 years of probation."

She asked, "What for?"

He told her, "Simple possession of stolen weapons."

She asked. "What did your wife or girlfriends have to say about it?"

Frequency replied, "She asked me to leave her alone the day I reported to prison. She was my girl-friend, I've never been married."

"Oh, well her loss," Erica said. Then she pulled into the computer store parking lot and said," Come on let's go get these computer supplies you so urgently need."

Freq felt like a kid in a candy store. All of the latest computer equipment was at his fingertips. He had read about a lot of it, but what he was looking for was not there. He decided to ask the young guy walking around with an Ipod on. It was kind of hard to get his attention, until he saw Erica and asked if he could be of any assistance.

Erica said, "My friend is looking for some computer components but what he's looking for isn't on the shelf."

Ipod dude looked perturbed. He acted like he didn't want to help us after he saw that she was with me. I gave him my list anyway.

Ipod dude said, "I have to talk to the store owner about this list."

Freq asked, "What's the problem?"

He said, "It not really a problem, but the stuff on your list is kept under lock and key. Only the owner can help you."

Freq asked, "So what are you waiting on?"

Ipod dude started to reply, "Look dude..."

Freq interrupted him and said, "My name is Frequency."

The young man said, "Sorry, my name is Ken."

"Well, Ken can we get the owner out here so I can purchase my components?" Ken said, "Ok," and ran to the back to get the manager.

Frequency turned to talk to Erica, but she wasn't there. He looked up and down the aisle, but he didn't see her. He was just about to go outside when he heard Ken and some guy arguing while coming out of the back room.

Ken walked over to Frequency and said, "Here's the guy that wants these parts.

Freq laughed and said, "What's happening EoW?"

The owner of the shop was an old friend from college. EoW gave him a hug and said, "Where the hell you been?"

"I told him I had to lie down for a while after that trial."

EoW said, "I heard that, but you ok now?"

I said. "Of course, but I'll be doing much better if I can get those parts on that list I gave to Ken."

EoW said, "I have everything you need, except it is already in a liquid cooled case."

"Liquid cooled," said Frequency, "I thought that wouldn't be ready for another year?"

"No my friend," EoW said, "I have only one and I will let it go for $5000 with operating system."

"Well I won't need the OS 'cause I still got CMAX.

"Now don't bullshit me," said EoW, "he should be overloading his memory banks by now."

"Damn near," said Frequency, "that's why I need those components."

EoW said, "I'll let you have it for $4500 with a 5-year warranty."

"Deal!" said Freq, "charge it to this account."

EoW told Ken to ring it up. Frequency told EoW to load it up in that tricked out car. Frequency then turned his attention to looking for Erica.

He was about to head outside when she said, "Looking for me?"

He turned to face her and she said, "I want to show you something."

Freq followed her to a special room that was in the back of the store. This room had all of the latest car audio equipment. She was looking at the newest flip down monitor. She then went over to the console and started the navigation program. She made that thing work like it was part of her hand. She told him having access to equipment like this drives her excitement level to its highest peak. Freq could understand her excitement. He was the same way when he designed the CMAX program.

Erica turned to Freq and kissed him. She pressed close to him and his manhood came to life. Erica pulled away and said, "I could take care of that here, but we'd probably get arrested for indecent exposure."

Freq said, "You're right." They pulled apart and headed for the car. Ken and EoW had the liquid cooled boxed up and ready to go.

Erica whistled and said, "When you go shopping, you go shopping!"

They laughed about it, loaded up the box, and pulled off.

Erica told Freq, "Hold on tight cause I have a package to unwrap." She made the Element surge into performance mode. She turned up the sound system which was playing "California Love" by Tupac. The little Element moved around the corners and straight away like an Indy car. Before you knew it they were pulling into the driveway of Freq's house.

Erica jumped over into the seat with him and started to kiss him. She was hungry and this man was the meal on the menu. Freq had to gain control of the situation. He did not know this woman, and he had no condoms with him. She pulled his head to her breasts and let him get a mouth full of them. Freq sucked on her nipples but knew he needed to get into the house. CMAX was in the final stages of the security protocol program and he had to be there just in case there was a problem. Frequency then came up with the perfect solution. He reached down between her legs and got a hand full of womanhood. Erica came to her senses and made him stop.

"Not out here," she said." That was what Frequency wanted to hear. He opened the door and pulled Erica out of the car. She pulled Frequency to her and said, "You shouldn't keep a woman waiting."

Freq went to the back of the car and got the box out of the trunk. He went to the house and put in his code. CMAX announced "Security offline." Frequency then opened the door and let Erica in. She walked in and was quite impressed. The house was very clean and nicely decorated.

Freq said, "Make yourself comfortable. I've got to put these components up. I'll be back shortly."

He closed the door behind him and told CMAX to go into full surveillance mode. Freq pulled the liquid cool system out of the box and placed it in the custom case for CMAX to make the transformation. CMAX stated that he would go offline for 2 hours. Frequency knew he would be at his most vulnerable with CMAX offline. He turned on his security system and left all cameras and microphones turned on.

Now he had to turn his attention to the beautiful woman in his house. As he walked into the room where he left Erica, he saw that she was looking at his certificates of accomplishment. Frequency asked, "Do you wanted something to drink?"

Erica said, "I have you for that. Just take me to the room where I can get more comfortable."

Freq said, "Follow me," as he led her to his bedroom.

Freq rolled over and nobody was there. He rose up in bed and looked for Erica, but she was not there. Freq got out of bed and pulled on his pants. As he went toward the kitchen, he remembered walking Erica to the door earlier. She had to be at work early so no harm, no foul. Freq thought about last night's festivities and smiled. That woman had it going on in the bedroom. She made Freq smile with just the thought of it.

Freq went into the bathroom and took a long hot shower. As he stepped out of the shower, he heard the sound that was music to his ears. "CMAX IS ONLINE".

Freq asked CMAX how the upgrade went. CMAX acknowledged and replied ALL SYSTEMS ARE GO. CMAX then reported that the liquid cool system increased its performance by ninety-five percent. CMAX would run surveillance scan programs to ensure that nothing had gone wrong while he was offline. Freq stated that would be fine, went to his bedroom and got dressed.

It was not long before CMAX detected a problem. The worm program needed to be taken down and destroyed. Freq stated that CMAX should pull the information out of it, name it, and then send the worm to the federal courthouse in any state of its choice. CMAX stated that he did not have a choice only logic. Freq told CMAX to send the worm to Washington. With all the problems they already have, one more would not hurt. CMAX acknowledged. Freq then told CMAX to name the file "The Gathering."

Mack Master got back to his office and pulled the file on Mr. Frequency Hunter. The info that it contained brought Mr. Master's interest level to an all-time high. The file read:

A 36-year-old who prosecutors say high jacked computers to damage other computer networks and send waves of spam across the Internet was sentenced on Monday to 2 years in prison.

Frequency Hunter, a well-known member of a group of master level computer geeks called "FREAKS" who pleaded guilty in January to federal charges of conspiracy, fraud and damaging U.S. government computers, was given the longest sentence for spreading computer viruses federal prosecutors said.

He was sentenced to 24 months in prison and two years of supervised probation by U.S. District Judge Warren Hill, who also ordered him to pay $250,000 in restitution to the U.S. Naval Air Warfare Center in China Lake, Calif., and forfeit to the government some $100,000 in illicit gains.

"Your worst enemy is your own intellectual arrogance in believing that somehow the world could not touch you on this," Hill said in sentencing Hunter.

Hunter was accused in the original 25-count indictment of hijacking some 500,000 computers using "worms," or programs that surreptitiously install themselves on computers so they can be controlled by a hacker.

A worm net is a network of such robot, or "zombie" computers, which can harness their collective powers to do considerable damage or gather huge amounts of financial data.

Prosecutors say the case was unique because Hunter was accused of profiting from his attacks by selling access to his worm nets to other hackers and planting "worms," software that causes your computer to send financial information to be harnessed, then destroys the infected computers.

In entering the guilty pleas, Hunter admitted using computer servers he controlled to transmit malicious codes over the Web to scan for and exploit vulnerable computers, which he then controlled as zombie machines.

Mr. Master was trying to think how much information this man held when he was interrupted by a call from the receptionist. He answered the phone

The receptionist said, "Two gentlemen from the FBI office are waiting to see you".

"Send them in," he told the receptionist.

Soon there was a knock at his door and two men walked in wearing black suits. They pulled out their badges and stated that they were Agents Marks and Bartworth.

Mr. Master shook hands with the agents and asked, "How can I help you gentlemen?"

They said that they were interested in one of his parolees, one Mr. Frequency Hunter.

Mr. Master said, "I was just going over his file. Mr. Hunter appears to be an amazing intellectual."

The agents said they knew all about him. It had taken them seven years to finally get enough information to get him.

"We had to use an informant close to him to get enough information to make him plead guilty," said agent Marks.

"So why are you guys here?" asked Master.

Marks said, "Now we need Mr. Hunter's help. The FBI has been trying to crack an elite pedophile ring with no success. One of Mr. Hunter's worm programs has compromised their main computers. We need the information that the worm program has gathered."

Mr. Master asked, "Why doesn't the FBI just use some of their abundant resources to get the information?"

Agent Bartworth said, "We've tried, but we haven't been able to get anything."

Mr. Master looked at both agents then asked, "So what does this have to do with me?"

"You have been the first of any kind of justice official to get close to him," They both said, "so we need you to be our inside man."

Chapter 2

NICE GUY

Freq had been having a semi-productive day. He had been on several job interviews which went very well. He did not care about the amount he made as long as it was a salaried position. Freq rode around to several computer shops looking for a job, but he knew he was over qualified. He was not discouraged.

He was looking forward to seeing Erica again. It had been 4 weeks since their first night together. Freq drove around in his old Trans Am. He tried not to show it, but he was a true American car nut, especially the GM brand. Freq stopped at the light and a Honda Element pulled next to him. He glanced at the car because he did not want to stare. It was Erica's ride, but Erica was not in it. A Dude was driving and smoking a cigarette. That usually doesn't mean much, but most people won't let a stranger smoke in their car. Dude had the music loud and was dancing in the driver's seat. Freq felt low but he was not going to let that get to him.

The light changed and they both took off. Freq got onto the interstate and decided to let the TA open up. The motor sounded like music. Freq decided while he was out he would get a cell phone. He needed one to be able to have constant contact while he was out of the house.

He stopped by the local Verizon store and asked, "Is Don 1 was still employed here?"

The clerk said, "Not only is he still here, he's the new owner/operator."

Freq smiled, just thinking about his good friend stepping up in the world of business.

The clerk asked, "Would you like to speak with him and who might I say is looking for him?"

Frequency told the clerk his name and then the clerk went to the business management area to get Don. Freq stepped away from the counter and started looking at some of the new cell phones that were on display.

There were numerous phones with all kinds of gimmicks and gadgets that came with them. Then Freq saw the ultimate phone. It was called a Smart phone. It was part PDA (personal digital assistant) and part cell phone wrapped in one neat package. Freq was looking at all of the features, when he heard a familiar voice. Freq turned and it was his old pal Don 1. Don 1 grabbed him and gave him a hug and a firm hand-shake.

He said, "It's good to see you, Frequency. Looks like you're here for the latest Smart phone.

"Of course," said Freq. "I need the phone that has the best of what technology has to offer."

Don 1 said, "Come back to my office; I have some-thing you might be interested in."

Don 1 and Freq stepped into Don's office, which was setup nicely. Don1 went to a closet in his office and pulled out a FedEx box.

Don said, "This phone just came in. It's the only one like it in the city."

Freq and Don opened the box and were like two fat kids in an all you can eat candy store. The phone was a silver one-piece unit.

Don said, "It runs the latest Microsoft mobile OS with WI-FI, Bluetooth, and a host of other features."

He said, "This phone can handle up to a 50-gig SD card. The largest on the market now handles only 8 gigs."

Freq did not care. He had to have it.

Don asked, "Is CMAX still online?"

Freq answered, "Of course."

"Then you would love this, Don said. "This thing has full time wireless access and streaming video incoming and outgoing."

"Hold up, you mean I can take CMAX with me wherever I go?" Freq asked.

"That's right," said Don. "Matter of fact let us try to get it connected and see if CMAX can find it."

Don asked Freq for his info to put in the computer and Freq gave it to him immediately. Then Don told Freq that his old cell number, 481-8180, was still active and in good standing.

"Cool," said Freq. "Go ahead and activate it on this phone.

Don put in all the necessary information and got the phone activated. Don then gave the phone to Freq.

To Freq's amazement, the new phone had pulled all of his old information and phone numbers inside. Freq was overwhelmed. He told Don that it would probably take him a week to learn about all the features.

Don said "You got plenty of time as long as you stay out of trouble."

Freq said, "You can count on that."

Don then said," Go on and try to bring CMAX up on the phone."

Freq then dialed the Mac address to CMAX and entered the proper access transition codes. The phone took a while to connect but within two minutes, Freq heard the familiar voice of CMAX asking for the proper access codes and bio scan. Freq typed in the command using the phones QWERTY keyboard then placed his right thumb on the screen. The biometric scan that CMAX used worked across the cell phone interface. CMAX acknowledge and said, "Biometric scan accepted. How do you do Sir?"

Don and Freq were ecstatic they could not believe what was happening. Don told Freq he had to buy that phone and Freq reached into his pocket and gave him his check card. Don ran it through the computer and the processor stated "accepted."

Freq then got his card back and asked CMAX to activate voice command. Then Freq told CMAX to give him a status report. CMAX stated, "ALL is well," and "system is at 100%." Freq felt as if he'd just won the lottery.

Don 1 asked Freq if he had found a job yet.

Freq said, "No, but I'm still looking."

Don 1 said, "Freq I have an opening in my Tech. Support Dept. if you want it."   Freq   told Don1,"I'll, take it!"

Don said, "It doesn't pay very well."

Freq said, "That okay, I just need something to keep my probation officer off my ass."

 Freq decided to go to New York Suit Market and pick up on the three suits special. He used his new phone to find the address, and then used the navigation program to find out how to get there. Freq jumped into the TA and headed to the market.

He was just enjoying the drive when CMAX came online and told him there was a problem with the worm program. Freq asked CMAX to give him the full status. CMAX told him that the Fed's were monitoring the computer the worm program got the "Gathering" file from. Freq told CMAX to shut down all worm programs except that one. Freq told CMAX to use trace route bombs on all files and then keep monitoring the "Gathering." CMAX stated "Done deal." Then went offline.

Freq stepped on the gas of the TA and hurried his shopping experience at the suit market. He picked out three suits and all the accessories he needed with them. He even picked up three pairs of shoes.

He went to check out and the young woman at the counter gave him a flyer for a party at club "RISQUE." Freq thought about it and thought to himself it would be nice to go out and kick it. He put the address of the club in the navigation program and thought about going by there on his way home. He had nothing to do so why not. He loaded his new clothes into the car and headed for the club. The club was not too far from his house. It was hidden in plain sight. Freq turned the music up and followed the instruction of the navigation program. Freq found the club with no problem. He liked what he saw and decided to come back later.

He was about to leave when he saw a familiar car. It was the limousine that Erica had picked him up in. Freq blew it off when Erica's Honda pulled in front of the limo. The Dude that he saw earlier got out of the car and started tapping on the limo's windows. He was walking around the car screaming her name pulling on the car door handles.

Erica stepped out of the back of the club and confronted the guy. He pushed her and started shouting at her. She stood her ground and they started fighting. Erica caught him hard in the stomach with a knee and he backhanded her. He hit her in the stomach and she folded over. He tried to knee her in the face, but she got a hand full of his testicles. Dude gasped for air then punched Erica in the head. Erica let out a scream and grabbed her head. Dude raised a knee and caught Erica in the stomach. Erica folded over and fell to the ground. Dude kicked Erica in the face.

This all happened so fast and before Freq could get to them. Freq ran over and grabbed a piece of a 2 x 4 lying on the ground. Freq got to Dude, swung the 2 x 4, and popped Dude upside the head. Dude, did not know what had hit him. He folded up like an old chair. Freq was about to pop him again, when Erica jumped between them. Freq could not believe it. This dude had put his hands on her and here she was protecting him.

Freq dropped the board and got into his car. He knew with all of the commotion that the police had been called He did not need their company... He looked at Erica as he pulled off. She just stood there crying and trying to explain. Freq stepped on the gas and let the TransAm ride. Freq headed for home, cause as of that moment, home was the best place for him. Freq could not believe everything that had happened. The whole thing could have been avoided if he hadn't been such a nice guy.

Erica was pissed! This nigga had just put his hands on her and messed her up with somebody new. She picked up the board and walked over to Dude. When the police arrived. They pulled their weapons and told her to drop the board. Erica complied. They ran up on her, handcuffed her, and put her in the backseat of their car. Then they ran to help Dude, who was just getting up off the ground.

The guy in charge of the club's video surveillance system called the police when he saw Dude attack Erica. He was trying to explain to the police what happened up until he had some temporary camera problems. The man told the police he had live video up until Dude kicked the woman in the face. After that, the system went out and didn't come back on until the police pulled up.

The officers went over and arrested Dude. They released Erica and asked her if she wanted to press charges.

She said, "At this moment no. I just want to get the limo back and go home."

Erica got into the limo and headed to her job's garage to turn it in. Dude had messed up her plans. Now she had to go and doctor on herself to fix all the bumps and bruises. Erica dropped off the limo, then had a cousin come pick her up and drop her off at home. She thanked him for the ride and promised him she would be all right. Erica got into the house and started to undress. She ran very warm water in the tub so she could soak her aching body. She knew she was not going to be able to work with her face messed up like it was. She decided she would use some sick days until her face healed. As for everything else, she knew that time healed all and that no one got a free ride including Dude.

Frequency chilled at his house. He decided not to go anywhere but to work and back home. Occasionally, he would go to the computer store or the maintenance shop for car repairs. Other than that, he and CMAX just hung out and put together some brilliant plans for future patents and a couple of new companies.

Frequency had not left the house and just rode around in two months. He wanted to make sure that he had not been identified when he hit Dude with the two-by-four. Frequency was greatly disappointed.

He did not know the whole story between the Dude and Erica. He sure could use some female company right now, but he didn't let that bother him. He decided to go and visit the computer store to see what new gear EoW had. Frequency went to the garage and started the old TA. He pulled the car out of the garage and headed for the computer shop.

EoW was just coming from the back of the store when his clerk asked for a high-end video card.

EoW said, "I would have to pull the item from stock so let's make sure this is the card the customer wants. Did you do the demo for the client in the demo room?"

The clerk said, "No, I didn't ask."

EoW then explained to his clerk, "To ensure that a customer gets the right product, always offer them a demo. That way you make sure that it's going to work properly for them."

The clerk said, "Okay, I'll go ask."

EoW told him, "Don't worry 'bout it. Since I'm already out on the floor I'll do it. EoW then proceeded to the counter to find the customer. He saw a very nice looking woman at the counter with her arms folded.

He asked, "Can I help you?"

She said, "I'm waiting for the clerk to come out with an NVIDIA Gamer Video card. I want to try it in a system that I'm having built.

EoW introduced himself and asked for the specs on the computer.

She asked him, "Why? And by the way my name is Denise."

EoW said, "We have a complete computer demo room where you can put in specs from any computer. It will configure it and let you see if the specification would meet your needs."

This system and the program was the brainchild of EoW, Don 1, and Frequency working together. They designed the system to react as any computer would with any kind of parts in it.

EoW said, "Follow me into the demo room and I'll demo the system for you. Denise was excited and followed EoW inside. She watched as EoW put the code on the lock and heard it click and automatically open.

He escorted her to the terminal and put in a second code. The system's 60-inch screen lit up and the door shut behind them.

Denise asked," Will it open again?"

EoW said, "Sure, it has to close or the noise from the speakers would vibrate the whole store. Denise was impressed.

EoW then asked if she would rather type or use voice recognition. She chose voice. EoW typed in to the computer, "Begin voice protocol." The computer came online and said acknowledge. It then asked for the specification for Denise's computer. First, it asked for the processor, then how much ram, next it asked for hard drive size and speed. It asked what type of video card. It then asked for what type of fan used for cooling CPU. Next, it asked for power supply size. Last, it asked for what type of media drives used. Denise gave all of the information and the computer asked her to acknowledge if she was ready to try her specified computer.

Denise answered, "Yes," and the screen displayed "Wait during configuration." Suddenly the computer came back online and said this is how the specified computer would run using Windows XP OS. It then asked her to choose her gaming experience. She chose "Hitman3". A door opened and a Microsoft game pad came out. The computer then stated "Begin". Denise grabbed the game pad and started playing the game. EoW pulled two theater type chairs up and let her sit down and play.

As she was playing EoW told the computer to auto configure to meet her playing needs best. The computer acknowledged the command and began showing the spec changes at the bottom of the screen as Denise played. Every time there was a spec change the computer would announce the change and by how much. Denise was over the top!

She was really getting into the game, which made her horny. She could not believe the system that she was playing on and how well it responded. She finished the level she was on and EoW had the computer printout the newly adjusted specs of Denise's computer. Denise took the sheet and read it. It showed the downfall of her existing design and the upgraded hardware that would make it great. Denise was so excited that she hugged EoW and kissed him dead on the lips. EoW was caught by surprise and fell back into the chair. Denise fell on top of him and decided to make EoW an offer he could not refuse. She told him, if he could make that computer play some music she could dance to, she would purchase the upgrades needed from him today.

Not one to miss a sale EoW said, "Program 15." The music started up and Denise stood up and began to dance. EoW felt as if he had his own strip club going on, without a whole bunch of naked women.

Denise looked at EoW and decided to indulge herself in a little foreplay. She dropped down between EoW's legs and unbuckled his pants. She then reached under him and pulled his pants and underwear down to his thighs. She reached inside of her purse and pulled out a raspberry flavored condom. She opened the pack and placed the condom in her mouth. EoW was on swoll when she put it in her mouth and started stroking up and down.

Denise stopped and looked at EoW and said, "I love giving head after I finish playing video games."

EoW said, "Oh, go ahead and enjoy yourself. Don't worry I will not disturb you. Denise said, "Well!" and went back to stroking EoW's manhood.

EoW just laid back and enjoyed the free service from this very nice looking woman. He made sure he had the demo room locked for at least an hour or until the program was stopped. The way this woman was handling her business, he was not about to stop her.

Denise was enjoying her raspberry condom. She had so many saved up from her last fun party. With her boyfriend out of town on business, she'd had nobody to use them on until now. She knew all she had to do was keep the rhythm going and this man would fill her condom. She wanted to feel the real thing, but maybe she'd get another chance later. Right now, she just wanted to see him explode from her oral gift. That was not a problem; because she was working EoW like the one. She was possessed. She could feel the muscle jump in her mouth as he was about to cum. Denise felt her own body shake as she got an orgasm while giving head to a complete stranger. She dismissed it for now and said that she would discuss that with her therapist at their next meeting.

EoW thought I have to make sure I get this chick's number. He grunted and shook as he exploded a load into her mouth. He grabbed the back of her head and pushed down as she began slurping on his manhood like a straw. EoW's body was shaking to the very end. Denise sucked on his manhood until it went limp. She then carefully removed the condom not to spill the contents. She tied it into a knot and threw it into a nearby garbage can. EoW had gotten up and pulled his pants back up.

EoW asked, "Can we stay in touch?

Denise said, "I hoped this wouldn't be the last time I saw you."

EoW said, "So what's your number?"

Denise said, "Give me yours and I will call you."

EoW pulled out a business card and gave it to her.

Denise took the card and said, "I'll send someone for the parts on the list."

EoW said, "Sure I have them in stock so just let me know when."

Denise said, "I will call you by tomorrow morning."

"Cool," said EoW. "We open at 8:00 a.m."

Denise said, "Okay so can we go out now?"

EoW said, "Oh, sure." then told the computer to end program. The big screen shut down and the music ended. The doors swung open and the two went back into the store.

EoW walked Denise to the door and said, "I look to hear from you soon."

Denise said, "You most definitely will," as she went out of the store and got in her car. She started the engine and zoomed away.

EoW was on cloud nine. He had just got the knob polished and now he could go in his office and chill for the rest of the day.

Frequency pulled into the parking lot and noticed that business was light. He got out of the car and went into the office to wait for EoW. EoW had just come from the men's room when he walked into his office and saw Frequency.

EoW laughed and asked, "What's on your mind?"

Frequency said, "I'm getting stir crazy being cooped up in that house."

EoW said, "Go to a club or something, I know there's plenty in this city for you to do. Go ride your motorcycle and swindle somebody out of some money. That usually makes your day."

Frequency thought about it and said, "Yeah, I could go out for a ride. I probably will do that as soon as I leave here. How's business?"

EoW said, "Business is steady. Light on the traffic, but in the green on the spending."

Frequency liked hearing that, especially after spending so much money on the experimental weapon. EoW then pulled up a new distributor he thought Frequency would be interested in. The name of the equipment was "Dyno-Drag." It was a portable drag strip for motorcycles and light cars.

Frequency read the specifications on the setup and asked EoW, "Where could you run it and what would you charge per run?"

EoW said, "Talk to Webb about it because that's his area. I'm just showing you one way to tap into the racing events."

Frequency's mind started rolling with ideas to make this "Dyno-Drag" pay off for him. He told EoW, "Get in touch with the distributor and have him call me on my cell. I have to go to the street races tonight to see whose king of the strip."

EoW said, "Okay, just holler at me later and fill me in on the details."

Frequency said, "Sure thing." Then he jumped into the TA and headed for home. He decided to get out his old 85 Yamaha Virago and take it for a ride.

EoW made the call to the distributor of "Dyno-Drag." When he looked into the video monitor he noticed a familiar face in the store talking to his clerk. EoW got up and went into the main store. As he walked up, he noticed that it was the same young woman who'd come into the store with Frequency a while back.

She turned to EoW as he walked up and said, "Hello. You might not remember me. I came into the store with a friend of yours couple of months ago."

EoW knew who she was talking about, but he did not call his name. He just said, "Oh yeah, your name is..."

"Erica," she said.

EoW asked, "How may we help you today?

Erica sensed that calling Frequency's name was not a good idea. She asked for a USB hub for her computer.

EoW took her over to the aisle that had the hub and told her it was on sale. He was admiring the way she wore her camisole and camouflage outfit and trying hard not to stare at her breasts.

He told his clerk, "Mark the item down to the sale price and make sure you enter her for a chance to have a customize home computer or car system."

Erica said, "Thanks," and went to the counter to pay for her hub.

EoW made sure he got a good look at this fine woman as she walked away. He understood why his friend was upset about her and her Dude problem.

Erica gave the clerk the info to enter her in the giveaway, got her bag from the clerk and left the store. She was in a good mood. Erica was planning to do some more shopping, but she had to go by her job first to see when she was scheduled to go back to work. She thought about catching a cab since her Dude had not shown up with her car. Erica had left messages and gone by his apartment. She still couldn't find him or her ride. She made up her mind to file a stolen car report as soon as she got home. Erica got on a city bus and decided to take it to her job since it was directly on the route.

Kendra sat on the back of Dude's ride enjoying his tongue between her thighs. He was going to town on her clit making her shudder with pleasure. She could not believe that her co-worker gave up a man who could make a woman feel like this. Kendra pulled his head deep between her thighs as she came.

Dude was just in it out of spite. He was pissed off and was trying to get even for what Erica had done to him. He knew Erica could not stand Kendra, so he'd been messing with her on the side. Now that Erica had 'broke bad' on him, he would get even with her by sexing Kendra in her car.

Dude rose up from Kendra's thighs and kissed her deeply on the lips. He then crawled into the hatchback area, where he had already prepared for this little escapade.

Kendra knew Dude and Erica were going out, but she didn't care. She was about to get off again and Erica had nothing to do with it. She pulled her panties completely off and got into the back of the vehicle with Dude. She unzipped his pants and started sucking his manhood enough to get it up, but not enough to make him cum. She wanted to get on top and she was not going to mess it up by blowing him off. As soon as he was stiff, she got on top and started riding him. She wanted to get a good hard orgasm to make this rendezvous worthwhile. Kendra knew she should not be having sex on the back lot of her job, but she was the only person scheduled to be in today.   Kendra was enjoying riding Dude and making him buck up as she used her Kegal muscle to massage his manhood. She was really enjoying the thrusting as he pushed up into her. Dude knew he had to go deep inside this woman if he wanted to get more from her so he reached up and grabbed her shoulders from under her arms. He then started using her body for leverage to pull her down deeply onto his engorged member. This sent Kendra over the edge as her orgasm hit and screamed as it flowed endlessly.

Erica had just gotten off the bus and walked to the office of the limo service. She knew it was open for business. She had spoken with the owner earlier and he said Kendra would be there and would have her schedule.

Erica walked to the door and pushed the buzzer. No one answered. She waited a little while, and then decided to walk around to the back. Maybe Kendra was in the garage. Erica went around to the garage but nobody was there. Eddie, the mechanic, was just finishing an oil change when he saw Erica walking around. He waved and she walked over to him.

Eddie asked, "How're you doing?"

"Fine," she answered.

Eddie asked, "You ready to come back to work?"

Erica said, "That's why I'm here to get my schedule."

Eddie said, "I saw Kendra here earlier. "Go check and see if she's around at the back office."

Erica said, "Okay thanks Eddie." She walked around to the back office and was caught off guard when she saw her car parked under a nearby tree. She reached into her purse and found her keys. As she walked over to the car, she heard someone inside screaming. She went to the back of the car and used the keys to open the hatch. She was shocked to see her co-worker on top of her man.

Kendra had just finished her orgasm when she felt someone grab her by the hair and pull her out of the vehicle. Kendra crawled and barely made it to her feet as she was being pulled. She reached and grabbed the arm of the person who had her by the hair and twisted it as violently as she could. She broke loose from the person and when she looked, she saw it was Erica.

Erica let go of Kendra's hair when Kendra twisted her arm. Now she was looking directly into the bitch's face. Kendra decided to try to hit and run. She threw a hard wild punch at Erica but Erica moved and countered by kicking her in her stomach. The air rushed from Kendra's body and she doubled over.

Erica grabbed a hand full of hair again and started to hit Kendra in the face. Kendra tried to block the punches, but Erica was too fast. Kendra reached for Erica's throat. She grabbed it in a choke hold. Erica kicked Kendra in the stomach again and then punched her in the jaw. Kendra spun around from the blow and tried to run. Erica kicked the back of her foot and made her fall. She jumped on Kendra's back and started banging her head against the ground.

Dude had gotten up from the car and was watching the two girls fight. He was a little upset that he did not get to bust a nut in Kendra, but this fight was rather arousing. Dude saw Erica take the upper hand. He knew there was going to be a problem if Erica whooped this girl. He wasted no time. He went over, grabbed Erica and slapped her hard on the back of the head. This knocked Erica forward into Kendra's head. Kendra's head hit the ground so hard it knocked her unconscious. Erica rolled over and got to her feet as fast as she could. Dude looked into Erica's face and saw that she was pissed. He said, "Calm down before you make me do something we'll both regret."

Erica was beyond pissed at that point. She got into hitting range and fell to one knee. She knew he was still on hard from Kendra and would not be expecting this. She punched him dead in the testicles. Dude fell to one knee and lunged toward Erica. She moved to the left and let him hit the ground. She kicked him in the ribs and heard him lose all of his wind. She then kicked him right between his legs.

Dude was through. He knew he had to get up and get moving or this woman was going to kill him. He waited until she was ready to kick him again. He reached down and threw a handful of gravel in her face. This temporarily blinded Erica. Dude rushed her on wobbly legs and had enough strength to tackle her. They fell to the ground with him landing on his stomach and Erica falling onto a grassy strip. Dude saw his opportunity to run and took it.

Erica rebounded from the tackle, got up and ran after him. She was going to make him pay for all he'd done to her. She saw him run toward the garage and knew she could find something in there to beat the devil out of him. She saw him limping and knew that she had done a good job so far. As she entered the garage, she saw the jack handle on the floor. She picked it up and decided to make this the last time he put his hands on her.

Eddie, the mechanic, saw Dude run into the garage and screamed at him. The next thing he saw was Erica with his jack handle. Eddie quickly left the garage to go get help 'because he knew something had definitely gone wrong.

Dude ran out of the garage into the parts storage area. Erica knew there was only one way out and she headed straight for that exit. Dude ran to the door and opened it. Erica swung the jack handle and hit him and the door. Dude fell to the side and tried to run again. Erica threw the jack handle caught him on his ankle. Dude fell in pain and tried to crawl away. Erica was right on him, beating the back of his head.

She started screaming at him to turn around, but he wouldn't so she just kicked him with everything she had. This turned out to be a mistake. Dude kicked Erica's other leg from under her and she hit the ground hard. He got up and tried to hit her in her face but she covered up. Dude elbowed Erica in the back of the head and she collapsed.

Dude stood over Erica and laughed. He said, "You are one tuff bitch," as he started to unbuckle his pants. He pulled his belt off and started to whip her. She jumped every time the belt bit into her skin. He kept on swinging and screamed, "You don't know your place, stupid bitch. Now I'm gone finish with you what I started with that other bitch."

He hit Erica again with his belt and she started to scream and cry. He jumped on her back and pushed her to the floor. Erica was worn out. She had no more fight left.

Dude pulled up her skirt and saw that the lacey camisole she was wearing had a button crotch. This would make it easy for him to take advantage of the situation.

Erica felt him unbutton her camisole and tried to fight him off. He pushed his entire weight on to her back and made her gasp for air. He was hard from seeing her exposed body. He grabbed her head and screamed in her ear as he sodomized her. "Fight like a man; get fucked like one, Bitch."

Erica could barely scream as he pushed himself fully into her. She grunted in pain with each thrust. She resisted at first then she relaxed and let him have his way. This sent Dude over the edge as he fell into a rhythm and stopped paying attention to her.

Erica struggled to turn her head as she looked for a weapon to get him off her. She caught sight of the same jack handle that she had used earlier. Erica knew that if she rose up just a little bit she could reach the handle and get him off.

Dude reached his peak when Erica rose up and busted that nut he had been holding. He couldn't believe how good it felt to cum. Then he felt a very sharp pain on his head. He opened his eyes and felt something warm running down his face. The jack handle had hit him right between the eyes. Dude rolled over in pain which freed Erica.

She got up slowly from the ground and limped over to Dude. She started hitting him everywhere she could with that jack handle. Dude was screaming as each blow caught him on another body part with a cracking sound. Erica finally got what she wanted when one of the blows caught him directly across the bridge of his nose. She then hit him in each eye.

She knew she was going to be in trouble, so she decided to make it worth her while. She got ready to hit him with everything she had left, when someone took the handle from her. It was Eddie with the police. Erica had never been so glad to see anyone. She collapsed in his arms and blacked out.

Erica came to in an ambulance. The paramedics told her she would okay eventually. When Erica looked around, she saw Eddie out there talking to the police. She could see police cars and officers all over the place. Some were pulling records out of the back office. She did not understand why and she really didn't care. For now, she just wanted to get the hell away from there. Erica was feeling the pain from both of the fights she had just been in. In addition, the throbbing coming from her behind let her know Dude had had his way with her. She shrugged it off for now knowing that the pain she was in was great but his was even greater. Erica heard the paramedics close the door of the ambulance. She dozed off as it started to move.

Frequency was just finishing the tuning of his old school motorcycle when he heard breaking news on the radio.

"A local woman was assaulted at a well-known limousine service," The broadcaster announced. "The woman fought off her attackers injuring both of them. One of the attackers was part of a fraudulent company using limos to escort underage teens being used in a prostitution ring. Kendra Johns was secretly transporting the teens to service an as yet unknown proprietor. More arrest will be made as evidence is gathered and presented. The other unknown attacker received blunt trauma throughout his body and is in a coma. The woman attacked, who has only been identified as "Erica," was severely beaten but was able to fend off and injure her assailants. She was taken to a nearby hospital where she is presently listed in stable condition."

Frequency knew exactly who they were talking about and hurriedly finished working on his motorcycle. He then had CMAX go online and find out as much information as possible and get it back to him immediately. Next, the phone rang and Freq saw that it was EoW.

He answered the phone and EoW started shouting about Erica. Frequency told him to calm down because he could not understand a word coming out of his mouth. EoW took a breath and repeated what he'd said. Erica had just left his shop before she was attacked.

Frequency thought for a second, then told EoW, "Rewind the surveillance tape to when she came into the store. Make copies of it and have it ready for the police when they come to question you. Remember do NOT volunteer any information if they do not ask for it."

"Are you going to see her?" asked EoW.

"I'll try but first I have to wait until the police presence dies down. I do not want to take any chances on anything dealing with the police," Frequency said. "And did you hear that the broad in the limousine shop was transporting teen prostitutes? That might be a lead within itself. "I'm going to check it out as soon as I can. Have you contacted the "Dyno-Drag" equipment distributor?"

EoW said," Yeah, they'll be putting a package together as soon as possible."

"Cool," said Frequency, "I need you to send flowers to Erica and make sure everything is okay with her."

EoW said, "Frequency, I thought you were through with her."

Frequency said, "Like I've always said it's my curse to be a nice guy."

Chapter 3

Who Would've Guessed?

Mr. Master now had the kind of case on his hands that he'd always dreamed of. He was now working with the Fed's to solve a major case. The key was parolee Hunter. He had to stay cool with him and let him know that the Feds were on to him. Mr. Master had thought about the information that came from the compromised computer. He knew that once the information was given to the agents all hell would break loose. He laughed to himself recalling how the agents said they were still trying to break into the specified computer. Frequency Hunter did it in 2 hours right after he was released from prison! Hunter hadn't even been in the same room with a computer in two years! Now Mr. Master had to go to the place where Mr. Hunter had been hired and do an interview with the owner. It was standard procedure for all newly released federal prisoners.

Don 1 had just opened the shop when a customer walked in. Don told him that he was not open for business just yet. The man reached into his jacket pocket and produced an ID card and a badge.

He said, "I'm Federal Probation Officer Master. I'm looking for the owner of this business."

Don figured this was coming and was well prepared. Don told Mr. Master, I've been looking forward to talking to you."

Don escorted Mr. Master back to his office, where they sat down and discussed the pros and cons of employing Frequency Hunter.

"Don said. "I'm aware of everything dealing with Mr. Hunter. Mr. Hunter was honest about his stint in prison and the reasons for it. He told me he'd be on probation for two years. He even told me about the hefty fines he has to repay."

Mr. Master was taken surprised. Usually a parolee doesn't tell a potential employer about their history. Mr. Master knew that Frequency was ahead of him in this area so it was no longer necessary to waste Don 1's time. Mr. Master told Don that he would be in from time to time just to monitor Mr. Hunter's status, nothing to the point of interfering with his job though.

Don said," That will be fine," and walked Mr. Master to the door.

As soon as Mr. Master pulled out of the parking lot Freq walked in through the private entrance in back. Freq and Don had a long history, much longer than the two let on. Don 1 is one of the other members of "FREAKS." He knew Freq was not going to give them up when he went to trial and as a matter of fact, Freq had invested heavily in Don 1's cell phone shop. Freq made sure that all of the members of "FREAKS" had stable businesses. He also made sure that everybody owned the buildings their businesses occupied.

Don 1 laughed as Freq walked in looking like he had a million in the bank. Freq told Don what was going on with the last worm program and that it may have come upon some information that the Fed's might be interested in.

Don asked, "What do you want to do?"

Freq said, "I need to assemble the team, but I have to do it in a setting that won't blow anyone's cover."

Don came up with a great idea. "How about a "get out of jail party" at club "RISQUE?"

Freq said, "I've already had one run in at that club He explained what had happened the last time he'd been there. Don laughed and said, "Always Mr. Nice Guy."

Freq laughed and said, "We can just go to the club and have everybody meet there. No formal invitations cause they would just tag all the people who show up."

Don said, "I'll notify the rest of the "FREAKS, and let them know what's up."

Freq then laughed and said, "Now let me get to work!" Freq. went to his area and logged on to the system. Don ran a tight ship. Everything was accounted for and nothing came into or out of the shop without a bar code.

Freq knew that when he gave each person within their organization foundation money, they would use it well. EoW had the computer shop. Don1 had the cell phone shop, M Webb had the car shop, and then there was Mr. White. Freq had not spoken to the other two, but he knew that day was coming. He knew everything with Webb would go smoothly, but the business with

Mr. White could turn ugly. Oh, well. He couldn't let that bother him right now. He'd just deal with today's tech support problems and other business at hand. Freq was deep in thought when he was relieved by one of the other employees and told to go see Don.

Don told Freq to come in and close the door behind him. Freq followed his instructions and sat in a chair across from Don. Don told Freq everything he'd found out about Mr. White and how he robbed everybody. Then Don gave Freq some info that really hurt.

He said, "Mr. White was the source of the leak that sent you to jail."

Freq laughed, he was not about to be a hot head and do something stupid. That would play right into Mr. White's hand.

Don was confused. "What do you want to do about it?" he asked.

Freq asked, "Who all did he hit up for loot?"

"All of the FREAKS got hit," Don said, but you sustained the most damage."   Freq said, "I need to go see M Webb. He's the one who'll be the hardest to control behind this. Let me head there now."

Don told Freq, "Do what you got to do. I got your back so take your time."

Freq said, "Go online with CMAX if you need to reach me. Any other means of communications might already be compromised."

Freq jumped into the TransAm and made a bee-line to M Webb's custom shop. He was already strategizing 'because he knew he had to have a plan to give Webb to keep him from pulling out the heavy artillery to go to war.

M Webb was working on a customer's car. He was also trying to keep his mind off his financial problems. He could not believe one of the FREAKS had robbed them all and locked up their leader! There was gone be some shit here shortly...

Webb heard tires burning, and smoke started coming in from the parking lot. He couldn't even see what he was working on! He knew that only one thing could make tires smoke like that: pure horsepower! Webb went over to the wall switch and turned on the vent. As the smoke cleared, he saw a familiar figure walking toward him. It was Frequency Hunter.

Webb grabbed Freq and said, "Man it is good to see you!"

Freq told Webb, "I knew I had to see you first. Let's talk business."

Webb said, "Come to my office."

Freq said, "Naw man, let's ride like old school."

Webb said, "I'm driving." Then he told one of his employees, "Finish this up for me. I'll be back shortly." To Freq he said, "Follow me."

Webb went to the back of the shop and pulled the cover off a 1975 Pontiac Catalina with a 400 cubic inch big block engine and 22-inch rims.

He smiled and said, "Now this is old school!"

Webb and Freq jumped into the car and Webb let the horses run wild! That old school car smoked the tires and took off like a bat out of hell! Freq laughed as Webb stepped on the gas and turned the music up.

Webb knew the procedure for when it was time to talk business. He made sure he hit a couple of corners, and then ran for a while to make sure they weren't being followed.

Webb turned down the music and said, "How soon can we handle our business with Mr. White?"

Freq laughed and said, "Soon my friend, very soon. First we have to make up for the loss of one of the FREAKS. Then I have some business that I'll need the team to help me take care of. After that, Mr. White will have the full and direct attention of the group."

"Now that's what I am talking bout!" said Webb.

"So do you have somebody in mind to replace White?" asked Webb.

"Yeah, there's this dude who was locked up with me," Freq said. "He'd bring some much needed muscle to our group."

Webb said, "If you say so. What you need from me?"

"The FREAKS are going mobile," Frequency said. "No more houses filled with computers. We're going to need a van... no a truck. Something big with enough power to carry us and run all our equipment."

Webb thought about it for a moment then said, "I have an idea, but it's going to take me awhile to put it together."

Freq said, "Take your time 'because I want it done right." He handed Webb an all-black American Express card.

Webb asked, "What is this?"

Freq told him, this was a type of credit card that has no limit. Vendors who know what this card represents usually shut down the rest of the store just so they can focus on this card holder."

"Ah Shit!" shouted Webb. "I am going to act a fool with this."

Freq then said, "Keep in mind we still have a mission of "V" for Vengeance."

That made Webb step on the gas pedal and head back to his shop. He knew now that Freq was out and okay, and that shit was about to happen. He almost felt sorry for anyone who would dare to cross their path.

Freq and Webb got back to the shop and Webb asked, "You still driving that TransAm?"

Freq said, "As soon as I take care of Mr. White, I'll put some new horses under my feet."

Webb told Freq, "I'll see you later," as they pulled into the parking lot.

Agents Marks and Bartworth were in their office when they found out they had been assigned a new supervisor for the pedophile case. Agent Layrock was introduced to the gentlemen. Layrock was known throughout the agency as a hardnosed by-the-book agent. His attention to detail was impeccable.

Agent Layrock asked Marks and Bartworth about the case. They brought him up to date on all that they had so far. He was not happy. They told him of all the obstacles they'd run into while attempting to crack the access code of the pedophile database. Layrock already knew how much progress they had made. He had already gone over their notes and files. "He'd even devised a plan to quickly move them further along.

Agent Layrock said, "You two are going to interview all involved parties again." The two agents then shared their plan with Layrock. Their ace would be none other than Frequency Hunter.

Agent Layrock immediately had them pack their bags for full mobilization. He wanted a team of the best computer experts that the Fed's could commandeer. Layrock was already familiar with the capabilities of Frequency Hunter. He knew this man was like a modern day Robin Hood. Wherever Hunter couldn't go, he could make his computers go.

Layrock remembered going after one of Mr. Hunter's friend, Mr. White he thought the name was. This 'friend' was so greedy and low down Layrock had wished he could arrest him instead of Hunter. No matter. The outcome of that case earned him a promotion and a serious bonus. Now agent Layrock would have to try and do it again with no inside help.

Agents Marks and Bartworth had all the equipment and manpower they needed in place. They were instructed to have the plane loaded and ready for takeoff ASAP. The agents all knew they were in for one big technological adventure. Layrock suspected that Mr. Hunter knew they'd be watching him so they would have to move with precision every time they went near him. The tiniest slip would put them so far behind that by the time they got caught up, he would have disappeared into cyberspace. Once the plane was loaded and ready to go, the agents steeled themselves to challenge one of the biggest and best computer hackers of all times.

Mr. Master was notified that a full team of FBI agents were coming to work on the pedophile case. Mr. Master didn't know what to expect or exactly what his role would be. He was excited! He knew that he could make something happen for the future of his government career. He was headed to the air base on the outskirts of town to meet the agents. He was given explicit instruction not to inform anyone of their arrival. Just as Master reached the base, he saw a big C130 cargo plane land. A convoy of trucks and cars drove down the ramp as soon as it was dropped. Next a black Suburban pulled up and three agents got out. Two he knew; the other one was new to him.

Agents Marks and Bartworth approached Master and shook his hand. Then they introduced him to their supervisor, Agent Layrock. Layrock shook hands with Mr. Master then got right to business.

"I'm going to have my team set up 24 hour surveillance of Frequency Hunter. If they watch him long enough, he's bound to make a mistake. When that happens we'll move in and get the information we need to bring down a major pedophile syndicate."

Mr. Master then brought the agent up to date on what he had seen and the whereabouts of Mr. Hunter. Agent Layrock was surprised to hear that he was working in a cell phone shop as a technical support person.

Mr. Master told the agents about Mr. Hunter's home. "He has setup a few voice command robots, but nothing major. His house is missing the one thing that should be present--- a computer."

Agent Layrock then said, "This guy is good. He knows how to hide the most sophisticated system available where nobody can find it."

This time, he addressed the whole team, "If Hunter has any inkling that we are on to him, and we might as well pack up and go home now."

One agent stepped up and asked, "What about an inside person?"

Agent Layrock said we don't have a lead on anyone who was close to him." Agent Payne stepped up and said, "Why don't we try to get in through his job? I can act like a customer having phone trouble and try to get to know him."

Agent Layrock was not cool with his female agents going undercover, but since Mr. Hunter has a non-violent history he gave the idea some thought. He finally agreed to let her go undercover. Layrock told the other agents to find out anything and everything they could about Mr. Hunter.

Layrock told them, "Hunter's the key to this whole investigation, so we will leave no stones unturned."

Agent Layrock pulled Mr. Master to the side and asked him "Is Mr. Hunter the partying kind?"

"No," Master said. "All he does is go to work and go home. I viewed a video of him looking at flat screen video equipment at the local electronics store. I asked the salesclerk that waited on him and he told me Hunter said the prices were too high."

Agent Layrock thought for a second and then asked, "When is his first payment due for restitution?"

Mr. Master said, "In about 30 days give or take a few."

"Okay," Layrock said, "let me know as soon as he brings in a payment."

"He's not," said Master, Most likely we'll get a payment directly from his bank."

"Well can't we monitor his spending to see where he's spending his money and how much he's spending?" asked Layrock.

"We have and majority of his spending is with online merchants, said Master. "He's having the stuff shipped to his house."

Agent Layrock had a bad thought. He knew from past experiences that they couldn't get anywhere near his home without him knowing it. That would be a grave mistake because it would blow the Fed's very thin cover. Agent Layrock knew that he had one small chance if agent Payne could get next to Mr. Hunter. He had no choice but to gamble with it.

As soon as the Fed's had all of their equipment unpacked and ready, Agent Payne began setting up her undercover information. She knew that she couldn't leave anything to chance. Frequency Hunter was a very intelligent man and he was one case that was going to push their equipment and computer knowledge beyond its limits.

Agent Layrock had the surveillance team crank up their equipment and use GPS to locate their mark. He also had them restart attempts on cracking the main frame that held the information they needed. His computer staff had been chosen from the elite colleges around the world. These people were at the top of their game long before they came to work for the FBI.

Frequency's worm program had been in and out of the main frame. His trace routes had been exploded by spam bombs. He used this tactic so the programmers on the other end wouldn't know that they'd been infiltrated. Frequency also left himself a little present of a timer program. Most computer programmers didn't search for this type of program because they tied in with the expiration of the main operating system. This would be a way he could exploit the main frame when the time came.

Frequency knew what he had from inside the computer; he just couldn't get a location from it. The person who set up this mainframe was good! But he did leave out one small detail which his worm program took advantage of and then closed the door behind itself. So in all the mainframe got a free fix from the master computer cracker.

Frequency laughed to himself as he could hear the reporter on the news calling him a "HACKER." That was one name he did not like being called. He did not take down networks or do damage to any networks that did not deserve to be damaged. He had to admit that he would crack codes and copy Intel that would help his cause in any way. Frequency was home doing his usual internet searches when CMAX alerted him that the Fed's had activated one of the computers involved in his last online case. Frequency activated voice command and told CMAX to begin security protocol "4433." CMAX said, "Acknowledged." Basically, 4433 stood for 'hide.' Frequency knew that the Fed's knew he had something to do with the information from the main frame computer. He was still trying to figure out the naming conventions of the main frame and the coding of each individual. He had each individual file but this # 5646766-2489 he could not figure out. This number was in a multitude of places and it had various amounts of money tied to it.

The biggest point was that it had the highest encryption level that Frequency had ever seen on a file. Frequency told CMAX to set up a tracer on the one computer so when it linked into the network, it would connect into the entire FBI database and infrastructure. Frequency knew that this would alert him to when they were close and keep him up to date on any information they might have.

Agent Layrock had just set his laptop down and turned it on. He went out of the office to get a cup of coffee. What he didn't know was that he'd released Frequency Hunter's program into his infrastructure. Agent Layrock sat down and started going over all of the files he had dealing with this pedophile case. In real time, Frequency saw what he saw. Frequency liked this agent's style -- he was thorough in his investigating techniques. He didn't take anything for granted. Frequency knew this was the key to keeping him from going back to prison. He would pass on small leads through the computer to keep the Fed's close as a backup. They surely needed muscle. Frequency did not send out any programs to look for information because he knew that would trigger an alarm to let the Feds know that their security had been breached.

Frequency did have a gift for the agent. He saw that they were going to use the government GPS system to track him. He saw that they had an agent assigned to place the tracking device at the cell shop. Since they wanted to track him, Frequency decided he would give them a vehicle to track. He made a mental note to hook up with a friend of his to get a truck. He would let them track the truck wherever it went. He then had to make sure that none of the guys introduced him to anyone new. Nine times out of ten, Frequency knew they would try to come at him that way, so that meant no new faces. He knew that he had to stay in the back of the tech support center of the cell shop, because that would be a perfect place to stay out of the lime light.

CMAX announced that the Fed's had just initialized their high gigahertz security frequency. They are in full force, Frequency thought to himself. He knew they would come and get their network online. He learned from the last time that whenever the Fed's do anything, they put their network up for secure transmissions. Frequency didn't blame them 'cause If he had the time he would set up his own He made a mental note to do just that and put one in place.

He started thinking about how the Fed's like to set up shop. He tried to remember everything that they did to catch him last time. This time there will be no Mr. White to open the door for them. Mr. Master was the first person to come to mind. He knew that Master had the layout of his home and knew about the robots. What he did not know was that CMAX controlled everything.

He then decided to move CMAX, and he had to do it in a big way. Frequency started working out ideas on how to keep the Fed's at his back door at all times, but have that back door ready to move whenever they got ready to kick it in. He knew that the guys would be affected by the Fed's, but they didn't know enough information to get them involved. Frequency was very proud of his group. They held up through everything the Feds threw at them the last time. They did not let him down, except for Mr. White. He had not thought that his good friend would be that greedy and take him out like he did. Frequency knew Mr. White had some tough characters working with him, but they really didn't involve themselves with him. He would spare the Hudson Brothers and Rome. All others that got in the way would be victims of a pissed off computer whiz.

Frequency started designing a special kind of bullet for a special kind of gun. This bullet was made of a special polymer that would not penetrate the skin but would give one helluva shock that would render a person defenseless. Frequency knew that as a convicted felon on probation, he could no longer carry a fire arm. He did not want to take a chance and get pulled over with a gun near him, because that would be the end. He and CMAX started working on the design using detailed specifications from the "EMP design." Frequency wanted to be able to fire this device at a target and hit it with enough amperage equivalents to equal that of a heart defibrillator. This would disable the target without killing them. Frequency also knew that if he could pull this off the patents alone would be worth millions. But before he could sell it he had to make sure that it would work.

He used the modeling from all kinds of futuristic weapons to come up with a three dimensional design. He then had CMAX begin testing of the 3d model. CMAX finished testing and gave Frequency a list of components needed for assembling the weapon. Frequency laughed at all of the hospital equipment he had to come up with. He pulled up all of the companies he had invested in. He always invested his money as a ghost partner to small companies needing his computer expertise. Frequency always made sure that he had access to their computer systems so whenever there was a problem, he could consult with the companies and get the problems fixed in no time. Then he would be provided with access to an account for his computer equipment purchases. That was his big secret that kept the Feds at bay. They could never trace any components or computers directly to him. Frequency looked into a particular account and saw that it was perfect for the equipment he needed. He put in the order and had the equipment delivered to

the location for pick up. He would then set up designated pick ups by EoW who would eventually deliver
the equipment to him. Frequency knew that everything had to be done precisely with nothing left out.
He knew that he was about to face the biggest challenge of his life and one mistake would cost him
dearly. Frequency had CMAX open up a visual call to
EoW.

EoW was at the computer shop answering calls and
selling computers as usual. He knew that a lot of shit
was getting ready to happen, and he knew that the
crew was going to be in the middle of it. He had just
hung up the phone when he got a message from CMAX
to go to a secure area. EoW knew that something was
going down and he had to put his game face on. He
went into his office and put his code into his computer.
A red laser scan went around the room to check for
any taps or bugging devices. The computer gave a
green light that signaled "ALL CLEAR." EoW then
accepted the call.

Frequency and EoW started talking about what was
happening. Frequency said, "The Feds have set up shop
here. They want to use me to get to this mainframe
computer."

EoW asked, "Why don't you just give them the information?"

Frequency said, "I can't 'because I received this information while I was in prison. They'd have to lock me
up again, and I'm not about to go through that again."

EoW said, "I can understand that."

Frequency gave EoW detailed information on the equipment he's ordered. "I had most of it delivered to these places. I need for you to send a different person to each location to pick up each package."

EoW said, "You know you can count on me."

Freq added, "Make sure that none of the boxes have been opened. I don't want the contents compromised or contaminated. If the box is open send it back."

EoW said, "No problem, I'll take care of it right away. Hey, what ever happened to that fine young lady you were with that day?"

Frequency said, "She had too much drama going on for me, and now that the Fed's are in town, I can't take a chance with anyone."

EoW asked, "What about Doc?"

Frequency's heart damn near stopped he was silent for a long while. EoW waited and then got concerned when he did not get an answer.

EoW asked, "Are you okay?"

Frequency finally spoke up and said Yeah, I'm okay."

EoW knew he had hit on a touchy subject. He immediately jumped to another subject. "What about the experimental clinic? We left some serious items out there."

"I know," said Frequency. "I hope we never have to use it, but if we do it's enough to fight a street war."

EoW then gave Frequency an update on the computer shop's finances. He told Frequency, "We need to sell off some of the stock purchased while it's at a premium."

Frequency said, "I trust your judgment, go ahead with what you think is best."

EoW told Frequency, "I'll make sure that all items will be ready tomorrow." Frequency said, "Be careful, and to be ready for anything."

They both signed off, and EoW began to schedule all of the pickups he needed to have done for Frequency.

EoW was a character like none of the other crew. He was as diverse as he was silly. He was always looking to put another female's name in his book of laid maidens. The next day, EoW wanted to make sure that he did not lead anyone back to the crew so he got himself ready for a little masquerade.

First, EoW told the clerk, "I have to go out and run some errands."

He always had to pick up new computer components from different warehouse distributors, so this would be like any other time. Next, EoW called up his cousin Angie. She was always down for making money and she knew just the right kind of people to help EoW with this particular task. EoW went to Angie and told her he needed to pick up some packages but it had to be done on the down low. Angie immediately called up her friend Mike, who worked for a local delivery company. She knew that she could make Mike come over.

Angie said, "He would have to make up his own runs, then he can use the truck for two hours."

EoW said, "I'll have it back before then."

Angie said, "I have to go freshen up before Mike gets here. As soon as Mike and I come in the house, you should in the truck and handle your business."

EoW said, "Okay," and went outside to wait for Mike.

It wasn't long before the delivery truck showed up. Mike pulled up to the driveway and was getting ready to get out when he saw Angie come outside. Angie ran over to the driver side of the van and opened the door. Mike was surprised when she jumped into the van and gave him a big kiss. Mike had been trying to get with Angie for weeks and now here she was all over him.

He was about to push Angie away when she said, "I finally got rid of the excuse that was keeping me away from you." She reached down into Mike's crotch and said. "We can do this here or in the house."

Mike damn near threw Angie out of the truck! He got out and slammed the door behind him. He remembered the keys in the ignition, but didn't care. Angie laughed as they went into the house. She got Mike inside the house, locked the door, and pushed herself against him. Her kissing and grinding was making him crazy!

Angie really was not interested in Mike, but when EoW needed a favor she would sell her left tit for him. EoW had paid off a big debt to a local drug dealer and gotten her cleaned up. She thought about the countless times the drug dealer had used her body for his own pleasure. She remembered the times he had let other women use her for their own enjoyment. She dismissed the thought and got back to the present with Mike. She was going to make him go to sleep and then wait on EoW for compensation.

EoW had jumped into the van and started to make his rounds. Before each stop, he changed his appearance to look like a different person. EoW had to be very careful not to mess this up. He did not want Frequency to go back to jail. He had done this many times before changing his accent and image just to pick up packages. He did not want to be recognized by of the delivery drop's personnel. He remembered the training manual Frequency gave him on how law enforcement personnel look for patterns in people to solve a case. It was quite funny to see how many people get profiled, then making the small mistakes that eventually get them caught. EoW had made numerous stops and was watching his time as he went about collecting the items that Frequency had ordered.

Meanwhile, Angie felt Mike pull her up from in front of him. Angie thought she could just blow Mike off and he would cum. This didn't happen. Mike had nothing to be ashamed of between his legs. Angie was actually aroused from giving Mike head. She tried everything in her repertoire to make him cum, but Mike would not shoot. She tried to deep throat him but gagged. That's when she noticed that Mike was bigger than she had thought when she started. Angie hadn't expected Mike to excite her, but she was wrong.

Mike had been waiting for a girl like Angie a long time. Angie had a body to die for, and a face that should be in a beauty magazine. Mike was only 21 and he knew that Angie was damn near 30. He would see Angie come by the delivery shop from time to time headed to the local store. He had watched other guys try and talk to her, but she turned them down. He remembered the day he got her number, when she was coming from the market with an armful of groceries and her bag broke. He just happened to be outside cleaning his van. He helped her collect her items, and then gave her a ride home. When they got there she asked him to help her get the groceries in and offered him a drink. He remembered when he got a call and couldn't stay. He remembered leaving and she gave him her phone number. Now he was getting head and was about to do more.

He pulled Angie up and started kissing her full on the lips. Angie was surprised and then she joined in. They quickly stripped out of their clothes and Angie guided him to her couch. She lay on the couch with her legs spread and Mike was right on top of her. Her body was moist and ready. Mike entered Angie and pushed until their bodies were touching. Mike didn't move he just wanted to enjoy the feel of this woman.

Angie released a gasp because Mike went to a spot where no man had been. Her body released a small orgasm that made Angie scream. She shuddered as the orgasm increased. Mike held Angie close as he rolled onto his back to let Angie be on top.

Angie was in control and she wanted Mike to know it. Angie started grinding like a woman possessed. She was screaming, pulling at Mike's shoulder, and trying to make him explode inside her. Mike was not going to climax anytime soon. He had just masturbated that morning while watching two of his co-worker was get it on in one of the vans. Mike was looking up at the woman on top of him. She was really grinding and sweating as she fulfilled her pleasure. Angie's body collapsed as she reached orgasm again. She could not believe Mike was hanging with her. She mostly dominated the men she slept with ever since she cleaned herself up. This one was not going away easily and she liked it.

Mike was mesmerized by the look on Angie's face as she climaxed on top of him. He did not want to stop he rolled her over on her stomach mounting her from behind. Mike entered her body forcefully.

Angie let out a gasp as Mike thrust into her deeply not leaving room for anything. Angie made sure he had all of her at his disposal. She was not going to let this man leave unsatisfied. Angie started pushing back onto Mike to make sure he penetrated deeply with each thrust. Angie knew that another orgasm wasn't far off and she had to make this man cum. She tried to hold back, but her body spasm as the orgasm took everything that she had as she called out his name.

Angie opened her eyes and there was Mike. She was at a loss. She had never been in a position where she had come so hard with anyone. Angie grabbed Mike's head and pulled him hard to her. She kissed him deeply and told him he could have anything he wanted from her. Mike was still hard and his manhood was throbbing.

Angie got up and went to her bedroom. She grabbed a bottle of baby oil and then she went to the bathroom and got a towel. She went back into the room and told Mike to lie on his back. She then poured baby oil on his throbbing member and started jacking him off. This drove Mike crazy! Her hands felt so good wrapped around him. Angie knew she was going to make him cum, but she did not want to waste it she poured baby oil on her body and then got back on top of Mike. The baby oil had them slipping around on each other. Mike was at the height of excitement while Angie was jacking him off. He was thrusting long strokes trying to achieve an orgasm, when he pulled out and it popped into her behind. Angie's mouth opened as she pushed down to receive Mike's gift. Mike exploded into Angie and froze. He had never experienced anything like it before. Angie clinched her cheeks to hold Mike's manhood in place until it went limp.

Mike was totally drained, but concerned. He thought he had hurt Angie, but she told him he could have anything and that meant anything. Mike looked into Angie's eyes as she bent over and kissed him. Mike was through and was not about to ask this woman to get up. He just enjoyed her touch and her soft kisses as they lay there in each other's arms.

Mike was startled as Angie pulled from him and went to the bathroom. She came back shortly with a wet cold towel. She started cleaning up his manhood and stomach. She played with his abs and kissed each one ever so softly. Angie enjoyed everything about

Mike's body. He had a six pack and he was in great shape. Angie could not stop looking at him and thinking how she almost let him get away. Mike was drained, but he was so happy. He closed his eyes and just enjoyed Angie's touch.

Mike was in another world when he thought about the rest of his deliveries that needed to be made. He was going to be late and that had him jumping up looking for his clothes. Angie was startled by Mike's reaction. She did not know if EoW had brought the truck back yet. Angie couldn't give him anymore pleasure because she was exhausted. Mike had his clothes on before she could think straight.

Angie asked, "Can you come back tonight"

Mike stopped and stared at her. He said, "Sure, as soon as I get off from work." Angie ran into the bedroom and threw on a robe. She looked out of the window and saw that EoW's truck was gone. She went back into the room where Mike was fully dressed. She told him, "Come back no matter how late it is."

They kissed and Mike jumped into the van and drove off. EoW walked up to the house and knocked on the door. Angie came to the door.

EoW shouted, "Damn! You look like you been in a fight!"

Angie opened the door and the way she walked EoW knew what kind of fight she'd been in.

He asked, "Are you alright?"

Angie looked at him with a smile and said, "Never better."

EoW sat in a chair and said, "Looks like you got more than you bargained for."   Angie said, "Yeah, and as soon as he gets off I'll be getting more."

EoW burst into laughter as Angie tried to get upon her wobbly legs.

Angie asked, "How did the deliveries go?"

He said, "It's a done deal, and it's all good." EoW gave Angie a package.

Angie said, you don't have to pay me, I've been well compensated."

EoW laughed and said, "Yeah that's cool, but it won't pay the bills." He put the package on the table and left.

Angie went into the bathroom and started to run herself a bath. She had a date with a man who was not going to be leaving without pleasuring her some more.

EoW had made all of the pickups and notified Frequency, so he went back to his shop to see what was going on. As he arrived he saw that all the gamers were inside looking for the new gaming video cards that had just arrived. EoW had 20 pre-ordered cards, and he'd ordered 20 extras just in case.

As he walked in the store, the clerk said, "All the pre-ordered cards have been picked up, and ten of the twenty extras have been sold already!"

Profits will be up for this week thought EoW. Now I need to get the parts that Frequency ordered to him.

To the store clerk he said, "I'll be in my office going over today's sales." EoW went and ran the usual security scans. When he got the green light, he opened the safe and pushed the bio reader to make the underground chute to Freq's house open up. He put all of the packages on the chute's loader and closed the door. He knew CMAX would take over and he could relax until it was time to meet. EoW knew his friend was still messed up about DOC. He hoped having those parts to work on would take his mind off of his disappointment. As EoW began to balance the books for the day, he made a mental note to go by the club and get him some action. He had earned the right to enjoy a pleasurable evening with a beautiful woman.

Frequency was reading the information he got from Agent Layrock's computer when CMAX announced that packages had arrived. He shut down the ghost link between the two computers and had CMAX bring up the three-dimensional rendering of the weapon they had designed. Frequency pulled all of the packages out and started putting them into their assigned places in his makeshift lab. CMAX controlled the robots and had them start mixing polymers and designing boards to create the EMP pistol. Frequency then decided to give the new weapon a name --- The SHOCK-D. He just smiled at the name and continued working on some of the last design specifications. As he worked, he made a quick adjustment to the design, to allow him to select the voltage according to the size of the target. Frequency sat back and let CMAX and the robots create another masterpiece and this time, someone was going to get hurt.

Chapter 4

MADDNESS

BDB was asleep in his cell when he heard the familiar sound of the guards doing their night count.

He heard one of them say, "Let's split up so that we can hurry up and finish."

He heard the keys jingling and saw the beams of the flashlights as they went about their job. BDB was having a hard time because he had gotten word that he was being released early thanks to some new evidence found in his case. He knew he had a lot to do. He had no family and no way to make money on the outside. He was nervous about what would happen to him once he was released.

The guard's light snapped him back to the present. He jumped up and said, "Turn that damn light off!"

Then he heard a familiar voice that should not have been there. He went to the bars and saw the cage controller that made a habit of flirting with him.

BDB asked, "What's going on?"

She started to laugh and said, "I thought I had more time to get to know you, but now that your friend done gone and got you released, I guess I better get what I want before you're gone."

BDB looked confused, until he felt her hands between the bars. She reached straight for his manhood and it came to life as soon as she touched it.

She smiled at BDB and said, "Let me go down and introduce myself." The guard dropped down and started filling her mouth with BDB's manhood. She was not going to stop until she got what she wanted. She'd had her eye on him for years, and had watched him stand his ground with every man who challenged him. He was dealt a bad hand but he still stood proud. She knew she was his first in a very long time, and she knew she would see him again.

BDB was losing it! It had been awhile since he'd felt the touch of a woman and this woman was blowing his mind. He wanted to just enjoy the moment so didn't try to hold back. He felt his body convulse with pleasure as he released ten years of waiting.

The guard held him in her mouth until she was sure he was spent. She got up and asked, "What's my name?"

He said with a smile, "Ms. Sunshine."

Sunshine said, "And don't you forget it!"

BDB said, "Are you crazy? We will see one another again."

Sunshine walked away and BDB went back to his rack. He nodded off to sleep so fast it was funny. And he had a big smile on his face.

The next day when BDB heard his number called they told him to go to the Administrative Building. The day that he had dreamed of a million nights had finally come. He walked in the room, signed all the paper-work, and was given some clothes to change into. Of course they were the same the clothes he wore when he came in and they did not fit.

BDB looked at the guard on duty and told him, "Give these clothes to Goodwill 'cause there's no a thing I can do with them."

BDB put on a pair of warm-up pants and a t-shirt. He had on the same Nike shoes that he'd been wearing on the inside. The guards escorted him to the outside exit and told him to go to the parking lot once he was outside. BDB didn't care 'because he was prepared to walk if necessary to get away from there.

He shook hands with the guards and said, "I will not see you guys later!" He walked out to the parking lot, and was getting ready to head for the nearest phone when he heard a car coming. It was a black car and it was coming straight for him. BDD jumped out of the way as he heard a familiar voice.

Frequency Hunter jumped out of the car and said, "I haven't ever seen you move that fast!"

BDB's face lit up like last year's Christmas tree.

Freq told BDB, "Get in and let's go take care of some business. We need to get you some decent clothes!"

BDB felt like a burden had been lifted. Being in the car with Freq gave him peace of mind. He relaxed and they headed to the Big and Tall men's store. It didn't take long to get there, and Freq told the ladies to 'freshen the big man up.'

The girls asked, "What was the occasion?"

Freq answered, "FREEDOM." Then he handed the girl at the counter the Black AmEx card. She looked at it, and then pushed a button on the side of the register. Less than a minute later, six more sales clerk came out to assist. One clerk escorted the other customers to the door and told them that they'd have come back after noon.

BDB was tripping 'because he'd never seen anything like this.

Freq told the girls to take care of everything he needed from head to toe. Then he told another clerk to take the stuff that he had on and make sure every piece was burned. He gave BDB a cell phone and showed him how to use it. Freq told the ladies he wanted his friend to have enough clothes for at least a month. He left BDB with the ladies and headed for the cell shop.

CMAX came online and told Freq that EoW and Don1 had viewed the Gathering file. The next bit of information was disturbing. To make matters worse it, the judge who had sentenced Freq to prison was a card-holding dues paying member of the group of pedophiles! Frequency knew a lot of shit was going to hit the fan, and he had to have something in place when it did. He got on the phone with the FREAKS and told them they needed to meet. They all agreed and Webb said he would supply the pickup. Freq then had CMAX set up the meeting spot and they all went on about their business.

Freq went to the nearest Bank of America and talked to the manager. Mr. Davis knew Frequency and greeted him with a smile. Freq told Mr. Davis what he needed for BDB.

 Mr. Davis said, "Just bring him in and I'll take care of everything."

Freq said, "That's great! We'll start him off with what's in this envelope." He shook hands with Mr. Davis, left the bank, and headed back to the BIG & TALL shop to pick up BDB.

BDB was happier than hell on a sunny day. He was freshly dressed with clothes that fit him perfectly. He had on new everything and he had a couple of phone numbers for a little female company later. He needed only one more thing to make things right --- FOOD. He was about to use the cell phone when Frequency pulled up.

"Get in so that we can go get some sustenance," Freq told him.

BDB asked, "Get some what?"

Freq laughed and said, "That is FOOD."

BDB laughed hard and said, "Man, I had just realized I am hungry as hell when you pulled up."

Freq headed to a popular soul food restaurant. While they were riding, BDB handed Freq the AmEx card.

Freq asked," Did you get everything that you needed?"

BDB said, "Yeah, and that they said all the stuff would be delivered to your house."

Freq said, "That's cool so now let's get some eats!" They pulled into the parking lot of the restaurant and the smell of good food was heavy in the air. BDB and Freq went inside and were seated by the hostess. They got the menu and ordered full three-course meals.

The waitress said, "You guys must be hungry." Freq just smiled and started to talk business with BDB.

Frequency gave BDB the low down of his situation. BDB didn't understand a lot of the particulars, but he was down for whatever his friend needed.

When their meals came out, Freq told BDB, "Eat hardy 'cause we still have more business to take care of." They dug in and finished everything. Freq had ordered a bottle of wine with their meal, so he made a toast to FREEDOM with the last of it.

BDB took a big swallow and said, "It's been a long time since I've tasted a good wine."

Frequency pushed his plate from him because he was full. BDB ordered more food. He finally got full and Freq paid for their meals.

Freq then took BDB with him to the bank. When they go there he introduced BDB to Mr. Davis, and then left them in the bank office to talk business. At first, Mr. Davis was taken aback by BDB's size. Once he collected himself, he started telling BDB about his new account. He had BDB fill out all of the necessary papers and sign the signature cards. He took a picture of BDB to put on the card for security reasons.

BDB was astonished when Mr. Davis told him how much money was in his account. He already had five thousand dollars in the bank, and he hadn't been out of prison 12 hours! Any thoughts of backing out now were out of the question. BDB had Freq's back for from that minute till he told him he didn't need him anymore. For anyone to mess with Freq, they would have to come through BDB.

Mr. Davis then asked BDB, "Do you have any idea what kind of business you want to start?"

"I want to have my own landscaping business," BDB said.

Mr. Davis accessed the bank's computer and pulled together a detailed list of everything BDB would need to get the business going. He also gave BDB a special order form to go to Don1 and get a Smartphone with a software package on it that would handle all of his invoices.

Mr. Davis asked BDB" Do you have any ideas for your company's name?"

BDB pulled out an old piece of paper that he and Freq had written on when they were still locked up. It had all of the details for his business.

He gave the paper to Mr. Davis and said, "Frequency put this together for me."

Mr. Davis took the paper and said, "I'll take care of everything. All the necessary materials and supplies will be delivered to Mr. Hunter's house."

BDB said, "Okay, I'll be looking forward to it."

Freq saw BDB come out of the bank so he blew his horn to let him know where he was parked. BDB jumped into the car and the two headed for the house. They were at Frequency's house in no time. BDB was amazed when CMAX came online and greeted them.

CMAX then gave a status report and let them know that they had one hour before it would be time for their meeting.

Freq showed BDB where his room would be. It was very spacious and well decorated with its own bathroom. Everything was neat and clean, but in a manly way. BDB made a mental note that when he got his own place, it would be just as well kept. The next thing that caught his eye was the huge bed. And just like a big kid, he went and jumped right in. The bed absorbed the weight of his very large frame and didn't even grunt. "Now this is living," he thought.

Freq had made sure the bed was sturdy enough when he'd bought it. He had told the salesman that the bedroom furniture was for a very tall, large framed man.

The salesman said, "Another Green Mile,"

Freq said, "Exactly."

So now BDB was lying in bed and was about to doze off when two words came to mind: BUBBLE BATH. He went to his bathroom and started the water. He looked in the cabinet and there it was, Mr. Bubble. BDB grabbed the bottle, opened it up, and poured an ample amount into the tub. Before long, the tub was full of tepid water and bubbles. He undressed and jumped into the tub. He stretched out his legs and was amazed that the tub was big enough. He sat back and just let his body soak. He laid his arms on each side of the tub and felt a button. He sat up, looked at the button, and realized he didn't know what it was for.

BDB didn't want to mess up anything so he shouted for Frequency.

Freq told CMAX to activate the intercom. BDB was startled when a little TV monitor rose from the side of the tub and there was Freq.

Freq said, "Hey, there's no need to shout. You can communicate with me from anywhere in the house at any time."

"No shit," said BDB, "What else can I do?"

"The tub you're in is also a whirlpool. All you have to do is push the button on the side and it'll come on," Freq told him.

BDB pushed the button and the jets came to life hitting BDB all over his body. He hadn't felt this relaxed in too many years.

Freq said, "You can watch TV or listen to music by making a selection from the monitor's touchscreen."

BDB just sat back and let the water soothe his soul.

Freq told CMAX, "Open up a dialog box just for BDB."

"That way, you can have access to most of the general commands," he told BDB. "Anything beyond the basics has to be authorized."

CMAX said, "Acknowledged", and put the necessary commands in place.

While BDB enjoyed his bath, Freq was busy putting together all the information from the Gathering file. The group consisted of nine individuals who basically ran a syndicate of pedophiles. They all had high status jobs with six figures salaries, and they all used different organizations to find their victims. Freq separated the group into five categories, and assigned one of the FREAKS to each category. Freq made a list of the individual's names. They were Cupcake, Mama's boy , Gay Mack , Elevator Man , Madame & Big Trouble, Johnson City, Banker and Judge. Freq put each name on a piece of paper so his people could randomly select a name out of a hat. He figured if the Feds come after him he'd need to have substantial to keep from getting locked up again. Freq knew that once the Feds found out it was his worm program that gathered the information on the pedophiles, they would try to revoke his parole. All of the information his crew amassed had to be solid.

Frequency then got on the phone and started checking in with the FREAKS. Each one answered on the first ring and gave him progress report. As soon as he hung from one, he would call another until all their business matters were completed and he was satisfied that they were in order.

He heard movement in the background which was of course BDB waking up from his nap.

BDB came into the room where Freq was sitting and asked," What's on the agenda?"

Freq told BDB "We're going to see what the local nightlife has to offer."

BDB smiled and said, "Man, that's something I've been looking forward to for years."

Frequency told him, "Just put on some nice slacks and shoes so we can blend in at any club. We want to see what's happening, but we don't want to draw too much attention."

BDB said, "Give me ten minutes to change and I'm ready."

Freq said, "Cool 'because I need to change clothes too."

Frequency put CMAX into full security mode and mobile mode so he could have access from his Smartphone. Freq then called Don 1 and said, "Me and the Big Man are going out if you want to join us."

Don 1 said, "I'll pass. I already have a very hot date."

"Alright, we'll catch you later," Freq said.

As Don1 hung up the phone, his doorbell rang. He opened it and a very beautiful lady stepped in. Terri was a customer Don 1 had met at his store. She dropped the digits and he had taken his time trying to get to know her.

Terri was a little perturbed because she just knew she had the right package for this man. She was well educated, she had her own business, and she maintained a six-figure checking account balance. This was nothing that she went around bragging on, but it was a plus in her book. She told Don 1 she was open for dinner and a movie, but he had brushed her off. He had said he was busy that night but promised her he would make it worth her while. Well that was 3 months ago, and she was ready to move to the next level. Terri knew that she was an aggressive person, and she was used to having her way. She could not figure out why this man was so hesitant.

Don 1 had all the information he needed about Terri. He knew that if he played her slow, she would get all bent out of shape. Then things would move at a pace he wanted. Don 1 had already made reservations at one of the best restaurants in town called the Blue Fish. The movie theater was only five blocks from the restaurant. Don knew she was ripe with anticipation, so he didn't waste any time getting her to the car and in the restaurant.

Terri had insisted on driving. She had told him, "If you drive as slowly as it has taken is to get together, the city will be shut down for the night before we eat!"

Don laughed and said, "You wouldn't appreciate a man who would take you out to dinner then have you pick up the tab."

Terri laughed and said, "You got some money. You just like being a little too conservative."

Don1 walked around and opened the driver's side door for Terri's. She did not try to hide the abundance of thigh showing when she swung her legs into the car. She had purchased everything she had on specifically for this date. She had already decided that Don1 was going to get laid tonight as long as he didn't do anything stupid.

Don1 closed the door and admired Terri's choice of automobile. She had a brand new Lexus convertible, fully loaded with a set of twenty-inch rims. Don1 was impressed. His Pontiac GXP could not top that, but it was affordable. Don1 got in and they headed for the restaurant. They were soon inside the restaurant ordering their food and drinks. Don1 was making small talk when he saw his good friend EoW walk into the restaurant.

He had a nice looking young lady on his arm as usual. Don1 got up from the table, shook hands with EoW, and introduced EoW to Terri. EoW was very impressed with Don1's taste in women and gave Don1 the look that meant approval.

Terri caught that look too, but she waited until his friend left their table before she did anything about it. Once EoW and his date walked away, she then reached under the table and lightly patted Don1's crotch. Don1 smiled and looked at her.

Terri said, "If you like what you see on the outside, just wait 'til you get to feel the inside."

Don1 damn near jumped up and said "check please," but he had to maintain his composure. Terri was impressed to see that Don could remain so cool with the pressure she was applying.

She thought to herself, "Before the night is over I will bring this man to a boiling point!"

Don1 did not forget what Terri had said and done as he paid for their meal. As they headed for the car, he thought, "I have to do something to light a little fire under Miss Terri." True to form, when they got to her car Don1 pushed her gently against the car and laid a slow, deep kiss on her. Terri was a bit surprised, but she accepted the kiss with open ambition. Don1 pushed against her to let her know she had his full and undivided attention. To make his intentions a little more clear, Don1 ran his hand down the front of her dress and lightly caressed her inner thigh. Terri moaned softly as Don went beyond her thighs and lightly touched her womanhood.

Then he abruptly pulled away from her and said, "Come on or we'll be late for the movie."

Terri damn near fainted at the way he had her going. She reached into her purse, gave him the keys to the car, and told him to drive. Don1 helped her into the passenger seat then ran around to the other side of the car and got in.

Terri looked at him and said, "You have to promise to take it easy."

Don1 asked, "Are you talking about you or your car?"

Terri laughed and said, "The car silly. It hasn't been broken in yet."

Don laughed as Terri hit the button to drop the top. After all his kissing and caressing she needed some air! Terri was looking at Don1 trying to make up her mind if she was going to make it to one of their places before she was all over him or after. She was about to say something smart when Don1 ran his hand up her thigh. She started to stammer as his hand caressed her oh so gently. She put her hand on top of his and enjoyed the pleasure his hand was giving her. She released a small shimmer of an orgasm just as they arrived at the theater. Terri pushed the button to let the top up on the car. As soon as it was latched back in place, she got out of the car. She felt the night air blow onto the wetness between her thighs. She thought, "This man's breath is the next thing I want to feel there." Don got out of the car and Terri was there waiting. She grabbed his hand and they walked into the theater together.

Terri told Don, "I'll choose and pay for the movie." She chose a movie that had been out for some time that she had seen, but Don hadn't.

Don said, 'I've been so busy trying to maintain a green status in my business that I haven't taken much time out for myself."

Terri understood what Don was talking about because her father was the very same way. She remembered the stories her mom used to tell her about how she'd have to damn near force her father to go out and have a good time. Terri had a thought: "Maybe mother should have tried what Don1 and I are going to do tonight." She got the tickets and ordered Don a beer.

How did she know he drank beer? It seems he's not the only one checking up on someone. The two went deeper into the theater on a side where there were hardly any patrons. They found their movie and went inside. It was empty except for the two people cleaning up. They walked up to the front corner seats and sat down. Their seats made it easy to stretch out and enjoy the movie.

Don1 knew he was going to get lucky, he just didn't know how far Terri was going to let him go. He looked at his watch and saw that they were 5 minutes ahead of schedule.

Terri looked at Don and said, "Thank you for a good time tonight."

Don said, "It's my pleasure."

Terri said, "No it's mine, and I have wet panties to prove it."

Don smiled and said, "I'm glad you enjoyed it."

Terri reached over and pulled Don in for a kiss. It was a long wet kiss that was interrupted by the beginning of the movie and other moviegoers starting to come in. Terri let out a soft "damn," as a couple sat not to far from them. She looked over at them and they decided to move to the other side of the theater. Even in the dark, Terri could see that the woman was wearing a skirt shorter than what she had on. It did not bother her, but the woman was tall and stout. Terri dismissed it because she had something else on her mind. She turned back to Don who was watching the movie and enjoying his beer.

Don noticed Terri looking at him and turned to her. He finished off the beer and had to turn his head abruptly to burp. The two laughed and Don pushed the armrest from between them so he could pull Terri closer. They started to kiss until Don opened his eyes and saw the other couple tripping.

When Don stopped kissing her Terri looked at him and asked, "What's wrong?"

Don said, "Don't turn around 'because it's some nasty shit going on over there."

Terri was thinking the worse, because she was probably about to do the nasty herself. She looked at Don again and said, "What's wrong now?"

"Just don't pay them any attention," Don said.

With that she turned around saw the big woman in the extra short skirt straddling her date's face. The killing part was that 'she' was not a woman but a man dressed as a woman. The man with the skirt on was getting a blowjob from the other guy!

Don was furious. He got up and left the theater. Terri was right behind him. She went to the counter and demanded to see the manager. Then she and Don told him what was going on. The manager quickly dispatched security and had the police called. Security dragged the male couple from the theater and held them till the police arrived. Don got a good look at both guys, and thought he recognized one of them. He put it at the back of his mind as the police showed up and arrested the couple. They said they would be charged with public indecency and several other offences. Don1 and Terri received vouchers for a years' worth of movies for their trouble.

They decided to leave the theater and go for a drive. It was an uneventful drive until Don asked Terri, "How can I make up for tonight's fiasco?"

Terri was not going to let those punks ruin her night. She reached over to Don and unzipped his pants. She pulled his limp member free and asked, "If I make it rise will you let it shoot?"

Don pulled Terri to him and kissed her deeply. She pulled away from him and said, "Save that for later. Right now get me to a bed so I can finish what you started." Then Terri started giving Don some toe curling head. She wanted to see if he could handle himself while he was being handled.

Don headed straight for his apartment. He did not hit the brakes too hard because he did not want her to have a reason to stop.

Terri felt Don come to life and challenge her tongue in every way. She was determined to finish Don off before they got into bed. She wanted him to feel the pleasure of her mouth before he got between her legs.

Don was out of this world! He could not believe he was even with this woman or that she was giving him the best blow job of his life! He knew he was close to his place when Terri started drawing him in further. He was amazed at how she would not quit.

Terri was starting to get tired when she felt Don start thrusting forward to meet the down strokes of her mouth. She knew she had him where she wanted him so she put forth even more effort.

Don pulled into the parking space right next to his car at his apartment. He felt his body tense up as he let go an extreme orgasm. He felt his manhood surge and his eyes damn near crossed as his body convulsed with pleasure.

Terri lost all inhibition and swallowed deeply. She was playing for keeps and this meant everything was going to be hers for the enjoyment. She drank every-thing Don released and would not let go until he went limp.

Don was totally gone. He had to have this woman and he could not imagine letting her leave. He opened his eyes and there was Terri with the biggest grin on her face.

Don said, "Now you know you aren't finished don't you?"

Terri answered, "There's not enough room in the car to do what I really want."

Don fixed his clothes and started fumbling with the door handle. He got out of the car and ran to the passenger side. He helped Terri out and hit the key fob to lock her car. He grabbed Terri by the hand and walked with her into his apartment building. They got into the building and went straight to the elevator. Don pushed the button to take them to his floor and pulled Terri to him. She turned her back to him and pushed her nice round behind directly into him. She enjoyed the feeling of having Don behind her. He had started kissing her neck when the elevator door opened. They were on his floor. Terri pulled Don's arms around her as they walked to his door. She reached into his pockets and played with him. He was getting hard again and she was about to take full advantage of it.

She grabbed his keys and gave them to him. He quickly unlocked the door and they went in. Terri asked Don where the bathroom was. Don took her to the bathroom and told her he'd be in the den when she came out. Don went to the den and turned on the TV. He was very pleased with how the night was going.

Terri went into the bathroom and closed the door. She reached into her purse and pulled out her little survival kit. It had a small toothbrush, tampons, toothpaste, condoms, and a pair of panties with a matching bra. She had always carried her kit in her purse just in case. She quickly brushed her teeth, and then sprayed some flavored body spray under her skirt. She was about to walk out when she got an idea. She pulled off all her clothes except for her shoes, panties and bra. She stepped out of the bathroom and looked into one of the two doors on the hall. The first door was the room she was looking for; Don's bedroom. She had to give this man credit. His room was clean and neat. Terri climbed into the bed and pulled back the covers. She then called to Don.

Don didn't know what to think, so he got up and headed for the bathroom. As he stepped into the hall he saw the bathroom door was wide open, but nobody was in there. He went to his bedroom door and was greeted by a vision he had dreamed of many nights. This smart, sexy, beautiful woman was in his bed with barely any clothes on. He did not hesitate as he started stripping out of his clothes. He was in such a hurry his hands fumbled with his socks, then his pants, and then he damn near ripped off his shirt! As he did, the tent that his erection had made out of his underwear was clearly visible. Terri was happy with what she saw and helped Don get into bed. Don started to kiss Terri and was pleased that she had freshened up for him. He reached under her bra and pulled it up to expose her breast and gave each one his attention. He slowly made his way down to her belly button, where he had to taste every crevice. He moved further down and noticed the strings on either side of her panties. He quickly untied them and totally exposed this woman to his eyes. Don looked at her shaved body like it was a five star meal at the best restaurant in town.

He licked his lips and started to indulge himself on her womanhood. Terri's head went back as Don started giving her some of the best oral gratifications she'd had in years. She raised her buttocks so that he could get both hands full of her voluptuous body. Don had his face pushed deeply into her body. He wanted to make sure she was given the same amount of pleasure that he had received earlier. Don was then presented with a gift of Terri pleasure. She orgasmed hard as he continued to pleasure her with his magnificent skills. Terri pulled Don up until they were face to face and planted a kiss on his wet lips.

They kissed deeply as Don entered her body for that long awaited pleasure session. They were moving in unison with every thrust. Terri was totally lost in this man's power. Don was in another world trying to ensure that this was not the last time he saw this beautiful woman. He was not about to upset Terri in anyway. He wanted to make sure that she was there to stay.

Terri was into her own little fantasy when another orgasm made her gasp and pull Don into her even deeper. Don knew that he was not going to last much longer so he pulled away from her.

She felt Don's hands on her hips as he turned her over. She rolled to follow his lead. She lay on her stomach and offered herself to him. Her body was already wet from multiple orgasms. Don positioned himself behind her and thrust forward. This drove Terri wild as she found herself moaning with each thrust. She was losing control and liking every minute of it. Don was overjoyed at the pleasure he was giving and receiving. Terri was pushing back against Don's thrusts when he dropped his full weight down on her back. She was wild with passion as he turned her head and stuck his tongue in her mouth for a long passionate kiss.

Terri released his tongue and asked him in the height of passion, "Let me stay tonight."

Don replied, "No way in hell are you leaving tonight!"

Terri returned her mouth to his as Don started thrusting harder. She knew he was about to cum and she was coming with him. Terri lost it and said, "I Cumming!"

Don thrust deeply into her body as his body released every ounce of semen he had. He let out a deep growl as Terri wiggled hard to make sure his body dumped everything it had into her. They both collapsed as their orgasms finished simultaneously.

Terri pulled Don closer to her and said, "I hope you're still happy in the morning."

Don laughed and said, "The only way I wouldn't be happy is if you're not here when I wake up." They exchanged kisses as they started to doze off to sleep. Terri felt like she was in heaven as she felt Don's arms around her.

Don was just happy not sleeping alone. He asked Terri, "Would you like something to drink?" His answer was her heavy breathing which let him know that his guest was now fast asleep. He was not about to mess this up, so he got comfortable and dozed off too.

Terri awoke to the sound of her cell phone ringing. She cleared her eyes and then her head. She looked around, and then she remembered she'd had one heck of a night! She was happy with the outcome, and she was about ready for another round. She rose up in bed and saw that Don had cleaned up. He'd left his shirt on the bed for her to use as a robe. Terri smiled as she put on the shirt which fit her perfectly. The apartment was filled the aroma of banana pancakes and eggs. She walked to the kitchen and found Don just a-cooking! He had everything set up: coffee was brewing, orange juice was on the table, and table was set. Terri went over and gave him a big kiss.

Don said, "As much as I wanted to wake you, I decided to let you sleep. Now that you're awake, it's time to eat."

Terri laughed and smacked him on the butt. She asked, "are you trying to play for keeps?"

Don laughed and said, "I thought I told you I don't play."

Terri said, "Shut up before I have you for breakfast!"

She smiled and Don started serving her breakfast. He made sure she had plenty to eat as they both sat and enjoyed breakfast. Don decided to turn on the TV while they enjoyed their meal. He went to the local news channel and was tripping at some breaking news.

The news anchor stated that, "A young teen that had been missing for several months was found last night at a local movie theater. The teen was being sexually assaulted when a couple in the theater saw what was happening and notified the authorities. Thanks to the diligence of the couple, this young man who'd been missing for so long was now being treated

at a local hospital before being released to his parents."

The reporter then showed a shot of the movie theater that Don and Terri visited last night. He then
showed the same man who had been dressed like a
woman last night! His name was Newman Freat, but
on the street he was known as Nefertiti. They had
arrested him and he was being held without bond in
the local jail.

Don was tripping out! He looked at Terri and said,
"Well don't that beat all!"

Terri said, "Look at me. I have myself a real life he-
ro!"

Don just couldn't believe it. He said to Terri, "I almost just walked away without doing a thing about it."

Terri saw the concern on his face. She quickly got
up from her chair and went to him. She said, "Just
think about it. There's no telling what that man has
done to that poor child. You just helped that boy get
back to his family."

Don said, "You're right," and then they kissed.

Don pulled his lips from Terri's and said, "Go on
and finish your meal. I have something for you."

Terri got up from Don and he pinched her bottom
gently. She giggled as she went back to finish eating.

He went into the bedroom and heard her cell
phone ringing. He said, "Your phone's ringing!"

She asked, "Will you bring it to me?"

He grabbed the phone and took it to her, then
stepped into another part of the apartment where his
washer and dryer were. He had cleaned and washed all

of her clothes. He had spent the extra money to get one of those dryers that doubled as an at home dry cleaning service. Her clothes were as fresh, as if they'd just come from the cleaners. She was greatly surprise when he took the clothes to her.

He heard her say, "I'll be on the first flight out and we'll make the arrangements then." Terri hung up the phone and gave Don a passionate kiss. He asked her if everything was alright.

Terri said, "My brother was injured this morning in a boating accident. That was my father and mother calling. They want me to go see what he'll need since I'm closer. I told them I'll help out as much as I can until they can get here."

Don didn't want her to go but he knew he had pressing matters to take care of too if he was going to help Frequency. He was not going to let any of that interfere with the time he was spending with Terri. Terri had to get back to her apartment and get packed.

While she was dressing, Don pulled out his laptop and logged into the Cell Shop security camera system. He went back about two weeks and what he saw shocked him. It was the same guy in a skirt that had been arrested at the movie theatre with another man. He played back the video and the skirt guy kept calling the other dude Gay Mack. He had not thought any-thing of it until now. The dude called Gay Mack was a pimp. He made sure that all of his people had commu-nications. Don remembered that he ordered Sprint phones with the two-way radio feature so that his people would not use a lot of minutes. Don then decided to look into the store's database for more information.

He was just about to really start digging when Terri walked into the room looking as good as she had the previous night.

She asked Don, "Are you part Jamaican?"

He said, "No, why?"

Terri said, "Because you do so many different jobs," as she started laughing.

Don got up from his laptop and embraced her.

They started kissing and Terri had to stop him. She said, "Did you just clean me up to get me all soiled again?"

Don said, "If I have no problem with it, why should you?"

Terri said, "I have no problem, but after what happened last night, I know I would miss my flight! Will you walk me to my car?"

Don got up and escorted her to her car where they shared another passionate kiss. This time, it was Don who pulled away from Terri because he knew she had to get on a plane. He also knew he had to find out more about the dude in the skirt.

Don told Terri, "Call me as soon as she gets a chance."

Terri said, "Sure will, and I'll get back here as soon as I have my family taken care of."

He let her get into the car and watch her drive off. Then he went back into the house to finish reviewing the video. He played back the part in the video when Gay Mack said that he paid a pretty penny for the work on the skirt guy. The skirt guy was evidently a well-known transvestite. This dude was pimpin' dudes! "Now that's some sick shit," thought Don. How can a man, let another man make him suck and fuck guys for money, then bring all of it back to him? Those had to be some weak-assed dudes!

There was some sick shit going on with this dude. It looks like he's turning young boys into young girls. Now that's one sick dude who deserves to be hanged by his balls!   "Where is all this coming from?" Don thought to himself. He could not explain it and he didn't even want to try. "All I know is that this world is getting sicker by the day with no end to the MADDNESS in sight!"

Chapter 5

Long Haul

Frequency had everything in order for the meeting. He finally got BDB out of the tub. Dude had bubbles everywhere meaning he had finally gotten relaxed. They jumped into the TransAm and sped off toward the designated meeting area.

BDB asked, "Do y'all always meet this way?"

Freq replied, "Meetings are always carefully planned and executed down to the very last detail. I'd never have met with one of the FREAKS alone. The group is not designed to operate that way. We always meet as a group."

He continued, "The day I got arrested, Mr. White called me with a fictitious emergency. After I arrived, he started asking a bunch of 'How To' questions. I went into details about how to make the program work not knowing that he was wearing a wire for the FEDs. I made a huge mistake. I dropped my guard for some-one I thought was a friend, and he turned out to be a whistleblower. White and the Feds also made one big mistake. They didn't have enough solid evidence to put me away for life. Now that I'm back on the pavement, I'll get some 'V' on the whistleblower as soon as I can get this other matter out of the way."

BDB asked, "What will you do if they come to the house looking for you?"

"Don't worry about that my friend," Frequency said, "CMAX is more than capable of handling any unauthorized person on my property." They pulled into a parking garage.

Freq told BDB, "Follow me and I'll explain everything else when we get to the pickup area."

They went down a couple of flights of stairs and then out of one of the parking garage exits. Just as they stepped out onto the sidewalk, a big black Chevrolet custom truck pulled up and the door opened. Freq and BDB climbed inside and greeted the rest of the FREAKS.

Freq laughed and said, "Webb you've outdone yourself this time!"

Webb was grinning like the cat that swallowed the canary. He pulled the truck away from the curb and headed to the local Racetrack. The designated area was perfect! Who would look for a team of hackers in a motor sport park?

Freq introduced BDB to the crew. "EoW is our computer hardware specialist, Don1 is cellular and networking specialist, M. Webb is transportation and master detail mechanic. And of course you know me: Frequency Hunter, all around computer expert."

Don1 said, "Yeah right," and they all laughed.

BDB then spoke up and told the guys about himself, not leaving out any of the details. After he finished, the guys wanted to know how he felt working with a team of computer nerds.

BDB stated "You guys aren't nerds; you're the best in your fields. If the world can't deal with that, it'll have to deal with me."

"Now that's what I am talking about," said Webb, "now we have some muscle that ain't scared to take on the idiots." Webb then brought the crew up to date on the custom truck he was driving.

Series III 20' GARAGE MOTORHOME STARTING AT $39.900

- Series III Standard Features
- Air Conditioner
- Microwave
- Sleeper Sofa
- 48" counter and single sink in Kitchen
- Dinette that converts to a bed

- Oak trim
- six foot oak cabinets
- 1 Lower Kitchen cabinet
- White ceiling
- 110 interior lighting
- 6- 12 Volt reading lights
- 110 Volt interior receipts GFI
- Base to accommodate full size bed in back of conversion- motor home
- Bunk over the Cab
- Stool
- Full size shower
- 6 gallon Electric hot water heater
- Carbon monoxide and smoke detectors
- Fire extinguisher
- Receiver Hitch
- Lower storage compartments with weather sealed doors
- 50 gallon fresh water
- 60 gallon black water
- 60 gallon gray water
- .040 Smooth Exterior Sheeting
- Curb side door
- Flexible weather seal between cab and conversion
- Easy access between cab and conversion
- Series III Optional Features
- 8 Cubic foot Gas Refrigerator
- 2 burner cook top

- LP tank, mounting and hook up 20,000 BTU LP furnace
- Additional 25 gallon fresh water tank
- Leather sofa and cushions
- Day/night window shades
- AM/FM CD with 2 speakers
- 20" & 30" LCD with 360 degree satellite antenna
- Satellite remote system
- 7.5 Watt Diesel Generator
- 10 K Diesel Generator
- 12 K Diesel Generator
- 14' awning
- 20' awning
- Electric Step
- Hardwood Floors
- Oak Paneling

"And to top it off it has a custom liquid cooled cabinet for CMAX," Webb said.   Frequency was hyped! He knew now how he would throw the FEDs off when they come looking for them. He told the guys, "The FREAKS are going all out mobile. With this vehicle, we can really set up shop and gather more than enough information to clear up this mess that White dropped on me." Freq pulled out a pad and started laying out plans on how to equip the truck with all the necessary computer equipment.

EoW was all ears as he started making calls to get the items Freq would need ordered. Don1 put together a serious cellular network that was Bluetooth capable.

He would also set up interactive monitoring of cellular towers to help them know who is in the area transmitting signals. That would help them keep tabs on law enforcement vehicles and personnel at all times.

Webb said, "BDB and I will go to my shop and kick this thang up a notch. I'll add a bully dog propane injection kit and a Bank's dual turbocharger setup. We'll also add a bigger tank for gas and make sure there's enough voltage to run all the computer systems."

Freq said, "I like everything that's come out of our meeting so far. I'd say it's been very productive so far."

Then he got to the next item on his agenda. He pulled out his names and found a plastic bag in a cabinet. He put the names in the bag and had everybody pull out one. EoW pulled out Mama's Boy. Don1 pulled Madame & Big Trouble. Then Webb pulled Johnson City, and BDB pulled the Banker, Freq reached in and pulled out Cupcake. When EoW reached in again and pulled Gay Mack, the crew had to laugh at the look on his face. Don1 was about to pull again but Freq stopped him saying that he already had two. Webb reached in and pulled Elevator Man and BDB then pulled out Judge.

All the guys got quiet and BDB was confused.

Freq told BDB, "I believe Judge is the ring leader, so you'll have to play him close but smart."

BDB said, "I have the perfect idea to get to him."

Freq said, "Cool," then he reached inside the bag again, but the bag was empty. He decided to add Mr. White, an outsider, to the list.

He said, "I'm adding Mr. White to this group with the code name Whistleblower.

Don1 asked, "Why did you call him Whistleblower?"

Before Freq could answer, Webb shouted, "Because he's a snitch and his bitch ass needs to be hung by the balls!"

The guys all started laughing and Freq said, "I plan to make sure the Whistleblower pays for what he has done to the group as a whole and to me. Now that we have some work to do let's get this party started! Webb, get BDB some wheels and get this truck ready for CMAX as soon as possible."

Webb said, "This truck has a name."

Freq said, "You named it already? So what is it?"

Webb said, "Long Haul."

"So now you guys can get Long Haul ready for service because we've got a lot of info to gather but not a lot of time to work with," said Freq.

The crew all agreed and Webb got them headed to the next drop off point. Freq told BDB to ride out with Webb. Don1 and EoW knew exactly what to do. This wasn't the first time they had to work as a team, but this time they had a lot more at stake. Webb and BDB dropped off EoW and then Don1. They took Long Haul to the shop where Webb planned to do all the required modifications to the truck. He had already pre-ordered the parts for the engine mods and had a grease board with a list of all the things he needed to do.

BDB looked at the board and said, "We have our work cut out for us."

Webb said, "You don't have to worry 'bout a thing. I have a crew of mechanics that'll be in shortly to help us with this job."

BDB asked Webb, "Why are you all so loyal to Frequency? Why not just accept the things White did and walk away?"

Webb said, "Freq taught us all we knew about computers and business. He set us up with our own individual accounts and made sure we all had a secure future. When Mr. White turned over on us, Frequency made sure he was the only one the authorities could find. .Freq took the full onslaught of the Feds investigation. It was as if the rest of us in the group didn't exist. The Feds only found the evidence that Mr. White gave them about Frequency. Freq is a true friend that deserves much more than our loyalty. Until we can give him more, our loyalty will have to suffice."

Webb heard the chime from the security system. He turned on the security camera monitor and it was the mechanic crew.

The guys came in through the main door and were awe struck when they saw Long Haul. Kenny, the leader of the crew said, "When you said this truck was large, you meant LARGE!"

Webb laughed and said, "I want this thang to run like a scalded dog!"

The crew went to work on the engine modifications, and Webb and BDB started setting up the interior for CMAX. Webb and BDB got the 360 degree satellite online first so they could get CMAX linked in and have all the detailed instructions needed straight from him. It wasn't long before they heard the familiar voice of CMAX giving them step-by-step details of the intricate case needed to support his special operating systems.

BDB had to go out and get Freon and a compressor from a local A/C repair shop. He knew of the shop because it was owned by an old friend. Blue's A/C Repair was closed for business and he was about to leave when he heard the knock on his door. It was strange because the knock had a familiar rhythm to it. Blue knew there was only one person who knocked like that. He opened the door and sure enough there was his old friend.

He greeted BDB with a smile and said, "I can't believe my eyes!" as they shook hands. "Come on in, you want a beer?" They sat for a while and chatted, reminiscing about old times.   Blue asked, "What brings you to the shop?"

BDB told him what he needed and what they were building.

Blue asked, "Can I be of any assistance?"

BDB said, "You're the A/C man. Your expertise would be greatly appreciated." They gathered up the parts specified by CMAX, then headed to the shop. Blue brought all of his A/C repair tools because this was one serious cooling system that BDB was trying to put together.

BDB got back in Webb's shop truck and headed back to the shop. Blue followed closely so he wouldn't lose him. They got into the shop and BDB introduced Blue to Webb and the crew. Webb then introduced

Blue to Long Haul. Blue went inside and saw all the intricate design.

He said, "I'm going to need my tools from the truck. This is going to take some time!"

Webb said, "You have until morning." As he handed Blue an envelope with 10 k in it.

Blue opened the envelope, then pulled out his cell phone and called his girlfriend. He said, "I won't be in for dinner today, but I need you to make reservation for Vegas tomorrow." He didn't give her any details as he hung up the phone. He got started on the system. By morning he was done. He was the last one to get finished.

Blue stood up from his work and went to the driver's area. He started Long Haul up and the truck roared to life. He looked at the instrument panel and everything checked out. All the guys had crashed in the shop. They started coming around one by one looking at all of the work that had been done in one night. Webb and BDB had crashed on the shop couches. They jumped up and said, "Everybody get in and let's go for a ride!"

Webb traded places with Blue and had BDB open the shop's large rear doors. He pulled the truck out and hit the automatic button to close the door. Webb opened the door to Long Haul and BDB jumped in. Webb started grinning like he'd just won the lottery. He steered the big truck around the corner, then onto the main street. He pulled right up to the light next to a hyped up import car.

Webb revved the engine and black smoke poured out of the exhaust. The dude in the import car revved back. Dude laughed thinking that this truck was easy pickings. The light turned green and Webb stomped the gas pedal to the floor. Long Haul's tires let out a deep screech unheard from a truck of this magnitude. The import took off and, to the amazement of the guy driving it, the big truck was right there beside him. The dude was awe struck as he went through the gears and the big truck stayed right beside him. He was really floored when the big truck started pulling ahead of him. The last thing he remembered was the driver of the truck and the grin he had on his face.

Webb pointed Long Haul onto the interstate and headed to EoW's shop. He knew EoW and Don1 would be ready to do their part for Long Haul. Webb drove the interstate for a while before he jumped off and stopped at IHOP to buy breakfast for all the fellas. He pulled into the parking lot and parked with no trouble. He unlocked the doors and the whole crew jumped out, still buzzing with excitement. They knew that their modifications were top of the line and flawless. The shop crew, Blue, Webb and BDB ate a hearty breakfast then returned to the shop. Webb paid the crew very generously for their work and sent them on their way.

Blue gave Webb and BDB his cell number and said, "If you ever need anything else just call. You guys know how to put money in man's pocket!" He jumped into his truck and headed for home. He still had to explain to his girlfriend everything he'd just experienced.

Webb called Don1 and asked, "You ready for Long Haul?"

Don1 said, "I'm waiting for FedEx. They should be delivering within the hour. I'll put everything together in the shop."

Webb said, "Cool. I'll contact EoW and see if he's ready."

Don1 said, "I'll holler latah," hung up.

The door of the shop started to rise as EoW arrived in his Nissan Xterra SUV full of computer goodies. EoW jumped out and said, "All set to get CMAX's new home ready!"

Webb asked," What all do you have?"

EoW said, "I went beyond the specifications that Freq gave me."

BDB looked confused, so Webb told EoW to explain what was up.

EoW started up. He said, "The specifications that Freq gave me were for a top of the line computer two years ago. Technology has changed exponentially since then. CMAX will now have eighteen of the hottest processors money can buy, ten terabyte hard drives and a digital sound system like none other. It will be linked to every monitor within the vehicle making it totally interactive. No keyboard will be needed thanks to voice command and you already know about the cooling system. CMAX will control and monitor everything within Long Haul. This will be one bad ass setup when we get done!"

BDB was still lost, so EoW said, "Only the Feds and major corporations will have something like this."

That's when BDB understood.

EoW went inside Long Haul to get started. Webb told him, "Me and BDB are going to leave and get some much needed rest."

EoW said, "I'll call when I'm done."

EoW went to work and BDB and Webb jumped into the Catalina and took off. Webb took BDB to the Toy Store car lot. There they talked to Mr. Sherrod and got BDB a work truck. It was nothing fancy just something for hauling lawn equipment and pulling a trailer.

BDB told Webb, "I'm going to use my lawn service business to infiltrate the Banker and the Judge."

Webb said, "That's a great idea. but what about the lawn service they're already using?"   BDB   said, "I'll just convince them to take a vacation."

Webb laughed and said, "Meet me back at the shop tomorrow."

BDB jumped into his new truck and pulled off. Webb jumped into the Catalina and headed home for some rest.

Back at the shop, EoW was joined by Don1. The two of them worked until they had finished all of the computer specification and the cellular network. Long Haul was ready for the main ingredient, the CMAX operating system.

Freq was at home doing research on a way to enable Long Haul to render any vehicle defenseless. He was reading an article on an electromagnetic bomb. He wasn't trying to set off a nuclear bomb, but he wanted to use similar technology to disable any electronic device. The article had some interesting points. It said:

High power electromagnetic pulse generation techniques and high power microwave technology have matured to the point where practical E-Bombs (electromagnetic bombs) are becoming technically feasible with new applications in both strategic and tactical Information warfare. The development of conventional E-Bomb devices allows their use in non-nuclear confrontations. The ElectroMagnetic Pulse (EMP) effect was first observed during the early testing of high altitude airburst nuclear weapons.

The effect is characterized by the production of a very short (hundreds of nanoseconds) but intense electromagnetic pulses, which propagates away from its source with ever diminishing intensity governed by the theory of electromagnetism. The ElectroMagnetic Pulse is in effect an electromagnetic shock wave.

This pulse of energy produces a powerful electro-magnetic field, particularly within the vicinity of the weapon burst. The field can be sufficiently strong to produce short lived transient voltages of thousands of Volts (i.e. kilovolts) on exposed electrical conductors, such as wires, or conductive tracks on printed circuit boards, where exposed.

It is this aspect of the EMP effect which is of mili-tary significance, as it can result in irreversible damage to a wide range of electrical and electronic equipment, particularly computers and radio or radar receivers. Subject to the electromagnetic hardness of the elec-tronics, a measure of the equipment's resilience to this effect, and the intensity of the field produced by the weapon, the equipment can be irreversibly damaged or in effect electrically destroyed. The damage inflicted is not unlike that experienced through exposure to close proximity lightning strikes, and may require complete replacement of the equipment, or at least substantial portions thereof.

Commercial computer equipment is particularly vulnerable to EMP effects, as it is largely built of high density Metal Oxide Semiconductor (MOS) devices, which are very sensitive to exposure to high voltage transients. What is significant about MOS devices is that very little energy is required to permanently wound or destroy them. Any voltage typically in excess of tens of Volts can produce an effect termed gate breakdown which effectively destroys the device. Even if the pulse is not powerful enough to produce thermal damage, the power supply in the equipment will readily supply enough energy to complete the destructive process. Wounded devices may still function, but their reliability will be seriously impaired. Shielding electronics by equipment chassis provides only limited protection, as any cables running in and out of the equipment will behave very much like antennae, in effect guiding the high voltage transients into the equipment.

Computers used in data processing systems, communications systems, displays, industrial control applications, including road and rail signaling, and those embedded in military equipment, such as signal processors, electronic flight controls and digital engine control systems, are all potentially vulnerable to the EMP effect.

Other electronic devices and electrical equipment may also be destroyed by the EMP effect. Telecommunications equipment can be highly vulnerable, due to the presence of lengthy copper cables between devices. Receivers of all varieties are particularly sensitive to EMP, as the highly sensitive miniature high frequency transistors and diodes in such equipment are easily destroyed by exposure to high voltage electrical transients. Therefore radar and electronic warfare equipment, satellite, microwave, UHF, VHF, HF and low band communications equipment and television equipment are all potentially vulnerable to the EMP effect.

It is significant that modern military platforms are densely packed with electronic equipment, and unless these platforms are well hardened, an EMP device can substantially reduce their function or render them unusable.

Frequency found a device called a High Power Microwave Source or the Vircator.

The Vircator is of interest because it is a one shot device capable of producing a very powerful single pulse of radiation, yet it is mechanically simple, small and robust, and can operate over a relatively broad band of microwave frequencies.

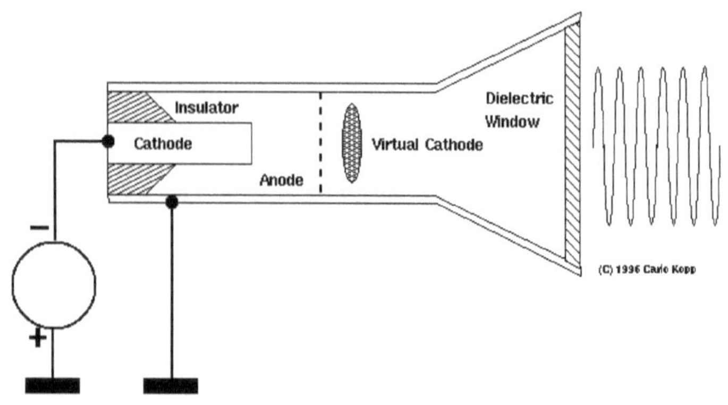

FIG.3 AXIAL VIRTUAL CATHODE OSCILLATOR

The physics of the Vircator tube are substantially more complex than those of the preceding devices. The fundamental idea behind the Vircator is that of accelerating a high current electron beam against a mesh (or foil) anode. Many electrons will pass through the anode, forming a bubble of space charge behind the anode. Under the proper conditions, this space charge region will oscillate at microwave frequencies. If the space charge region is placed into a resonant cavity which is appropriately tuned, very high peak powers may be achieved. Conventional microwave engineering techniques may then be used to extract microwave power from the resonant cavity. Because the frequency of oscillation is dependent upon the electron beam parameters, Vircators may be tuned or chirped in frequency, where the microwave cavity will support appropriate modes. Power levels achieved in Vircator experiments range from 170 kilowatts to 40

Gigawatts over frequencies spanning the decimetric and centimetric bands.

The two most commonly described configurations for the Vircator are the Axial Vircator (AV) (Fig.3), and the Transverse Vircator (TV). The Axial Vircator is the simplest by design, and has generally produced the best power output in experiments. It is typically built into a cylindrical waveguide structure. Power is most often extracted by transitioning the waveguide into a conical horn structure, which functions as an antenna. AVs typically oscillate in Transverse Magnetic (TM) modes. The Transverse Vircator injects cathode current from the side of the cavity and will typically oscillate in a Transverse Electric (TE) mode.

Technical issues in Vircator design are output pulse duration, which is typically of the order of a microsecond and is limited by anode melting, stability of oscillation frequency, often compromised by cavity mode hopping, conversion efficiency and total power output. Coupling power efficiently from the Vircator cavity in modes suitable for a chosen antenna type may also be an issue, given the high power levels involved and thus the potential for electrical breakdown in insulators.

Frequency started putting his idea into CMAX for his design of turning an EMP into a scanner that could be fired from Long Haul. As he set up everything in a virtual environment, he kept running into obstacles and failures. Not one to give up easily, Frequency had CMAX pull more information for him to use in his EMP design. One fix was "Coupling Modes" which in assessing how power was coupled into targets; two principal coupling modes were recognized in his research:

• Front Door Coupling occurs typically when power from an electromagnetic weapon is coupled into an antenna associated with radar or communications equipment. The antenna subsystem is designed to couple power in and out of the equipment, and thus provides an efficient path for the power flow from the electromagnetic weapon to enter the equipment and cause damage.

• Back Door Coupling occurs when the electromagnetic field from a weapon produces large transient currents (called spikes, when produced by a low frequency weapon) or electrical standing waves when fixed on electrical wiring and cables interconnecting equipment, or providing connections to mains power or the telephone network. Equipment connected to exposed cables or wiring will experience either high voltage transient spikes or standing waves which can damage power supplies and communications interfaces if these are not hardened. Moreover, should the transient penetrate into the equipment, damage can be done to other devices inside.

A low frequency weapon will couple well into a typical wiring infrastructure, as most telephone lines, networking cables and power lines follow streets, building risers and corridors. In most instances any particular cable run will comprise multiple linear segments joined at approximately right angles. Whatever the relative orientation of the weapons field, more than one linear segment of the cable run is likely to be oriented such that a good coupling efficiency can be achieved.

Frequency added this mode and tried the 3-d model again with a much improve success rate. He then started putting together an equipment list. Most of the stuff could be bought at the higher end electrical shops. Frequency had CMAX make the necessary orders and arrange to have them delivered to various companies with which he was affiliated. Freq knew this wouldn't lead any Federal agents to his door.

Freq gave EoW a call and told him of his success with the EMP scanner 3-d model. EoW told Frequency that they were finished with all the modifications and were ready for the main ingredient.

Freq asked, "How soon can I upload CMAX to the new system?"

EoW answered, "Immediately; in fact I'm already en route. I hope you have some food in the house."

Frequency said, "Bring Long Haul on so I can get started. I've got plenty of food and beer too!"

EoW said, "I'll pick up Don1 and we'll be arriving shortly."

Frequency knew he had to put this package together and get it off to the patent office as soon as possible. He gave CMAX a series of commands to put everything together for the EMP and get it ready to ship off via FedEx. Frequency realized that as soon as this hit the patent office with his name on it, the Feds would come a knocking. He decided to create a fake company, and have Don1 do all the necessary paperwork to get it legitimized. He also decided that he'd call the company "emps, inc." The company would specialize in the making of children's talking computers. He then put on paper a fictitious board of directors and executive staff. He'd done this before with other ventures, and with friends like Don1 and EoW, Frequency knew the company would appear to be both legitimate and profitable

CMAX announced that a vehicle was approaching. Frequency had CMAX bring all cameras online and he saw Long Haul pulling into the driveway with EoW at the wheel. Frequency got up from his desk and went outside to meet them. He walked up to the door of Long Haul and it opened automatically.

Frequency stepped in and said, "I am impressed. Not bad for one nights work."

EoW said,"You've got Webb's crew and BDB to thank. .They worked all night to pull this off."

Ok then what do you two have for me to see?" asked Freq.

EoW began the demonstration with Don1 right there to back him up. Frequency was incredibly impressed with the system they'd designed. Once they finished their demo, Don1 pushed the button to turn on the communication system. CMAX announced that he had full access to all system functions inside and could commence backup immediately.

Frequency asked, "What's the down time for this procedure?" CMAX calculated all of the processes and said that he'd be down for 12 hours. Frequency didn't like the sound of that. He knew they still had a lot of information to gather before they could take CMAX down for 12 hours.

Don1 told Freq, "If we do the main backup tonight all that'll be left to do is to move all of CMAX's artificial intelligence information via secure wireless connection."

That gave Freq some hope. He knew that the crew would be defenseless without CMAX fully online. Then he came up with an alternative idea.

Frequency asked the guys, "Did you put in a 10/100 switch like asked?"

EoW said, "No." Freq was about to explode when Don1 said, "Instead we put in a 100/1000 switch."

EoW said, "Gotcha!!"

Frequency went to the onboard keyboard and linked in with CMAX.

First, Freq activated full voice command and CMAX acknowledged. Next, Frequency had Don1 and EoW give CMAX all of the system specification they put in. After that, Frequency had CMAX recalculate all of the procedures. The new specifications knocked the down time for system backup to 4 hours with no trace data left behind.

Frequency loved hearing that! He then had CMAX brief the guys on their new business endeavor. He gave Don1 all of the paperwork and patent information. He gave EoW the information for all of the tracking numbers for FedEx.

EoW looked at all the descriptions of parts and said, "Damn dog! We making a bomb!"

"No," said Freq, "just an EMP scanner to help keep the haters offs our backs." Frequency had CMAX send all the FREAKS details of the inner and outer workings of the EMP scanner via their individual cell phones.

He told EoW, "Make sure that Webb and BDB don't go out and use this thing before it's time."

Don1 laughed and said, "I can just see Webb disabling cars and then selling his mechanical services to them." They all had a good laugh on that one.

Freq said, "I need for you guys to get Long Haul hooked up to CMAX's main frame to get the backup started."

EoW went into the back compartment and pulled out a long network cable. He plugged one end into the 100/1000 switch of Long Haul and started pulling the other end into the house. The door on Long Haul closed, but it did not damage the cable. EoW, Don1, and Frequency went into Freq's house and down to the basement to access CMAX's mainframe. Frequency took the cable from EoW and plugged it into CMAX's mainframe Ethernet port. CMAX acknowledged with, "backup process has begun."

Frequency saw the lights in his house dim momentarily. The power CMAX was using was incredible! Frequency and the fellas decided not to sit around and watch the light show, so they went upstairs to eat and watch some TV. They went into the kitchen and saw that Frequency had plenty of food. He had just gone to the grocery store yesterday. Freq went into the room where the 50-inch LCD TV was. He told CMAX to activate TV, but nothing happened. Frequency was puzzled, but EoW grabbed the remote, blew the dust off and pressed the power button.

Don1, who was laughing hysterically, said, "Freq's got to learn to watch TV the old fashion way!" Then all of them started laughing.

When CMAX said he'd be down, Freq did not think that all of the systems would be down. Well it'll just be a couple of hours, and then everything should be okay. Frequency sat back and watched TV with the guys and talked about old times. It felt good to be sitting with them knowing they would be ready for anything once CMAX was totally migrated over to Long Haul. Freq started thinking about what he needed to do to get Mr. White and put an end to that pedophile group once and for all. The ideas that came to mind made him think more of the long haul ahead.

Chapter 6

Cupcake

Frequency had just finished working on his plans to roll out his new business the Dyno-Drag portable drag racing center. The center was basically a big trailer with 2 steel Dyno monitor wheels set up to see if a potential rider or vehicle is ready for the real quarter mile. Frequency loved seeing the diagnostic review of a run on the Dyno to see what changes, if any, needed to be made. He installed the last of the software needed to run the Dyno Drag program, and then put every-thing away till later. Frequency decided to head out and see what was happening on the street racing circuit.

He opened the garage and cranked up the old school Virago. He pulled out into the driveway and hit the button to bring his motorcycle to life. The exhaust note was loud and strong. Frequency put on his helmet and gloves and set out on a night ride. He rode down toward the outskirts of town, where all of the biker groups and wanna be groups hung out and raced. Frequency had not been out in years and rode the old school bike because he knew he was rusty. He felt the night breeze blow on him and seemed to smile as he rode. Frequency rode through the crowd, and then parked the side of the road. A couple of Hayabusas shot down the street starting off tonight's festivities. Next R1 vs. Gsx1000 lined up and went down. After that, a couple of tuner cars lined up and went down. A familiar face pulled up to the line and riding a limited edition red Hayabusa. A young cat on a Honda pulled next to him and laid money on the line. This meant there was about to be an all out drag war. A nice looking young lady came out between the two bikes and held up a rag. The two bikers revved up, then took off when she dropped her hand. Frequency had to give the young cat credit. He jumped the red Hayabusa, but that was about it.

The red Busa settled in and walked the dog with the Honda. As they came back up the street the young lady took the money over to the red Busa and the winner took the money. The rider of the bike noticed Frequency and rode over to him. He got to Frequency and parked his bike. He took his helmet off and Frequency realized it was his friend KP. KP was the reigning King of the Street. Frequency got off his bike and gave him a firm handshake and a hug.   KP asked, "Where've you been?"

Frequency gave him the low down on the double cross by Mr. White.

KP said, "Mr. White is a low down dirty dog that needs to be dragged by the balls!"

Frequency said, "That time might just come soon. I'm putting something together to handle Mr. White."

KP then asked Frequency, "What the hell are you riding?"

Frequency said," This is an old school project that I've been working on."

Frequency threw KP the keys and KP took it out for a ride. KP was a serious crotch rocket rider, but he found himself enjoying the old school cruiser. He came back and parked the bike. He and Frequency sat back and watched the night's festivities unfold. KP told Frequency about How he won 'King of the Street' and that now he pulled 25% on all races sanctioned throughout the city. Frequency told him about his new business venture, the Dyno Drag.

KP said, 'I've heard about it, but nobody in the circuit has had the capital to make it happen here."

Frequency threw out some numbers to KP and saw that he was interested. Frequency then threw the pitch that got KP's full support.

He said, "No more payoffs to the cops."

KP smiled and said, "You know they're going to come after you when you cut into their money."

Frequency said. "You know they're going to go after Mr. White when he cuts into their money."

KP thought about this, and then laughed. He said, "Frequency you one sneaky motherfucka!"

They both laughed hard as one of KP's bikers rode up and said a female was out their knocking down his bikers on the set. KP was not concerned because she hadn't knocked off a real contender yet.

When the biker told KP, "She's after Little Charlotte's pants," KP became concerned.

"Who is Little Charlotte? asked Frequency.

"Little Charlotte weighs about 125 pounds soaking wet, but she rides a dime like it was stolen."

Frequency had been off the circuit for a good while so he asked, "What is a dime?"

KP said, "That's a 1000cc motorcycle that runs with the big boys." Frequency nodded then asked, "So what's the problem?"

KP said," Sounds like we got ourselves a "dab"."

"Say what?" said Frequency.

KP said, "A dike on a bike."

Frequency laughed so hard he damn near fell. He followed KP to the straight away where the races were going down. He and KP saw a GSX1000 pull up and park. It was little Charlotte and her bike called "Dime". Charlotte was a dark skinned lady with a nice athletic shape. She walked up to KP and said, "This dike bitch wants my ass."

KP asked, "What do you want to do?"

Charlotte didn't look real sure, but she said, "I'll take the run."

KP looked at Charlotte and said,"You know what happens if you lose right?"

 Charlotte looked at KP and said, "I'm strictly dickey and I do not do fakes."

"Ok," said KP, "I'll make the race happen." He went onto the strip where the races had been staged, and saw a Ducati Monster S2R 1000. It had a custom paint theme that made it look like a chocolate cake. KP figured out how she was beating his guys when she walked up. She was a stout, nice looking woman, but you could see that no man was getting next to her. The bike was naked, with no fairings and fenders to make it look like a crotch rocket. The woman stepped up to KP and said, "What do I have to do to get a race?"

KP laughed and said, "I heard you been knocking down my riders and now you up for some high stakes riding."

The woman said, "So you must be the King."

"That I am," said KP, "and with whom do I have the pleasure of speaking?"

She said, "My name is Cupcake."

Frequency overheard her and had to get a closer look. He knew he had information on someone called Cupcake, and wondered if this could be the same person under the code. He moved away from KP and the group and pulled his cell phone out of saddlebag on his motorcycle. He activated voice command, and then had CMAX pull the file on Cupcake. CMAX cross referenced everything in the Gathering file and said, "We have images and voice patterns to cross refer-ence."

Frequency said, "Hold that information and get ready for a cross check." He headed over to KP and whispered, "I'll back Charlotte's run one hundred percent."

KP asked Cupcake, "What did you bring to the ta-ble?"

Cupcake had given up a lot just to get the motorcycle she was on. She had belonged to a couple of riders called Fire and Ice. She'd done whatever they told her for several years until she was able to work her way out from under them. They used her for sexual gratification on many different occasions. She accepted the fact that two women were her masters until she came up with a way to get them to leave her alone. She won her freedom when they lost her in a race to Madame & Big Trouble. Madame and Big Trouble toyed with her for a few months, and then they put her to work recruiting teenaged girls. She liked having the freedom to move around without any repercussions other than when Madame needed to get her rocks off.

Cupcake hated when Big Trouble came around because he knew how to hurt a woman. When she refused to do as she was told with Big Trouble, Madame gave her an alternative. Madame told Cupcake to bring them something fresh to replace her and she'd never have to worry about Big Trouble again. Cupcake turned her first teen girl in one week. She found her at the local adolescent center. Her name was Tricia and she was a temperamental young girl. Cupcake played right along with her and in no time she handed her over to Madame and Big Trouble. They got her pulling down $2500.00 a week. It didn't matter to Cupcake that this girl was still a child. She enjoyed receiving large amounts of money from Madame. Madame also satisfied her sexual needs whenever Big Trouble wasn't around. Cupcake decided that using Madame's car all of the time was not a good idea so she went back to Fire and Ice and asked them to teach her to ride.

They told her that they would teach her whatever she wanted to know as long as she agreed to spend a week with them. Cupcake knew what they wanted and she agreed. Not only did they teach her how to ride, they also taught her how to win races. Cupcake remembered the bike as they pulled it out of their storage unit. They said a man had lost his bike and his manhood to them on that very day. Cupcake did not react because she'd been witness to many a men trying to mount these two women. She'd also seen these same two women turn men away with their deflated egos between their legs. Cupcake pushed her past out of her mind and dealt with the present.

Cupcake told KP, I want Little Charlotte, and I won't settle for anything else." She had watched Little Charlotte ride and knew what she was capable of. Cupcake had it in her mind that when she won Charlotte, she would have her own girl to help bring in some money.

Charlotte stepped up to KP and said, "I'll run this bitch, but she's got to have something more than a bike."

KP looked at Cupcake and said, "If you lose you belong to my crew,"   Cupcake said, "I'm strictly down for the ladies -- no man's land."

KP figured that and said, "You got to bring ass to get ass!"

Cupcake said, "I only brought cash. That should be enough."

KP asked, "What you got?"

Cupcake pulled out 10k and threw it at KP's feet.

Now that changed the game for KP. He picked up the cash which was bank wrapped for authenticity.

Charlotte knew she didn't have that kind of money, but that's when Frequency stepped in.

He walked up behind Little Charlotte and said, "I got your back and you better not let me down."

Charlotte started up the 'dime piece' and did a burn out. Cupcake started her bike and did the same. The two ladies lined up on the mark in the road and awaited instructions.

KP stepped up to the ladies and handed each a cylinder of nitrous oxide.   Charlotte screwed her bottle in place and so did Cupcake. Cupcake was nervous because she had run with NOs only a few times. Now she had to make it count. Cupcake got on the line and revved her bike to 3500 rpm. She wanted to launch hard and fast, but did not want to pop a wheelie. That would have ensured her loss.

Charlotte revved to 4000 rpm. She knew her bike would come off the line perfectly at that rpm. The two ladies' eyes were focused straight ahead of them. .

KP went out on the street between the two bikes and held up his hands. He dropped them simultaneously and the ladies took off! Their bikes roared down the street like lightning! Cupcake was good and was shifting the Ducati like they were one. She hit the bottle of NOs in fifth gear and her bike lurched forward hard.

Charlotte had run a smooth race, keeping the Ducati close as she waited for Cupcake to blow her bottle of NOs. As Charlotte had expected, Cupcake blew it too soon. Charlotte released hers and the Dime piece lurched forward and passed the Ducati right at the finished line! Charlotte stepped on the rear brake and let the bike come to a screeching halt. She did a celebratory donut and headed back to the starting line.

Cupcake was sunk; she could not believe she'd just lost. She turned her bike around and headed back to the starting line. As she got to the line, she saw KP, Charlotte and some other guy talking. She rode up to them.

To Charlotte she said, "Good race." Charlotte nodded and walked away.   KP stepped up to Cupcake and said, "You need to leave since you lost. That's the way we operate."

Cupcake wanted a second chance to win the right to challenge KP. So she asked KP, "How about another race?" But this time all she had was the clothes on her back.

KP laughed and said, "Ok I'll let you race Charlotte again only this time the loser gives up their riding gear."

KP called Charlotte over and told about the second race and the new stipulation and she agreed.

Cupcake didn't have anything else to lose but the clothes on her back. She spoke up and said, "This race is engine only."

KP looked at Charlotte as she nodded her agreement. The ladies went back to the starting line and prepared for a second run. KP sent riders down to the other end to make sure both ladies would come back up to adhere to the stipulation. KP went between both bikes to the starting line and held up his hands. Cupcake revved her engine up to 4500 rpm this time and Charlotte did 4200 rpm. KP dropped his hands and the bikes took off. Cupcake and Charlotte both shifted at the same time, dragging the rpm level to the red before each shift. The ladies were side by side when Charlotte pulled herself lower to her gas tank, to give herself a slight wind advantage. The 'Dime piece' edged forward just at the finish line to give Charlotte the win again! Charlotte went through her celebratory donut at the end of the track and headed back to the starting line.

Cupcake slowed her bike and started to ride off until she saw the other bikers waiting down at the end. She put on brakes, turned the bike around and headed for the starting line. Cupcake pulled up to the line and handed KP her helmet.

KP laughed and said, "I didn't win your stuff, so pass that shit to the little lady."

Cupcake went to Charlotte and handed her the helmet.

Charlotte laughed and said, "You can keep your helmet and your boots, but everything else you need to let drop."

Cupcake knew the rules so she didn't hesitate to strip down to her bra and panties.

Charlotte said, "Don't forget those 'because they belong to me too."   Cupcake said, "You really going to leave me out here naked?"

Charlotte said, "Just like your bike so you should feel at home."

Cupcake took off her bra and panties and let them fall on top of the pile of clothes. She went to her bike and was about to leave when Charlotte walked over and gave her a stern warning.

"Next time you try to trick one of our riders you're going to come up missing." Charlotte had one of the other riders bring her some gasoline, which she poured on Cupcake's clothes and them ablaze.

When Cupcake saw this, she cranked her bike and headed straight for home. She was freezing as she took all of the back streets and routes to get home. She was so glad that she made it home without having to stop near anyone. She pulled her bike around to the back where she kept a spare key for the back door in a fake rock. She took out the key and let herself in. She was furious but had no one to blame but herself! She went to the bathroom and jumped into the shower.

The water started off cold and then heated up. She stood in front of the water and just let her body soak. She stayed in the shower for a while before she got out to dry off. She reached for a towel as someone handed it to her. She jumped when she realized what was happening. Big Trouble was standing there smiling at her. Cupcake tried to scramble away, but he grabbed her. He pulled her close so she could feel his hard-on. She didn't want that thing in her! She was about to try and bargain her way out of it when Big Trouble threw her into the room where Madame was sitting.

Cupcake relaxed as she heard Madame say, "Take it easy on my number one recruiter."

Big Trouble went over to Madame, who started rubbing his massive hard-on. Madame told Big Trouble, "Go to the car and I'll take care of that shortly."

Big Trouble turned toward Cupcake and Madame hit him on his swollen member. She said, "I'm going to handle that dick in the car and I'm not sharing!" Big Trouble grabbed his hard on and left.

Madame turned her attention to the naked Cupcake. She told Cupcake, "I heard you lost the clothes off your back and I couldn't believe it."

Cupcake nodded in the affirmative and told her what happened.

Madame laughed when she got to the part about setting her clothes on fire. Madame asked, "How much money you got left?"

Cupcake said, "Enough to keep the lights on."

Madame looked at Cupcake then reached into her purse. She pulled out two thousand dollars and laid it on the floor between her legs. She said, "This is the down payment on the next teen you bring me."

Cupcake crawled over to get the money, but Madame put her right heel on Cupcake's right shoulder.

Cupcake knew she'd have to give Madame some lip service for the money 'cause Madame never let any good head go to waste. Especially since she knew Big Trouble was about to fuck her brains out for getting between him and Cupcake.

Cupcake went between Madame's legs and started giving her a good licking. She knew that if she took too long and Big Trouble came back in, she and Madame were going to be screwed. Cupcake dove into Madame's crotch hard, not missing a spot. She went to the area where Madame would cum just by blowing on it and it worked like a charm. Madame let out a squeal as she achieved an orgasm. She pulled Cupcake's head in further until she finished her orgasmic trip. Madame pulled Cupcake up and they started kissing full on the lips. Madame stood up in front of Cupcake and slapped her hard on the face.

She said, "You better not go back out there racing because we've got a lot at stake. I can't afford to have one of my recruiters getting caught doing dumb shit like that."

Cupcake understood and wanted her own thing. She watched out the window as Madame walked to the car where Big Trouble was standing, still holding his hard on. Madame walked up to him and started unzipping his pants. His hard member popped out and Madame started giving him some head. She turned and sat on the seat with his manhood still in her mouth and stroked it deeply. She then slid into the car and Big Trouble hurriedly jumped in. The driver of the car took off as soon as the door in the back closed. Cupcake was still horny and she still had the same problem. She had to find teen girl for Madame!

She went to her bedroom and got her favorite vibrator. She decided that she would think better after a good hard orgasm and some sleep. She pulled out the vibrator and inserted it deeply into her wet womanhood. She worked the vibrator around every inch of her wet tunnel till she exploded with pleasure. She knew that she would find someone for Madame, but she decided she would also pick up an extra for herself.

Madame couldn't believe how crazy Big Trouble was this time. He was so deep inside of her she could barely breathe! He was humping her and shaking the car as they drove down the street. Madame could not stifle the cries of enjoyment as Big trouble reminded her who was in charge when it came to the bedroom. Madame felt Big Trouble cum as he lunged forward so hard that he made her hit her head on the door. Madame's eyes glazed over as she achieved the last of many orgasms. She held Big Trouble close as his body shuddered at the end of a hard orgasm. Big Trouble wanted to roll over but Madame held on to his manhood. She was trying to make him lay there and not get up. Madame knew if she let him up he might get another hard on and she just couldn't handle any more.

Big Trouble had something on his mind. He asked her, "Do you think Cupcake will come through?"

This shocked Madame because he never seemed concerned before. Madame released him and said, "Don't worry; it's all taken care of."

Frequency had more than enough info on Cupcake. He used his phone to get video of her. Cupcake was one of the people who were messing around with the adolescent children. He had one disturbing image of her strapping on a dildo and raping a very young girl. He knew that he could pass this on to the Feds, but they might grab her prematurely and send the rest of them packing. Frequency knew that he had to let his team in on what he'd found out. He had CMAX send the information out via text message to the guys. Then he told them to use the information from CMAX to cross reference anything they could find on any of the names they'd been given. He told all of them that each name was a nickname of sorts for a person within the group. Frequency ran the license plate off Cupcake's bike. The department of motor vehicles came up with a Camille Cup and her last known address.

Cupcake awoke from her sleep to a sunny day. She went into the bathroom to freshen up. After that she put on some clothes and headed for the adolescent center where she volunteered. She went to the center for only one thing, and that was to turn out another teen girl. Cupcake thought about all the girls she had moved from the center. She had to be cautious because the center hired a new clinical director who watched everything going on in the center like a hawk. Cupcake had not met her, but she'd heard that she scrutinized everything. Cupcake got to the center and noticed the car parked into the spot labeled Clinical Director. She parked on the side of the building where there were no cameras. She knew that to pull a girl from here you had to do it from this side of the building or risk getting seen.

Cupcake went into the center and talked to the front desk clerk. The clerk gave her an access key id that allowed her to go to certain areas. Cupcake had her card changed out to an administrative level by one of the former employees before she left. The woman was eager to let Cupcake please her and that opened the door for Cupcake to get what she needed from the center. Cupcake went into the area for runaways and saw the face of a girl named Kim. Kim was a runaway that Cupcake had been working on. Upon seeing her, Kim ran up and hugged her around the neck. Cupcake returned the hug but made sure she didn't go any further.

Kim said, "I have someone I want you to meet." She took Cupcake by the hand and led her over to Keynesia, who was new to the center and had been on the streets before that.

Cupcake saw the wildness about her and knew that she would be an easy target to flip. She shook hands with Keynesia and asked, "How are you doing?"

Keynesia said, "I'm fine and I'm happy just being off of the streets."		Cupcake said, "Tell me about yourself."

Keynesia said, "I'm15 years old and I'd been on the streets for about six months before coming here. I was abused by my older sister's boyfriend and my parents are dead."

Cupcake knew she had hit the jackpot! She was talking with the girls when a lady in a business suit walked by.

Kim saw her and said, "Hello Doc."

Doc responded with a wave and kept on walking. Cupcake watched her walk all the way out of the area. Something deep inside Cupcake made her want that woman. Doc was attractive with a nice shape from behind. Cupcake wanted to follow her, but she had to take care of the business at hand. She made a mental note to find out more about the lady called DOC.

Cupcake asked Kim, "Who is that woman?"

Kim said, "That's the new director of this center."

Cupcake knew she might have to bump heads with this woman, and hopefully something else.

Kim thought about her plan to leave the center and she hoped Keynesia would help her. Cupcake already had Kim wrapped around her finger and used it to her every advantage. Kim was so totally lost in Cupcake's words. Cupcake had already helped get her out of trouble several times. The last time, Kim kissed Cupcake and she had returned the kiss. Cupcake then sternly warned her that she couldn't let anyone else know, and Kim agreed but only if Cupcake would help her get out of the center. Cupcake agreed only if Kim followed her exact instruction on when and where.

Kim saw how cupcake looked at DOC and got jealous. She decided to get in trouble to make Cupcake have to come to help her again. She made up her mind to go to the North wall, where the boys hung out. She waited till Cupcake went to make her rounds. She headed that way and heard someone following behind her. She looked back and saw that it was Keynesia.

She grabbed Keynesia and asked,"What do you think you're doing?" Keynesia was shaken up by Kim's roughness. She said, "I just don't want to be left alone."

The girls made it over to the north wall and saw all the boys standing around talking about girls. Keynesia laughed when she saw one of the boys playing with himself. The boy heard Keynesia and chased after her. The rest of the boys followed and chased both girls. They tried to run but didn't get far.

The boys asked the girls, "What are you laughing at?"

Keynesia grabbed the guy who'd been playing with himself by the crotch and told him," You don't even know what to with it!"

All the boys turned toward Keynesia as she unzipped the boy's pants and started jacking him off. Another boy walked up to her with his pants down and she started doing the same to him.

Kim backed away as they gathered around Keynesia with their pants down.

One boy pulled out some Vaseline and gave it to Keynesia. She put it on his hard on and really started stroking up and down. This one and the others shared the Vaseline with Keynesia. She had done this and more before. Keynesia had been gang banged by older boys, so this was just another day for her.

Kim was backing up and moving away when she backed into someone. She turned and saw it was

Cupcake. Kim immediately began begging for forgiveness and said, "I'll do anything for you, Cupcake, as long as she if you don't tell."

This was the moment Cupcake had been waiting for. She told Kim to be at the south parking lot tomorrow, then shook her and made her promise. As soon as Kim promised, Cupcake made her go back to the girls' area.

Keynesia was really enjoying the control she had on these boys. Two of them had blown their loads already and left. She was jerking the last two off, when she saw Cupcake walk up. The boys squirted on her arms and it was too late for her to play it off.

Cupcake made the boys head back to the male side of the center, and then turned her attention to Keynesia. Keynesia wasn't afraid of Cupcake 'because she had already peeped her game. Keynesia tried to walk past Cupcake, but Cupcake grabbed her. Keynesia resisted and they tussled for a while before Keynesia pulled Cupcake to her and kissed her on the lips. Cupcake didn't resist and put her hands between Keynesia legs. Keynesia gasped for air as Cupcake used her experience to get her off. By then, Keynesia was putty in her hands and Cupcake knew she could turn her over to Madame to collect the rest of her money. Cupcake started talking harshly to Keynesia telling her, "Give me that pussy," with each thrust inside of her. Keynesia gave in to her with an orgasm that had her biting Cupcake's neck. Keynesia's knees buckled and Cupcake let her fall to the ground.

Cupcake stood over her and said, "You will run away tomorrow and go where I tell you. I'll pick you up and you'll never ever have to come back to the center." Keynesia agreed as she and Cupcake headed back to the center.

Doc saw when Kim came back into the surveillance area and then Ms. Cup and Keynesia. She made a note to check Ms. Cup's log to ensure that the infraction was notated properly. Doc had been made aware of how many adolescent girls had run away from this center. She got the position because she used her education as a defender of children. That's how she got her nickname. Doc laughed when she thought about her past and the friend that she no longer wanted to see.

She wondered sometimes how he was doing, but that was a short thought because one of the alarms went off. Doc ran down the hall to the alarm board. There was a light going off in the girl area that meant one thing -- girl fight. Doc rushed over to the area to see to girls stripped down to their panties and pulling and hitting at each other. Doc sent in two male counselors to break up the melee. The girls where the same two that Doc had seen come into the surveillance area. She immediately had them locked in confinement rooms until morning. Doc then had volunteer Cup called to her office. Ms. Cup had been doing her rounds when the alarm sounded. It was company policy for the counselor making rounds to continue doing so until rounds were completed. Ms. Cup finished her rounds and headed for the Directors office.

She made it to the office and was told to come in, so she walked in and said, "You called for me ma'am?"

"Just call me Doc, and why were you and two of the girls out of bounds earlier?"

Cupcake said, "I'd heard about the two trying to sneak off to the boys' area. I headed there myself and saw the girls watching the boys masturbate. I ran the boys off and chastised the girls before escorting them back to the appropriate area. I've written all of this up in my log, and notified the male counselors of the incident."

Doc said, "The same two girls got into a fight just now, and both of them are in confinement rooms."

Cupcake knew that her cover might be blown if one of the girls decided to talk. She asked Doc, "D you want me to set up disciplinary action for them?" Doc said, "No, I want to talk to the two before any disciplinary jobs are assigned for them."

Cupcake became nervous, and knew she had to get to the girls before Doc did. She decided to take another route. She looked at Doc and asked, "Can I work overtime tonight for a co-worker?"

Doc didn't think anything of it and said, Sure, no problem."

Cupcake asked "Do you need anything else?"

Doc said, "No, that will be all for now."

Cupcake left and went down to the employee locker room. She grabbed her cell phone and called her co-worker, Sarah. Cupcake said, "Don't bother coming in tonight. I'll cover for you. I'll let you have one of my evening shifts in return." Cupcake went into action as soon as she saw Doc head for her car. She wrote down her license tag number, then called Madame and had her check with her connection at the DMV to find out where she lived. Cupcake went into the main circuitry room and loosened one of the sprinkler heads just enough for it to drip a little bit of water. She went to the main counselor's area and waited for the camera in the containment room to go out. It took about 15 minutes for the containment room cameras to go blank. The head counselor on duty called maintenance and had them dispatched.

He then called to Ms. Cup and said, "Go and sentry the containment rooms until maintenance gets them back online."

Cupcake rushed to the room where Kim was first. She stepped into the room and Kim jumped into her arms.

Kim said, "I'm so sorry for fighting with Keynesia, but she made me jealous when she told me that you'd been with her. I want to be with you too!"   Cupcake told Kim, "You can only be with me if you don't say a word of this to anybody, especially the Director."

After Kim agreed, Cupcake kissed her deeply and began unzipping her pants. She reached into Kim's panties and started to caress her like it meant her life! Kim was in another world as Cupcake pleased her in a way she'd never felt before. Kim fell to the floor and pulled Cupcake on top of her. Cupcake did not stop until Kim climaxed. Kim's eyes were glazed over as Cupcake pulled her hand from her panties.

Cupcake licked her fingers and said, "What a sweet little girl." This made Kim jump back into her arms and say that she loved her and would do anything for her.

Cupcake said, "Hold that thought, because I'm going to get you out of here for good." Cupcake left her room and went to the other confinement room, where Keynesia was pacing back and forth and trying to figure out how she was going to get out of the predicament that she was in. She was brought back to reality when Cupcake walked into the room and closed the door behind her. Keynesia knew that she was in trouble, so she prepared herself for a battle.

Cupcake saw Keynesia knuckle up so she slapped her hard on the face. Keynesia fell to the floor and Cupcake was on top of her. Cupcake spun her around so that she was straddling her back and started to use one of the sanctioned choke holds to make Keynesia settle down. Keynesia dropped her head to the floor and started crying.

Cupcake got up and said, "You stupid bitch, you almost ruined everything!" She got into Keynesia's face and made her swear on her life that she would not tell the Director anything about their plan.

After Keynesia promised she asked, "Please make me feel good again." Cupcake said, "After you get out of the center; I'll make sure you have more than enough." Then Cupcake left Keynesia in the containment room and went back to her duty as night counselor.

Doc arrived at work and had her assistant pull all of Ms. Cup's logs. She then went to see both of her girl's in their containment rooms. She went to Keynesia first and asked,"What caused the misunderstanding between you and Kim?"

Keynesia didn't want to tell Doc the truth so she lied. She said, "Me and Kim like the same boy. We got into it because we both wanted to be with him."

No matter what questions Doc asked, Keynesia didn't change her story. Doc left the room unsatisfied with the answers she got from Keynesia, so she went to the other room to talk to Kim. Doc knew something was wrong as soon as she stepped into the room.

She found Kim laying on the floor masturbating. Doc had two other female counselors come into the room and stop her. Kim was saying over and over, "He will be mine, He will be mine." Doc knew this was a dead end so she left the room and went back to her office, where her assistant had left copies of Ms. Cup's logs. Doc examined each entry with the scrutiny of a homicide detective. She found nothing out of place, until she noticed that Ms. Cup had befriended all the girls who had run away in the last few months. Red Flags went up immediately in Doc's mind, but she didn't want to alert any of her staff just yet. She was still trying to get a feel for who was with her and who was not. She sat that issue to the side to deal with later.

Doc called in one of the older counselors and asked, "How did you all deal with in the past that had been put into containment?"

The lady said, "We usually took them to the Farm and let them work on the highway picking up trash."

Doc asked, "Who usually does this?"

The counselor pulled her roster and said, "That would be Sarah."

Doc told the counselor, "Contact Sarah and let her know we have two more girls for road duty."

The counselor did as she was told, but when Sarah got the news, she quickly told Cupcake. This was the break that Cupcake had been waiting for! She would get both girls, and then she would return to work the next day like nothing had happened. Cupcake thought about the Director and put it in her mind to ask her out for drinks.

The next day everything was going as planned in Doc's eyes. Sarah had the girls from confinement and was headed to the farm. Doc was satisfied with Ms. Cup's log entries so she went ahead and dismissed that issue. The day was going great until Doc got a call from the county authorities. Their two girls had attacked Sarah and run off.

Doc's first concern was Sarah's wellbeing. She asked, "How is she?" and was told that Sarah was bleeding from the head, but would be fine. She had a mild concussion so they had transported her to the local hospital.

Keynesia and Kim had run the length of the farm and down to the train tracks. They waited a while before a truck pulled up and the door opened. They both jumped into the back and the truck drove to a motel about 20 miles from the farm and stopped. The girls got out and went to the back of the hotel. At the back of the hotel, they found a change of clothes. Both girls changed then walked to the pay phone. The phone rang and a familiar voice asked if they were ready. They both said yeah as another car showed up. Keynesia walked over to the car and was told to get in. Kim tried to follow her, but was told to wait for the next vehicle. The car pulled away leaving Kim behind. Kim wasn't happy about being left behind, but at least she didn't have to be with Keynesia

Cupcake pulled into work to use the center's workout facility. As soon as she got in the building, she was confronted by the Director. Cupcake was in full chill mode, and assured the Director that she had nothing to do with those girls running away. Doc was furious! She had all outside programs suspended until further notice. Her stress level was in the clouds, so she decided to go work out in the center's facility. She told her assistant to let her know immediately, if she heard anything about Kim and Keynesia. As she went into the ladies dressing room to change, she saw that Ms. Cup was already there. Doc spoke, but kept moving. She went to her locker on the other side of the room and began to undress. Doc let her guard down and just wanted to get on the treadmill. She was already in great shape and when Cupcake saw her out of her business attire, she immediately wanted her. She watched Doc put on her workout tights and go to the treadmill. Doc had on her headphones to drown out all other noises.

Cupcake got on the bicycle behind Doc and just watched her like a perverted fool. She wanted to jump on Doc and turn her out! Doc didn't think about the woman behind her. She was just trying to work off some of the stress from the day. Cupcake reached down between her own legs and started to bring herself into a frenzy while she watched Doc bounce up and down on the treadmill. She almost got caught when the overhead announcement center called for the Doc. Cupcake was soaking wet between her legs, but she played it off as if she had been sweating. She said, "Got to get into the shower now, whew!" Doc smiled and didn't think anything of it. She went to the nearest phone and called the clinic operator.

Cupcake hurried and went to the shower area. She got into the shower where she could have the best view of all of the other showers. Cupcake stripped hurriedly, got into the shower, and turned on the water. She stood to the side as it heated up.

Doc finished her call and decided to get in the shower and call it a day. She stripped down and wrapped herself in a towel. She went into the shower area and chose a stall. She could hear another person in the shower, but she couldn't see her for the steam. Doc pulled the towel off and let her shower begin. She got under the water as soon as the temperature was right, got her soap and lathered up from head to toe. Cupcake was in perverted heaven. She was watching Doc and masturbating at the same time. She had got down on her knees and was finishing her big climax, when Doc's soap slid over to where she was. Doc had soap in her face so she did not open her eyes. Cupcake quickly grabbed her soap and started to walk toward Doc. She got really close to Doc where she could see every inch of her body. Cupcake was livid with lust, she had to have this woman and she was going to get her rather she wanted her or not! Doc ran her face into the water and was able to open her eyes.

She was startled when Ms. Cup was directly in front of her.

Ms. Cup held up Doc's soap and said ever so calmly, "You dropped your soap."

Doc took the soap from her and said, "Thank you." She felt very uncomfortable. She hurriedly finished showering then ran out of there to get dressed. Doc dressed just as quickly and was walking out of the area when she was joined by Ms. Cup.

Ms. Cup asked, "Did you have a good work out?"

Doc said, "Yes I did."

Ms. Cup then told Doc, "I've worked myself into frenzy and now I'm famished!"

Doc agreed and said, "I'm going to get some food."

Ms. Cup asked, "Would you like to join me for dinner?"

Doc said, "No, thank you though."

Ms. Cup walked Doc to her car and then wrote down her number on the back of a business card. She gave it to Doc as she was getting into her car and said, "If you change her mind just give me a call. Maybe we can catch a movie or just hang out."

Doc politely said, "I don't think so. I'm going home to cook dinner and get some rest." As she pulled out of the parking lot, she thought briefly about how persistent Ms. Cup was. Then she put it out of her mind. She was going home to cook herself a good meal and get some sleep.

Cupcake was gone over the edge! She damn near jumped into the car with Doc. She had to have her and she would not wait another minute. Cupcake had already made arrangements for Keynesia and Kim to get picked up. She would deal with Kim after she had the good Director for dinner and dessert.

Chapter 7

Doc

What a way to finish the day! Doc decided that she would go home and cook herself a dinner and then watch a little television. She got into her car and started driving home. Doc turned on the radio and tried to let her stressful day at work just go away. She drove her normal route, and decided to stop by the store to pick up a few items. As she got a shopping cart she noticed that some new Cajun seasoning were on sale. She couldn't pass them up. Cooking Cajun style made her think of growing up in Louisiana. Next, she went to the meat counter and picked up some pork chops and steak. One her way to check out, she grabbed a six-pack of sodas.

Doc was excited about trying the new Cajun seasoning. She got to her place in no time, and felt the relief of another long work day that was over. She parked her car, gathered her groceries, and went inside. Doc turned on the entry lights and went straight to the kitchen. She put the groceries down and went to her bedroom to change into something comfortable. She stripped down to her panties, then put on her favorite shirt and lounge pants. She slipped on her house shoes and went to the kitchen to do some Cajun style cooking.

She turned on the TV and started prepping the meats. She hummed her favorite tune while she prepared the food. All of a sudden the doorbell rang. Doc was not expecting company so she eased her way to the door. She looked through the peep hole and nobody was there. She opened the door, looked out and still nobody was there. She turned and closed the door. She went back to the kitchen and picked up where she left off preparing her meal. She started humming again but then got quiet.

She turned down her TV and heard children outside playing. She figured the kids were the reason for her doorbell ringing. As she started to reminisce about 'the good old days' when she was a little girl, the doorbell rang again. Doc went to the door and peeped through the peep hole. Nobody was there. She opened the door and there stood the cutest little Girl Scout

"Would you like to buy some cookies?" she asked.

Doc asked, "When do I have to pay for them?"

The little girl said, "You can pay for them now, because I have them with me now."

Doc said, "I want one box of Thin Mints."

The little Girl Scout smiled and said, "That will be $3.50."

Doc said, "Stay right there while I go get your money." She went to her bedroom and got the money out of her purse. Then she went back to the door and paid for her cookies.

The little girl said, "Just step outside and I'll bring the cookies up to you."

Doc dashed back to the kitchen and moved the skillet off the eye. No sense starting a grease fire just to get cookies. Doc stepped outside and the little girl met her on the porch with one box of Thin Mint cookies. Doc went back inside, closed and locked the door, and after laying the cookies on her kitchen counter, started to finish cooking her meal. As she turned around, she noticed that her pan of meat was not on the stove where she'd left it. She turned to look on the counter and was hit hard on the side of her head.

Doc fell to the floor and, when she tried to move, found that she couldn't. Whoever hit her had jumped on top of her and was pulling at her clothes. Doc tried to fight back, but her attacker was very strong. She felt herself being dragged, and then felt more blows to her head. With each blow, she became more disoriented. She tried to think of a way to save herself, but found her mind was too foggy. Her attacker ripped off her shirt and roughly grabbed her breast. Doc started to scream, but her attacker hit her in the mouth. Doc fell back to the floor and tried to crawl away. Her attacker kicked her in the back bringing her another dose pain.

The attacker grabbed Doc and put something in her mouth, then taped her mouth shut. Doc felt her hands tied separately, each above her head. The attacker then grabbed her legs around her ankles and secured them to keep her from kicking. The attacker started breathing heavy as Doc's panties were pulled down to her ankles. By this time, Doc was crying and screaming into the gag in her mouth.

The attacker had her lying on her stomach, and was fondling her buttocks. Doc was horrified as her attacker went the kitchen and she heard them rambling through the kitchen. The attacker came back and again moved behind Doc. Doc felt something cold roll between her legs, then she felt her attacker's hand caress her buttocks again. She knew what was about to happen, but she made a promised herself she would not give her attacker the satisfaction of hearing her scream.

The attacker toyed with the Doc for a while, smacking her on her buttocks, and then sodomized Doc with his fingers. Doc felt him pushing one finger in at a time in an effort to make her scream. She bit down on the gag in her mouth and willed herself not to scream. She could hear her attacker breathe harder as the attack continued. Doc felt the attacker remove his fingers, then felt his hot breath on her buttocks as his fingers were replaced by his tongue. She could feel she was being violated through her vagina and rectum.

Doc lay bound on the floor and heard her attacker begin to unbuckle his belt. Again, she knew what was about to happen. She tried to think of anything other than the situation she was in. There had never been a day in her life that she wanted vengeance on anyone until this day. She promised herself that, if she made it through this attack, this person was going to pay! At that very moment, her attacker poured something on her, and then penetrated her with such a forceful thrust that her body was forced open. Then her attacker started to thrust violently and repeatedly like a wild bull. The attacker looked at the Doc and decided she was too good not to enjoy. Her body was perfect in every way and that excited her attacker even more. He put one of his hands under her shoulder, and used the other to push her head down. He would torture his victim until she submitted, and then kidnap her .But this is one tough lady who does NOT plan to submit! The attacker thrust and thrust until he was deeply winded.

Doc lay on her stomach in more pain than she'd ever felt before, but was not about to give in to this monster. She felt her attacker get off her and realized she could still hear the children playing outside. She wished for a miracle, or a weapon, or anything that would make her attacker stop. All of a sudden, she felt a sharp pain in her rectum that made her tense up as her attacker entered her anal canal.

The table that her right hand was tied to slid closer to her and she was able to grab hold of it. Doc pulled the table quickly and the lamp fell off to the floor. She grabbed the lamp as she turned over on her back and her attacker fell to the side. As her attacker moved to contain her, Doc swung the lamp and hit her attacker squarely on the side of his head. The attacker stumbled, got up, and ran out the door.

Doc scrambled to her feet and tried to run after her attacker, but she'd forgotten that her feet were still bound. She tripped over the table that had fallen and hit her head. Doc tried to look up as she started to pass out. The last thing she remembered is seeing her fleeing attacker back through the door he'd left open and hearing the children screaming outside.

Doc awoke in the hospital surrounded by a sea of people. Her sister Krystal and her husband Jay, her mother and step-father, and several of her co-workers and friends. She sat up in bed and felt the return of the pain from her attack. As much as she wished it had been a dream, Doc realized it was a real life nightmare.

Her sister and mom were so relieved that she was awake and alert.

"You're going to be okay," her mother said.

Doc tried to smile, but found that she couldn't. Her attacker had busted her up pretty good.

Krystal said, "The little girl that had sold you the cookies saw your attacker run out of your house. She screamed and a couple of adults came running to help her. She told them what she saw, and they ran to your place and found your door open and you lying in the floor bound and gagged. They called the police and an ambulance."

Doc was so grateful tears came to her eyes. She said, "I'll be sure to thank that little girl and my other rescuers as soon as I can get out of here."

Krystal wanted to know everything, but she knew her sister was exhausted and in a lot of pain. She was right, because Doc felt like she'd been hit by a truck! Every inch of her body ached, especially her rear end. She remembered everything, and she knew that as soon as she healed, she would be on the hunt for the person who had done this unspeakable thing to her.

Cupcake lay in bed with her girl Kim directly next to her. Cupcake had enjoyed a long evening of turning out this new girl. Kim was totally exhausted from all the girl sex that Cupcake put her through. She was totally committed to Cupcake now, and would do whatever Cupcake told her to do. Cupcake started remembering how everything last night went wrong. She had Doc right where she wanted her and she slipped up. She hadn't seen Doc grab that lamp, but she sure had felt it! The bulb in the lamp broke when Doc hit her and had shocked and burned Cupcake on the side of her head. Cupcake went to the bathroom and looked in the mirror. Just above her temple was the swollen burn mark. She touched it lightly and it hurt. She went to the medicine cabinet and found some ointment to put on it. Then she used her hair to cover it up. Cupcake was glad she didn't have to go to work today, because she knew the center would be buzzing with talk of what happened to the Director. She was getting wet just thinking about how she had the naked body of Doc all to herself.

She was brought back to the present when she felt Kim's arms around her waist and felt her fondling her clitoris. Cupcake turned in her arms and kissed her. Kim wanted to make Cupcake feel as good as Cupcake had made her feel numerous times the night before. Kim knelt in front of Cupcake and pushed her legs apart. She pushed her tongue directly between Cupcake's thighs and to her wet vagina. Cupcake was thrilled as she settled back on the counter top and let

Kim's inexperienced tongue find its way to her hot spot.

Kim had the taste of a woman in her mouth for the first time. She started slowly, and then increased the intensity as she found that she enjoyed the taste. Cupcake hadn't had a woman pleasure her in ages, so she was ecstatic when her orgasm came down. She grabbed the back of Kim head and pulled it deeper into her body. Kim hugged Cupcake's thighs and knew she had pleased her new mate. Cupcake's legs shuddered as the orgasm ran its course.

Then she pulled Kim up and kissed her deeply until Kim pulled away and said, "Let me make you some breakfast."

Cupcake smacked Kim on her naked behind as she went into the kitchen to start breakfast. Cupcake waited until she heard Kim opening cabinets in the kitchen before she reached behind the toilet and pulled out a black strap-on dildo. It was the same one she had used in the attack on the Doc, and she knew she needed to get rid of it. She wrapped it in an old towel, walked out of her bathroom, and back to the bedroom. She gathered the other clothes from last night's attack, put them all in a dark trash bag, and placed the bag beside the garbage. Cupcake then went into the kitchen where Kim had finished making breakfast, kissed her and thanked her for a wonderful breakfast. Kim giggled with excitement as she watched Cupcake eat.

After they finished breakfast, Kim cleaned up the mess and turned on the TV. The news was on and they were talking about a woman who was attacked the night before. They showed the woman and Kim's jaw dropped. She started screaming to Cupcake and Cupcake went into the room. Cupcake pretended to be shocked by the news report. She smiled inside when she heard that they thought the attacker was a man, and was sure she'd get away with it because those idiots were looking for a man!

Kim turned to Cupcake and asked, "Where's Keynesia?"

Cupcake shouted, "Don't you ever mention that name again!"

Kim was surprised and confused, but said, "I'll never say it again if you don't want me to." Then she went over and hugged and kissed Cupcake. Cupcake held Kim close as the thought of what Keynesia might be going through occurred to her too.

From the time Keynesia got into the car, she wondered, "What have I gotten myself into?" A woman named Madame had her brought in so she could dress her up. Madame had Keynesia put on several different outfits and took pictures of her in each outfit. Then she had Keynesia put in a room where she was stripped naked. There was a bed and a TV in the room, but nothing else. Next, they asked her what kind of food she liked. Keynesia told the person on the other side of the door, and a few minutes later they brought her exactly what she asked for. Keynesia ate her fill, then sat back and watched TV for a while.

Before long, a big man walked into the room and told her to come with him. Keynesia tried to ask a question but the big man just grabbed her and put a mask over her face. Keynesia did not try to struggle because he was way too big for her to fight with and win. He guided her out of the room by her shoulders and into a corridor. They walked around a bunch of corners, then into a room where Keynesia heard the door close behind her. Her mask was removed and she saw she was in a very nice room. It looked to Keynesia like it was fixed up for royalty. She heard Madame's voice and turned to see Madame seated and having a drink of some kind.

Madame said, "Come sit beside me."

Keynesia went over to Madame and was told why she had been brought here. Madame gave Keynesia 2 options, "Option one is that you can do as you're told and be rewarded for it. Option two is you don't do as you're told and you become another victim."

Keynesia said, "I like the first option as long as it means I never have from go back to the center." She reached for the cup Madame was drinking from and took a sip from it. It was very strong and made Keynesia cough.

Madame said, "In due time child, you'll learn to handle such strong elixir." Then she grabbed Keynesia hand and guided her to the bed. She said, "You're being groomed to start learning how to please Madame and her clientele." Madame then grabbed the back of Keynesia's head and pulled her close. They began to kiss and Keynesia opened Madame's robe. Madame's was totally naked underneath and Keynesia knew exactly where to go. She started on Madame's breast and worked her way down. She spread her legs and dove in to her wet, wanting womanhood. Madame enjoyed the touch of her newly found apprentice and let her feed off her pleasure juices.

What Keynesia did not know was that they were being watched and were about to be joined by the Madame's man, Big Trouble. Big Trouble was in the corner of the room watching and waiting for Madame to release him. He was hard as a diamond watching the little lady please his woman. Big trouble saw Madame lay her head back, then heard her scream as she orgasmed in the little one's mouth. Madame called to Big trouble and he quickly went to her. She knew he'd be crazy with lust knowing she was with somebody else, and there was only one way to keep him cool.

Madame rose up and told Keynesia, "Your next task is to please my man Trouble."

Keynesia looked at the huge man as he stood next to Madame's head. Madame reached to his crotch and started playing with his hard on. She told Keynesia, "Come and get it!"

Keynesia climbed from between Madame's legs and went to Trouble. Madame exposed Trouble to Keynesia and she knew immediately that she'd bit off more than she could chew. He was huge! She'd never been with a man this size before.

Madame saw her hesitate so she put it in her mouth and begin stroking it up and down. Then she pulled it from her mouth and put it in Keynesia's mouth. Keynesia followed her lead and tried to do the same but gagged. Trouble knew he and Madame would be working on this girl for a while. Madame instructed Keynesia on how to properly give head without gagging. They went through several position changes with Madame teaching Keynesia every step of the way. Trouble was hyped and ready to really get into one of these women. Madame was not going to let Trouble into her body because it always took her some time to recoup when he was done. No, Madame was going to let Trouble bust out this new girl and teach her who was in charge.

Frequency had just pulled up outside Cupcake's house and seen Cupcake and another girl get on her bike and leave. Before that, Cupcake had pushed the trash to the curb. Frequency saw that she had left a bag full of shredded papers on the side. Shredded papers told Frequency someone was trying to destroy potentially valuable information. Frequency got out of the truck he was in and grabbed the entire bag of shredded papers. He noticed how heavy it was and but thought nothing of it. He threw it into the back of the truck and left. He'd take the papers to EoW who had connections with a crew with equipment that could tell him exactly what was on those shredded papers.

Then Frequency got a call from Don1 that almost made him drive off the road. "Doc was attacked in her apartment last night," Don1 said.

Frequency was livid! It felt as if he couldn't breathe. Even though Doc broke his heart, he would never have wished something like this on her. Frequency was quiet while thoughts of Doc ran through his head.

Don1 asked, "Are you alright? 'Cause this next thing is really going to piss you off."

Frequency asked, "What could be worse than that?"

Don1 said, "The police have named you as a suspect."

The truck Frequency was driving came to a screeching halt. He was off the chain mad and ready to make somebody pay for it. He tried to think of anyone who'd want to do this to Doc and only one name came to mind. "WHITE," Frequency said aloud. He knew he needed to have his stuff together because he knew the police were probably already heading to his house. Frequency started driving again and headed straight for home.

He was in the cell shop truck, but he knew Don had no problem with that. Frequency got home and there waiting for him were Mr. Master and a police officer. Frequency walked up and spoke to both gentlemen as if nothing was going on.

Mr. Master was cool about the whole subject as they went directly to why they were there. Mr. Master could tell Frequency was struggling to keep some strong emotions in check. That let him know they were barking up the wrong tree. Mr. Master and the officer finished asking all of the official questions, and then Mr. Master stepped outside and started asking Frequency about different kinds of computer processors and networking. Frequency peeped his game and told him only about the older equipment on the market, not any of the new stuff. He remembered that Mr.

Master was working with the Fed's who were trying to get into his computer worm program.

Frequency asked Mr. Master, "How is Doc doing?"

Mr. Master said, "I haven't been privileged to see her because they've granted access only to close family and friends."

Frequency knew that he could see her if he really wanted to, but he didn't want to stir up the past. He invited Mr. Master and the office to come inside, but they declined saying the officer had to get back to the investigation.

Frequency turned to Mr. Master and said, "Do me a favor. Keep me updated on the Doc's condition."

Mr. Master said, "Sure. I can tell it's important to you."

As they drove off Mr. Master got on the phone with Agent Layrock and gave him the 411 on Doc and her association with Frequency.

This was the kind of insider information that Layrock needed to help him get into Frequency's house. Once inside he knew he could find the computer with the worm program on it and crack one of the biggest pedophile rings in the history of the department.

Doc had been in the hospital several weeks and was ready to go home. The hospital crew had been wonderful, but she just wanted to go home. She had thought seriously about what she would do when she got her apartment, but hadn't come up with anything concrete. She had her family there to help her as they walked back into the place where the attack happened. The apartment hadn't been touched since the CSI team had processed it.

As she looked around, Doc said, "Pack up all my things because I can't stay here."

Krystal helped her back to the car as she told Jay, "I'm taking her to Mom's house."

Doc said, "Rent a storage unit and just put everything in it."

Jay said, "I'll take care of everything." Then he called his friend Juan at the computer store and said, "I'm moving my sister-in-law and I need some able bodies. I'm willing to pay for the help."

Juan stayed broke, so any time there was a chance to make money, he was down for it. Juan asked his boss, "Is it was ok if I go help a friend move out of an apartment?"

EoW knew business was extremely slow that day, so he told him to leave. EoW was putting his little investigation into full swing and trying to help Frequency with the worm program. He got some information from Don1 about the dude who bought all those cell phones, and then he got his address from Don1's database.

He said, "I think I'll go over there on the weekend while the shop's closed for repairs and find out what's up with that dude." EoW also dropped off Frequency's bag of shredded papers to his partner, LabRat, who had set up his own little crime lab at a storage unit in the old part of town. He knew his mom, who owns the joint, wouldn't mind as long as he wasn't blowing up anything or making Meth. EoW was checking out a couple of nude photos from the web when he got a call from LabRat. "Hey man, you gave me more than just shredded papers," LabRat said.

EoW asked, "What else was in there?"

LabRat said, "There was a pair of pants, a shirt, a mask, and a strap-on dildo wrapped in a towel with blood and some kind of oily residue on it. I'm running tests on all the clothes and fluids to see who or what they belong to."

EoW was tripping thinking that Frequency had raided some dike's pleasure chest leftovers. EoW laughed at the thought and would save that bit of information for later so he could rag on Frequency about it. He went back to searching the addresses of all the cell phones the dude had purchased.

Juan arrived to help Jay move all Docs' stuff. After looking around he asked, 'What the hell happened here? What's with all this police tape?"

Jay said, "It was my sister-in-law that was attacked the other night."

Juan said, "I'd have to move too if that had happened to me." They stopped talking and started breaking down the furniture. Jay had a POD delivered and found out they could just put everything in it and leave it to be picked up later. It took most of the night to get all her stuff loaded, and the two men were totally worn out.

Jay said, "I wish my sister-in-law and her man hadn't broken up. If they'd stayed together, this would never have happened."

Juan asked, "Where was the dude when this happened?"

Jay said, "They broke up over a year ago and she made him stop coming over. Dude was cool and they seemed to be happy. I remember the time when we went riding in his black TransAm and ended up crashing in a small town in Tennessee. We had a good time, me and Frequency."

Juan cut in and said, "You mean Frequency, as in Frequency Hunter?"

Jay looked surprised and said, "Yeah that's him. You know him?"

"Know him," said Juan, "the computer shop I work in is owned by his friend EoW."

Jay put two and two together and said, "No wonder Frequency always had the latest computer technology." Jay asked, "Can you hook me up with Frequency?"

Juan said, "I can't but EoW can."

Jay said, "I need to meet with EoW as soon as possible." Juan was about to leave when Jay asked, "Did you forget about the money I owe you for helping me?"

Juan said, "You don't owe me anything."

Jay looked confused until Juan said, "I can't take money for helping out a friend of Frequency Hunter's because I already owe Frequency too much."

Jay jumped into his car and headed to his mother-in-law's to meet his wife, Krystal. He called her told her what had happen with Juan.

Krystal knew Doc's ex was connected, but she didn't know to what extent. She told Jay, "Don't mention that you got help from Frequency to Doc. As independent as her sister was, finding out that Frequency had been involved would just upset her." Krystal could not understand her sister's reason for breaking up with Frequency. She did know that once he found out what had happened to Doc, all hell would break loose! Someone would definitely pay for hurting her sister."

Jay and Krystal went back to see if Doc wanted to go out and get something to eat.

Doc said, "Thanks but no thanks. I just want to rest."

Krystal did everything in her power to keep from telling Doc that Jay got help from an associate of Frequency. Of course, Krystal was terrible at keeping things from her sister. She was so glad Doc didn't ask how Jay got everything packed up so quickly.

Jay hurried Krystal out of Doc's room and he and Krystal went to the Blue Fish Restaurant for dinner. They were enjoying their meal when Jay got a call from Juan. He'd made it back to the computer shop and told EoW the whole story about the move. EoW had to talk to Jay first and make sure he was on the up and up.

Jay told Juan they were finishing their dinner.

Juan said, "Yeah, we know."

Jay asked, "How do you know where we are?"

Juan said, "Frequency told us."

Then a man joined them at their table and introduced himself.

"My name is EoW," he said. "How is Doc doing?" EoW had asked Frequency to have CMAX use the coordinates of his cell phone to pinpoint Jay's location EoW was nearby, so he decided to drop in on them and check Jay out.

Jay smiled and said, "Juan told me you know Frequency."

Know him?" said EoW, "he's like a brother to me! So how is Doc?"

Krystal said, "She's worse for wear and pretty worn out, but she's recovering."

"Is she still in the Hospital?" asked EoW.

"No, she's at my mom's house."

Jay said, "The house is still off limits to Frequency. I can only go to certain parts of the house myself."

EoW laughed and said, "The old man still tripping."

Jay and Krystal exchanged a look that meant 'this guy really does know Frequency.'

Krystal asked, "How is Frequency doing and where has he been hiding?"

"He's fine," said EoW, "as a matter of fact, this is him calling now."

EoW answered his phone and listened to what Frequency was saying. He knew this would make his friend's day so he said, "I've got someone here who wants to ask you a question."

He gave his phone to Krystal and she asked, "Frequency, what does a girl have to do to see her brother-in-law?"

Frequency said, "Is this Krystal?" When she answered yes, Frequency said, "Tell EoW to put his phone in video conference mode."

She told EoW what Frequency said, and he punched a few buttons on the keypad and told Krystal to hold the phone a few inches from her face.

Krystal could see Frequency and he could see her. Frequency said, "You look well. So where's Jay?"

Jay moved over next to Krystal and the three of them started to talk about old and new times. Krystal said, "Jay and I are forbidden from mentioning your name in the house."

"Yeah," said Frequency, "Doc got that wild independent streak set and decided that she needed time alone. She won't accept my calls, and refuses to see me."

Jay and Krystal laughed and said, "We told you she was feisty, but you wouldn't listen!"

Frequency laughed with them, and then he received an urgent message from CMAX "I've got to take care of this immediately. Yall go by the cell shop and ask for Don1. He'll update your phones so you all can talk to me anytime."

Krystal asked, "What are you going to do about Doc's situation?"

"That's a done deal," said Frequency, "you two just do as I requested and keep me informed on the Doc's progress."

EoW's phone screen went blank and Krystal gave it back to him.

Jay asked, "Are you the guy who owns the State of the Art Computer Shop?"

EoW said, "Yes, why do you ask?"

Jay said, "I'm getting started as a computer consultant, and I could use a reliable distributor."

EoW said, "You're Juan's friend, right? I guarantee that if you follow Frequency's instructions you'll have no problem getting your business going."

Jay said, "Thanks for the advice."

EoW said, "No thank you. You don't know what that phone call meant to my friend." As EoW left their table, he got a call from Frequency asking about the shredded materials in the bag. EoW told Frequency about the clothes and the dildo, that LabRat was running fluid samples against all of the fluids found in the bag.

Frequency said, "Pick me up and take me to the LabRat."

EoW said, "Cool 'cause I'm not too far from your house right now. He knew Frequency held back a lot when it came to the subject of Doc. He knew his friend was going to do everything in his power to find out who'd hurt her. EoW pulled up to the house and Frequency got in.

Frequency threw a small spongy item in the air and EoW caught it and asked "What in the hell..?"

Frequency cut him off and said, "Whatever you do, don't squeeze it."

EoW immediately dropped it on the seat and asked, "What is it?"

Frequency said," It's similar to the projectile from the SHOCK-D weapon. This is enough to take out one person for a few minutes. Once embedded in the EMP device, the effect would be magnified to equal the power of 2500 regular gun rounds."

EoW's mouth dropped and he said, "WOW!"

Frequency said, "The rest of the devices should be finished and ready for testing very soon."

EoW asked, "What are you going to do with that?"

"Depending on what LabRat tells me, nothing for the moment."

EoW headed for LabRat's place. It was a long ride and EoW could tell that Frequency had some heavy thinking going on. He saw the storage sign where LabRat's place was and turned in. They parked beside an older model convertible Jaguar.

LabRat came outside hyped up on coffee and no doze. He was jittery in a comical way and he was just as hyped on his findings. EoW introduced Frequency and LabRat reacted as if he was in the presence of royalty. Frequency looked at EoW and they both just shrugged their shoulders. LabRat took them into his work area and broke down all of the test results he had run.

He told them about everything from the fibers of carpet to the pieces of glass and wire found in a light bulb. He said, "The oily residual was some kind of cooking oil. I found two types of blood from two different areas." Frequency and EoW were definitely impressed.

"One type was on a small shard of glass from a light bulb of some kind. The other type came from the end of this," he said as he pulled out the strap-on dildo.

Frequency and EoW both jumped back and hollered, "WHOA!!"

LabRat said, "I also found that the blood on the end of the dildo was in the towel. Now what I can't figure out is if the blood is from a male or female. I'm still running test on that."

Frequency asked, "What about the paper shreds?"

"Oh yeah," said LabRat, "here's what all that paper was about." He went to a makeshift computer keyboard and typed in his password, then pulled up the computer generated papers and let Frequency and EoW read for themselves. The papers were from a center that dealt with runaway adolescents. The papers looked like some kind of log listing the names of teen girls who had run away from the center. All the pages that LabRat pulled up gave the same information but, but each page was for a different teen girl. One of the girls was only 13 years old.

Frequency looked at EoW and said, "This bitch is kidnapping and raping these young girls."

EoW said, "She's probably taking them to some pilferer of girls and selling them off."

Frequency said, "We need proof before we can pass this information on."

EoW told Frequency, "You need to go back and find out more about this one."

Frequency said, "Oh I plan to, but I need you to get me some kind of listening device."

EoW said, "I've got those video camera smoke detectors that were in storage."

Frequency thought about it, and came up with an ingenious plan to get them installed in their house.

Frequency told EoW, "Get them to me as soon as possible."

LabRat's computer made a sound that surely said a new hard drive was needed. EoW and Frequency looked at each other as LabRat smacked the top of his computer and it came back to life and the printer started printing.

LabRat told Frequency and EoW, "Both of the blood samples came from women."

Frequency asked LabRat, "What do I owe you?"

LabRat said, "Just sign this for me." It was a copy of the newspaper that had Frequency on the front page the first time he was indicted for computer hacking. LabRat was a true aficionado in the computer realm, otherwise known as a nerd. To LabRat, having Frequency in his lab was an honor.

Frequency signed the paper and told LabRat, "You need to get out more often Man. That sure is a nice car outside. How long have you had it?"

LabRat looked at Frequency and said, "I don't have a car."

Frequency asked, "Whose drop top Jag is that outside?"

LabRat told Frequency, "Wait a minute," as he grabbed the phone to call his mom. He talked on the phone for a minute then hung up. He turned and told

Frequency, "It's my mom's car, and she had the car for over a year now."

EoW laughed and said, "Now you see why they call him LabRat."

Frequency and EoW laughed and told LabRat that they would be in touch. When they made it down the street, Frequency told EoW, "Set the LabRat up FREAK style."

"How am I going to do that? asked EoW, "I don't know anything about a crime lab."

"Don't worry about that," said Frequency, "CMAX will get the information we need from the Fed's lab, then we'll duplicate it and make it five times better."

EoW nodded and headed to the computer shop. He and Frequency arrived at the shop and went in through the back door. They went directly to the storage room and found a whole slew of spy shop devices still in the crate. Frequency looked at EoW in disgust.

"I thought I told you to sell all of this stuff a year ago," he said.

EoW looked as if he'd just swallowed a bug and said, "I did but the guy never picked it up."

"Who was he?" asked Frequency.

EoW said, "I don't remember, but I've got an address from the payment check."

Frequency told EoW, "Send me all of the information tomorrow and I'll settle it once and for all." He picked out the equipment he needed plus a couple of phone taps. He told EoW, "Come take the TransAm to Webb for a tune up tomorrow."

EoW knew that Frequency was going to use his truck to plant the devices in Cupcake's crib. EoW started seriously thinking about getting himself a new set of wheels.

Frequency woke up the next day when CMAX announced that EoW was on the premises. When he'd made it home the night before, he'd had a few too many drinks. Frequency got to the front door as EoW was taking out the t-tops. EoW loved to drive the TA, but hated bringing it back.

He told Frequency, "You look like shit!"

Frequency saluted him with his middle finger and said, "If you wreck my car I'll have your head."

EoW knew he wasn't going to bring him that car back for quite a while. Frequency didn't care because he had plenty to drive and that happened to be his favorite. Frequency went back into the house and got showered and dressed. He knew he had to get to Cupcake's house right as she left for work. He put on some blue khaki pants and a light blue shirt. He put on black Lugs boots to make him look like a repairman. He got into EoW's truck and headed to Cupcake's house.

He made it in time to see Cupcake and a young girl getting on a motorcycle. Frequency made sure he got a good look at both of them as they put on helmets and left. Frequency pulled up to the curb as Cupcake's neighbors left out of their side of the duplex, got into their car and left. Frequency sprang into action, walking to the back of the duplex, and quickly using an automatic pick on the door. He walked in the duplex looking for a smoke detector, but couldn't find one.

This pissed Frequency off 'cause he couldn't use the one he had with the camera in it. He looked for a phone but there was no phone either! Frequency was really pissed till he found a laptop under the bed. He quickly tried to go online and found that Cupcake was jacking the wireless signal from her neighbor. Frequency went online to the website that he stored worms on and loaded one on Cupcake's laptop.

He got all of the information he needed and started to leave until he accidentally clicked on a file and it prompted him for a password. Not being one who could resist a challenge, he tried to crack the code. Frequency thought that he must be rusty because it took him a few tries to get the password. Then he froze when he clicked on the file inside and saw that it contained pictures from a camera phone.

Cupcake had pictures of Doc! Frequency started clicking on more files until he found the pictures that made him almost go berserk. Cupcake had a picture of Doc tied up and naked! Frequency shutdown the laptop and put it back under the bed. He made a hasty retreat out of the duplex and hurriedly walked down the driveway and back to EoW's truck. He was so pissed at Doc! She could have told him she was...

Frequency never finished that thought because he now knew, who had attacked Doc, and he had all the proof he needed. The next time Cupcake uses her laptop, he'll have even more. Frequency wanted to kill Cupcake but he knew they'd lock him up forever if he did. He began to put a plan together to get this bitch and, when he did, Doc would be there to make the judgment call.

Frequency started the truck and headed for home. He knew that soon he would have to start the next phase of the CMAX move because he was getting deeper into the pedophile thing than he wanted. And now that his beloved was involved, the stakes were far greater than he had ever imagined they could be.

Doc sat in the bedroom of her mother's house and watched TV. She had been granted a leave of absence until she was released from her doctor's care. The doctors told her there would be no permanent damage. They said all of her physical wounds would heal in time. In her mind there would always be the fact that she had been attacked in her own home. She wanted to call Frequency so bad and just let him make everything better, but she knew he wouldn't hold to her religious beliefs, He would hunt the person who did this down no matter what. The end result would be that someone's life would be taken and once again Frequency would be taken from her life. Doc felt conflicted by the mere thought of having Frequency back in her life. They were an off-the-chain couple who had no regards for other people's thoughts when they were together. She thought about all the good times they'd had, and then shook it off. She opened her Bible and began to read, then stopped and thought about something Frequency once said to her. He'd said that his arms were too short to box with God, but all others would catch hell! She never knew what that meant, but she had a feeling she would soon find out.

Chapter 8

GayMack

Frequency gave EoW a call but didn't get an answer. That's because, at that very moment, EoW was standing outside someone's residence and couldn't take a chance on being heard. He was in the process of following up on information Don1 had given him. He had left his cell phone back in the car so he could get a closer look. The house belonged to a Richard Inman, an eccentric nightclub owner who had the gay scene on lock. His club stayed packed, and did not close until five a.m.

This dude was hard to track until his clerk said, "You know, they called him GayMack because he pimps a bunch of young boys."

EoW almost puked when he heard this! He knew he'd have to handle this one with a long handled spoon. His next move would have to be perfectly planned and flawlessly executed in order to be successful. EoW put on his night vision goggles and got an eye full of the sickest, most repulsive scene he'd witnessed in a while. This dude had transvestites and young boys all over his property, even walking around his pool in two-piece bikinis. Some even had on silk robes. A couple of the boys were swimming, but the others were just lying around like items on a freakish menu. He moved to another side of the yard and saw a young dude giving a guy with tits a blow job. Another guy had a transvestite in the buck.

It was just one big fag orgy EoW thought to himself until everyone just froze. He swung his head around and saw the main dude, GayMack himself, walk into view. EoW could tell by the way GayMack was dressed and how the others treated him that he was definitely king of this castle.

EoW left the area where he was and went back to the car. He knew he would need more than night vision goggles, but that was all he had with him. Then he thought about all of the equipment in storage that never got picked up and decided with a smile that he would put it to very good use.

He slipped out the back way and walked right into a small nice looking woman. "Excuse me," he said, and then realized he was not talking to a woman. The woman said, "My name is Bobbie. I think you should come to visit me at my home."

Bobbie gave EoW a card with something written on it, which he put in his pocket just before he ran to the car. He hurriedly cranked the car and sped off. EoW headed straight for his store. Upon arriving, he did some research and found out that GayMack owned a night spot called The Gallery. Then he found out who his suppliers were. EoW saw that one of his competitors had GayMack's business on the computers that controlled all the lighting and disc jockey's equipment in his club. He came up with the perfect idea.

EoW was transfixed by the power of the TransAm. No matter how far he pushed it, the car responded very well. He wished Frequency would sell the car to him, but he knew that was not happening. EoW knew that Frequency had already been offered some nice money for the car, but he wouldn't sell it. Before long, he was back at his store. He went inside and started putting the equipment that he needed in a bag to make it easier to take with him.

EoW had just finished loading up and was headed back to the car when his cell phone vibrated. It was Frequency on a secure line. EoW let his Bluetooth auto answered the phone as he jumped back into the car.

Frequency told him, "I've found out who attacked Doc."

"Who?" asked EoW, "Mr. White's crew?"

"No," said Frequency, "it was that dike bitch, Cupcake."

"No shit!" yelled EoW "Where did you get that information?"

Frequency told him, "I ran across pictures of Doc on Cupcake's laptop. One of them almost made me lose it!"

EoW was floored! He couldn't believe what he had just heard.

Frequency said, "Get in touch with LabRat again and have him test the blood samples he has against the sample the hospital got from Doc."

EoW asked, "Where do you want LabRat to run the files from? The boy has a piece of junk for a computer system, so it could take a month to access the hospital's mainframe with the equipment he has."

Frequency laughed and said. "Take him a laptop from inventory and put it on my bill."

"No problem," said EoW, "I need a little assistance on my current project any way." EoW told Frequency what he'd found out about Richard Inman. Frequency asked, "Who is that?"

EoW said, "He's the man behind the GayMack file."

"Are you serious?" asked Frequency.

EoW brought him up to speed on everything he had seen at Inman's house, including the transvestite who passed him a business card.

Frequency asked, "So what's on the card?"

EoW pulled the card out of his pocket and read the glossy raised pink and teal lettering aloud: 'Ms. Bobbie the Pleasure Peacock.'

Frequency had to laugh 'cause he knew EoW was not cool with the gay scene. "Hold on," he said, "the card has something else on it: 'See the show at the Gallery. This card worth free admission for two.'

EoW said, "Our competitors have all of GayMack's business."

Frequency then thought about the EMP round, and then he and EoW said it almost simultaneously. But EoW's idea was a bit more in depth than Frequency's.

Frequency's plan was to just destroy their computer's circuitry.

EoW said, "Let's buy up all the replacement parts first, and then blow all of their equipment. GayMack will be forced to buy from us, and we can make sure that a worm is already in place."

"Absolutely ingenious!" Frequency said, "Go ahead and follow through with your plan."

EoW said, "First I have to go back and get some nasty shit from GayMack's little party on night vision video. Then I'll be ready to pop the circuitry at The Gallery.

Frequency and EoW set up a time to meet so Frequency could give him the EMP round. Frequency took the specifications given to him from EoW. He had all of the equipment specified by EoW purchased and then he went back to his work out. They would meet after EoW had enough footage from the night's party.

EoW was headed back to GayMack's house. He parked one block away and found a spot that gave him a clear view of GayMack's backyard. Lady Luck was on his side because the house behind GayMack's was vacant and for sale. He climbed on top of the garage and crawled around until he found the perfect spot. EoW opened the bag and pulled out all the hardware he needed, got everything setup, then starting shooting video.

He saw the person that he'd first thought as a woman. 'Ms. Bobbie' was on a platform that was being carried around by six men wearing tight gold shorts. Ms. Bobbie was holding a gold flask filled with some kind of liquid. The men put Ms. Bobbie down and stood around him. Ms. Bobbie removed the bra like top to expose a pair of silicone breast implants. He drank from the flask then lay back and removed the rest of his clothing exposing his manhood to the onlookers. The six men began removing their pants and masturbating themselves. Another guy walked over to Ms.Bobbie and squirted some kind of oil all over them. The guys started in on Ms. Bobbie and did not spare the rod.   They filled every part of her with one of them. Ms. Bobbie let out a gasp as one after another penetrated him. They pounded his body with ruthless abandon. As soon as one finished, she'd reach for the next until the last of them had finished. Ms. Bobbie was then given a special treat for providing the night's entertainment. GayMack walked in with a young boy who couldn't have been more than 13 or 14 years old. EoW wanted to interfere, but he couldn't blow his cover just yet.

GayMack took the little boy over to Ms. Bobbie, who was totally gone on the liquid he'd consumed earlier. The little boy was presented to Bobbie as a sacrifice to the pleasure peacock. Ms. Bobbie had been in this situation on numerous occasions, and had turned many a boy into victims of the pleasure pea-cock. He loved drinking his wine and ecstasy mix, and had no qualms about having his way with anybody that GayMack gave her.

EoW packed up most of the equipment, but left the night vision camera hidden on the roof and still record-ing. EoW climbed down and went to the car. He was looking for something to cause a distraction but found nothing. He got Frequency on the phone and was frantically trying to explain what was about to happen to the boy.

Frequency got CMAX online and said, "Slow down long enough to give CMAX the address; I have a surprise for GayMack and his crew."

As soon as EoW gave him the address, CMAX had the location and the EMP weapon's scope aimed in that direction.

EoW asked, "What's going to happen now?"

Frequency said, "I'm not sure since this is the first test." Then he hit the enter key and set off a chain of events that happened in a matter of milliseconds.

EoW saw the lights flicker then go off completely in and outside GayMack's house. He heard people shouting and saw them running out of the house. The next thing EoW saw was Ms. Bobbie being escorted by GayMack into a waiting Lincoln Navigator, the two of them being driven away. GayMack's other guests followed suit, jumping into their cars and leaving in a hurry as well. Next, EoW saw the little boy walkout of the house naked and covered in some kind of red oil. He seemed confused and appeared to be drugged. EoW waited until all of the cars were gone; then he went to the little boy and covered him with a towel he found in the car.

EoW started talking to the little boy and found out his name was Dean. He told a most chilling tale. "I was in an elevator at the hospital when someone snatched me up, made me ride in the back of a truck inside a bag until we got here."

EoW could tell Dean was scared and disoriented. He asked, "Did they do anything to you?"

Dean said, "That man thing was about to rape me when the lights started exploding. That thing threw something at me that got all in my mouth. I can't remember much after that."

EoW said, "I wish I could take you home myself, but I can't without messing up this investigation. But there's a very nice family in that house over there who'll help you get home. I'll check on you once the investigation is over." Then he pointed Dean in the direction of the house, disappeared back through the brush, and jumped into the TransAm. headed for Frequency's house. EoW was half way to Frequency's when he remembered the camera he'd left recording on the roof. He knew he couldn't go back tonight so he came up with an idea of how to get it back without causing a stir.

EoW made it to Frequency's place in no time and went straight to the bathroom, where he puked until he thought his guts were coming up! Once he finished, he came out and told Frequency everything he'd seen and heard at GayMack's party.

Frequency said, "I promise that this dude is going down!"

EoW told Frequency, "GayMack is too clean at this point. We don't have anything on him. He didn't touch anything last night; he just sat back and watched."

Frequency asked, "You think you can make it to the club?"

EoW said, "I wouldn't miss it for the world. I need to set up an appointment with the realtor who's showing the house I used to shoot the video."

Frequency asked, "Why?"

EoW said with all of the excitement at GayMack's, I forgot the camera." Frequency laughed and said, "Under those circumstances, I can certainly understand."

EoW asked, "Do you mind if I crash at your crib?"

Frequency said, "No problem. Now that BDB has his own crib, you can use my guest room."

EoW made a crack about the EMP. He said "The next time you decide to use that EMP, maybe you should dial it down a bit. It's been a very long time since I've seen fireworks like that!"

Frequency laughed and said, "Maybe I will; maybe I won't."

'Ms. Bobbie' had been totally wasted on that elixir he'd been drinking the night before. He overhead GayMack on the phone talking about a fire and telling someone to make sure no one was still in the house. Ms. Bobbie sat up on the couch and began to remember the events from the night before.

He asked GayMack, "What happen to my new little friend?"

GayMack said, "That little fucker got away when the lights exploded." Ms. Bobbie got up off of the couch and went into the bathroom, where His stomach exploded as he vomited the last remnants of his special elixir from last night. He finished, and then turned on the shower. He knew that GayMack was not happy with the outcome of last night's party, but it wasn't his fault. He jumped into the shower and cleaned himself up. He was tired, but was also eagerly looking forward to tonight's show at The Gallery.

Ms. Bobbie finished his shower and went in the kitchen where GayMack had one of his servants cooking breakfast. Ms. Bobbie walked over to him and kissed him.

GayMack smacked him hard on the ass and said, "I am really confused about what happened with the lights last night. That whole house had to be fried to cover our trail."

Ms Bobbie said, "I'm so sorry about that fiasco. Don't worry, 'cause I plan to make it all up to you tonight at The Gallery."

Now that statement alone made GayMack smile. He pulled down some major dollars every time Ms. Bobbie put on one of his shows. He knew he had to get ready for some of his other clients too, so he needed to put the word out that he needed some fresh young talent. The younger the talent, the more money he could make. GayMack did not care about age or sex, he just cared about the money he made peddling their flesh.

He had Ms. Bobbie on a leash and planned on keeping him close. Ms. Bobbie turned every girl and boy that he had in his stable. He loved to watch him entice and enrapture each new victim, turn them out, then put them to work. He had a talent that GayMack controlled. Bobbie had killed for him before and would do again if he asked. GayMack was thoroughly enjoying his reign as King of the Gay Scene. He made it a point not touch the help except for Ms. Bobbie. With his hands in so many other business ventures, he couldn't take a chance that his insatiable sex addiction would mess up his money.

GayMack still couldn't for the life of him figure out what had caused the lights at the party to blow like they did. It had left a colossal mess for him to clean up. and he had just bought that property from somebody who was up to their eyeballs in debt. GayMack had blackmailed her into giving up the house by videotaping her with an underage boy. When she saw the video, she was happy to give up her house as payment for it. GayMack had her in the palm of his hand and was not through with her yet. At least he knew he had insurance money coming from the fire that destroyed the house. He knew they had to pay this woman off 'cause he had sent her out of town so they couldn't say that she set the fire.

Ms. Bobbie finished her breakfast and told Gay-Mack, "I'm going to the club to make sure everything is in place for tonight's show."

GayMack said, "Make sure they test all of the equipment before the show, because I don't want a repeat performance like last night."

Ms. Bobbie gave him a kiss and left. He had the driver take him straight to the club's private entrance. Bobbie was met at the door by the club's manager. He briefed Bobbie on all of the goings on at the club and exactly where they were on the final touches for his show.

'Ms. Bobbie' walked out on the stage and saw people working like bees in a hive to get The Gallery ready for the big show. He knew everything was going to be perfect, so he decided to have himself a little fun before he had to perform. Ms. Bobbie walked around to the backstage area where crews of electricians were working on a light array. One tall guy with a nice body caught his eye. Dude saw Ms. Bobbie looking at him, but he did not want any dealings with a transsexual. He turned and went to work high up on the scaffold to tighten up the light array. It was hot and he was sweaty. Ms. Bobbie saw him turn and walk away and then climb up high to get away from him. He started to go up and get the guy, but was distracted when a familiar face came into view.

EoW was a nervous wreck! He had stepped into a place where he was totally uncomfortable. He moved around stiffly, making sure he was not touching anything. He was about to turn and leave when he saw the person he was looking for.

Ms. Bobbie walked up to EoW and said, "You're mighty early."

EoW said, "I wanted to have a chance to give you my business card and inventory package."

Ms. Bobbie took the information, motioned for the club manager to come over, and handed the packet to him. Bobbie introduced the club manager, Carl to EoW, who couldn't help but notice that Carl became ex-tremely nervous when he came near Ms. Bobbie.

Ms. Bobbie then told Carl, "That all for now. You can leave." Carl left as though his feet were on fire! Ms. Bobbie asked, "Are you going to make it to the show tonight?"

EoW said, "Unfortunately, I have a prior engagement that won't allow me to make it."

Ms. Bobbie then said, "Follow me and I'll give you a tour of the club."

EoW was nervous, but incredibly alert as he walked around the facility. He took inventory of all the computer equipment they were using to make the club work like a well-oiled machine. He had everything that he'd need in stock, so he was ready to enact his plan when Ms. Bobbie asked him to join her for lunch. He knew he couldn't stomach much more of Ms. Bobbie's company and was about to come up with an excuse when Carl walked up and said there was a problem that needed to be handled immediately.

Ms. Bobbie looked at Carl and said, "Looks like I'll have to give you a rain check on lunch."

EoW was so happy to get out of there that he bumped into the disc jockey and knocked some of his equipment out of his hands. EoW didn't want the stuff to break, so he reached out and caught all of it but a very small piece that came off came off. EoW gave the DJ the rest and said, "Stay right there. I'll get the other piece." He searched the floor and found that it was the handle off some kind of light fader. He had his back to the DJ when he found the piece which had just enough room in it for the EMP round. EoW quickly pushed the round inside, and then palmed the fader control so that dude couldn't see it.

He walked up to dude and said, "My bad. I'll help you to the disc jockey station."

The DJ said, "That's cool," and handed EoW the equipment.

EoW told him, "I found the knob that fell and since it was my fault, I'll put it back on for you."

Dude said, "Cool. It's always falling off. I'm going to replace this equipment as soon as I finish this gig tonight."

That was music to EoW's ears! He helped dude get to his station and handed him a business card as he said, "If it's got a computer chip in it, I either have it or I can get it."

Dude told EoW, "Look, my name is Travis and I'm not into the Gallery scene, but I need the money to buy new equipment."

EoW said, "I can understand that," as he left. He found his way out of the club, got into his Nissan Xterra and left. What he didn't know was that the doorman at the club took down his license plate number and saved it for Ms. Bobbie.

EoW turned up the music in his truck and headed for his meeting with the realtor. He was happy that his plan was coming together nicely so far. His cell phone vibrated and he saw that it was Frequency.

Frequency said, "I don't know what's going on but I have some potentially bad news. Somebody is running a DMV check on your license plate."

Oh How I Hate That!!!!! EoW thought to himself. Then he remembered who his partner was and said, "Can you find out who is checking up on me?"

Frequency said, "I've already done that and I changed registration to show the address of the computer store."

EoW said, "The staff of the Gallery was probably trying to find out if I'm legit. Now I know my plan will run flawlessly!"

When he got to the house the realtor was waiting for him. She walked up to him and said, "Hello, I'm Vanessa. Just call me V. Let's get started."

EoW was there to look at the house and get his equipment, but he found himself looking even harder at Vanessa. He followed her around the house and asked a number of questions. EoW needed to get V out of the house. He went upstairs and looked out of the back bedroom window. He was at a loss for words after what he saw. The house where the gay orgy was staged had been burned to the ground!

V walked up beside EoW and said, I had no idea that house had caught on fire. I'll be right back as soon as I get my camera so I can take some pictures."

EoW said, "That's fine, I'll wait for you." This would be the break that he needed. As V went down the stairs, EoW went out on the back deck and climbed to the side of the house where his equipment was still set up. He hurriedly packed everything in the duffle bag, threw it on the ground next to the tree, climbed back onto the deck and acted like he was trying to get a better view of the charred remains of the house.

V came up the stairs looking for EoW and, when she didn't see him, called his name.

EoW answered her and said, "I'm on the balcony out back."

V joined him and started taking pictures.

EoW loved seeing her bend over the balcony because she was one fine woman.

Of course, V knew EoW was checking her out, and she made sure he had enough to entice him. V knew that EoW had been in contact with Frequency Hunter. She had been assigned the case by agent Layrock. Her job was to keep up with all of the acquaintances of Mr. Hunter. V turned around quickly and saw just what she wanted to see. EoW was admiring her attributes when she turned and asked him about the house.

He came to his senses and said, "I'd like to think on this one. Can I get back to you?"

V reached into her purse and gave EoW her business card. EoW pulled out one of his own and said, "You can call me for any computer problem you might have, night or day. I will personally take care of it for you."

V smiled at him as she walked past him and headed to the outside of the house. She said, "I'll give you a call in a couple of days."

EoW said, "Sure thing." Then he got in his truck drove away.

V waited until EoW was out of sight before she made a call to agent Layrock. She told him, "Contact has been made. I'm leaving this location to set up for another visit."

EoW went about 7 blocks up the road, then made his way back to the empty house. He pulled into the driveway and went to the backyard where he had dropped the duffel. He got to the tree, picked up the bag, and found that everything inside it was still intact. He was inside his vehicle and about to leave when another vehicle pulled into the driveway and a lady got out.

She ran up to EoW and said breathlessly, "I'm the real estate agent assigned to this house. I've been trying to call you and let you know I was running late."

EoW was about to say something about the other lady, but decided he'd play along with this lady. She told him her name was Samantha, but he could call her Sam. Sam led him on a tour of the house, and EoW played along as if he hadn't already seen it all. He went through the entire tour and then exchanged information with the real realtor this time. As soon as he left the house, he called Frequency and asked, "What is really going on?"

Frequency said, "We'll talk about it at LabRat's place."

EoW was totally spooked, and when he got to the Rat's place he did not feel any better. Frequency wasn't outside, so EoW went inside to see if Frequency was inside with LabRat. Then he got really confused.

EoW asked Frequency, "Where's the TransAm?"

Frequency said, "It's in the shop so I'm on the scooter parked outside."

"What scooter?" asked EoW?

Frequency said, "The one I just gave LabRat for transportation."

"Oh," said EoW, "is it a nice one?"

Frequency said, "It has a 650cc motor in it and 120 on the dash."

EoW was impressed and said, "That's a whole lot better than nice!" then LabRat came in just as excited. He told Frequency, "I love my new set of wheels! Now I'll finish up the rest of the experiments I was working on. I'm ninety-nine percent sure that the blood on the sex toy and the blood work that the hospital had on file is the same."

Frequency knew without a doubt that Cupcake had assaulted Doc.

EoW told Frequency, "Stay focused and we'll get that bitch later. What should I do about the fake realtor?"

Frequency said, "Play along with her." He knew that they were going to try to get to him through his friends, so he knew exactly what to do.

He told EoW, "Just wait her out. She'll come around you trying to see if you'll mention my name or if you and I are hanging together. If we don't let them see us together they have nothing to gain from you."

EoW knew just what to do from there. Now he had a way to get Ms. Bobbie off of his jock, and he would use the feds to do it! EoW felt as if the weight of the world had been lifted off his shoulders.

Frequency asked LabRat, "Did you finish all of the nanobyte experiments I gave you?"

LabRat said, "I've finished all of them and added some refinements that will make it work, but the injections are still untested."

Frequency said, "I want you to take all of the information and go see an old friend of mine. She'll take over from there and she probably could use the help of someone with your talents."

LabRat said, "I'm on it!" and started getting the experiments together for transportation.

Then Frequency turned to EoW and said, "Soon you'll be needing a new ride."

EoW asked, "Do you have something in mind?"

Frequency told him, "Go get something that fits your style. Can you drop me off at BDB's place?"

EoW asked, "Do you think your ride is tapped?"

Frequency said, "Not yet, but as soon as they do it, we'll make it conveniently disappear."

EoW knew Frequency was up to something, but he could not put his finger on it. The two of them helped LabRat get the scooter loaded and sent him on his way then they got into EoW's SUV and headed for BDB's place.

BDB had purchased the perfect place for his home and landscape business. It was on the outskirts of town and had plenty of room for his equipment and vehicles. Frequency had set him up with all of the computer equipment and teaching programs to get him into the intermediate stages of computers. BDB had learned a lot in a short period of time, so he was no longer afraid that he might break the computer. He had all of his billing and accounts set up, and he'd learned how to do backups and set off worm programs. He had also learned how to download and upload all types of data and images. Frequency didn't leave any stone unturned when it came to teaching BDB how everything worked

BDB was just unhitching his trailer when he saw EoW and Frequency pulling up. He walked to the truck and just smiled. He was glad to have some company at his new place. EoW and Frequency got out of the SUV and followed BDB around as he showed them his place.

He took them to his computer room and the two guys got to work. They logged into CMAX and had him see what the Fed's were up to. Agent Layrock had installed an entire video array on his laptop. Frequency used the array to look at all of the personnel in the area. EoW did not see the person, who called herself Vanessa. Frequency went into the agent's daily log and found the information that told him EoW was also being monitored by the Feds.

Frequency told EoW and said, "You need to check your ride every day to see if it is tagged."

EoW nodded and asked, "What do I do when it is tagged?"

Frequency said, "Take V for a ride then we'll get you a new one."

EoW loved the sound of that cause he had been looking at a convertible that had his name all over it.

Richard Inman had a meeting in an undisclosed location. He needed to see one of his 'recruiters' as he called them. The guy showed up and was calm when Richard told him he'd lost his last recruit.

Richard paid for another recruit and said, "Make sure this one is a girl."

The recruiter said, "I'll need more money because the cops are hot when a young girl comes up missing."

Richard then called his recruiter by name. He said, "Benjamin Dover am I hearing you whine?"

Benjamin Dover wasn't one to complain. He had grabbed more kids than any recruiter who worked for Richard Inman. Ben said, "I'm the most ingenious of all of your recruiters. While you're running around being the GayMack, I'm busting my ass snatching up kids for your decadent lifestyle."

Richard walked closer to Ben and said, "Don't forget that I'm the one who helped you to have any life outside of prison – period!"

Ben looked like he wanted to kill Richard, but he knew he would be the next to die if he did. Richard reached inside his suit and gave Ben another package filled with money. Ben took the package and walked away. Richard made a mental note to introduce Ben to Ms. Bobbie. He appreciated Ben's work, but he did not like his attitude.

Benjamin Dover would bring Richard any young kid that he requested. Benjamin had a way of making a young child disappear from a building via the elevator shaft. That's why he was known as the 'Elevator Man.' Richard had found out about him many years ago and used him as much as possible. He liked Ben's style and the fact that he didn't leave any evidence that brought the cops to his door. Richard went to his car and placed a call to another one of his recruiters. He told the recruiter to come to the Gallery to discuss some business. Then Richard had his driver take him to the

Gallery where he'd been told there was a problem with tonight's big show.

Ms. Bobbie was in a zone, when he felt her partner orgasm inside of him. Carl lay on his back as he busted a hard nut inside of Ms. Bobbie. Ms. Bobbie had worn his behind out earlier and now Carl had to return the favor. Ms. Bobbie got out of the chair he had decided to let Carl mount him on, still excited and wanting more. Bobbie pulled up her pants and told Carl to get back to work. Carl knew then that he did not pleasure Ms. Bobbie enough. He pulled up his pants and went to the men's room to clean himself up. Ms. Bobbie was on the prowl looking for the electrician he'd seen earlier. She wanted him more than ever! The sex with Carl just made him more excited and he was determined to be pleased by someone other than himself.

Ms. Bobbie went back to the lighting area and was disappointed to see the electricians had left for the day. He was in a frenzy looking for a quickie sexual experience and was just about to go masturbate when he saw his next pleasure piece.

Mario had come to the Gallery to deliver the flyers for tonight's event. He was bending over when Ms. Bobbie walked up on him. Mario turned to face him and asked, "What's up?"

Ms. Bobbie peeped his style immediately and asked,"Would you like the VIP treatment?"

Mario was down so he said, "Sure."

Ms. Bobbie grabbed his hand and led him to her dressing room. He hurriedly pulled him inside and they started kissing. Ms. Bobbie grabbed Mario's hand and put it on the bulge in his pants. Mario grabbed the bulge and started to stroke it. Ms. Bobbie hurriedly pulled his hard on free and had Mario on it. Mario let Ms. Bobbie know that this was not his first time. Ms. Bobbie was totally enraptured by Mario's oral skill. Bobbie knew that he wouldn't be able to hold back his orgasm, and Mario wasn't about to let him. Ms. Bobbie grabbed the back of Mario's head and started pumping erratically. His orgasm came and Mario drank deeply, not leaving a drop to spare. As soon as he depleted his semen, Bobbie pulled Mario up to her mouth and the two kissed deeply. Ms. Bobbie then went down on Mario and found out immediately that Mario had more than he could swallow. Bobbie still would not stop giving him head as he pulled his pants off. As soon as Bobbie was naked from the waist down, Mario turn his back to him and started sticking his tongue into his rectum. Mario had made it up in his mind that he was going to make this transvestite spend some of that money on him. He saw that Bobbie had some very nice breast implants. Mario pulled his tongue from Bobbie as he saw some body oil on a cabinet. He grabbed the oil and poured some on Ms. Bobbie and some on his throbbing manhood. Ms. Bobbie gasped for air as Mario entered him hard and fast. He did not waste any time before going deep inside of Ms. Bobbie.

Ms. Bobbie had been with a lot of men, but none had gone as deep inside of him as this guy was. Ms. Bobbie found himself letting out gasps of air each time Mario thrust deep inside of him. He was trying not to scream, but this dude was hitting him just right. Ms.

Bobbie looked down and saw cum spewing out of his manhood as he let out a scream of pleasure. Mario knew he had Ms Bobbie, so now he could bust his own orgasm. He grabbed Ms. Bobbie's shoulder and pulled back on him hard. Mario saw this guy walk in and stare at them, but he didn't care. He came hard up inside of Ms. Bobbie, and growled deeply as his orgasm shot deep inside of Ms. Bobbie. Ms. Bobbie collapsed on the floor as Mario released him.

GayMack started to clap his hands in appreciation of what he'd just seen. He had never before seen Ms. Bobbie so overcome by any man.

GayMack threw Mario a towel and asked, "What's your name?"

Mario told him and asked, "Are you the GayMack?"

Richard answered him by saying, "That's what I'm called around here." Then Mario asked, "Are you doing any hiring?"

GayMack said, "After what I just saw you don't need to look for a job, you already have one!"

Mario asked, "What am I going to be doing?"

GayMack said, "You'll be Ms. Bobbie new assistant, with an emphasis on 'ass.'

Mario then realized that Ms. Bobbie was still on the floor with her ass up in the air, so he reached down and helped him up. Ms. Bobbie stood up on wobbly legs and was amazed at what she'd just experienced.

GayMack said, "Go on and get ready for the show."

Ms. Bobbie saw a look in GayMack's eyes that said he meant business, so Ms. Bobbie limped his way into his dressing room shower. This was one time that he definitely bit off more than he could chew.

Mario followed Ms. Bobbie back to her dressing room and waited for him to finish up in the shower.

Ms. Bobbie got out of the shower and saw Mario sitting there waiting on him. He was excited but cautious; since he knew he couldn't fool around with this young man again and mess up the Gallery's big night. Bobbie asked Mario, "Where are you staying?"

Mario said, "A rooming house down the street."

Ms. Bobbie told him "You're going to be helping me from now on. As soon as I get finished with my show, we're going to get you cleaned up and make you more presentable."

Mario felt as if he'd hit the jackpot! He told Ms. Bobbie, "I won't leave your dressing room until you say so."

Ms. Bobbie walked over and kissed his new boy toy. Then he went over and started to dress for their big night.

EoW was very nervous about the date he had setup with 'V.' He knew that everything she would tell him would be a lie, so he had to be cool and not let her know that her cover had already been blown.

Vanessa had already contacted agent Layrock and told him about tonight's date with EoW. She wore a long dress with a very high split to highlight her curves. Vanessa had her backup pistol in a holster up high on her thigh. She knew she had to go up that high just in case they went to a venue that searched for weapons. She wasn't worried because Agent Layrock sent a team of three agents along for the date. Vanessa arrived at the restaurant where EoW asked her to meet him, and was pleased to find out that the restaurant was like a small villa in Italy that served some great seafood and pasta.

EoW was dressed in a single breasted suit that made him look debonair. He was impressed when V walked in and the dress she was wearing made him forget she was an agent for the Feds. EoW stood up and waved V over to his table. He pulled her chair out for her and V made a mental note that he was a gentleman, and then sat down.

EoW sat down and asked, "Would you like some-thing to drink?"

V said, "Sure."

EoW told the waiter, "A glass of red wine for the lady."

V smiled at his selection and looked at the menu until she found a selection that met her approval and ordered it. EoW also ordered and they sat back and conversed as they sipped red wine and waited for their meal.

EoW stuck to small talk and talked about the house that she had shown him.

V talked about the house that had been burned to the ground. She said, "I found out that the local fire department got the call only after most of the house was already engulfed in flames. They say that it was arson, and they have assigned an investigator to it."

Their meals came and they ate and enjoyed their time together. EoW had programmed his PDA to remind him about the party at the Gallery. He pulled his phone from his inside pocket when it vibrated and acknowledged the reminder.

V asked, "Do you have an appointment you need handle?"

EoW told her, "I'm trying to get the owner of this club to buy his computer equipment from me."

V said, "The Gallery is known as the gay scene of the city."

EoW said, "I know that, but sales have been down this year and the owner is making major purchases from my competitor."

V said, "I can understand that. What are you going to do about it?"

EoW told V, "I've been invited to the Gallery for some kind of big show tonight, but I'm not going."

V said, "You should go. I'll go with you to protect you from the man-eaters."

EoW laughed and said, "Do you think it would be good for business?"

V said, "The owner will see that you at least showed up for his big party, even if your competitor doesn't."

EoW hadn't thought of it that way, so he decided to go. He asked, "Will you go with me?"

V said, "I wouldn't miss it for the world!"

The two got up from their table as EoW paid for the meal and left a nice tip. They went out to the parking area and decided to go in Vanessa's car, a BMW roadster. EoW knew this wasn't her car, but he would enjoy the ride for tonight. They buckled up and headed for the Gallery.

It didn't take long to get there, and as they pulled up on the property, the lights and glitz was in full swing. GayMack had pulled out all of the stops for this one. He had a Las Vegas style affair going with VIP parking. V and EoW were both impressed. They handed the VIP invitation to the valet and he called for an escort to take them in. Richard met them on a red carpet and took them inside past the metal detectors. V was so glad that she didn't have to go through the metal detector. She was going to have a good time tonight and she was going to teach EoW a step or two.

EoW was a little nervous. Here he was in a club where he had set a device to knock out the place's electrical system and he was there with a federal agent. He played his part well, watching the entire extravaganza that GayMack had set forth. The show started without a hitch and Ms. Bobbie had a chance to show off all of her talents. She was in her zone and her show was riveting. Richard Inman went on stage and thanked everyone for coming out, then turned the rest of the night over to the DJ. The music started and people filled the dance floor. V grabbed EoW's hand and led him to the dance floor.

Richard Inman stood in his office talking to one of his recruiters. Cupcake had come to the Gallery to get her payment for turning Keynesia over to the Madame. Richard paid her and told her to stick around and enjoy herself. The two left his office and went to join the festivities. Richard had his bodyguard escort him out to the VIP area.

Cupcake went out on the dance floor and looked around. There she saw a very nice looking woman in a black dress dancing with a dude. Cupcake was not interested in the dude, but the woman had her mesmerized. Cupcake made her way to the floor and started dancing behind the woman in the black dress. V was really enjoying dancing with EoW when she felt someone dancing really too close for her comfort. V turned to protest and found she was staring another woman in the face.

The woman introduced herself as Cupcake.

V looked her in the eye and told her, "I'm not interested."

Cupcake came on strong and asked, "What's your name?"

V turned to ignore her and Cupcake grabbed her hand.

V snatched back her hand and stopped dancing. She told Cupcake "If you enjoy living, you should keep your hands to yourself."

Cupcake smiled at her and said, "I'll check you later," and walked away. She decided to get ready for a feisty pickup. She wanted to see what was under that black dress even if this woman didn't want to play with her. Cupcake waited for the DJ to start the laser light show up. She knew that the lights would be off and she could touch up the girl then leave. The DJ started the show and Cupcake went to make her move.

V had just gotten into her groove, when she felt someone groping her breast. She looked and saw EoW and knew it was time to teach this perverted woman a lesson.

EoW was about to say something, when he saw V grab and then flip a person on their back. She then threw a punch that hit the person dead on the jaw. EoW looked closely and saw that it was the woman who had danced too close to her earlier.

EoW grabbed V and told her, "Let's get out of here before security comes to investigate."

V came to her senses and followed EoW to the exit. They moved through the crowd and made it out without another incident.

EoW asked, "Where did you learn to fight like that?"

V said, "I take martial arts classes on a regular basis."

EoW and V made it over to the valet parking area, where she gave the valet her ticket. and he went to get her car.

While they waited, V explained, "That woman grabbed my breast! She's lucky all I did was flipped and punch her."

The valet pulled up with V's car and she and EoW left. EoW had forgotten all about the EMP round he'd planted when V said something about the parking lot lights flashing. Then all the lights went out.

EoW said, "I sure am glad we weren't still in there when it happened."

EoW and V had an enjoyable conversation as they made their way back to his vehicle.

Once there V asked, "Can I have another chance to teach you some dance moves?"

EoW said, "Sure, just give me a call." He got out of V's car and said goodnight as. V pulled off. EoW got into his SUV and headed for home. He thought about how well tonight went and how much business he was looking for in the morning. He even considered hooking up with a little female company, but decided against it. Instead, EoW went straight home and got into bed.

Chapter 9

The Elevator Man

Benjamin Dover had just left his meeting with Richard "Gay Mack" Inman, well paid but distraught. He knew that when Gay Mack had to issue out extra he usually wanted something in return. Ben knew that if he did not want to be a boy toy for Ms. Bobbie or Gay Mack, he had to come up with something that would top all of the other recruiters.

Richard had been watching TV when he saw that the director at one of the teen centers had been attacked and assaulted at her home. He knew that Cupcake worked at that center and that she was taking girls from the center and passing them on to the Madame. He wondered if she was dumb enough to be mixed up in the assault.

Ben knew that they all had been pulled into an organization with power in high places throughout the world. He was not afraid of the henchmen that they'd probably send after him, but he was afraid of being caged up like an animal. All his life, he had been locked in rooms and forced to work for his family. His father was a hard man who made sure that Ben learned how to work with his hands whether he wanted to or not. Ben remembered the beatings that he'd endured whenever he defied his father to go play with other children his age. He vividly remembered his father hanging him upside down and whipping him till he was unconscious. Ben's father forced him to learn all about the elevator maintenance business and secured his future within it. Ben eventually stopped fighting against his father and went along with his program.

Even after his father passed Ben continued his father's disciplined work ethic and became a well-respected craftsman in his field. Ben embraced his father's business and took it to new heights that his father could never have imagined. Ben had secured the majority of the city's elevator repair contracts and had begun designing newer elevator systems for new construction projects.

Ben had another talent that helped him secure funds for the business during the days when business was dead. He became a recruiter for Gay Mack when he bought the building his father's business was in. Gay Mack had the capital and the credit to buy the building when Ben did not. He even sent Ms. Bobbie and a few of his henchman to evict him out of the building. After a long fight and after he slapped Ms. Bobbie around a bit, Richard entered the premises and made him an offer to come to work for him. Ben agreed, with the stipulation that Richard would sell the building back to him for 15% over the cost at which Richard bought the building. Richard agreed and so their partnership began.

Richard started him out small, and then moved him into larger jobs as he got better. Richard had him snatching kids, young boys mostly, but Ben didn't care as long as Richard and his crew stayed away from him and his business. Ben opened the envelope and found a set of instructions inside. Gay Mack was requesting the biggest snatch that Ben had ever attempted. He wanted four boys and two girls, and they had to be between the ages of 13 and 16.

Ben was trying to imagine why when he remembered that Gay Mack was getting ready for another organizational meeting with the big bosses. Ben put the instructions in his pocket and started counting the money. There was $15 k in one envelope and $20 k in the other. Ben immediately put the money away and headed for his business to map out a strategy by which he could snatch so many children in one week without getting caught. Ben knew his best time was at night and that every job had to be in a building with an elevator. He laughed at the name Elevator Man that Richard had given him; He used the elevator shafts as an escape route in all of his capers, and knew the ins and outs of every kind of elevator in existence. He made his living repairing elevators, and he had a hustle that also involved elevators.

Ben made it to his office and parked his truck in back. He went straight to the maintenance closet and entered a code in a keypad on the back of a shelf. The shelf wall opened and he went inside. Ben had set up a staging area for all of his alternative equipment. He had gear designed for mountain climbing re-engineered for elevator shaft repelling. He had de-signed all kinds of electric pulleys and nets to help him in his extracurricular activities. Ben went to the safe and put the money from GayMack inside. He had to do this job and maybe one more before the building would be his outright. Ben smiled knowing he would soon be through with Gay Mack and his crew of fairies.

Ben locked up his staging area, then went to check out the van that he used for his night jobs. It was an average delivery van except that it had a containment area for holding his latest victims. Ben knew his van would have to perform flawlessly, so he decided to get the engine checked out. He removed all of his special-ized gear first just in case. If anyone went inside, they wouldn't find anything that would reveal his alternate hustle. As Ben grabbed the gear, one of his small grappling hooks got caught between the door and the back bumper, but he didn't hear it fall. He finished putting up his equipment and headed for a nearby maintenance shop to have the van checked out.

Webb was still handling customer repairs and all of the research he needed to do to help Frequency. He was burning the candle at both ends and was dog tired! He hadn't found any more information on any of the subjects assigned to him. He went to the shop and used his computer to review all of the images connect-ed to the Gathering file and the file called Elevator Man. He still couldn't find anything that indicated a specific person or anything that adequately described any individual. Webb looked for anything that could help him find out anything about this person but came up empty.

Webb called Frequency and asked him to use CMAX to pull information. CMAX broke the images down and put the images into files. CMAX then began to match the images to known images advertised in all of the business in the city. CMAX used all of its resources and finally came up with a partial image that had a matching piece with a company in the city. CMAX pulled the information and sent it to Webb's cell phone. Webb couldn't quite make it out so he decided to deal with it later.   He needed to get away from the shop for a while and get out for some fresh air. He wanted to drive one of his cars, but they were all blocked by his new slab tow truck. Just like that, Webb jumped into the new truck and took off. He was having a blast just blowing off some steam. He took the truck out on the interstate, opened it up, and found that it had power to spare! Webb was sure it could haul anything he needed to pick up. He pulled off the interstate and into a gas station to refuel. He was winding down, but was still on a high from opening up that truck. Webb went inside and paid for a fill-up. As he walked back to his truck, he saw a guy walking up the side of the road who looked like he had been walking for a while.

Ben had been walking for six hours after his van decided to quit on a stretch of interstate where there was no communication and no traffic anywhere in sight. And to top it off he had left his cell phone at home! He saw the tow truck and finally felt as if there was help ahead. Ben walked toward the truck and started looking for the driver.

Webb saw him coming and asked, "Can I help you?"

Ben said, "My van broke down and I've been walking for six hours looking for help."

Webb told Ben, "I have a shop across town and this is a new truck that I'm breaking in."

Ben said, "I'm willing to pay whatever you charge."

Webb said, "I'm not the truck driver, but I'll do the best I can."

Ben said, "That's all I can ask."

The two jumped into the slab truck and headed for Ben's broken down van. Webb called the guys in the shop and told them what was going on, and of course they cracked jokes about the boss doing tow duty.

Webb hung up the phone and asked Ben, "Do you have any idea what's wrong with your van?"

Ben said, "I was just riding along and the thing just shut down and would not crank again."

The two continued their small talk as they drove until they got to the van. Webb got on the phone to ask his tow truck driver, Mickey, how to hook up a van to the truck. Webb finally got the van loaded and was headed to the shop, where Mickey was already preparing for the broken down van. Webb and Ben rode on into the shop without a hitch.

As they pulled up, Ben asked Webb," Can you guys handle corporate accounts?"

Webb said, "My guys can handle anything you can throw at them." Ben watched as Webb and the guys dissected his van like surgeons in an operating room. They found that the van had a bad voltage monitor and a bad cable going to the battery. Corrosion had built up on the circuits and eaten through all of the cables. Webb went back and told Ben the news.   Ben asked, "How long will it take to fix?"

Ben said, "It should be finished in about 20 minutes."

Ben was surprised and asked Webb, "What do I owe you for the job?"

Webb told Ben, "You don't owe me a thing for the tow, but the service charge for the van is a hundred dollars."

Ben was so happy he gave Webb a fifty dollar tip and one of his business cards.

He said, "I have a fleet of 10 vans and 10 trucks for my business. I'd like for your guys to handle all my repairs from now on."

Webb was excited about his new customer, and thought that was the icing on the cake for the shop!

He said, "As soon as I get your contract worked up, I'll call you so we can finalize the deal."

Ben said, "I can have my lawyer draw up the contract and have it sent over at the first of the week."

Webb said, "Thanks Ben," as they shook hands and one of the guys pulled the van out and gave Ben the keys.

Ben got into the van and headed back to his office. His latest dilemma was solved and over. so Ben could finish planning his 'assignment.'

Webb told the guys that they could shut it down and call it a day. He also told them they'd be getting a raise when the contract with Ben was in place. It wasn't long before all of the guys had left and Webb was the only one there. He finished the last of the cleanup and, as he turned to leave the shop, he found something on the floor of the maintenance shop. It was some kind of hook, but Webb had no clue what it was for. He threw it on the shop's counter and decided to finish up the transaction from Ben's repair.

Webb activated his computer and scanned Ben's business card into the repair shop's customer database. Webb saw the name Benjamin Dover owner of Dover Elevator R & D. Webb made sure that all of the information was in the system, and then shut down the computer for the night. He decided to get cleaned up and step out on the town. Webb pulled out his old school Mustang convertible and did a burn out as he left the shop.

He got to his house and went straight in and took a shower, letting the water relax and wash off the day's stress. Webb finished his shower and dressed for his night out. When he walked out of the bathroom, he saw that a whole hour had passed since he'd walked into the bathroom. Webb smiled and thought to himself, 'you just can't rush art," as he put together an outfit for the night. He decided to go with shorts and a fresh white tee. He put on his signature medallion and grabbed a fresh white baseball cap with a W in the center. Webb sprayed on some smell good and then headed for the car.

He had the mustang detailed earlier so it was primed and ready to go. He started the engine and then roared off to the festivities. Webb decided to go down to the park on the river to see if he could pull something proper. He enjoyed the scenery at the park on the river, and. he could always go down there and find a decent spot to park and chill. He was surprised that there was a big crowd tonight and he wasn't able to pull down on the strip. He decided to try one of the back streets to see if there was another way to get in.

Webb kind of wished he'd driven the truck cause then he could just drive through the grass to his destination. He got to a side street and it was packed too. Then he saw a spot to park his car so he parked, locked the car up, and started to head into the crowd. Webb saw police lights and, as he walked farther into the crowd, he saw police cars and people standing around. He spotted an officer that he knew and asked him what was going on.

The officer name was Pete and he told Webb, "A young boy just went missing at one of the high rise buildings. The boy has run away before, but this time building security did not see him leave."

Webb said, "Maybe the little joker's just playing a prank."

"We don't think so," said Pete. "This is the fourth boy tonight to go missing from a high rise building."

Webb said, "DAMN! Now that is totally fucked up!"

Pete said, "The police department has nothing to show where they went. It's as if they just vanished into thin air."

Ben had just finished dropping the boys off at the location where Ms. Bobbie had told him to leave them. He was told that he would be paid when all of the 'orders' had been filled. Ben listened to the radio as a special bulletin came across the air waves to notify listeners of the missing boys. He knew he had done well, because the announcer said that there were no signs of struggle or foul play in the disappearances of the children.

Ben then turned his attention to coming up with a way to find two young girls to complete GayMack's order. He thought about the center where he'd fixed an elevator about a month ago. It was a part of the Criminal Correction for Adolescent Teens complex. He remembered that they kept the runaways and drug offenders on the tenth floor. He also remembered seeing two girls that stuck in his mind as perfect for the grabbing. He decided to go for it.

Ben headed straight for the building and it did not take long for him to get there. He knew he could access the building from around back through the sewer tunnel. Then he'd go into the elevator shaft and climb up to the floor where the girls were housed.

Ben pulled his van around and made sure it was parked out of sight. Then he grabbed his equipment and the knockout drugs to ensure a quiet escape. He pulled all of his equipment through the sewer and into the elevator shaft. He set up the net to catch whatever he dropped into it. He came up with the idea while watching an old Tarzan movie in which trappers caught lions in nets. Ben always mapped out every building he worked in just in case he had to make a hasty escape. He got all of his equipment in place but couldn't find one of his climbing clips. He looked in each of his pockets but still couldn't find it. He found one similar to it and decided to use that instead. Ben sprang into action using several ropes and pulleys to get himself up into the elevator shaft.

He got to a certain height and waited for the elevator card to come down. He hooked himself to the bottom and rode the card until it got one floor lower than the floor he wanted to go on. Ben used a key that was made for elevators to pry the doors open just enough for him to slide past the car and without it hitting him. He knew the building was heavily secured and had cameras everywhere. He knew that the elevator doors went to floors and would just open and then close. He remembered the guards saying that the kids were always pushing the buttons then jumping out. That would be a special part of Ben's plan.

Ben pulled himself up to the tenth floor and waited for the elevator to stop. As soon as it did he hit the cut-off breaker inside the shaft to cut power to the system. As soon as he did this the alarm went off and alerted the guards. He waited patiently as he listened to the guards try to fix the elevator before calling for a repairman. Ben waited and then felt his cell phone vibrate. He ignored it because he knew that it was his dispatcher telling him about the problem with the elevator.

Ben pried the doors open enough to see out. The floor was empty and the camera was turned in the opposite direction. Ben knew that it was a 360 degree camera that was powered by the same power source as the elevators. He personally made sure of that when he had linked the building's camera system into it just in case he ever wanted to sneak a peek.

Ben moved like a cat to the area where the runaways were held, but it was empty. He cursed because he knew better than to try something without checking all the components first. He hurriedly got back into the elevator shaft and descended to the elevator car. He carefully slipped around it and then back to where he had his equipment staged. He gathered up all of his equipment and went back through the sewer pipe and to his van. He put all of his equipment back, and then drove off in his van. He hurriedly drove to his office where he changed into his business uniform and went back to Criminal Correction for Adolescent Teens to repair the broken elevator. Ben arrived back at the building disgusted, but not letting it show. He knew he should have come by the place before attempting something so brazen.

Ben walked up to the main entrance and signed in. The guard on duty called for an escort to take him to the problem elevator. Ben played the role like he didn't know what was going on and started his troubleshooting routing.

He told the guard, "I'll have to go get some grappling equipment because the problem seems to be in the shaft somewhere."

The guard said, "Do whatever you need to do because the building is empty except for some construction workers."

That broke Ben's heart because it totally corrupted his plan. The guard then gave him some very useful information.

He said, "They use some of the runaways for cleaning the lower level areas. We have to watch them closely since the cameras are down for the construction period."

Ben almost did a flip because now he knew how he could get what he needed and push Ms. Bobbie and Gay Mack out of his life forever! He moved around in the shaft then sat still and pretended to work on the elevator. He kept an eye on his watch to ensure that he'd be able to submit a big invoice for this job. After about an hour of doing nothing, Ben climbed up and turned the elevator back on. He made it to the car when it started to move. He just sat on the top of it and waited until it came to a stop.

Ben was about to pull the hatch and climb down into the car when two teenaged girls got in the elevator. He decided not to move because he didn't want to scare them.

Amber and Marie had been in the building cleaning and planning a way to escape. So far their plans had been foiled when the elevator broke down. They got into the elevator and discussed their new plans They talked out loud, thinking that they were the only two there.

Ben heard them say that they would come out of the same sewer pipe that he came in through. He knew he had to move fast and would not have time to go get his other van, so Ben came up with a way to temporarily blind them so they couldn't see the markings on his van, He would have to be very fast. Ben heard Marie say that if they got caught she'd do whatever it took to persuade them not to turn them in. They seemed very desperate for girls so young.

Ben felt himself getting aroused, and decided he would have both of them before he gave them to Gay Mack. He was deep in thought when the elevator car stopped and the girls got out. He waited about 3 minutes and then climbed down and finished his business transaction. The guard signed the invoice and Ben headed straight for the exit which led to the sewer line. Ben was excited and nervous all at once! He got to the area where the pipe opened up and ran to the entrance. He looked into the wet area and saw no footprints so he knew he had gotten there before the girls. Ben went back to his van and positioned it so that the headlights were pointing directly into the sewer entrance. For added insurance, Ben went to the back of the van and got a powerful light to help blind the two girls as they exited the drain pipe. He got tape and made a couple of rags to put around their eyes to keep them from seeing where he would take them. Ben wished he had his other van, but there was no time. He tried to calm himself down as he prepared to wait for the girls to arrive. Ben sat in the van and accidentally dozed off. He was startled when he dropped his big light onto the floor. He woke up and looked at his watch it was 3:00 o'clock in the morning! He figured something had gone wrong so he decided to leave.

Ben forgot that he'd left his lights on bright when he turned the van off. As soon as he started the van the bright lights came on and there were the girls just making it to the end of the sewer line. Amber and Marie froze in their tracks. The van and lights scared them stiff. Ben saw them and quickly grabbed his stuff as he ran toward the girls. He turned on the other light and it was five times brighter than his headlights! Amber and Marie did not move.

Ben yelled, "Move to your right slowly and don't try to run."

Amber screamed, "I can't see!"

Marie started negotiating immediately. She said, "You can have whatever you want as long as you don't turn us in."

Ben kept quiet as he grabbed Amber first, taped her hands behind her back, and put the rag around her eyes. He led her to the back of the van and put her inside. Then he grabbed Marie and moved her out of the mud and to the side of the van. Ben spun her around to tie her hands behind her back, but he let her get too close.

Marie might have been a teenaged girl, but she'd been having sex since she was thirteen. She grabbed his crotch and stroked him gently. Ben was already excited and could not control himself. Marie knew she had him and was not about to go back to the detention center, so she turned and fell to her knees. She rubbed her head against Ben's hard on and started to put it in her mouth. She knew this would be a guarantee to get him on her side. Marie caressed his hard on with her lips through his pants, which put Ben over the edge. Marie grabbed the zipper and hurriedly freed Ben's throbbing erection. She gave Ben a blow job like her life depended on it. Marie treated him like the many before him only better. She was not going to let this man or anyone else take her back to that center. Marie sucked Ben into her mouth deeply and slowly let him pull out. She showed Ben that she had skills like a woman twice her age. Ben was totally lost inside of this young girl. Before he knew it he was coming and coming hard. Marie felt his erection spasm and did not withdraw from him. She cupped his balls and squeezed ever so gently which made him explode deeply inside her. Marie swallowed and continued to stroke Ben until his knees buckled and he went limp.

Ben came back to reality and quickly pulled up his pants and grabbed Marie. He turned her around, taped her hands, and put the other rag around her eyes. He took Marie to the back of the van and put her inside with the other girl. Amber heard the door of the van open and felt another body being pushed inside. Amber hollered out Marie's name and Marie said kiss me. Amber slid to her and felt her breast with her head and then found her way to her mouth. As soon as Amber kissed Marie, Marie exchanged Ben's semen with her. Amber knew this meant that Marie had secured their fate. They would not go back to the detention center for the moment. The two kissed and put on a show for Ben. Ben could not take his eyes off the two girls as they put on their sexual performance.

Ben slammed the door shut and hurriedly got into the driver's seat of the van. He sped off and headed for his usual drop off spot. Ben knew he was finished with Gay Mack and Ms. Bobbie so he thought to himself, why not have some more fun before he turned the girls over to them. Ben decided to head to an abandoned warehouse, where there were some old studio apartments. He drove the van inside the building and into the freight elevator. He knew nobody would think anything of it because he had always worked on the elevator system.

He got to the top floor and got the girls out one at a time. He took them into the bathroom and washed them up. He had them get into a bed in the middle of the room before he told them to take off their blindfolds. All they could see were the white sheets and bright lights all around them. Amber and Marie looked at each other and strained to see who they were with.

Ben instructed the girls to finish what they started in the van.

Amber quickly said, "It sure would be nice if you'd join us." Ben was preparing himself just for that by putting on some whiteface makeup and blacking out his nose and eyes. He waited until the girls got into a position where each girl had their head between the other legs. Amber and Marie were not strangers to pleasing each other, and this was one of their favorite positions.

Marie had a mouthful of Amber when she felt Ben penetrate Amber's body. Amber gasped for air as Ben thrust deep inside her. Marie immediately started caressing Ben's testicles with her tongue and sucking them in deeply as Ben penetrated Amber. Amber was so totally engrossed in the sexual pleasure she was receiving that she orgasmed and collapsed on top of Marie.

Ben pulled out of Amber and Marie consumed his erection as soon as he did. Marie rolled over so that she was on top of Amber. Ben pulled out of Marie's mouth and penetrated her body. Marie gasped and started pushing back onto Ben's forward thrusts. The two of them started sexing as if it was a title fight! Neither wanted to give in to the other, but Marie finally conceded and orgasmed with a scream. Her body shuddered hard as the orgasm ran its course. Amber moved around and kissed her friend for she knew she had achieved a pleasure that they both now shared.

The two girls laid Ben on his back and started giving him a double blow job. They wanted him to cum and they were not going to stop until he did. Ben was out of control so he just let the girls do whatever they wanted to him. Both girls were sucking his erection as each one covered an area that the other missed. It wasn't long before Ben orgasmed and the girls shared the semen like it was their last meal. Ben sat back and let them finished him off. He was not about to stop them until he heard the other elevator start to move.

Ben jumped up and ran to the right of the white screen. He threw on a jumpsuit and grabbed a nine millimeter Berretta he had on a table nearby. He screamed to the girls not to move if they wanted to be free.

Amber and Marie did what he said and did not move. Ben quickly got to an area where he could see everything that came out of the elevator, but they could not see him. When the elevator doors opened up Ben froze. The first person he saw was Ms. Bobbie in one of her usual miniskirts. Then a couple of body-guards and Gay Mack himself came in. They went straight for the center where the girls were. Amber and Marie stood up and were grabbed by the body-guards.

Ms. Bobbie started looking them over and said, "Come out, Come out wherever you are, Benjamin."

Ben knew he was in trouble cause this fool called out his name. He ran to go whoop Ms. Bobbie, but another bodyguard was waiting for him and tripped him up. Ben hit the ground and the bodyguard kicked him sharply in his ribs. All the wind that Ben had flew out of his body like a bird freed from a cage.

GayMack walked over to him and said, "Ben you're a fool for fucking these girls before I gave them the once over. I've had these premises under surveillance for years so I could watch you come in and out of here." GayMack then walked over to the girls and looked at Amber like she was a piece of fine meat. He licked 2 of his fingers and pushed them deep into Amber's anus.

Amber let out a scream and Ms. Bobbie laughed and said, "Looks like we got ourselves a virgin piece of ass."

GayMack said, "Not for long." He went over to Marie and did the same thing. Marie pushed hers back onto his fingers to let him know that she could take it. Marie had been sodomized by the guards and other women so much that it did not bother her; in fact she had become accustomed to it. Gay Mack was excited by this and decided to finish the deal with Ben.

GayMack told his guards "Go put the girls in the car for transport." He went over to Ben and kicked him in his other side. Ben screamed in pain.

GayMack told Ms. Bobbie, "Bring the briefcase."

Ms. Bobbie went and got the briefcase that Ben had prepared for the transaction to pay off GayMack. Ms. Bobbie opened it up and saw that it was filled with the payoff money.

GayMack asked, "Is it all there?"

Bobbie said, "Yes it's all here."

"Good," said GayMack as he reached into his inside pocket and threw the deed to Ben's building on the floor.

Ben grabbed the paper and opened it. When he saw his dad's signature he knew he was done with them and their perversions.

Gay Mack was about to leave when he suddenly turned and kicked Ben again. Ben curled up to protect his paperwork as Ms. Bobbie joined GayMack and the two kicked Ben several times.

Gay Mack told Ms. Bobbie,"Finish the deal."

Ms. Bobbie pulled out his penis and urinated on Ben. He told Ben, "You're lucky I just busted a nut before we got here, because otherwise I'd be getting into your ass." Ms. Bobbie stood and kicked Ben dead in the testicles.

Ben lost whatever senses he had left and passed out.

Ms. Bobbie and GayMack went to their car and left.

GayMack asked, "Are you happy now that Ben is gone?"

Ms. Bobbie said, "Can I celebrate with you to show how happy I am?"

GayMack asked, "What would you like?"

Ms. Bobbie asked, "Can I have you for a drink?"

GayMack told the driver to close the window separating them from him, then gave Ms. Bobbie an ecstasy tablet and a drink of wine. Ms. Bobbie swallowed the tablet and the wine and stretched out on the floor of the car. GayMack sat in the seat and watched as the pill took effect. Ms. Bobbie started touching himself gently and erratically. He started jacking himself off and then looked at GayMack. He unzipped his pants and started giving him a blowjob. He was gone on the ecstasy and could not control himself. GayMack had some oil that he kept for his personal use and he let Ms. Bobbie oil him up good. Ms. Bobbie mounted the GayMack's erection and stroked his own at the same time. It wasn't long before he erupted in his hand and quickly put them in his mouth. He was totally out of it when GayMack pushed him off of his and placed it in

Bobbie's mouth. Ms. Bobbie swallowed his semen and would not let go. GayMack just relaxed and let him do what he did best. Ms. Bobbie then started jacking off again. When he got on ecstasy he was good for multiple orgasms. Ms. Bobbie lay in the floor of the car and jacked off a second time then fell asleep. Gay Mack picked up the phone and waited for someone to answer.

He told the voice on the other end, "I have everything in place and I'll be expecting payment."

Ben got up off the floor and immediately got into the shower. He was sore as hell from the beating he'd just taken. He would get his revenge, but first he had to heal. He cleaned himself up, and then took the clothes that he had worn and burned them. He got back into his van and started it up. He pushed the buttons on the freight elevator to take him to the bottom floor. Ben drove out of the elevator then onto the street. He knew something was wrong as soon as he drove a few inches. He stopped the van and got out to find that all four of his tires had been slashed. Ben looked for his radio and saw that it had been smashed. He then went to a hiding place in his van where he kept a prepaid cell phone in case of emergencies.

Ben remembered the towing service that helped him out before and decided to call them again. He called the number and Webb answered the phone. Ben made up a story so that Webb wouldn't find out about the girls.

Webb asked, "Where are you?"

Ben told him and Webb dispatched the slab truck. Ben hung up the phone and waited for the tow truck. He didn't have to wait long before the truck was there to pick him up. He told the driver to drop him off at the elevator repair shop.

The driver asked, "Are you okay?"

Ben said, "I will be after some rest and relaxation."

The driver dropped Ben off then headed for the shop. He got there and gave the van to Webb. Webb gave the van the once over to ensure that he inventoried everything that was in the van. Webb did not want to be liable for any of Ben's missing equipment. Webb got to an area of the van where a small door had been cut into it. Webb did not try to open it, but he did make a mental note of it. When he picked up a tool box and moved it, the little door opened. Webb looked inside and saw a mini recorder built into it.

Webb stopped the recorder and pulled the disk out. He went to his shop's office and closed the door. He put the disk into the computer and went online with CMAX. Webb had CMAX play the disk. CMAX told Webb that this disk was encrypted and he would run the protocol to break it. It didn't take CMAX long before he told Webb that he had several files for him to view. Webb sat and watched as the inside of an elevator shaft came into view. It was a camera that was attached to some kind of helmet camera. Then he watched as the person wearing the helmet went in an elevator car and grabbed a boy and then disappeared back up into the elevator shaft.

Webb watched this several times until he finally saw something he recognized. Webb told CMAX to copy all of the files on the disc and CMAX responded with "ACKNOWLEDGED." Webb went back out to the shop and looked for the hook he had found earlier in the week. He found it right where he had left it and went directly to his office. Webb had CMAX zoom in on the hook and it was a perfect match. He then put two and two together and came up with the fact that Benjamin Dover was the Elevator Man!

Webb called Frequency immediately and told him what he had discovered.

Frequency said, "Have EoW hook up a link into the same disc drive that he got the file from."

Webb said, "I'll do that and then head out for the next assignment on his list. I think I have more than enough evidence on this dude."

Frequency said, "Don't let him know, you're onto him, at least not just yet." Webb hung up the phone then put everything back in place exactly like he'd found it. Webb could not believe that Ben was the guy taking all of those kids. Webb put in a work ticket to get the van repaired and back to Ben.

Ben was back at his apartment resting. He was sore as hell, but now he had his father's business back! He would rest for now, but he would get even with GayMack and his people. And he knew just how he could do it. It was time for the rendezvous of the elite and he knew exactly where and when. Ben was going to make them all pay while he planned to come out smelling like a rose.

Chapter 10

Mama's Boy

EoW had just made it back to the computer shop after helping Webb set up a link in a repair van. He was putting some new hand held gaming devices on the shelf when a nice looking lady came into the shop and asked about a USB camera for a laptop.

EoW went over and introduced himself, then "Can I be of assistance?"

"Hello EoW," she said, "my name is Carla and I'm interested in a USB camera." He took her over and showed her the cameras that he had in stock. He was very professional and very careful not to flirt with her. She wore a t-shirt but no bra, and the jeans she wore hugged her figure like a leather glove. EoW told her about all the camera's features.

She said, "I want a camera with ip addressing capabilities for my son's room. My husband and I are going out of town and I want to be able to monitor what my teenaged son is doing."

EoW said, "Wait a minute. I think I have the perfect camera." He went and got the X10 USB wireless camera setup. He told her, "You and connect it to the phone line and monitor it from anywhere in the world."

"I want two of them," Carla said.

EoW went to the counter and told the clerk, "Ring up two of these and I'll bring them out."

Carla asked, "Do you all handle installation too?"

Since he wasn't one to turn away a dollar he said, "Yes we do if the customer requests it." He gave Carla his card and set up an appointment for the installation of the cameras. EoW walked Carla out to her car and loaded up her new equipment. She got inside and drove away.

EoW thought hard about seeing if Carla was willing to have a fling with him, but he could tell the lady was not going. He just shook his head and chalked it up as a loss for her.

Carla got on her phone as soon as she left the shop and called her husband Paul. She told him, "I found something to keep an eye on our son while we're out of town."

Allen was big for his age at six foot three and about 185 pounds. He was handsome and she watched him very closely. Some said she was obsessed with him, but she paid them no mind. Carla knew that Allen was into the little girls at his school, and did everything in her power to keep them away. Allen was her husband's son from his first marriage. After his wife was killed in a car accident, she and Paul hooked up and got married. Paul was a decent, good man and he loved her like no one else ever had.

Paul suffered a stroke two years into their marriage. Carla was there for him, but she longed for a partner who could handle her in the bedroom. Paul was just no match for her after his stroke. Carla didn't have the heart to tell Paul, so she took matters into her own hands. She started with toys and masturbation, and then graduated to a couple of her female friends who were in the same situation.

One night after Paul had finished his business on top of her and fallen asleep; she got up and took a shower. As she got out of the shower, she heard someone giggling outside. She grabbed a robe and went to the window to check it out. She caught a glimpse of Allen and one of the girls from his school. Carla heard Allen tell this girl Jenny to stop because his folks were just upstairs. Carla wrapped and tied her robe as she went downstairs to get a better look.

When she got downstairs, she saw Jenny grab Allen's crotch and heard her say, "Come on, and just let me see it."

Allen was a shy kid and, as far as Carla knew, hadn't been schooled about sex. Jenny, on the other hand, already had a reputation for her hand jobs. She wanted Allen because no one else had him and she wanted the bragging rights of being his first.

Jenny said, "If you don't let me see it I'll scream and say you tried to force yourself on me."

Allen knew she'd do it too cause he'd heard it from the other guys on the team. He said, "Step back and I'll show you."

Jenny stepped back as Allen unzipped his pants and pulled out his erect member. She was about to grab it when Carla stepped out of the shadows.

"What are you two doing out here this time of the night?" Carla asked.

Jenny turned on the waterworks and said, "Allen told me to do it."

Carla smacked Jenny hard on the cheek and said, "You need to stop lying Missy because I overheard your whole conversation! You need to leave."

Jenny was shocked at being busted and angry. She looked at Carla and said, "I'll get even if it's the last thing I do!" She stormed off the porch, went to her car, and burned rubber as she left.

Carla then turned to Allen, who was still holding his erection. She tried not to look down, but couldn't help herself. Allen was well hung for a boy his age, and Carla found herself getting aroused. She quickly turned away and told him to go take a cold shower. She went and pulled out a vibrator so she could satisfy herself. After that night, Carla found herself more brazen about walking into her stepson's room. She had watched him masturbate in the shower and acted as if she was just a concerned parent. She was amazed at how he could stay hard afterwards. Carla knew she had a problem, so she turned to one of her close girlfriends for help.

Maxine knew she was a sex addict and had no qualms about it. She fucked or sucked whoever was available when she got the urge. She had already slept with most of the people in her neighborhood including the women. When Carla told her what was happening, Maxine knew exactly what she was going to do.

Maxine asked Carla, "Are you ready for our relationship to move to another level?"

Carla enjoyed being with Maxine and knew that she would be sexually fulfilled if she let Maxine handle it. She kissed Maxine and said, "I'm ready for anything."

Maxine said, "Give Paul a sleeping pill Friday night so we can have the whole night to ourselves."

When Friday came Carla did exactly what Maxine had told her, and to top it off, she had sex with Paul before the pill kicked in. As usual, Paul came first and fell asleep. Carla took a shower afterwards to get ready for Maxine.

Meanwhile, Maxine showed up and Allen let her in. Allen didn't have a clue that Maxine had plans for him, so he just let her in as usual.

As she came in, Maxine said, "Give me a hug."

She was by no means an ugly woman and she was dressed very provocatively. Allen felt himself getting aroused by the embrace, and Maxine felt a little extra on her thigh and knew that it was time to get the party started. She acted as if she didn't notice the lump in Allen's shorts as he turned to go to his room. Maxine smiled as she thought to herself how she and his step mother were about to enjoy all of that and then some. She went to the bar and poured herself and Carla a glass of wine, then dropped some ecstasy into Carla's glass and stirred until it was dissolved. Maxine sat on the couch to wait until Carla came down.

Allen went upstairs to tell his step-mom that Maxine was downstairs waiting. Carla had left the bedroom door unlocked and Allen walked in on her. Carla was just pulling on her robe and Allen got a full naked shot of his step-mom, before he turned away and said he was sorry. Carla didn't say anything.

Allen said, "Miss Maxine is downstairs," then left her room. Carla knew that Allen would not come out of his room, because he was embarrassed. She did not want to keep Maxine waiting, so she decided to run downstairs to let her she needed a few more minutes. When she got downstairs, there was Maxine in a very low cut dress.

Carla asked, "What's the occasion?"

Maxine said, "It's our coming out party!"

Carla looked confused as Maxine walked up and kissed her on the lips. Carla hesitated at first then pulled Maxine in for a deeper kiss. Maxine reached around and squeezed Carla's ass. Carla pulled away and Maxine brought her a drink.

She told Carla, "Drink up; I have a surprise for you." After Carla drank half of the wine, Maxine led her over to the couch. Maxine started to kiss Carla again then asked Carla to suck her cock. Carla was really confused, but said agreed anyway. Maxine went to her purse and pulled out a strap-on dildo. She showed it to Carla and Carla started to laugh. Maxine put it into Carla's mouth and Carla started to stroke it.   Maxine knew that the wine and ecstasy were starting to kick in, so she told Carla, "You keep playing with that until I come back from the bathroom." Then Maxine grabbed the half glass of wine and went upstairs to look for Allen.

She found his room and quietly opened the door. She saw Allen in his room jerking off. His little encounters with her and his step-mom had him hard as a brick! Maxine jumped into his room and scared the hell out of him.

Allen froze because his dad had caught him masturbating once and told him that he would cut his penis off if he caught him beating his meat again. Allen immediately said, "Miss Maxine please don't tell my father."

Maxine said, "I won't tell if you let me do that." Of course, Allen agreed and did not move as Maxine walked up to him and grabbed his hard member. She was impressed by the size of Allen's hard on. She looked at Allen as she stroked him ever so slowly, then handed him the glass of wine and said, "Drink it or I will tell your father."

Allen swallowed the wine so fast he barely tasted it. Maxine said, "Now I'll give you a reward for being such a good boy." She took out two bandanas and covered Allen's eyes with one and his mouth with the other.

She said, "Come with me. I promise won't regret it." Maxine led Allen to the top of the stairs and said, "Stay here and don't move." Then she went back to Carla who was really gone on the ecstasy now. She had the dildo stuffed deep down her throat and was moaning like a mad woman. Maxine got to Carla and pulled the dildo from her hands, whirled her around a couple of times, then covered her eyes with a bandana. Maxine got Allen, who was also under the influence of the ecstasy Maxine had put in the wine. She carefully brought Allen down the stairs and made him lie on the floor on his back. She got Carla and led her to where Allen was laying. Carla was so high she didn't even know where she was! She heard Maxine say, "Now finish sucking my cock." Carla grabbed what she thought was Maxine's hard dildo and began sucking it again.

Allen felt the warm wetness around his manhood and couldn't believe how good it felt. He thrust forward until he came and the wetness seemed to be pulling his orgasm out of him. Carla was hungry for whatever it was Maxine had shot into her mouth. She knew Maxine would not do anything to hurt her so she kept going. Maxine sat on the couch and watched as step-mother and step-son had sex with each other. She watched as Carla straddled her son's manhood and started riding him insatiably. Allen felt warm wetness around him again, and felt it move up and down faster and faster. He had heard the guys at school talk about how the girls got on top and rode them and now he was feeling it for the first time himself! He reached up and grabbed a nice set of tits and it made him harder than ever before. Carla was mad with lust and couldn't believe how great she felt. Maxine moved closer to both of them as she could hear Carla letting out the signs that she was having an orgasm. As soon as she said she was coming, Maxine removed her and Allen's blindfolds.

Carla thought back on that day and couldn't believe that she and her step-son were still fooling around. It had been a year since Maxine tricked them into sexing each other, and now Carla found herself guarding Allen like he was her boyfriend. There had been many such nights since that first time Allen got laid by his step-mom. Allen loved the way she acted when he told her he was going out and would be in late. He remembered all of the times she came to his room and shared his bed. His step-mom even let Miss Maxine get in bed with them for some really wild times.

Carla had built up a jealous streak where her stepson was concerned. She didn't want another woman anywhere near him. Paul thought it was special having his son and his new wife be so close. Of course, he had no clue that his wife and his young son were a lot closer than he thought. Carla and Allen did everything in their power to keep it that way. The secret weighed heavy on Allen, but it just made Carla more insatiable. Allen often caught his step-mom looking at him in a lustful way in front of his dad. He was so glad to hear that they were going on vacation without him.

Carla knew Allen would not approve of her putting in video surveillance to monitor him while they were gone, so she went to the professionals to get what she wanted.

EoW showed up during the morning hours when the house was empty except for Carla. She already knew this guy wanted to have sex with her so she thought she'd flirt with him just for kicks. She showed EoW where she wanted the main transmitter to be setup, and he got to work while Carla went across the room to watch TV. She sat with her legs slightly open to let him have a good look since she had decided not to wear anything under her housedress.

EoW couldn't help but look because she flaunted her nudity directly in front of him. He wanted to say something, but by then he had the transmitter installation completed. He was about to call Carla over to show her how to use the camera system when the doorbell rang. Carla stood up and ran to open the door and found Maxine standing there. Maxine had just gotten back in town and she just walked in like she always did, closed the door behind her, and planted a big kiss on Carla's lips.

EoW walked to the end of the stairs and got a good look at Carla and someone kissing. The person was another woman who was feeling up Carla. Maxine grabbed the end of Carla's shirt and pulled it up to smack Carla on the butt.

Carla said, "Stop! I've got the guy upstairs putting in the new camera system."

Maxine asked, "Where is he?" and went upstairs looking for him.

Carla followed her upstairs and found Maxine and EoW talking about the video system he'd just installed.

Maxine told Carla, "Come over here and show me some love."

Carla walked up to Maxine and kissed her on the lips. EoW would be happy to get with either one of these women!

Maxine told Carla, "Go on back downstairs. I want to knock off a little jet lag." As soon as Carla went downstairs, Maxine said, "I want to screw."

EoW stood up and let Maxine explore his crotch with her hands. He knew better than to mess around with a woman he didn't know without a condom, so he kept at least two in his wallet at all times. Maxine found what she was looking for, a good hard prick. Maxine had a mouthful of EoW before he could ask her what she wanted. She had a talented mouth and she knew she had to hold back if she wanted to get laid.

EoW was in the clouds enjoying this woman's oral skills. Maxine pulled away from EoW and let her thong drop. EoW reached into his back pocket, grabbed a condom, and quickly put it on before Maxine mounted him. Maxine dropped down low so she could get full penetration from this man.

EoW was not about to let this woman outdo him. He was having sex with her as if it was a prize fight. Maxine was just horny and determined she was going to cum as much as possible. Maxine was enjoying this ride and let her orgasm come down without resistance. She let out a gasp and collapsed on EoW's chest. EoW felt as if he'd won the championship trophy as he rolled this woman off his chest and onto her stomach. Maxine raised her behind so EoW could get some good penetration. He went back inside Maxine's body and thrust like there would be no end. He knew he was good for a least one good orgasm, but for some reason he couldn't get there. Maxine was already at her peak again and let go another hard orgasm.

Maxine accepted the fact that EoW would not cum as she thought she could make him, so she went back to do what she knew best. Maxine got between EoW's legs, pulled off the condom, and began to give him the benefit of her best oral skills. EoW's eyes rolled to the back of his head as she put her best work down on his erection. She did not miss a beat until EoW let out a growl as he came hard into her mouth. Maxine swallowed every drop, then leaned back to look at EoW.

She asked, "Are you married?"

He said, "No, I'm not."

Maxine asked, "What did you say your name is?"

EoW just laughed, pulled his pants on, gave Maxine one of his business cards, and then got ready to go back to the computer shop. He told Maxine how the camera worked and said, "I'll be looking forward to seeing you again."

Maxine said, "I enjoyed our rumpus and am looking forward to seeing you again too."

Carla came upstairs with a couple of glasses of cool sweet tea. She had heard the action between them from downstairs and knew they needed to cool down. She was looking forward to Allen coming home to help put out the fire between her legs.

EoW noticed that Carla would not look directly at him as long as Maxine was in the room. He explained how the video device worked to Carla and she assured him that she understood all of its features. Carla heard something downstairs and excused herself again. Maxine waited a few minutes then followed. EoW heard them talking loudly to someone, then he overheard Maxine say something about a Mama's Boy all grown up.

He heard Carla say "He's just fifteen years old and already he's about as tall as a tree."

EoW knew he could get into a lot of trouble for setting up a video source without consent, but he had a feeling that something just wasn't right about these women. He quickly did the setup and had the device transmit to dual ip addresses. He hurriedly got out of set up and picked up all his equipment.

Maxine walked in and said, "I'll escort you to your truck."

EoW and Maxine went out different doors so that whoever came into the house would not see him. As he got to his vehicle, Carla came out to pay for the installation service for the camera system. Carla even paid him a little extra saying that she was very pleased with the end result.

EoW said, "Thank you," and politely left.

Carla told Maxine, "I need to go spend some time with Allen before his father gets home." Maxine just laughed, got in her car and left. Carla knew that Maxine had her little secret and would not hesitate to use it whenever it was convenient. Carla didn't care at that moment. She got the USB camera and went into Allen's room, where he was just turning on his computer.

Carla said, "I have a gift for you," as she pulled out the camera and handed it to him. Allen was ecstatic and could not wait to install it on his laptop. Allen didn't know that his step-mom had a hidden agenda behind this camera, and she was not about to tell him. As soon as he got it installed he went to thank his step mom for his new camera.

Paul pulled into his driveway happy to be going on vacation for a week of relaxation with his wife. His doctor had given him a clean bill of health and prescribed some Viagra to help him out in the bedroom. Paul hadn't told his wife that he planned to talk to his doctor about his sexual problem, so he knew this would be a surprise for her.

Allen and his step mom had just finished their little rumpus, when they heard Paul come into the house. Allen panicked and Carla ran to the master bedroom to take a quick shower. Allen knew his room smelled like sex so he had to move quickly. He raised the window, lit a candle in the corner of the room, then went into his closet and grabbed his abdominal cruncher. He started crunching like his life depended on it.

Paul walked in and started calling out for Carla and Allen. He got no answer and decided to go to Allen's room. He opened the door and walked in and was hit with the smell of candles and sweat. Allen was in the room working out with his headphones on. Paul tapped him on the shoulder and Allen pretended to be surprised to see his dad.

Paul asked, "Where's your step-mom?"

Allen said, "I don't know."

Paul said, "Clean up your room because it smells like a sweat shop!"

Allen stopped working out and said, "Okay, I will."

Paul left Allen's room and Allen breathed a sigh of relief. A couple of minutes sooner and he and his step-mom would have been in a world of trouble.

Carla was just finishing her shower when she turned to see Paul standing in the bathroom. She said, "You scared me!" and he just laughed. Carla tried to walk past Paul but he wanted some affection. She hugged him and kissed, but did not want to do anything more.

Paul didn't think anything of it and said, "I have a surprise for you when we go on vacation."

Carla asked, "What is it?"

Paul smiled and said, "You'll have to wait and see."

Carla was glad that she was able to deter Paul from being intimate. Allen had her worn out! She knew it was noticeable when she walked, so she would make sure she walked behind Paul for the time being.

Paul and Carla had everything packed and were on the plane for their long awaited vacation. The flight was at night and Paul decided to take a nap so he'd be fresh when they arrived in Hawaii. Carla was surprised that Paul was so eager to take a nap, but she thought she'd make the best of it. She pulled out her small laptop and opened up an internet browser. She went to her shortcut menu and clicked on the ip address for the video surveillance system. The screen went black, and then Carla saw Allen's room. Just as she thought he had immediately turned on the camera to start chatting with his friends. Carla was amazed at how much information scrolled across the screen. It told her who he chatted with and for how long. Carla pulled out her little ear bud headphones so she could listen in on Allen's conversation.

Carla was like a surveillance camera operator in a casino, watching her step-son's every move thanks to the new system. She was excited and decided to shut it down and take herself a nap. She hadn't been asleep long when she heard squealing in her ear. She awoke to a plane with everybody asleep except for a few passengers. She moved her hand to her ears and remembered her ear bud headphones. Carla quickly opened her laptop and logged into the surveillance system.

What she saw on the screen made her gasp. Allen was in his room with five of her friends including Maxine. The women were all over him, and Maxine was leading the foray. Carla watched in horror as the women devoured Allen like fresh meat in an alligator pond. One woman after another straddled Allen and got her rocks off. Carla knew that Maxine had spiked his drink again so the girls could have their way with him. The shocker was when she saw Maxine give Allen some kind of pill and pour wine down his throat. Carla was really upset when she heard Paul start to awaken. She put the surveillance system into auto record mode and shut down her laptop.

Paul had not been on vacation in two years. He was having the time of his life and so was his wife. He could tell that she had something on her mind but he decided to let her keep to herself until she was ready to talk.

Carla knew she was only half-heartedly into this vacation and longed to be with Allen. She wanted to tell Paul everything, but she just couldn't bring herself to do it. She decided to try and leave all of the events she'd seen at home and enjoy herself on this fabulous vacation. Carla went and shopping and bought a two piece dress designed for the Hawaii state of mind. She bought new sandals to complement the dress, and then rushed to their hut to put it on.

Paul was out parasailing and riding water jet skis when he saw a familiar figure step out of his hut. He headed in and parked the water ski, then went to the hut. As he got closer he saw Carla looking magnificent in her new outfit, so he decided it was time to go get dinner and a night cap that he was sure she would never forget. Paul walked to Carla and kissed her lightly.

He told her, "Don't get too close or you'll have sand and salt all over your outfit!"

Carla smiled and said, "Go get cleaned up."

As Paul walked past her, she smacked him on his butt. Paul really got excited and rushed to get cleaned up. He pulled out a new outfit he'd purchased right before they left for Hawaii. He took one of the Viagra pills while he was in the bathroom, so Carla wouldn't know about the prescription. Paul stepped out of the bathroom looking like brand new money and Carla liked what she saw!

She went to Paul and gave him a big hug and a kiss. Paul shortened the kiss and told her, "Hold that thought for tonight's festivities." They went to the restaurant, had a marvelous meal, and did some dancing. As soon as they came off the dance floor the Viagra kicked in. Paul and Carla sat back down in their booth and he pulled her close to him. Carla didn't think anything of it until Paul put her hand on his crotch.

Carla was surprised when she felt an erection, and to her surprise, it was a strong one. She looked into Paul's eyes and he was grinning like he'd won the lottery! Carla was instantly excited and decided to see if Paul could handle the spontaneity of her next action. She unzipped Paul's pants and his erection rose up and stood firm. The booth that Paul had chosen was dimly lit and secluded. Carla looked around to see if the coast was clear and went down on Paul in the booth. He held his excitement as Carla started slowly stroking his erection and then increased her intensity. Paul looked around to ensure that his pleasure wouldn't be interrupted. Carla wasn't expecting Paul to last long, but he did, so she had to stop and catch her breath. She slowly rose from the table and looked at Paul. She was very much aroused, and she was sure that Paul was ready for her.

She stroked his erection with her hand and said, "I want you very badly."

Paul pulled her hand from his erection, zipped it up, and then called for the waiter to bring their check.

Carla was exhausted and happy. She and Paul went at it all night long in so many different positions she couldn't remember them all! She awoke and found herself in bed alone. She got up and walked to the bathroom on unsteady legs. She smiled as she walked and noticed that the soreness of their pleasure filled night extended up her backside. She remembered that Paul had pleasured every inch of her body, and didn't stop until they passed out from exhaustion. Carla remembered telling Paul things that Allen couldn't get out of her. She knew that night with Paul had ended her affair with Allen. She couldn't have both of them wearing her out! As Carla finished up in the bathroom she saw Paul coming in from an early morning swim.

He looked at Carla and decided that he was ready for another round. Carla was not ready for Paul, and when he bent her over she let out a squeal as he penetrated her deeply. She couldn't resist and let Paul have his way. Paul mounted Carla and made her orgasms a few times before he took his own pleasure. He collapsed on top of Carla and the two slept off the morning's festivities.

Allen was exhausted from his night with Maxine and her crew. He cleaned himself up and went to the kitchen for breakfast. He was sore from all the different positions and with all the different women and just wanted a break!

Maxine awoke and went to the kitchen, where she found Allen finishing breakfast and getting ready to leave.

She said, "You did very well last night."

Allen said, "I'm so tired!"

Maxine reached in her purse and gave Allen an envelope. When Allen opened the envelope he saw that it was full of money.

Maxine told him, "You've just been paid for your first orgy. You can make a lot more if you just hang with me and do as you're told."

Allen asked, "What about my mom?"

Maxine told him, "Don't worry, I'll take care of her."

Allen decided to go get some more computer equipment with the money he'd made from the night before.

EoW had just opened for business when his first customer of the day walked in. The dude showed up on a full size scooter looking for the latest PDA cell phone. EoW had one in stock and asked the dude if he had a cell phone already. Dude said yeah, but it was in his step mom's name. EoW asked for her name and dude told him. EoW recognized the name immediately and asked dude if his name was Allen. Allen said yes and EoW explained that his step mom had just purchased a camera system. Allen said yes and that it worked great. He told EoW how he used it to chat with his friends and recorded some of the party he had last night. EoW just listen and did not say a word. Allen just spilled his guts on how he got paid to have sex with a few older women. He told EoW that he wanted the PDA phone to help him organize his schedule because he was going to be a gigolo and needed to be able to better organize his time. EoW laughed and handed Allen the PDA that he requested. EoW told Allen the price and Allen pulled out the envelope full of money and paid him. EoW then told Allen that he would have to call his cellular service to get the phone portion of the PDA activated. Allen said cool and then left the store. EoW went to the back and linked in to Carla's assigned IP Address. He logged in and saw Maxine and a couple of older women getting dressed and talking.

EoW turned up the volume and heard the women telling Maxine how they enjoyed the boy she gave them last night and then gave her an envelope to give to him as a tip. They then asked Maxine how much would the next one cost and could she get this boy back again. Maxine told the ladies that it would cost 15K each and that they would have to provide their own transportation. The ladies told Maxine that they would be in touch then they left. EoW then watched as Maxine left and the room was empty. He then accessed the surveillance system hard drive and copied the entire file of the festivities. He then logged out and decided to view the file later.

EoW knew Maxine was scandalous but not to the point that she was a pedophile pimp and was using that boy to make money! Then he thought about his visit to the house and how Carla acted when Allen came home while he was still there. EoW vowed that he would view the entire file later. More customers were coming in but his employees hadn't made it in yet.

EoW finished viewing the entire file that he'd gotten from Allen's computer. He had logged on several times and saw how Carla and her step-son had started to fall out with each other. Somebody must have found out more than they bargained for, he thought.

Carla and Paul came home and busted Allen walking out of the house with two older women. Carla was absolutely furious and Paul took all of his stuff away. Allen played it cool and did not tell his dad about his new business venture with Maxine. He also didn't tell

Paul that he and his step mom had been having an affair.

Carla couldn't tell Allen that she knew about the whole sordid affair between him and all her friends. She also couldn't have sex with Allen anymore because Paul was back in the picture and he was not taking it easy on her. Carla didn't complain, because this is exactly what she'd longed for since he'd had his stroke. Paul was laying pipe three and sometimes four times a week. He made sure Carla was well satisfied whenever she opened up to him.

Allen was upset because he wasn't getting his step-mom's attention like he had before their vacation. He was on punishment now, and couldn't leave the house without one of them. Hearing Paul and Carla going at it during the night was driving him crazy! Allen finally decided to do something about it. He would wait until he heard Carla's passionate screams the next night and run away. He knew they wouldn't hear him if they were going at it.

Allen grabbed what he wanted to take with him and put it in a duffle bag. He very quietly walked past his dad's bedroom. The door was not completely closed, so he pushed it lightly and peered in. He saw Carla on top of his dad, sweating and screaming. His dad was pulling her down hard and making her squeal with each thrust. Allen walked away from the door and went downstairs. He grabbed his dad's keys and used the manual handle to open the garage. Then opened the storage room door and reclaimed all of his confis-cated items and added them to what was in his duffle bag. He got his scooter and pushed it outside of the garage, pulled the door down, pushed his scooter down the block, started it up and took off.

A week had passed since Paul had last seen his son. He was worried sick about him, but he felt in his gut that he knew that he was okay. Paul had a lot on his mind ever since Carla told him that she was pregnant. He knew that Allen would love to be there when the baby came so he could have a part in his little brother or sister's life. He hoped with all that was in him that the police would find his teenaged son and bring him back home.

Carla sat and watches as Allen and Maxine were talking somewhere near a lake. She still had access to Allen's computer and evidently Maxine had forgotten that she had access. Carla had not told Maxine or anyone else that she was pregnant. Her bigger problem was that she didn't know if Allen or his Dad was the father.

Carla knew her secret would come out sooner or later, but she didn't plan on being around when either found out. Carla found out that her father had died and left her with a considerable amount of money. She packed and made travel arrangements saying she had to handle his funeral and burial and that she'd be returning soon. She hadn't told Paul a thing! She felt sorry for Paul as she prepared to leave.

Paul waited until Carla was ready to be dropped off at the airport, then loaded up her bags and headed to the airport so she wouldn't miss her flight. Paul dropped her off and they kissed and said goodbye.

Paul promised that he would have Allen back by the time she returned. Carla smiled, blew him a kiss, and then boarded her plane. It was a very long flight to Naples, Italy, but it would be well worth it. Carla would start afresh once the plane landed. She waited until the plane took off, and then checked to see what Allen was up to. She went through her usual log in procedure, and got the shock of her life. Allen and Maxine were having sex with a transsexual while another man watched!

Chapter 11

The Whistleblower

Mr. White enjoyed life to the fullest! He had made his money with pure brain power, which means without even one hour of physical labor. He'd managed to stash away a small fortune and set himself up with a crew who had no problem following his orders, even dumping a body in the river. He sat in his modest mansion styled home admiring the women swimming in his pool. He'd been married once, but decided to dismiss her after he found out she had a fortune in investments. Once he and his shyster lawyer finished with her she was paying him alimony, and he would receive half of her inheritance!

Mr. White kept all his enemies close and kept them under his thumb. He had everything under control until he had a run in with Frequency Hunter. Now he owed Frequency, but had cut a deal with a federal agent to have Frequency locked up for two years rather than pay up. Mr. White enjoyed the fruits of his labor while Frequency was safely locked, away. He'd been able to steal money and merchandise from Frequency's whole crew for those two years.

Now that Frequency was out of jail and looking to get even, Mr. White had to beef up his security and keep out of sight for a while. White knew that he couldn't put his name on any business or contracts as long as Frequency was around because Frequency would just hack into the system and take everything that he owned. He thought long and hard about how to get rid of Frequency Hunter once and for all Mr. White knew that a plan like the one he had in mind would cost him a pretty penny. He was about to call up a couple of associates for the job but his phone rang. Mr. White was hesitant to answer the phone, because as far as he knew, no one had his private number. Against his better judgment he answered the phone and heard a familiar voice.

Frequency stood on top of the gate at the back of Mr. White's home and said, "You look like a fake Tony Montana sitting in that lounge chair."

Mr. White froze.

Then Frequency said, "If you move or make a sound it'll be your last."

Mr. White started to sweat because he knew Frequency had the upper hand. White asked, "How are you doing Frequency?"

Frequency said, "I'm fine. I need to pick up that package that you owe me."

White said, "I thought we had squashed that issue. My partners wouldn't like it if I had to liquidate their assets to pay you."

Frequency laughed and said, "I am going to get my package whether you hand it to me or whether I just take it!"

Mr. White jumped out of his seat and angrily said, "Frequency if anything or anybody should come up missing from my organization; I will hold you personally accountable!"

Frequency said mockingly, "Oh, so you've learned how to use some big words."

That pushed White over the edge. He shouted to his guards, "Frequency Hunter is nearby!"

The Guards ran all over the grounds searching for Frequency, but he was in the house calmly walking around. He knew Mr. White had set his house up like Tony Montana so he knew exactly where he would come now that he'd been threatened. Frequency pulled out his favorite knife made by Hibben and hid deep in the corner of Mr. White's getaway office. He looked around the room and realized it was set up just like the movie "Scarface." White had his video cameras and monitors set up by EoW, who had done a damn good job. Now Frequency understood why EoW wanted White's head on a platter. He had done all of this fine work and hadn't been paid a dime for it!

Frequency held still and got quiet as Mr. White ran into the room and locked himself inside. He sat down behind his desk with the monitors and started looking into every angle to see if he could spot Frequency. Frequency knew this was the perfect time to set off his plan. He pushed speed dial on his phone which signaled CMAX to start the pyrotechnics show on Mr. White's property. The explosions started and White jumped in his seat. He had the cameras going in every direction until he felt something cold and sharp at his neck and heard Frequency whisper in his ear, "Guess Who?"

Mr. White's face nearly matched his name as he sat face to face with Frequency Hunter. Frequency had grabbed one of Mr. White's swords off of one of his displays and now held it against his throat.

Mr. White went into negotiation mode immediately saying, "Surely we can work out a deal."

"No deals," said Frequency, "I gave you that chance and you declined." Frequency took out a pair of handcuffs and said, Handcuff yourself to that fancy chair of yours." After White reluctantly fastened one hand to the chair, Frequency put down the sword and did the same to the other. He also secured his legs and blindfolded White.

Then Frequency began to ramble around the room looking for a place where White could have hidden his money. White was the kind of man who listened to other people's ideas, then put his own twist on them. Frequency moved some books off of a shelf and uncovered a small safe in the wall. Of course, he immediately started to crack it, but then thought that was way too easy. White had learned a lot from Frequency and his crew and he made damn sure he used their ideas to hide things. He took Don1's idea to have a safe behind a bookshelf because that was one of the first places someone trying to rob him would look. Don1 told him to put a small amount of money and jewelry inside just to give them a little something to steal and then they'd probably leave.

White never imagined the person who'd be robbing him would be Frequency. He kept hollering, "You're awaking the sleeping giant!"   Frequency yelled back, "You should have thought of that when you decided to double crossed me!

Then Frequency found something odd in the wall of a small closet .It was a normal electrical box with ten circuits in it. Each circuit was labeled with an individual number. Frequency normally would have ignored this box, but all of the circuits were off.

Frequency laughed and said, "Good try White, but I think I found what I am looking for."

White started talking and frantically trying to convince Frequency not to touch anything in that room. Frequency looked at the box and then decided to try turning on the breakers, but nothing happened. He then turned them off one by one and still nothing happened. Frequency looked around the room and saw something that gave him an idea. Mr. White had a picture of him and his favorite street car., a Porsche 962 turbo. Frequency tried the circuit numbered nine, then six, and finally two. The wall beside Frequency slid open, and there was White's hidden treasure.

Inside the door was a room made of solid concrete with a giant cube in the middle of it. The cube sat on a metal plate of some kind. Frequency took a letter opener and threw it at the cube. A digital readout lit up and the numbers ran up and then settle back down to 110. Frequency figured it was some type of scale and went inside for a closer look. He touched the cube and found it was solid with some type of satin fabric covering it. Frequency pulled at the fabric and exposed a site that he had dreamed about. The 'cube' was a stack of nothing but hundred dollar bills! Frequency tried to guess how much money was in there, but decided CMAX would be faster and more accurate.

CMAX quickly calculated that one hundred and ten pounds of one hundred dollar bills equaled to five million dollars! Frequency walked out of the vault and directly over to Mr. White, then slapped the daylights out of him.

White really got scared and said, "You're going to pay for that."

Frequency then quietly said, "Dead men don't commit murder."   White got quiet and then Frequency told him, "Now I know why you doubled crossed me."

White started trying to break loose from the chair and shake like crazy. He screamed at Frequency, "Don't you touch any of my money!" Frequency slapped him again and said, "What Money?"

White got quiet and calmed down, he knew he had been tricked and he knew that Frequency was on to his stash.

Frequency said, "You owe me White. I won't break you but I will take what you took from me."

White just slid down in the chair and sat quietly like any beaten man would. But Frequency went to work and had CMAX calculate how much a million dollars weighed in one hundred dollar bills. CMAX told him twenty two pounds, so that's exactly what Frequency took. The digital floor numbers rolled up to eighty-eight when Frequency took the last of many freeze dried bricks.

Then Frequency closed the door to White's treasure room and said, "Now we're even."

Mr. White was through. His sanctuary had been violated and all he could think at this point was revenge.

Frequency was well on his way out of the house by the time the fire department showed up to put out the small grass fire from the pyrotechnics he had initiated before going into White's house. Frequency was tired but very satisfied by what he had just done.

He had kept his temper in check and hadn't hurt anyone even though they well deserved it. Frequency knew that he had just started a war with a person who he once considered a friend. And from the looks of where Mr. White's house when he left, it would be a war with casualties.

Frequency had borrowed Don1's car for the job at Mr. White's. He knew that all of the fellas had been cheated by White and his new crew. Frequency laughed at how he would make sure that all of his own crew was generously compensated for their losses. He knew that he couldn't just give the money to them right away, because White would pick off each person one by one till he got all of the money back. Frequency knew exactly where he would hide the money until everything that he had planned unfolded. He headed to the one spot where no one would imagine a million in cash would be stashed.

When Mr. White was finally freed from his chair, he was livid that it took his staff 2 days to get into his office. White cleaned himself up then made some calls to his key crew members to get his money back. He knew he couldn't tell anyone how much money he had stashed away because that would be his downfall for sure. He'd held that money for a very long time without anyone finding out about it until now. His greed was in full charge when he went into his secret room and saw that the scale indicated that his money now weighed less.

He quickly calculated that a million dollars was missing. He laughed to himself thinking that Frequency took the exact amount of money that he owed him and nothing more. Mr. White made a note of that and decided that he would kill him quickly instead of torturing him first. Mr. White put his satin sheet back over his money and quickly closed the door. He left his office because he knew he needed to change his whole operational setup. Then he changed his mind and decided to just get rid of Frequency Hunter and his whole crew.

When the Hudson Brothers showed up, someone met them at the door with a package and detailed instructions. The two immediately got into their car and left. As they drove away they opened the package and read the directions for an elaborate plan to wipe out a whole group of guys! The Hudson brothers knew that it was too big a job for just the two of them, so they started making phone calls to put their own crew of mercenaries together.

Mr. White watched as the package was delivered to the Hudson brothers and knew that everything he ordered would take place in due time. He went back into his office and discovered that Frequency had left something behind. It looked like some kind of computer part, but White didn't really know anything about them.

He knew he couldn't just go to Frequency and tell him he dropped something while he was robbing him. White laughed at the thought and decided to go see an old girlfriend who was deep into computers.

Mika was on her way to get some lunch when she received a call from Mr. White. She started not to answer the phone, but knew if she didn't he would just show up on her doorstep. Mika had just finish moving to a new area and did not want White messing up her new vibe. She was doing well for herself and didn't need any riffraff in her life right now.

Mr. White very nicely asked, "Can you meet me for lunch?"

Mika said, "No, I have other plans."

Then White said, "Wherever you want to go is fine and I'm buying."

Mika wanted to check out a new restaurant in town and told him, "I'll meet you there."

Mr. White knew that she'd be able to tell him what was up with the thing Frequency had dropped, so he got into his Porsche Cayenne and headed to the newest restaurant in town. He was there in no time flat and asked the hostess to seat him in an area that afforded him plenty of privacy.

He slipped her a fifty and told her, "I'm expecting a young lady to join me." Then he ordered a bottle of wine and patiently waited for Mika.

Mika showed up and was impressed with the décor of the restaurant, but a little perturbed when she saw that Mr. White had them seated in a dimly lit area in the back of the restaurant. She was not about to go through this with White again! The last time she found herself in this situation, she ended up with her ass in the air and the short end of the stick. His girlfriend had interrupted them while they were having sex in the car.

Mr. White didn't beat around the bush and got straight to the point. He told Mika, "Order your meal then I want you to tell him what this thing is."

He handed the device to her and she said, "It's called a jump drive and is used to backup data from a computer."

White asked, "Can you tell me what's on it?"

Mika said, "Sure but I'll need a computer with a USB port on it."   White pulled out a Sony laptop and handed it to her.

Mika was impressed because it was one of the newest models on the market. She turned on the laptop and inserted the jump drive. The drive contained addresses and client information of some kind. Mr. White looked at the data and tried to figure out what Frequency was doing with this information. He had Mika go online and research an address, turned out to be a private bank in the city.

White said, "Show me how to access the information again once I get home."

Mika said, "Sure," and preceded to do just that and teach him how research the information once he accessed it.

The waitress came and took their order. Mika was taken aback by how focused White was on the information and the computer instead of on her. She wanted more of his attention and decided that she was going to be late going back to work in order to get it. White and Mika finished their meal and decided it was time to leave.

He hadn't really given Mika much thought until she walked back to his Porsche with him. He remembered what she'd just done for him and decided to pay her for her services. White reached into his pocket and gave Mika a couple of hundred dollar bills. Mika accepted the money and opened the driver's side door of the Porsche for White to get in. As he sat down she reached for his zipper and unzipped his pants.

Mika started to finish where the two last left off. Mr. White was not one to stop a good blowjob so he opened his legs to give her some room. She didn't stay down long before she got up and sat in his lap. Mika was wet and White went straight inside. She pulled her thong to the side to ensure he had an unobstructed entry, then rode Mr. White and didn't care if anyone saw her. It was just so convenient that he'd parked beside a big tree and his Porsche was hidden by it.

Mr. White was enjoying this woman's pleasure and would definitely use her again to help him get even with Frequency Hunter. Mika was really lost in her own pleasure when her orgasm came down on her. She could not believe that she had just had sex in broad daylight. She became even more excited when Mr. White traded positions and started stroking her from behind. He made sure he was hitting the area where Mika enjoyed him the most, so that when he came she was well ready to let him sex her again.

When they had finished, Mr. White reached inside his Porsche and grabbed a towel off the arm rest. He cleaned himself up and Mika did the same.

He grabbed Mika and said, "You need to drop me some digits so we can stay in touch."

Mika reached inside her purse, pulled out one of her business cards, and handed it to him.

She kissed him deeply and asked, "Can we get together tonight?"

Knowing that he needed to find out more about the information on the jump drive, Mr. White told her, "I'll call you and tell you when and where to come."

Mika said, "I'm looking forward to that, so I'll be waiting to hear from you." Mika went to her car and headed back to work, but went to a nearby friend's house to freshen up first. Then she went back to work as if nothing happened, and lied to her husband about a problem with her car that he never got around to fixing. He promised her he'd take care of it, and she went back to work thinking about getting with Mr. White later.

Mr. White had figured out a way to change the code on his vault and then added a new security feature to it that would automatically close the door and alert him if someone got inside. White then taped a small razor blade to the underside of his chair just in case he got taped to the chair again.

To add another element of surprise, Mr. White affixed a small derringer to the bottom side of his desk and put an extremely loud sounder in his office in case he ever got locked in again. White was very proud of himself and what he'd accomplished that day. He knew he'd learned a valuable lesson from Frequency, so now he was going to figure out where Frequency was going with the money so he could teach him a lesson.

Frequency had made his way back from dropping off the money. He was headed home to see if White had taken the bait he'd left for him. Sure enough, old White fell for it hook, line, and sinker! White had hooked the laptop into his computer and the worm program that was embedded on it had infiltrated his video surveillance system. Now that everything White saw Frequency saw, Frequency needed to finish the link between White and the Banker. Frequency knew that BDB would need help getting information on the banker, so he decided to give him some help from Mr. White. Frequency knew White was a stickler for organizing information. He knew that BDB could use the little bit of information from White to find out everything Frequency would need to nail down the banker. Frequency laughed as he watched White trying to setup his house to prevent another break-in when Frequency had no intention of ever going back into that house.

He had gotten all that he needed and was preparing himself for something bigger. Frequency gave Don1 a call and asked, "How's business?"

Don said, "You need to get to the shop because your probation officer's coming by to pay a visit."

Frequency said, "I'm already en route, so stall him if need be." Frequency's favorite two words were Pontiac Power. He pushed Don1's GXP and it gave results. Of course, it was nothing like his old school TA, but it was sufficient. It didn't take long for Frequency to make it to the shop.

Don1 was there grinning like he saw someone slip on a banana peel.

Frequency asked," What are you grinning at?"

Don1 said, Master's got you jumping through hoops!" then burst into laughter.

Frequency laughed with him then went to his desk to pretend to do some work.

Mr. Master showed up about 30 minutes later and tried to get Frequency to talk about mainframe computers. Frequency knew this was a ploy to get information from him, but it wouldn't work. He played along without giving Master any information that he couldn't get from any search engine on the internet. Mr. Master wanted to drill Frequency on some of the questions Agent Layrock had given him, but he knew Frequency would have him utterly confused and frustrated. Master decided to ask Don1 some questions about how he monitored Frequency's technical processes per call.

Don1 knew that he was trying to get him alone so that he could ask him some other types of questions, so he had Mr. Master follow him to his office.

Once Don1 got into his office Master asked, "How does Frequency spend his time? Is he on the phone a lot with other people outside of his technical support calls?"

Don1 answered his questions as if from a script. Mr. Master got a solid answer for every question he asked. Master then thought that maybe the Feds are wrong this time. Maybe they just need to ask for Hunter's help instead of trying to steal the information. Mr. Master pushed that thought out of his head and ended his visit. He shook hands with Don1 and Frequency on his way out, got into his car, and drove away.

He didn't make it down the street good before he saw a car following him. He made a few subtle turns, then pulled into a parking lot and drew out his weapon. About four different Federal Agents jumped out and pointed guns at him. Mr. Master surrendered his weapon, then saw agent Layrock get out of one of the cars.

Layrock said, "You are no longer to have any contact with Frequency Hunter. I have one agent in and am working on another. We appreciate all your assistance to this point, but your services are no longer required. We want to be sure you don't interfere with our agents or accidentally blow their cover."

Agent Layrock said, "One of Frequency's old buddies is trying to find him, a Mr. White."

Mr. Master knew that things were about to blow up because there was no way Frequency would stay on the straight and narrow path if White went anywhere near him.

Master asked agent Layrock, "What are the feds going to do to stop these two from getting together?"

Layrock said, "I understand your concern because I'm concerned too. We need Mr. Hunter's expertise but Mr. White could be a huge obstacle."

Master acknowledge agent Layrock and said, "I hope the agency won't let Mr. Hunter down or get him hurt in the process of trying to use his expertise."

Agent Layrock said, "The Feds are in the business of protecting not harming."

Mr. White had Mika over and she was providing him with some valuable information. She was good at research, but she couldn't understand how Frequency had set up all of the information located on the jump drive. Mr. White had her looking for addresses all over the city. No sooner would she would locate an address and send someone there than they'd find out it was an arena or a building slated for demolition.

Whoever put this information together had them running around on a wild goose chase, thought Mika. Then she found something that had Mr. White extremely excited. It was the address of a bank that was known for holding large quantities of cash. White knew that he had found Frequency's next caper, and he'd make sure that Frequency would fail.   Mr. White got on the phone immediately and set up a meeting with the bank's CEO. He got to the bank's CEO easily by stating that he was about to open a very large business account with a direct cash deposit.

The CEO's secretary said, "Come to the bank in the morning and ask for Mr. Albe Wimple."

White hung up the phone and decided to celebrate his little victory with Mika, since she had discovered the information he needed.

Mika knew she was in for a long night and had one of her girlfriends back her story for the night. She and Mr. White decided to eat in and have a pleasurable night cap before she had to go home.

Frequency loved his ingenuity! He had made Mr. White clear up another question about the Gathering file. He took all of the information and sent it to BDB's cell phone.

BDB called Frequency as soon as he got the message and said, "I'll wait till the man leaves the bank and follow him to his house. After that I'll find the landscape company taking care of his yard and make them shut down for a while."

BDB knew he could kill the landscape company's equipment by tainting their gas cans. Then he'd just wait a while and go by the house when the yard was looking pretty bad. The homeowner would be desperate, and he'd be in like Flint! BDB knew that Frequency had a lot riding on the information he gathered, so he made sure that everything he put in place would work to perfection.

Mr. White was ready for his meeting with the bank CEO. He had a very eventful night with Mika and was glad to let her go back home to her husband. He made a mental note to send her husband a copy of the video he'd made while they were together the night before. White knew that if Mika didn't have a husband, she'd need somebody's help to maintain her current lifestyle. He also thought about how he could use her skills on the computer for some other scams he had in mind.

White stepped into the bank and went straight to the business office area. He pulled out his driver's license for identification purposes and handed it to the receptionist.

She said, "Good morning Mr. White. We've been expecting you," and escorted him to the big business area. She gave White a form to fill out and he decided not to go through the hassle.

Mr. Wimple stepped out of his office and went to meet Mr. White. He introduced himself, and White stood up to shake hands.

Mr. Wimple said, "Please follow me to my office."

Once there, Mr. Wimple cut straight to the matter at hand. White opened his briefcase and showed Mr. Wimple the large amount of cash inside. Mr. Wimple knew that he'd have to explain such a large sum of money to the bank, but he didn't want to do that just yet. He had a business venture with another client that White's money could help move along without the bank's involvement. Mr. Wimple didn't know Mr. White, but he did know an investment opportunity when he saw one.

Mr. White decided to ask for the bank's history of security infractions. Wimple went into his usual spill on the bank's security and how it hadn't been breached.

Mr. White interrupted and said just two words, "Frequency Hunter."

Mr. Wimple almost fell out of his chair! He started stuttering and trying to explain what happened with 'that detestable individual.'

Mr. White laughed as he saw Wimple's face beaded with sweat. White then told Mr. Wimple something that made him smile.

"How would you like to put Frequency Hunter back behind bars where he belongs?" White asked.

Wimple said, "I'm definitely interested. If you can make it happen, I'll even let you in on a very lucrative business offer."

Mr. White told Mr. Wimple, "I'll give you the details later once we secure a meeting place away from the bank. There are too many cameras around here to talk of matters so sensitive."

White and Wimple met as agreed, and put together a plan to get rid of Frequency and lock him behind bars for a long time. Then Mr. Wimple came out with the business venture he'd spoken of earlier. White was at a loss for words when Wimple mentioned Richard Inman and the investment he needed to get his club back online. Mr. Wimple and one of his constituents were the main backers of Richard Inman's organization.

White found out that the Gallery had experienced a major power surge that fried most of the electrical systems. Neither Mr. Wimple nor his constituents had the capital available to get the repairs done. And to make matters worse, the bank could not loan any more funds to anything associated with Richard Inman because he had already used it all!

Mr. White liked the deal and smiled at the 25% interest rate on the total amount loaned. He asked Mr. Wimple to keep his name off of any and all the associated paperwork, and Mr. Wimple assured him that he'd be totally anonymous.

White then asked, "Were you able to use any of the information on the jump drive?"

Mr. Wimple replied, "The information was used and his bank's security team is on it."

Frequency was in heaven! He was now into the bank's computer system and he had Mr. White and the bank's Mr. Wimple working together on some illegal investments. Frequency put together an elementary type program to make the bank's security happy. He began looking for the last person in the Gathering file. He had everybody in place except this one, and he knew that the only way he would figure it out would be through Mr. Wimple, the bank's CEO.

Mr. Wimple called Mr. White and said, "My bank's security found the program that Frequency Hunter was using. They have it quarantined to some dummy accounts. As soon as Frequency Hunter tries to move any money from any of those accounts he'll be immediately identified and the Fed's will be notified."

Mr. White thanked Mr. Wimple and ended the call.

Mr. Wimple then called his constituent and told him of the recent developments.

Mr. White laughed and thought about the look on Frequency's face when the Feds show up at his place to arrest him. White had snitched on Frequency once to get him locked up, and had no problem doing it again. Only this time, Frequency would be locked up with no chance of getting out. He laughed, sat back in his favorite seat, and turned on his favorite movie "Scarface."

Chapter 12

Madame

Madame sat back and enjoyed the fruits of her labor. She had successfully transformed her latest crop of wild teenaged girls into a fine batch of prostitutes. Madame had received word that they needed to shut down on taking in new girls for a while because the heat was on and the last sets of girls were making headlines. She wasted no time in moving all of the cash from their latest transaction into an overseas account setup by a mutual friend at the local bank. As long as they sent him young girls to get his jollies off, he would help them move the thousands of dollars they made pimping minors.

Madame felt some remorse at first, but once she and her mate Big Trouble got to making big money, all thoughts of remorse flew away in the wind. Madame emptied all of her belongings into a box, and then left the house where she'd been staying. She and Big Trouble routinely set up training houses where the up and coming girls could practice their trade. After they get familiar with the routine and comfortable enough with their 'trade' they move them out onto the streets to make money. Some of the girls end up in the corporate sector as secretaries with hidden agendas. Those make five times the money as the street girls, and they also set Madame up with great insider stock tips.

Madame had dreams of getting out of the prostitution business one day, but her need for high finances grew as fast as her talents. Madame had the best of everything from cars she rode in; to the clothes she wore, to the houses that she lived in. She'd never had to want for anything ever since she got with Big Trouble. She thought that she was just turning out another young dude when she met him, but the tide got turned on her. Big trouble got a hold of her and never let go. She had been with him for a few years now, and every time he put it on her she had to recuperate for a few days. Big Trouble has one of the biggest sex drives of any man she'd ever met, and she'd been with a lot of them. No matter what they went through he remained loyal to her and her short comings.

Madame was getting ready for her usual inspection of all the girls, when one of them showed up late. Madame would usually let her slide, but this time she was going to make an example of her. Gloria knew she was bigger than Madame and knew she was not afraid to fight. She'd had a big night at the local lodge and was worn out. She knew Madame was going to come at her hard, but she was prepared for it. Gloria had made it up in her mind to take on Madame and see if she could run the girls better than Madame.

Madame did her usual inspection of each girl ensuring that they gave her the proper amount of money for the services rendered. She considered herself a nice manager because she only took 60% of the girls' money after they'd been with Madame faithfully for a year. Before that year was up, she gave them just enough to survive on the street for one day. That prevented the new girls from trying to run away. Of course, Madame had a few try over the years, but it never took long for them to come back and start over from scratch.

Madame went to each girl and collected all of last night's payout.

One girl gave Madame two stacks of money and said, "I'm gonna have to quit because the police have started harassing me."

Madame said, "That's okay, just go back and make up for it tonight."

All the other girls were handing Madame their money until she got to Gloria. As soon as Madame looked Gloria in the eye, she knew there was going to be trouble. Madame purposely skipped over Gloria and finished collecting her money, then separated the money accordingly. She dropped each girl's money into separate bags and decided to handle Gloria.

Madame suddenly ran and jumped on Gloria, who was caught off guard. She fell to the floor as Madame put an elbow to her head. Gloria's head flew back and hit the floor hard. She tried to fight back but Madame had blindsided her. Gloria saw Madame reach for her hair and decided to hit Madame hard in her chest. She heard the wind come from Madame as she lifted up and pushed Madame off of her. Madame struggled to regain her breath before Gloria got to her, but she couldn't. Gloria jumped on her back and punched her in the back of the head. Madame rolled with the punch and got out of the way of Gloria's vicious kick.

Madame got to her feet and hit Gloria in the stomach and then upper cut her between her breasts. Gloria lost her breath and staggered backwards. Madame kicked her foot from under her and Gloria fell to the floor. Madame jumped on her chest and elbowed Gloria in the head several times. She then let her full weight drop down on Gloria and started to choke her. Madame came to her senses and released Gloria's throat as she gasped for air. Madame got off her then kicked her in the ribs as hard as she could. The rest of the girls stood back in amazement as Madame whooped Gloria.

Madame saw that Gloria was through, but she wanted to add insult to injury. She told one of the girls, "Go get me the biggest strap on dildo you can find." Madame pulled out a straight razor and cut the ass out of Gloria's clothes as she waited for the girl to bring her the dildo.

Once she had it strapped on, she said to all the girls in the room, "When you fuck with me I fuck with you, and I do not use Vaseline."

Madame straddled Gloria from behind and thrust the dildo deeply into her rectum. Gloria let out a deep scream as Madame grabbed a handful of her hair and pulled backwards. Every time Madame thrust into Gloria, she'd scream at her to submit. Gloria tried to resist but Madame was relentlessly pounding into her anus and pulling her hair. Madame had on a pair of stiletto hills and decided to dig them deeply into Gloria's calf. Gloria finally lost all of her fight and gave in. She collapsed as Madame pulled the dildo from her ass. Madame went to one of the other girls and had her unstrap the dildo. Madame walked back over to Gloria and gave her one last hard kick that made Gloria sprawl out unconscious on the floor.

Madame finally got all of the girls out to work except Gloria, who she left back at the apartment tied up. Madame still had not collected money from Gloria and needed to set things straight with her. Madame knew if Gloria didn't get herself together, she'd have to turn her over to the man of the organization. Madame hoped that she had beaten some sense into her and knew that she would find it out shortly.

She was sore from her tangle with Gloria, but she was somewhat satisfied with the outcome. She knew that she had to make an example of Gloria so she got herself ready for some S&M type shit. Madame pulled up to the apartment, decided what she was going to do, then opened the door and went into action. She closed the door behind her and went directly to the kitchen. She put some water on the stove and got it to a boil. She pulled out a meat injector and took off her shoes. Gloria was still on the floor with her hands and legs taped together. Madame took the pot of boiling water and stuck the meat injector into it. She filled the injector with boiling hot water, then stuck it into Gloria's rectum and squeezed in the hot water. Gloria immediately regained consciousness and began shaking and screaming.

Madame looked into her face as she begged for mercy. Madame walked around Gloria as she shuddered from the boiling water, knowing that she couldn't mess up that pretty face or mar that voluptuous body. Madame knew that their customers paid well for girls with no blemishes. She waited a little while before she pulled the meat injector from Gloria's ass and proceeded to inject more hot water inside her. Gloria screamed so much that she had no voice left to scream with. She knew she had really messed up, and now more than ever she knew she wouldn't do it again.

Madame pulled out the injector and sat down near Gloria with Gloria's head in her lap. Gloria was still nearly delirious with pain. Madame started talking to Gloria as if she was her little girl.

Madame told Gloria, "There are consequences for defying me."

Gloria just shook as Madame picked up the injector again, and pleaded with everything she had left and finally told Madame the one thing she really wanted to know. Gloria told Madame where her money was. Gloria's head hit the floor with a thud as Madame quickly got up and went through her things. She had no trouble finding the money and a little something extra. She found a little pearl handled pistol that one of her customers given her. Madame checked the pistol and found that it had no bullets or firing pin. Madame pulled the trigger and discovered the thing was just a cigarette lighter. She put the lighter back, but kept the money.

She went back over to Gloria and asked, "How long did it take you to make this money?"

Gloria said, "That's a week's worth of money. I could have made more."

Madame asked, "Do you want to live in peace or be found in pieces?"

Gloria said, "I'll do whatever it takes to get back in your good graces."

Madame held her hand out toward Gloria's face and Gloria kissed it in submission, and Madame pulled out her straight razor and cut the tape from her hands and feet.

Gloria stood up and said, "May I go to the bathroom to clean myself up so I can get to work?"

Madam said, "Yes, but you'd better hurry up because you're already behind."

Gloria moved as fast as her sore body would let her. She got into the shower and washed herself. She dropped her head in disgust for being weak enough to submit to Madame. She wanted to go back out there and fight again, but the soreness in her behind reminded her that the next time would be much, much worse.

She knew she could not sell her ass tonight, because Madame had ruined it. She'd have to just rely on everything else and try to get twice the amount for it than she usually charged. She hurriedly got out of the shower and threw on just enough clothes to cover up her assets, then stepped out of the bathroom and did just enough to her hair to make it look neat. She put on her makeup and told Madame she was ready to go.

When they got into Madame's little convertible, Madame took her to a different area than usual. Gloria knew exactly where she were, but didn't say a word as Madame told her to get out of the car. Gloria watched as Madame drove away, and then went to work. Madame knew that Gloria was out of her league in this neighborhood, but she knew that her man was watching and she'd be okay. Madame went to check on the other girls. She told them it would be a long night, so she was sure she wouldn't see them until morning.

Don1 had just shut down the shop for the night. He'd told his friend Terri that he had to do some heavy research and would be at a friend's house. Terri was cool with what she heard and told him she would call him later. she'd already broken one of the first rules as an undercover agent: don't get involved with anyone connected to the case you are working on. But she found there was something special about Don that made her forget that she was a federal agent trying to keep tabs on one of his employees. She felt guilty, but promised herself that she would NOT let this one get away.

Don1 was really into Terri, but he remembered what Frequency told him about new people, so he kept them away from each other. Don1 thought about tracking devices and all of the other tricks of the trade that the Feds used to keep up with people, so he changed directions and headed to EoW's house instead.

EoW was just about to leave when Don1 pulled up. He said, "I was just about to go out for drinks," Don gave him a look that made him change his mind and turn around.

EoW said, "There's nothing in the house to drink or eat so I need to go to the store."

Don1 headed straight for the broom closet and got a broom, and EoW went straight to his computer room and got a bug sweeper. EoW loved the signals they had set up some time ago, because they worked without saying a word. He went to work with the sweeper and found that both his truck and Don1's car had been tagged. They didn't touch them, but they knew now that Frequency's suspicions were now proven facts! They checked the house for taps and found none, so they started talking in EoW's computer room.

Don1 said, "I've come up with some of the information you asked me about earlier." He handed EoW a jump drive with all of the information on it. EoW said, "Now my task will be really easy because if you found one I'll surely find the other."

Don1 asked, "What do you mean?"

EoW said,"There's a broad on the street who's running a bunch of very young prostitutes. She's known to have one of the baddest dudes in the city as her manager, and I mean this dude is tough."

"How tough?" asked Don1?

"The dude retired undefeated as the city champion back street brawler, said EoW, "is that tough enough for you?"

Don1 looked as if he just choked down something he had no business eating.

EoW asked, "You okay?"

Don1 said, "Yeah, come go on a night ride with me."

EoW said, "Sure but we need Frequency to get us a set of wheels that haven't been tagged by the Feds."

Frequency called Webb and said, "I need you to help Don1 and EoW out."   Webb said, "You know I've got 'em covered and will make delivery as soon as I hang up." Webb hung up the phone and pulled the cover off the 5.0 Mustang he'd just finished working on. He needed a reason to test it out and no time was better than right now. He started the engine and let it run for a minute, then jumped in the car and dropped the top. He put it in gear and hit the button to open the garage door. He eased the car out and hit the button to close the door behind him as he headed to EoW's house.

Webb did not spare the horses as he sped to EoW's. He loved to hear the car run 'cause it ran like a scalded dog! Webb got to EoW's house and blew the horn. EoW and Don1 came out the house, locked it up, and jumped into the car with Webb.

Webb laughed and said, "I heard that you guys have bug problems." All of them shared the laugh and Webb pulled a burnout as they went up the street.

Webb asked, "Where are you guys headed?"

Don1 said, "We're looking for the spot where the street fights take place."

Webb said, "I don't know personally, but I know someone else who does." They headed to Webb's friend's house and Webb got out and knocked on the door. A dude came to the door and started talking to Webb. He and the dude shook hands and then both men walked to the car.

Webb said, "This is Dan and he's into the street fighting game. Dan's going to show us where tonight's fight will be held."

Don1 and EoW were relieved because they could have driven around all night looking for it without his help. Dan got in the car, and Webb introduced him to EoW and Don1. Dan started telling the fellows about the fight game as Webb drove them to the location.

Don1 asked, "How do they contact each other so they know when the fights are supposed to go down?"

Dan said, "We have a cellular network vendor out of state taking care of that."

Well Don1 quickly told Dan, "I can supply the same network with twice the security locally. I'd also be willing to discount the phones, if the sure numbers in their group are the correct size."

Dan said, "You've totally lost me with all that technical mumbo jumbo. I'll introduce you to the man who does understand all of it and can make a decision on it immediately."

Don1 said, "Cool, and if the deal goes down, I'll take care of you on the other side."

Dan said, I'm cool with that, because if tonight's fight doesn't go my way, I'll be needing all of the finances I can get!"

The four men stood in awe as they finally made it to where the fight was going to take place. A young girl dressed in a bikini walked into the roped off area and started announcing all of the contenders for all four of the night's brawls. Then she introduced the champ. Big Trouble stepped into the arena and everybody could see why he was the champ. This guy was big and he was built like a Greek statue! He looked as if he could break a man in two with his bare hands! Don1 made sure that he had his best business etiquette in check 'cause it looked as if he was going to be doing business with a monster.

Big Trouble got all of the night's business started with the betting and collecting of the money. As the night's festivities went on, Don1 and EoW mingled with the crowd passing out business cards and telling about their business services. As the last finale fight ended Webb, EoW, and Don1 were introduced to Big Trouble by Dan. The look on Dan's face had them worried because he looked as if he just lost his heart.

Big Trouble asked, "Which one of you guys are talking about a cellular business?"

Don1 stepped forward and said, "That would be me."

Big trouble threw Don1 his cell phone and Don1 told him all of its specs and limitations. Big Trouble was impressed and decided to try another test.

He asked, "What about the encryption piece on the phone?"

Don1 was in his element so he decided to show off. He took Big Trouble's phone, cracked his code, then made all of Big Trouble's contacts go to his phone.

Then Don1 then threw Big Trouble's phone back and said, "Make a call to anyone in your contact list."

Big Trouble tried but he couldn't get the phone to unlock. He got so frustrated that he crushed the phone in his hands. Everyone standing around him stepped back as Big Trouble regained his composure and said, "We'll be by your cell shop in the morning to do business."

Don1 said, "I'll be looking forward to it. If I can get a little information from you I can cut down your wait time."

Big Trouble laughed and said, "You've got nothing to worry about 'cause I'm bringing my woman to ensure that everything goes smoothly."

Then Don1, EoW, Dan, and Webb left.

As they drove away, Webb asked Dan, "Why were you so nervous up there with Big Trouble?"

Dan told the guys, "I went all or nothing on the last fight and my guy won. I've been trying to collect my money from Big Trouble. Big Trouble was supposed to send somebody by my house to drop off the money he owed me."

"Is that good?" asked EoW.

"I don't know," said Dan; "the last person who won some money from Big Trouble ain't around anymore."

Big Trouble gathered all of the equipment from the fight arena and put it in his trailer. He went over to the girls who collected the money and got it all.

He told them, "I'm ready to go so just get in my truck. Big Trouble knew he was in trouble with the little woman because he'd taken a couple of her girls off the street to collect money for his fights. He knew he'd have to square it up with her later so he decided to take the girls back to work. That didn't take long and he was soon headed for home. He drove by a couple of areas to make sure the girls were alright, and then he headed to his final destination for the night. Once he made it home he showered and went his favorite couch for a nap. Big Trouble left all of tonight's winnings in the main bedroom with a note for the little woman detailing how much he had lost and to whom.

Madame was just changing vehicles when she thought about her man. Big Trouble hadn't called her since the fights began and that wasn't like him. Madame knew it was almost time to get the girls off the street so she took care of that first. She picked up each girl and collected their money then she tried to call Big Trouble but got no answer. Madame didn't want the girls see her worry, but she did pick up the pace as she collected each girl and her money. She was down to her last one and, even though she was worried about Big Trouble, she prepared herself for Ms. Gloria.

As Madame pulled up to the pickup spot she didn't see Gloria, so she parked the van and got out to look around. She didn't see anybody, but she heard a muffled scream. When she ran around the building, there was Gloria with three guys all over her. Madame wouldn't have interfered until she heard one of the guys asking Gloria where the rest of her money was, and saw that the other two were raping her. Madame picked up an old piece of pipe and sneaked up on them. One of the guys pulled out of Gloria and started coming on her. Madame felt sorry for her because she could have been exposed to some kind of disease. The second guy also came but he stayed inside of her.

Madame was close enough now to hit the first guy across the back of the head. He hit the ground uncon-scious. The second one was trying to scramble to his feet, but it was too late. Madame hit him in the back of the head and then across his back several times. The last one was trapped under Gloria and she was fighting him like crazy. She grabbed his nuts and twisted with all that she had as the guy screamed in pain. His scream ended with a thud as Madame hit him dead in the head to knock him out.

Gloria was shocked when she received a hand from Madame to get up. She looked as if she had been through hell, but she'd be okay. She and Madame walked back to the pickup spot and Gloria told her to wait. Gloria went over to a spot where she'd hidden her money and got it, then ran back to the van and gave the money to Madame. Madame was happy now that all of the girls and their money were accounted for. Now she could find out what was going on with Big Trouble.

Madame had all of the girls back at the apartment and had finished tallying the night's money. The girls were over quota, and she was surprised to see that Gloria was top achiever for the night. Whenever a girl did that she was able to take the following night off to go to a health spa for some pampering. Madame knew that Gloria needed it and so rightly deserved it. She left word for the girls to be ready again tomorrow when she got there to drop them off, then rushed out and sped off in her convertible. She headed straight for Big Trouble's place because she still hadn't heard from him.

It took her about 45 minutes to get out to his place. She was relieved when she pulled up and saw his truck there still attached to the trailer. Madame had gotten herself all worked up worrying about him and so far everything seemed okay. She parked her car and walked into the house. She first headed to the bedroom and was relieved when she saw that he had set up a fight that night and everything went well. She also saw from his note that he lost a nice chunk of change to Dan. She'd decide on his fate after she found Trouble.

Madame stripped down to her black thong and bra set, then went to his closet and put on one of his shirts. Madame looked at her body and saw where she now had bruises from her melee with Gloria and knew Trouble would freak out when he saw them. She was tired and she knew Big Trouble would wear her out, so she went to the kitchen and made herself a good strong pot of coffee. It was going to be a very long night. Madame went to the den and saw Trouble on his favorite couch asleep.

She laughed because all he had on was a towel and it was standing up like a tent. Madame finished her coffee then walked over to Trouble. She got down between his legs and moved the towel to expose his hard-on. Madame loved to look at him while he was erected, and decided to wake him up with some oral pleasure. She started off slow and deliberate. She took her time and enjoyed every inch of his manhood. Madame would try between strokes to engulf him, but she didn't want to choke. She bounced her head up and down rapidly then changed the pace and took it in slowly. Madame slid her tongue over the head as pre-cum came out. She wasn't one to shy away from anything that Trouble offered her, and she could feel his erection throb as she stroked it with her tongue.

Madame made sure Trouble was not going to hold back as he usually did trying to get her to give him some ass. She was determined to finish him off before she rode him back to sleep. She pulled her mouth from his erection and placed his scrotum in her mouth. She hummed as she did this and was happy to feel the hand of her man on the back of her neck. Madame looked up to see Trouble smiling down at her. She pulled his sack from her mouth and squeezed it gently, but firmly.

She said, "You worried me sick by not calling like you were supposed to."

Big Trouble told her, "Save your fussing for later," as he reached to touch one of her breasts. His hand brushed across an area where Madame was sore and bruised and she let out a soft cry of pain. Big Trouble looked at Madame then jumped up.

He snatched the shirt she was wearing open and saw all of the bruises. Big Trouble was livid! Someone was going to pay. He forgot that he was in the middle of quality time with Madame, and she was not about to stop.

Madame grabbed him by the testicles and said, "Calm down," but he started huffing like an old bull. She knew she really had to put her skills to work because this was one mad man. Madame went down on her knees and really started to put in work with her best oral skills. She knew that she had to make him cum hard to get him back under control. Big Trouble tried to resist, but he felt himself giving in until he fell back on the couch and Madame felt his body jerk and heard Trouble growl as he orgasmed. His erection jumped in her mouth as he finally released his seed. Madame did not let one drop escape savoring the taste as something that was her own. She kept stroking him till he went limp and lay back on the couch.

Madame got up and poured herself and him a cup of coffee. She added all the fixing that he liked and took it to him. Madame gave him his coffee and watched him drink it. Then she told him about her night and how one of the girls had gotten out of hand and she handled it. She then told him how that same girl needed her help in the end and turned out to be the highest earner for the night.   Big   Trouble smiled at her and told her about his night and what happened to his phone.

Madame said, "You're on punishment for breaking your phone."

Big Trouble started pouting like a little kid and asked, "What am I losing?"

Madame looked at him as he stood up from the couch and saw he was getting an erection just standing there. Madame said, "Okay, I won't take it all away from you. But no back door sex until you get another phone and make up for worrying me so bad."

Big Trouble said, "Okay," as he picked Madame up and took her to the bedroom.

Madame knew she was about to go through a lot. She told him, "Don't overdo it because we have business in the morning."

Big Trouble had Madame in bed in no time. Madame was on top riding him until she orgasmed. Big Trouble rolled her over and started thrusting deeply inside of her. Madame accepted each thrust before they changed positions again. She rolled over on her stomach and let Big Trouble get behind her. It was not long before he collapsed on top of her, satisfied and sleepy. He and Madame both quickly fell asleep, exhausted but together as usual.

Madame awoke the following morning and went to take care of the business and the girls as usual. She left Trouble at the house with a list of things to do and a message that she would take care of the money he owed Dan. Madame knew that if she let Trouble take care of paying Dan, Dan would never get this money. She knew that it would probably end up in a fight with Dan becoming another victim of a vicious beating. She walked out to her car and headed to the apartment where the girls were staged. Madame got into the place and found that all of the girls including Gloria were ready to go.

She looked at Gloria and said, "I'm proud of you, but you won't be going out today. Even though we had a run in, you deserved a day off." Madame had everybody ready to go, when all of a sudden in burst Trouble. He was dressed and smiling saying hello to all of the ladies. Madame didn't like it when he showed up around the girls, but she had no say so in the matter.

Trouble walked up to Madame and asked, "Why didn't you wake me?"   She smiled and said, "I needed to take care of the morning business and you would have made me late."

Trouble smiled slyly then started eyeballing all the girls. His eyes settled on Gloria and he walked up to her. Gloria was so scared she couldn't move. She knew that Trouble was a big man who could break her in half without breaking a sweat.

Trouble said, "I know about the situation between Madame and you "Will there be any more problems?"

Gloria said, "No sir," as she looked at Trouble.

Trouble reached out to take her hand and Gloria put it inside of his own. He started to squeeze her hand and talk really low.

He said, "If you ever get another idea about putting your hands on Madame, the pain in her hand will be nothing compared to what I'll do to you. Do you understand me?"

Trouble was about to do something else when he felt Madame grab his forearm and say that that was enough. He let go of Gloria and told Madame, "Hurry up and finish because we have a business meeting that I don't want to be late for."

Madame rushed the girls to the van and hurriedly dropped them off at their areas. Then she took Gloria to the day spa for a much deserved day of relaxation. Madame hurriedly got back to the apartment so she and Trouble could head to Don1's cell shop to do business.

Don1 had gotten to the shop early and was anticipating a big sale with a new client who had big credentials and even bigger money. He was totally surprised when Terri showed up looking quite sexy. Don1 knew that he'd be distracted as long as she was there.

Terri said, "I made this visit to find out why you didn't make it to my place last night."

Don1 said, "Me and the fellows played poker at EoW's place all night."

Terri walked up and hugged Don1 and asked, "So when will you make up for last night?"

Don1 looked puzzled until Terri grabbed his hand and put it under her dress. Don1 had a hand full her nakedness and was about to take advantage of it, when the buzzer rang. He looked into the surveillance monitor and saw Trouble. Terri was not pleased when Don1 pulled away his hand and headed for the door. She looked into the monitor and decided to go into Don1's office and watch everything from there, as he grabbed a hand sanitizer from the counter top and rubbed some on his hands. He hoped that the erection in his pants wouldn't show as he went to greet his prospective clients.

Big Trouble walked in and was immediately impressed with the store's set up and the items on display.

Don1 walked up and shook his hand. Don1 gave him a firm handshake, but quickly let go. He remembered what those hands did to that cell phone and did not need to have his hand in a cast.

Big Trouble introduced Don1 to Madame and the three sat down to talk business.

Don1 said, "I can increase your security and set you up with a cellular network with twice the features of your old network.

Madame looked at Trouble and said, "I see why you were impressed with this young man."

Trouble said, "Tell her about the codes and the GPS feature that we can monitor from any computer."

Madame looked at Don1 and he started to explain, "I can set you up with a phone like this. After that, anyone within your network could be monitored from anywhere in the world, and you could pinpoint them to within five feet of their actual location."

Madame looked confused and then asked, "So if someone in my network has another type of phone I can find them anywhere within five feet?"

Don1 said, "Yes."

Madame asked, "Where do we sign up?"

Don1 pulled out the necessary paperwork and asked, "How many phones do you need?"

Madame said, "Twenty-five."

Trouble hollered, "What!!!"

Madame reached down and rubbed Trouble between his legs to calm him down.

Don1 was surprised to see Trouble signing the papers and watched as Madame coerced him into agreeing. Don1 got the phones from the stockroom then returned with them and pulled out the two master phones. He programmed them with the numbers they already had, then he surprised them by pulling all of their existing information into the new phones. Big Trouble looked at his and saw that it had all of the information from the phone he crushed.

He looked at Don1 and asked, "How did you save my information?"

Don1 said, "I did it when you gave me the phone to show me your encryption program."

Big Trouble said, "I like that. Go ahead and ring us up."

Madame had really started working on Trouble's crotch. He probably would have bought the whole store the way she was working his erection.

Don1 got all of the phones programmed and explained all the fine points to Big Trouble. He did everything in his power not to watch Madame and the way she was holding on to Big Trouble's crotch. She was bold and brazen about her sexuality with her man and he knew it. Big Trouble knew that if Madame wanted him to pay for something she'd really cut up if he said no.

Don1 got all of the paperwork signed and said, "I need to go to my office and ensure that all of the phones are working properly." He walked away from

Madame and Big Trouble and went to his office to program the phones without distractions.

When he got to his office, there was Terri sitting on his couch watching TV. Don1 said, "I thought you'd left."

Terri said, "I was about to until I saw that woman come in."

Don1 said, "She's a customer and that's her man." He turned on his security monitor and showed Terri how Madame was cutting up with her man.

Madame decided to give Trouble a quickie right then and there!

She asked, "Do you have a problem with me getting some candy?" Madame exposed Trouble and started kissing and licking his erection. Big Trouble started looking around to make sure Don1 wasn't coming back.

Terri looked in awe at how that woman just decided to do her man in the store. She looked over at Don1, who decided to hurry and finish programming the last of the phones.

As soon as he was finished, Don made some noises to let the couple know he was headed their way.

Madame released Trouble and said, "Wait till we get to the car." Big Trouble covered himself and hurriedly finished the deal with Don1. Don1 gave all the phone packages to Big Trouble and he took them to the car.

Madame shook Don1's hand and gave him a message. She said, "We like the way you handle your business so you'll be seeing more of us."

Don1 didn't know if that was a good thing or bad thing. He did like the large amount of cash he received and the information that he was going to get when they issued those phones.

Madame went to the car and finished making Big Trouble happy as they drove back to the apartment to issue out the phones to the girls. Madame told Big Trouble how they would use the phones to keep a track on the girls at all times. Big Trouble understood and loved everything about it. Later that night Big Trouble and Madame put their plan to work and it worked flawlessly. Big Trouble then turned his attention to Madame and made sure that she would be late in the morning.

Chapter 13

Big Trouble

Big Trouble was up before the break of dawn and decided to go out and walk his dog. He left his woman in bed asleep after a long night of pleasure. Big Trouble had just spent most of his fight money on a GPS tracking system for the girls. He enjoyed having a full night with Madame there for his entertainment. Usually she would give him a quickie, and have to rush off and work with the girls. But last night she'd put one girl in charge while she spent all of her time with him.

Big Trouble got his dog, Bear, and headed out across his twenty acres of land. The two just walked without a care or a plan, because that's the way Big Trouble wanted it. He'd bought the land and had decided to settle down with Madame until they had a run-in with the judge. After that, they had to increase their business of managing underage prostitute to cater to his sick ass. Big Trouble knew that if he could just get rid of the judge and his sicko associates, he'd be able to enjoy himself out on his land. He loved to take these long walks to keep his head clear.

He could remember the days of having to fight all the time just to make ends meet. Then he met Madame and his world turned upside down in a good way. They got together after one of his street fights. He had to break the other guy's arm just to get him to quit. Madame came up to him at the after party and started talking dirty to him in front of some other girls. The other girls tried to push her out of the way, but ended up getting whooped.

Then Madame came back to Big Trouble and said, "I'm not done yet. You need to come with me."

After seeing her put a beat down on all those other girls, Big Trouble wanted to know more about this woman. They ended up having sex in the back of the club. Ever since then Big Trouble and Madame had been inseparable. Big Trouble thought about how he went from barely making it to having the deed to 20 acres of land and a house.

He heard Bear barking and went over to see what he'd found. When Big Trouble got to Bear, he found an old refrigerator that he knew he hadn't put there, and a bunch of tire tracks. Big Trouble got really concerned when he opened the refrigerator. The stench reminded him of an old Meth junkie he knew. Big Trouble knew that he had a major problem that might bring the Feds around in a hurry.

Madame was just waking up and taking a good hot bath. Big Trouble had worn her out in every way sexually possible! She was letting her body soak in the hot bubbling water of the big Jacuzzi, when she heard Big Trouble's. ring tone on her phone. She raised herself just enough to reach the phone and answered it. She heard Big Trouble out of breath and screaming almost hysterically into the phone.

When she finally got him to calm down she said, "I'm on my way." Madame grabbed her robe and went to the gun cabinet to grab a shotgun and some shells. She grabbed the keys to Trouble's truck, and then used the tracking system on the phone to find him.

Madame drove the truck like it was stolen as she made her way to where Trouble was, and found him and Bear walking around pulling stuff out of the underbrush. It all looked like a bunch of trash to Madame as she stopped the truck a few feet in front of Trouble and got out with the shotgun.

She made it over to Trouble in a hurry and caught her breath. Big Trouble took one good look at Madame and burst into a good hard laugh.

Madame frowned and asked, "What the hell are you laughing at?"

Big Trouble said, "You in your bathrobe with that shotgun."

Madame said, "I brought this shotgun in my bathrobe because you sounded like you were having some major problems!"

Big Trouble stopped laughing and took Madame over to the refrigerator, then opened it up. Madame damn near vomited from the stench that came out of it.

Big Trouble said, "All of this stuff came from a Meth lab, which could have the Feds swarming our property like flies on elephant shit."

Madame knew that this was too much for Big Trouble to handle because if he did, somebody would end up dead. Madame said, "We need to have a meeting with the Judge.

Big Trouble agreed, because he knew if they handled it themselves it would just bring more heat on them. That was something neither of them wanted.

Madame walked back to the truck and put the shotgun inside, then called out to Bear and put him in the back. She told Trouble, "Give me your phone so I can call the Judge directly."

Don1 was at home doing nothing, so he decided to see if Big Trouble had used the new cellular network. He almost jumped out of his seat when all twenty five lights lit up! That told him that every phone they'd bought had been activated, so he could listen in or track any of them at any time. Don1 decided to listen in on Big Trouble first and heard him talking to another man about a Meth lab he'd discovered on his personal property.

He heard Big Trouble say, "I don't need any Feds snooping around my house. What can you do about it?"

The other guy said, "I'll send some of my own people down there to meet with you shortly. Don't contact me directly anymore."

Big Trouble asked, "Why?"
But instead of answering him, the guy just hung up.

Don1 knew that his system was clean and wouldn't leave traces that could be picked up by cellular detector devices. He decided to connect in to the line outside of the network he'd set up for Big Trouble and he saw why the guy hung up. He was using a cell phone that was dirty and could easily be picked up. Don1 made a mental note of that and decided to keep listening in on Big Trouble.

Big Trouble was confused about why the Judge wouldn't talk to him, so he called the Banker.

The Banker answered his phone and told Big Trouble, "The Judge got hit by a hacker so now he's paranoid."

Big Trouble asked, "How much information did the Judge give out?"

The Banker said, "We've all been compromised in some form or fashion."

Big Trouble went to his truck and sat down without saying a word.

Madame tried to get a rise out of him but he just pushed her away. She knew that something was really wrong. Big Trouble told the Banker, "We just wiped our old services and gone to one with a much better security system."

The Banker said, "I did too. The only one that didn't make a change was the Judge."

Big Trouble said, "I'm shutting down all communications with you guys until further notice."

The Banker said, "All meetings will take place face-to-face from now on in a designated meeting place."

Big Trouble had Madame go check on the girls while he took care of the business with the Banker and the Judge. She'd finally had a chance to finish her bath before she left. Big Trouble went to work immediately cleaning up all of the trash left by whoever was making

Meth on his land. He got a call from one of the Judge's people saying he was trying to find the area where the lab was. Big Trouble gave the guy directions and told him that he was already there cleaning up.

The guy said, "Oh, I see you now. I'm almost there."

Big Trouble asked, "How can you see me?" but the guy had already hung up. Then he heard a helicopter getting closer and closer, And then it landed a few yards away from him.

A couple of guys got out of the helicopter and started walking toward Big Trouble. When they got there, they introduced themselves as Mr. Woods and Mr. Jordan.

Woods said, "The Judge called us in because he was having problem with somebody setting up a Meth lab."

Big Trouble showed the guys everything he had found, and they started making phone calls, and taking photos and samples. It wasn't long before two more helicopters came in and Big Trouble had a whole crew of people moving around the site where he found the refrigerator.

Mr. Woods told Big Trouble, "Don't worry about a thing because we have everything under control.

Big Trouble asked, "Who are you guys?"

Woods said, "We're a task force set up by the government just to find and take down Meth runners and their labs."

Big Trouble asked, "Will I be in any trouble for this?"

Mr. Woods said, "You won't have anything to do with this. Just go on about your business as usual and don't return to this area of your land until further notice."

Big Trouble got in his truck and headed back to his house. He decided to go drive around and check out the rest of his land to make sure there were no more surprises.

Don1 was surprised to see Big Trouble in his shop again so soon.

Big Trouble said, "Tell me about the computer system that can do the tracking for me."

Don1 said, "My friend who was with me the other night handles that part of the business, but I'd be happy to put you in touch with him."

Big Trouble said, "If you don't mind, can you take me to his shop?"

Don1 was a little nervous about it, but he agreed. He told his store manager that he was headed to EoW's computer shop. He was so glad that EoW's place wasn't too far from his. Big Trouble insisted that Don1 ride with him and Don1 did in Big Trouble's F350 dually truck. The interior was customized and fit Big Trouble's personality like a glove.

Big Trouble told Don1, "When I do business with anyone new, I like to have the person who recommended the business with me."

Don1 understood that as a comfort zone, and he certainly didn't want Big Trouble to get uncomfortable.

Big Trouble apologized for the way Madame acted when they were in the shop together. He said, "When you got a headstrong woman like I got, you let them have their way and apologize to whoever got offended later."

Don1 just laughed and asked, "Do you really apologize?"

Trouble said, "No, but it sounded good saying it." Both of them laughed as they drove up in from of EoW's computer shop.

Don1 showed Big Trouble where to get the best computer system to meet his needs. He sent one of EoW's salesperson to get him and they quickly came back with him.

Don1 was just about to introduce EoW when Big Trouble said, "I remember him from the night of the fight."

EoW shook hands with Big Trouble, and then did a demo of the tracking software for him.

Big Trouble told the guy, "I have a bunch of dump trucks that I need to track and this will be perfect."

Don1 said, "You could track every truck and have it give you the statistics of each one if you'd like."

"What kind of statistics?" asked Big Trouble.

EoW said, "Like how long it's been sitting still or how many different locations it stopped at.

Big Trouble asked, "How much would it cost and how long would it take to set up?"

EoW said, "Me and Don1 could have it up and running in about an hour."

Big Trouble then took a look around the computer shop and saw the surround chamber that EoW had built. He asked, "What's inside that room?"

EoW said, "What's inside that room is the ultimate entertainment experience." Big Trouble headed straight for it. Once inside he wasn't impressed because all he could see was black walls.

EoW instantly went into his sales pitch about the entertainment chamber. He told Big Trouble about all of the sound proofing and speaker systems. He asked Big Trouble, "Are you in a hurry?"

Big Trouble said, "No," so EoW had him sit in the multimedia chair. Then he and Don1 left the chamber, and EoW started the program that showcased the entire chamber's special features.

While Big Trouble was in the chamber, Don1 and EoW had to talk.

EoW asked, "What in hell are you doing with Big Trouble?"

Don1 told EoW, "I had no choice because he was there in good faith."

EoW was confused so Don1 said, "Big Trouble didn't feel comfortable with references over the phone. He preferred to have people introduced to him face-to-face."

EoW said, "I guess you didn't want to make this dude uncomfortable."

Don1 said, "Now you've hit the nail on the head!" They two laughed and kidded around until the program finished running and they heard the chamber doors open. Big Trouble came out with a smile on his face, stretched and let out a big yawn.

EoW asked, "What did you think?"

Big Trouble asked, "How soon can I have that system installed in my house?" EoW's mouth dropped open and Big Trouble said, "Close it before the flies make it in."

Don1 burst into laughter and Big Trouble joined him.

EoW told him, "I can have all of the equipment delivered to your house after the initial inspection of the room that you want to turn into a chamber."

Big Trouble asked, "Can you come out and inspect it now?"

EoW said, "Let me get the tools I need and I'll be ready to go."

Don1 asked, "Is it okay for us to go ahead and install the tracking computer while we're out there?"

Big Trouble said, "Sure."

EoW asked, "Do you want me to go ahead and ring up everything?"

Big Trouble thought about it for a second and then said, "Only if you can ensure me that I won't be out of any more money and you can have it installed in less than one week."

EoW said, "It's a done deal!" and he and Big Trouble shook on it.

EoW and Don1 loved the setup at Big Trouble's house. His den was designed perfectly for the chamber. They'd already decided to do the installation themselves and split the money. EoW got all of his wiring specification put into his computer and it generated a detailed list of all the equipment he would need to install to make the chamber system work.

They told Big Trouble, "Call either of us when the equipment arrives, and we'll schedule your installation."

Big Trouble was happy with the two guys that Dan had introduced him to. He decided to send Dan a little extra present just for introducing him to them.

He called Madame and asked, "Have you taken care of that business with Dan yet?"

Madame said, "No, not yet."

Big Trouble said, "Send one of the girls by to take him the package from me and to give him a little present."

Madame was shocked to hear that. She started to ask Big Trouble what he was up to, but he hung up the phone.

Big Trouble signed all of the necessary paperwork and took the guys back to Don1's shop. He told the guys that he looked forward to seeing them later, and he pulled off.

Don1 and EoW gave each other high five as they went into the cell shop to talk. Frequency met them at the door.

Don1 and EoW brought Frequency up to date on the information they had on Big Trouble and Madame. Frequency told them what he did to Mr. White, but left out the part about the cool million in cash.

EoW asked, "How are all the other guys doing with their research?" so Frequency brought them up to date on all the info Webb had collected.

Don1 asked, "Did you find out what those numbers were for yet?"

Frequency said, "No, I didn't."

Don1 said, "Don't forget the 'gifts' we found under our cars."

Frequency said, "I'm putting something together that'll make those transmitters obsolete."

Don1 said, "I hope you do something soon cause the woman I've been hanging with likes to be alone with me, if you get my drift."

EoW then bust him out by saying, "She's got a nice ass and some hooters Too." Frequency burst into laughter as Don1 pushed EoW from the side.

EoW asked Frequency, "Have you heard how Doc is doing?"

Frequency said, "I haven't heard anything but I'd really like to know how she's doing myself."

EoW was about to ask him if he wanted him to check, but Frequency cut him off quickly by saying no.

Don1 then asked EoW, "What's up with you?"

EoW said, "I knocked off this one chick in the chamber, and I think the other broad is a Fed."

Frequency asked him, "What makes you think that?"

EoW said, "She dropped this dike chick in the club the other night like a hot potato!"

Don1 asked, "Why'd she do that?"

EoW said, "The broad came up behind her on the dance floor and grabbed her tits, so she dropped her like a sack of potatoes and we got out of there."

"Damn that was wild!" said Don1.

"Yeah, I think that messed up my chances of getting laid, which I hated because that chick was fine!"

Frequency said, "Why would you try to get laid by a woman that you think is a Fed?"

EoW asked, "Why not?"

All three of them had a hearty laugh behind that. Then Don1 went into his office to close down his store for the night. While he was working, he turned on his tracking software to see what Big Trouble was up to.

Big Trouble was just arriving to the area where Madame told him she was having a problem. As he got out of his truck there was one of his competitors talking crazy to Madame. Big Trouble got out of his truck and walked up directly behind Madame. Madame didn't hear him come up behind her because she was going off on dude telling him that he should leave before Trouble arrives.

The guy said, "It's too late for that,' as Trouble moved Madame out of the way. The dude's name was Whitaker and he supposedly had that particular area on lockdown.

Whitaker told Trouble, "You need to find another spot to send your girls."

Trouble said, "I told you almost a month ago that I was moving into this area so you had better step up your game."

Instead Whitaker went and got him some muscle from out of town. Whitaker told Trouble, "You're not the only big man in town."

Trouble looked at Whitaker and said, "If you think you got something, bring it on."

Whitaker held up his hand and waved. Next thing they knew a Hummer limo pulled up and five guys got out.

Trouble laughed out loud and said, "It looks as if you done got yourself a healthy set of male strippers."

The lead guy didn't like hearing that and started to rush Big Trouble but Big Trouble stepped aside and cold cocked dude with one to his jaw. The dude fell to one knee then got up. Big Trouble was surprised because most of the time that blow was good for a knock-out. The dude started to take off his shirt, but Whitaker stopped him.

Whitaker told Trouble, "You get the action set up, because it's time for you to step down."

Trouble told Whitaker, "When I finish with your boy I'm going to take over your whole organization and put you out of business once and for all."

Trouble watched as Whitaker and his five men got into the Hummer and left.

He told Madame, "Get the girls you dropped off here and move them back to our side until I finish this business with Whitaker."

Madame asked, "Are you going to fight all of them?"

Trouble said, "I hope not, but it looks as though I have no choice."

Madame had a look of concern on her face.

Big Trouble kissed her and said, "Don't worry; I have a surprise for Mr. Whitaker."

Don1, Frequency, and EoW listened in and heard everything! The three of them knew they had to be at that fight.

Frequency said, "Make sure you become buddies with Big Trouble and stay far, far away from his wild ass woman."

Don1 said, "My woman has already seen her and jumped me about her."

EoW said, "From the looks of Big Trouble, sex with her certainly ain't worth dying for!"

All three of them laughed and Frequency said, "I'm headed for home to check out what the Feds know so far."

Don1 and EoW asked, "What are you riding?" before they saw him get on a scooter.

Frequency told them, "I think they've tagged all of their cars and I don't want to take any chances."

EoW asked, "Is the scooter fast?"

Frequency said, "I had it up to ninety on the expressway."

EoW and Don1 asked, "Where did you get it?"

Frequency told them, "I got it at Al's Scooter Haven."

Both of them said, "Looks like we'll be seeing Al in the morning to get one." Frequency pulled off and left the guys in the parking lot.

He had promised his neighbor that he'd only be gone a short while and would return his scooter soon. As Frequency pulled up in his neighbor's driveway he was sitting on his porch drinking a beer. Frequency got off the scooter and sat beside him. Al asked, "How did you like the ride?"

Frequency told him, "I think you've got three sure fire sales coming in the morning!"

Al reached in his cooler and offered Frequency a cold Miller Genuine Draft beer, which Frequency accepted and took a hefty swallow. The cold beer was very good, so Frequency thanked Al and continued to drink.

Al said, "A car pulled into your driveway while you were gone and then pulled back out."

Frequency asked, "What kind of car was it?"

Al said, "I didn't get a chance to see it, because it left before I could get outside." Frequency said, "Don't worry about it, probably just somebody who was lost."

"Yeah, you probably right," said Al. "Anyway I got to go. I've got company coming over and I need to freshen up." Frequency said, "Thanks again for the beer, Al. I'll see you in the morning."

Al was shocked to see Frequency and his friends the next day.

He met them at the front of the store and asked, "You guys want to see my new line of scooters they just delivered?"

Frequency asked, "What about the one I borrowed last night?"

Al told Frequency, "That one is the last of a dying breed."

Frequency then asked, "Is the new one anything like the one I borrowed last night?"

Al smiled and said, "Oh, it's so much better!"

Don1 said, "Better is always good in my book."

EoW asked, "Do you have them ready to go?"

Al escorted them to the back of the shop and showed them the new line of Yamaha scooters. The guys were impressed that they started trying them out and looking for the color they wanted.

Frequency asked, "What are the specs on these scooters?"

Al said, "They have 650cc engines and a top speed of about 110 untouched, and 160 if you do the unwarranted modifications to them."

Frequency told Al, "I'll make it worth your while if you make these scooters scoot straight out of the store," as he threw Al an envelope filled with hundred dollar bills.

Al smiled and said, "You just kept me in business for another month!"

Frequency said, "If these scooters perform like I think they will you won't ever have to worry about your business finances again."

Al told the guys, "Pick out the scooters you want and I'll have them ready in about two hours."

They chose their scooters, and then headed off to work out a plan for the night of the big fight. Big Trouble had made sure EoW and Don1 knew about the fight and would be there to see him in his element. EoW and Don1 had mentioned to Big Trouble that they'd be bringing a friend who was more like a brother.

Big Trouble had asked, "Why haven't you introduced me to him yet?"

EoW lied and said, "He's a big as nerd who just likes to stay in the house messing with all of his computer stuff."

That made Big Trouble laugh as he agreed to meet Frequency.

Frequency told EoW, "I'm a get you for introducing me as a stay-at-home nerd!" as they all had a good laugh.

Big Trouble was in the best shape that he had been in a while. Mr. Whitaker had been a thorn in his side and he was going to get rid of him once and for all. Mr. Whitaker didn't know that Big Trouble had conditioned himself for a fight with his biggest goon and the other four he had with him. Big Trouble made things worse by cutting Madame off. He knew being around her would sap his strength for fighting. He knew she would take it out on the girls, but he needed to get rid of Whitaker and Madame had to understand that. Big Trouble had left the main house over a week ago and had not seen her since.

He had a gym built away from the main house just for his style of exercise. He had his trainer flown in to help him get ready. Big Trouble knew that once he took out everybody he would have to clean up another area to get Madame's girls working in.

When he got with his trainer, he told him, "I'll have to break some bones fighting these guys. I hit the lead guy with one of my best punches and only knocked him to his knees before he got up ready to fight."

The trainer then had an idea. He told Big Trouble, "Wrap your hands like you're going to do the night of the fight." Then the trainer went outside and got a bunch of tree branches and cinder blocks that had been left from construction of the gym. Big Trouble watched as the trainer set the blocks and tree limbs up and told him, "Beat the bag and save your harder blows for the tree limbs."

Big Trouble had been going through the new training procedures and could not figure out how it worked. His trainer would interfere from time to time and make him hit a piece of wood just for kicks. Big Trouble did not have a clue to what his trainer was trying to do until they went outside of the gym. His trainer had him throwing punches in the air, and then all of a sudden, his trainer tried to hit him with an old tree branch. Trouble threw a punch and the branch shattered. He looked at his hand in wonder because didn't feel a thing! His hand worked as if it was hardened steel.

Big Trouble told his trainer, "Do it again," and he did. Just as the first one shattered, the second one did the same. Now Trouble had a secret weapon to use on the Whitaker crew.

The day of the big fight had finally come. Big Trouble was livid with the anticipation of seeing himself action again. Whitaker had set up everything and had a few old school players to make sure that everybody accepted the outcome of the fight. Big Trouble had really stepped in it when he said he would take on all five people, but he would stand by it. This was not the first time and this time, he was better conditioned. Big Trouble tried to keep his mind of Madame but it was very hard. He heard that Whitaker and his people were having their fill of the forbidden fruit.

Big Trouble drove to the designated fight area and saw that it was filled with eager fight lovers. He saw his guests and went over to talk with them briefly. EoW and Don1 introduced Big Trouble to Frequency. Big Trouble shook his hands and Frequency got a feel for his power. He'd felt power like this before when he first shook hands with BDB.

Frequency would not go into this now because he didn't want to throw off Big Trouble before the fight. Frequency decided to pull one of his own Aces out to show Big Trouble that he was rooting for him.

He pulled out a brick of one hundred dollar bills and told Big Trouble, "This is twenty thousand in cash that I'm putting on you."

Big Trouble told EoW and Don1, "I like him already!" then went over to get in the ring.

Mr. Whitaker had just finished enjoying one of Madame's young ladies' oral pleasures. He told her, "Get comfortable sweetheart cause I'll be back for the rest," then he rounded up his five men and headed out to the ring. He was all set to take over, and his first order of business was to put that bitch Madame back out on the street turning tricks. Whitaker took a look at his men then lined them up to take on Big Trouble. The first one would be Razor, then Anvil; next would be Buck, then Jack, and finally Cutter.

When Whitaker and his crew showed up, he went straight to Big Trouble and told him, "Put up your best fight because you'll be working for me as soon as you heal from this ass whooping."

Big Trouble told him "When I finish with your boys, I'm coming for you. I have an associate who would love to use you for a toy."

Whitaker was so angry, he tried to hit Big Trouble but his crew stopped him. Trouble just laughed and turned his back on all of them as the fights were about to start.

The announcer told everybody to get their bets in before he introduced everybody from Whitaker's crew. The crowd booed when each crew member's name was called, then really cut up when Whitaker was introduced. Next he announced Big Trouble and the crowd went wild! Big Trouble did his usual spin in the ring, then stood stock still and waited for his first challenger.

Razor stepped into the ring and shadow boxed his style of fighting. Big Trouble watched to see if this guy would show his weakness. He didn't show anything until he cracked his elbows just before the fight began. Big Trouble decided that he'd target his elbows in this first fight.

As soon as the bell rang, Razor ran straight for Big Trouble. He threw a series of punches to no avail. He tried a couple of kicks, but found no target. He went for a sure fire strike series that he was known for, but as soon as he went for it Big Trouble punched directly at his elbow. Trouble hit him solidly on the elbow and

Razor grimaced in pain. Big Trouble threw a series of punches which all landed solidly. Razor tried to block the next punch, but he didn't move fast enough. Big Trouble caught him directly on the temple. Razor couldn't shake off the impact as he felt himself falling to the floor. He tried to get up, but Big Trouble ended the fight by breaking Razor's arm at the same elbow he'd punched earlier. Razor's fight was over and Big Trouble put a notch for another fighter beaten.

Whitaker sat there without moving, as he shouted, "You just got lucky. You won't be able to make it through the next one."

Big Trouble just laughed and prepared himself for his next opponent. Anvil jumped into the ring and started attacking Big Trouble before the bell even rang. Big Trouble fended off his attack and caught Anvil in the chest with a high knee. Anvil backed off his attack and the bell rang to officially start the second match. Big Trouble didn't get a chance to scout Anvil for a weakness, so he just tried different techniques to throw Anvil off. It worked like a charm when Big Trouble scored a direct punch to Anvil's nose, which sent blood squirting all over Anvil's face. Trouble closed the deal when he threw a series of hard punches that all connected solidly. Anvil was knocked to the mat with an uppercut that sounded like thunder. He was unconscious before he hit the mat, and the fight was over.

Big Trouble looked at Whitaker and smiled. Whitaker called Buck over to him and whispered something in his ear. Buck nodded an acknowledgement and got into the ring. Big Trouble stood up and the bell rang. Buck used a jujitsu type of fighting style that Big Trouble had faced before. He knew that style was based on elbows and knees. Big Trouble waited for the bell to ring then went to the middle of the ring. Buck just stood there with his arms out. Big Trouble threw a series of punches with no results. Then Buck moved to the side and caught Big Trouble with a couple of short jabs to the chin. Big Trouble took the jabs then delivered a hard punch to Buck's head that knocked him to the ropes. Buck quickly recovered and caught Big Trouble in the stomach and head with a series of punches. Buck threw an elbow that caught Big Trouble on the side of the head, and then kicked him in his ribs. Buck went for an upper cut but missed, as Big Trouble threw a lumberjack swing that caught him dead on his left thigh. The blow sent pain throughout Buck's body and he tried to recover but it was too late.

Big Trouble knew he had hurt his opponent and decided to end the match. He threw a series of jabs that Buck blocked with ease. Buck didn't know that Big Trouble was setting him up to fall. Big Trouble came at Buck again, but this time he threw a hard punch downward, hitting Buck on the left thigh and shattered the bone. Buck hit the mat screaming, and Big Trouble turned his back and went to his corner. The referee asked Buck to continue but he couldn't. Big Trouble had knocked off another one of Whitaker's henchmen.

Whitaker called his man Jack and told him to handle his business. Jack got into the ring and waited for the bell. As soon as it rang he jumped into the air and caught Big Trouble with a kick to the face. Then he kicked out again and caught Big Trouble in the stomach. Big Trouble threw several blows but they didn't even come close. Jack was too fast for his punches! Big Trouble went for a grappling hold, but Jack side stepped him and hit him in the forehead. Big Trouble tried grabbing Jack, but Jack easily moved out of his way, and then hit Big Trouble several times. Big Trouble couldn't touch Jack due to his quickness. He knew he couldn't waste too much energy chasing Jack, and he knew that Jack would keep moving all night and hitting him at will until he was exhausted. Big Trouble came up with a way to slow Jack down.

Big Trouble rushed Jack knowing he would side step him. When he did Big Trouble stepped on his foot and punched him hard in the jaw. Jack couldn't believe it! He tried to regroup but Big Trouble had him where he wanted him. Jack tried to move around Big Trouble but he felt Big Trouble's weight increase the pressure on his foot. Big Trouble had his foot pinned under his foot and he was not about to release him. Big Trouble fell to one knee and delivered a crushing blow to Jack's right foot, making Jack scream in pain as he felt the ligaments tear and the bones crack in his foot. Big Trouble immediately delivered a solid upper cut to Jack's chin, which knocked him off his feet and to the mat. The referee went over to Jack and found that he was unconscious. He signaled for the bell and declared Big Trouble the winner.   Mr. Whitaker was furious! He couldn't contain himself as he went and got Cutter out of the limo. Whitaker knocked on the window and the door opened. Cutter stepped out of the limo and headed for the ring.

Big Trouble was sitting in his corner with his eyes closed getting himself mentally ready for the last fight of the night. He knew he would be in for the fight of his life, and he promised that he wouldn't give up. He opened his eyes and there was Cutter directly across from him. Big Trouble saw a younger version of himself in Cutter and decided to let him make the first move.

Cutter had been waiting for this fight and he was ready. As soon as the bell rang he walked over to Big Trouble and threw a straight right punch to Big Trouble's head. Big Trouble threw 2 punches and caught Cutter in the chest and head. Both men grabbed one another as they fought for position. Cutter pulled Big Trouble towards him and bit him on the arm. Big Trouble hollered as Cutter ripped the flesh from his arm.

Cutter laughed and said, "You taste sweet."

Big Trouble couldn't believe that this guy had just bit a plug out of him! He threw an elbow that caught Cutter upside the head. Cutter shook it off and hit Big Trouble in the lip with a straight punch.

Blood flowed from Big Trouble's lips as he threw a punch that opened a gash over Cutter's right eye. Cutter threw a right cross then left; both jabs hit their mark sending Big Trouble back against the ropes. Big Trouble sprung off the ropes and jumped into the air colliding with Cutter. He put his shoulder deep into Cutter's chest which knocked him off his feet. Cutter got to his feet slowly and was met with a knee directly to his forehead. Cutter fell back onto the mat and tried to get up. Big Trouble was all over him elbowing him in the head. Cutter caught several elbows to the head before he kneed big Trouble off him.

Cutter's face was bloodied and he was a little disoriented. He saw Big Trouble charge him and he swayed to the left and hit him hard in the ribs, then elbowed him to the back of the head. Big Trouble fell to one knee then threw an upper cup that caught Cutter on the jaw. Cutter staggered to the ropes then used them to launch himself into Big Trouble. Big Trouble and Cutter both fell to the mat and started trying to get up. Cutter shook his head trying to clear it from all of the hits that Big Trouble had landed.

Big Trouble knew his ribs were broken but he couldn't let Cutter know it. He spun around on his side and delivered a kick to the back of Cutter's head. Cutter grabbed his head as blood spurted from another gash. Big Trouble got to his feet despite the pain in his ribs. Cutter saw Big Trouble coming closer, so he made one last desperate attempt to stop him. As soon as Big Trouble stood over him, Cutter launched himself forward head butting Big Trouble in the ribs. Big Trouble felt his bones crack as he hit the mat in pain. He was hurt badly and now everyone knew it.

Cutter stumbled to his feet and took in the cheers from the crowd. He staggered over to Big Trouble and head butted him directly between the eyes. Big Trouble hit the floor screaming in agony. Cutter then placed a well-directed kick to Big Trouble's other side breaking more ribs. Big Trouble lay on the mat in a fetal position. All kinds of thoughts were going through his head, when he felt Cutter pick him up and throw him over his shoulder. Cutter had Big Trouble in a position where he could drop him on his knee and break his neck.

Cutter made the mistake of telling Big Trouble, "I enjoyed your woman last night and really look forward to making her walk the street for me." Then Cutter pushed Big Trouble slightly off of his shoulder then down hard across his knee.

Big Trouble moved his head just in time to prevent his neck from snapping. The blow hurt like hell, but at least he was still alive. Big Trouble thought about Cutter on top of Madame and all of his pain turned to rage. Cutter had turned his back away from Big Trouble and wasn't aware that Big trouble was now standing. The crowd yelled as Cutter turned around to see a very angry Big Trouble standing across from him.

Cutter screamed as he ran toward Big Trouble. The two met in the center of the ring and started trading blows. For every time Cutter hit Big Trouble, Trouble would hit him twice as hard until Cutter couldn't take anymore. Big Trouble kept swinging until Cutter fell to the floor a bloody mess and stayed there. The referee went over to him to stop the fight as Cutter got up and charged Big Trouble. The crowd went crazy!

Just like he'd practice with his trainer, Big Trouble turned and threw one of his most vicious punches, catching Cutter in the nose and sending the broken bones into his brain. Cutter's eyes rolled around then outward as he collapsed to the floor dead. Big Trouble stood in the ring and raised his arms outward when the bullets hit him in his shoulder and the right side of his chest. Mr. Whitaker held the 9mm pistol steady and laughed as he put it away. He turned to leave and was met with a barrage of fist and kicks as the crowd attacked him. They beat him senseless, but did not kill him.

EoW and Don1 jumped into the ring to try and help Big Trouble. They saw that he wasn't dead, so they called for an ambulance. Big Trouble was busted up badly, not to mention the two gunshot wounds.

The ambulance driver asked, "Who's going to ride to the hospital with this man?" but nobody answered.

Frequency, Don1, and EoW said, "There's too many of us to ride with him, but we'll meet you at the hospital and bring his next of kin with us."

The ambulance took off and the guys got together to come up with a way to help Big Trouble.

Don1 said, "Don't forget that I have all of Big Trouble's GPS information in the computer."

Frequency said, "I can make CMAX call Madame then hang up. CMAX initiated the command and, just like clockwork, Madame was alerted. Madame tried calling Big Trouble's phone but there was no answer. She kept trying until one of the ambulance attendants finally answered it.

He told her, "Big Trouble is being taken to the hospital and you need to meet us there as soon as possible."

Madame had been about to go into an orgy with a couple of the girls. She dropped everything and left for the hospital. She was crying hysterically as she sped across town to check on her man. She knew she should have been at the fight, but he'd made her promise not to come. Now he was being driven to the hospital in an ambulance and she was afraid she was going to lose him.

Chapter 14

Stuck On Stupid

As the plan that Mr. White put together was initiated, the demolition of Frequency Hunter and his entire crew was happening. Mr. White had done his homework, and now he was going after what he'd left behind. He had Don1 and EoW singled out in their own environments. He knew he couldn't attack them in their businesses, but they were fair game once they stepped outside. He had his henchmen, the Hudson Brothers, set up the hits, and had told them (A) not to be nice and (B) to make sure Frequency did not miss his one-way trip to the morgue.

John and Mark Hudson recruited some serious street muscle to handle this job. They had to make sure they had no direct ties to the hit. They couldn't be present, and they couldn't be tied to anyone who was present or involved in any way. If they were even minutely implicated, they'd most likely be locked up for a very long time. They had no desire to go to jail for Mr. White, especially not while he was still indebted to them. White was close to paying them off, and once he did they could sit back and leave all of his dirty work up to him.

Mark and John decided to split the jobs into three different events. First, John would take out EoW, then

Mark would take out Don1, after that both of them would take out the main ingredient, Frequency Hunter. They knew they had to get Freq away from his home,' cause Mr. White told them if Freq makes it to his house the end would come quickly for all who were against him. White wouldn't tell them what was in the house, but the brothers had an idea of how to keep Hunter away from his house. First John and Mark went to the computer shop, where they saw EoW closing up for the night.

John said, "Watch this." He used a laser pointer to flash a car that was parked on the other side of the street. Two guys got out of the car and headed straight for EoW. John and Mark sped off knowing that the planned hits had begun.

Next the two brothers headed to Don1's cellular phone business. Mark used tactics less brutal than his brother John. Mark had already sent two guys to rig a flammable liquid in line with Don1's fuel system in his car. To ensure that Don1 was inside the car when it went up, he'd make sure that he left it in a state of panic. So then they pulled up outside of Don1's cell shop and Mark's men used a laser pointer to signal that all was in place.

Don1 walked to his car and noticed a couple of guys walking away from his car. He screamed at them and they started to run. Don1 chased after them until one of the guys stopped and fired a shot. Mark knew it was time to leave so he and John pulled off and headed for Frequency.

Frequency was just leaving the movie theater. He had not seen a movie alone in years and it felt awkward. He was headed for his motorcycle when he noticed that the parking lot was full. He thought about the amount of money that was generated from the night's revenue. Freq got on his motorcycle and decided that he would take it out on a night ride as he pulled off the parking lot.

He hadn't gone far when he noticed a car following him. He blew it off as coincidental and didn't let it disturb him. Freq decided to see if the occupants of this car were really interested in him. He throttled up and the motorcycle responded magnificently! Not missing a beat, the car soon disappeared into the night life. Mark and John had to regroup since they weren't able to overtake Frequency and get rid of him once and for all. Now they were stuck as they tried to figure out where in hell he went on that motorcycle.

Mark came up with another idea. He told John, "I need to catch up with the girls in that motorcycle club."

John thought about it and said, "We can let one of them do our dirty work."

Mark said, "Now that's a good idea!" and they headed to the area where all of the serious street races went down.

Sure enough the GBG, Girl Biker Group, was in full attendance. They were notorious for taking the clothes off of inexperienced riders and taking the bikes of the experienced ones.

Mark and John were looking for the leader, Krystal. They found her sitting on her bike with her girl on the back. She had won her in a race for pinks and the dude ran off and left the lady standing. Nina was a stray that was just trying to make ends meet when she ended up with Krystal. She wasn't into women, but when you have nothing but the clothes on your back, you have to do what you got to do.

Nina saw John and Mark walking up and approached them to stop and talk.

Mark said, "I need to talk to Krystal."

Krystal saw Mark and John together and very quickly got herself together since it seemed like there was about to be trouble. Krystal had a run in with Mark before that caused her to get the ass whooping of her life. Mark did not take it lightly when anyone owed him money. She'd lost a few good women to the Hudson Brothers and still owed them.

Krystal told Nina, "Get off the bike," and Nina did so before Krystal dismounted.

Mark walked up on Krystal and grabbed a hand full of her hair. Krystal didn't scream, but Nina ran and got the rest of the GBG.

John started to laugh and said, "Krystal, when are you going to learn that we do not forget anything?"

Krystal became submissive to Mark and he said, "Now that's better. Just because you decided to take a woman lover doesn't mean that I'm through with you."

The GBG showed up and witnessed their leader in a submissive role. They knew that they were 21 deep and could take out these two men if Krystal gave the word.

John turned around and made an announcement. He said, "All you bitches have been working for me and my brother, so I suggest you settle down and listen to our little proposal."

The women didn't like what they heard so John put it another way. He pulled an army grenade out of his pocket and pulled the pin, then said, "If anyone moves I'll have the coroner dispatched."

The GBG stood still and silent.

John grabbed one of their youngest members and whispered in her ear, "You better not even flinch!" Then he took the grenade and hooked it inside the waist band of her pants and asked the group, "Do I have your attention now?"

The women answered, "Yes."

John told Mark, "I believe I have their undivided attention."

Mark told the ladies, "There's a biker riding around tonight that I need taken care of."

The GBG was cool with the idea of taking out one lone biker.

Mark added, "If you can verify that this biker is gone for good, I'll release Krystal from her debt to us."

The women all indicated that they understood.

Mark said, "You can release the girl now."

John pulled the grenade from the young lady's pants and pushed her to the group, as Mark turned to Krystal then reached around her and grabbed Nina.

Krystal started to move on Mark, but he did

something that froze her in her tracks: he passed Nina to John.

Krystal knew that if she just flinched, her girl would have been killed.

Mark grabbed Krystal and said, "You tell your girls to sit tight while you and this young lady escort me and my brother back to our car."

Krystal addressed the GBG and told them, "You all go on and finish racing, and none of you had better lose or the consciences will be severe."

Then she turned to Mark and said, "Let's walk."

John snatched Nina and headed for the car walking very fast 'cause he knew what his brother was about to do.

Krystal was his girl no matter what, and she knew this. She also knew what Mark was about to do to her. There was a part of her that couldn't resist Mark no matter what he did, but the rest of her couldn't stand him!

When they got to the car, John pushed Nina inside and she fell on the back seat with her legs open. He got an eye full of her nakedness because Nina could only wear underwear when Krystal gave her permission. He slammed the door knowing that he would hit that later.

Then John looked at his brother and said, "I'll be in the car."

Mark threw John the keys then turned his attention to Krystal. He grabbed her and she resisted until he slapped her firmly on her cheek.

Krystal rushed him and found herself being easily overpowered. She tried to escape, but Mark had a firm grip on her. He pushed her onto the back of the car and made her bend over backwards till she submitted. Krystal was now a woman for this man. She slowly slid down to her knees to address Mark's throbbing manhood. She knew she couldn't hit or bite him because she liked living. She knew John would kill her and the whole crew if she hurt Mark in any way.

Krystal reached up and started unzipping Mark's pants. He was already hard and waiting on her.

She took a deep breath then she opened her mouth to receive his manhood. She started off slowly and then increased her pace. Mark had Krystal by the back of the head and loved what she was doing. She knew that if she could keep Mark away from her she could live her life, but that was not happening. Mark was really getting into this blowjob. He had Krystal's head going like a pumping station in overdrive. Krystal began gagging from time to time because Mark was assaulting her throat. He was the only man that was touching her sexually, and this time he was not going to take it lightly.

Krystal's jaws started locking up on her and she knew she'd better not bite Mark so she slipped down and started caressing his jewels. That made Mark let out a moan and knew he had to have her. He would not take 'no' for an answer this time.

He pulled Krystal up by the hair and spun her around. She knew she was about to get fucked and she knew it was going to be hard. Her body was already wet just from touching Mark. She never could resist him once she gave him some head, and this time, just like the others, she had no choice. Her pants were down around her ankles and Mark was mounting her. She felt him enter her and her knees started to shake. Mark knew he was going to fuck Krystal and had it on the agenda to make her come back to him. He thrust forward and felt the wetness of her body and heard Krystal gasp as he was all the way in.

Krystal lay forward across the trunk of the car and let Mark have his way. Her body rolled with his to get the maximum penetration with each trust. Krystal felt herself coming hard. She reached back and grabbed Mark's arm as her orgasm came down. It made her shudder and say things that should have not have come out of her mouth.

Mark knew this was the moment he had been waiting for. The punishment began with some serious hard thrusts inside of her. Krystal was singing the song of good sex as her legs gave out on her and she came with harder intensity than the last time. Mark pulled out of her and turned her over on the trunk. He pushed her legs back over her head and reentered her body. Krystal felt another hard orgasm and just let Mark have his way.

John was in the car losing his mind! He heard Krystal on the back of the car and he was ready for his own action. John turned to the little lady in the backseat and witnessed her staring out the back window watching Krystal and Mark fuck. She was masturbating and had no shame about it.

John opened the glove compartment, grabbed a condom and said, "Waste not want not<" as he pushed Nina over and jumped in the backseat. Nina wasn't scared of John, but some perverted feeling in her mind wanted to watch Krystal being dominated by this man.

John was about grab her when she turned to him and said, "Hit it from the back, I've got to see them finish."

John didn't care what she wanted since he already had the condom on. He got behind Nina and started stroking. He went inside her body and heard her let out a grunt when he was all in. John started trusting hard and Nina was pushing back to receive him. It wasn't long before Nina let out a slight cry signaling that orgasm had been achieved. John was just getting started. He pushed into Nina harder with each thrust as he tried to bust that much needed nut. Nina was already going through another orgasm as she saw Krystal's legs go up in the air. Nina thought of the many times Krystal had her in that position. Nina thought of the many times that Krystal made her crawl to her and submit. Nina was enjoying the moment when John trust himself into her ass. Nina let out a muffled scream of pain as she bit into the leather of the seat, but John was in heaven as the wetness of this woman's body absorbed his sexual torment.

Nina watched as Krystal grabbed Mark's neck and shouted, "I still love you!"

Mark couldn't deny that this was why he was doing this anyway. He had Krystal talking just like he liked it.

He made her promise that when the night was over she would be in his bed.

Krystal shouted, "THE SUN WILL NOT FIND ME ANYWHERE EXCEPT WITH YOU!"

Mark had what he wanted and started thrusting like a mad man. Krystal was letting out grunts with each thrust. Mark had her now and she was not about to let go! He came hard with one last thrust that made Krystal release everything she had left. Mark didn't move another muscle, but instead just let the wind blow on his and Krystal's love connection. Then he lowered her legs. She tried to stand, but was a little wobbly.

Mark looked into Krystal's eyes as she pulled up her pants and said, "The sun better not catch you anywhere but with me!" Krystal knew what that meant and started walking away from him on her wobbly legs.

Then she turned to Mark and told him, "John can have the girl. Her name is Nina."

Mark shook his head and went to get in the car. As he opened the door he heard a grunt that told him his brother had already taken possession of Nina. He jumped into the car and headed for Frequency's house. He knew he had to leave notice that Mr. White had indeed been there. As he sped off heard his brother and Nina finish up in the back seat.

John pulled off the condom and had Nina clean him up. She was slow about giving a blowjob after sex, but this man was nobody to play with. Nina started giving John some head. His semen was tart, but that wouldn't stop her as she really went to work on him. She was really getting into it when she heard John's brother say that Krystal had given her away. That made Nina furious! She would have said something, but John was pushing down on the back of her head. She just continued bobbing her head up and down on John and hoping he'd hurry up and cum.

John was really enjoying Nina's work. This girl could suck the chrome off a trailer hitch! John knew that he'd have to keep her around, so he backed off on pushing her head down. Nina started to relax and turned her body so she could look at him as she worked on him.

She pulled her mouth away from him just long enough to say, I'm going to suck you dry!"

John couldn't believe what she said, so he hollered out to Mark, that "I'm going to see if she's really hungry."

Nina really started stroking on John's manhood, and was not going to let go until he was fully finished. She started sweating as she worked on making John cum. Mark heard slurping noises coming from the backseat so he turned up the music to drown out the sounds. Nina started working with the rhythm of the music. John knew he couldn't hold back any longer and he let go one hellafied orgasm that made his eyes damn near cross!

Nina went at him with even more intensity to make sure she didn't miss a drop. John thought he was drained, but Nina was still pulling on the last traces of cum when she sat up and asked, "Now am I worth keeping?"

John wanted to scream out HELL YEAH, but Mark would have had a fit. He just smiled and said, "We will see."

Just then, Mark pulled up one block from Freq.'s house. He told John, "Drop some fireworks on the house."

Nina wanted John and Mark to keep her around so she, "I'll do it."

John looked to Mark and got the okay, then gave her 4 grenades and told her, "Throw them in the house with the green roof."

Nina got out of the car with the grenades and ran toward the house. Once she made it around the corner, she saw the house in the middle of the street. She also saw that the people next door to her target had left their gate open. She slipped into the yard and saw an opening in the gate at the back. She was just small enough to slip through the opening, but as soon as she made it through, all of the motion lights came on. Nina pulled a pin on one of the grenades and threw it at the light, knocking it out. Then she pulled the pin on the other three grenades and threw them through the windows. Two of them made it through the glass, but she over through one and it went onto the roof and rolled off.

The grenade followed the slope of the roof, and then fell to the ground beside the gas main. Nina didn't stay for the results. She ran and jumped into the car just as the first grenade exploded. The sound was music to John's ears! He knew the grenades had a fifteen second delay, and they had worked like a charm. The other two exploded and flames erupted throughout the house. The fourth grenade was a charmer that exploded and ruptured the gas line. It shook the whole street as Mark, John and Nina drove away.

Frequency was enjoying his night ride when his cell phone started going off. He was riding down by the bluff's shore line when the phone vibrated. Freq pulled over and took his cell phone from his jacket pocket. The number "21" flashed across the screen. That number meant one thing only: EMERGENCY. Freq headed for home. He'd programmed the system to send out a simple numeric signal when any alarms where tripped. The constant vibrations meant that multiple alarms had been tripped.

Freq went into panic mode because he knew something major had gone wrong. He had turned the bike around and was headed for the house. He wasn't paying attention to his rear view when 2 riders pulled up on either side of him. Freq felt a hard thud on his helmet. One of the riders hit him on the helmet with something. Freq looked over at the rider. The bike sported a serious red flame job. He then looked over at the other rider's bike and it sported a serious blue iced paint job. Frequency knew he was in trouble. It was the two riders known as Fire & Ice, who were notorious for taking out riders on the racetrack. Most of the time, the riders they 'took out' never rode again.

Freq had a feeling that Mr. White was behind this, but for now he had to concentrate on getting away from Fire & Ice in one piece. He knew the bike he was riding was no match for the Suzuki Hayabusas. Freq just had to try and finesse his way out of the situation.

The rider on the red flamed bike aimed for Frequency's left arm and hit him dead on it. He felt a sharp pain shoot through the left side of his body as he saw the rider draw back for another swing. He waited until the rider swung and hit his gas tank. Then he grabbed the weapon and tried to yank it loose. It didn't work because the rider had a lanyard at the end of it wrapped around their wrist. Freq found himself in a tug of war with the rider on the red bike. He didn't notice that the rider on the blue bike had pulled out a chain and was getting ready to throw it.

Freq turned, but it was already too late. The rider on the blue bike threw the chain squarely into Frequency's front wheel. The chain seized the front end up and tossed Freq over the handlebars into the air. As Frequency was thrown from the bike, the safety lanyard built into his jacket was pulled. Instantly, the jacket and pants filled with CO_2 gas powered air. This was a new invention from a bike racer who'd had too many accidents and wanted to cushion his fall. The device worked perfectly! Freq felt his body stiffen as the air pockets filled with air. The bag in his helmet deployed and created a brace for his neck. Within seconds Frequency felt the impact as he hit the ground. His body tumbled as the forward momentum rolled him into a nearby guard rail.

Freq hit the rail hard, but he was all right. Just as he was about to try and get up, he felt himself being dragged very fast. He guessed that Ice had decided the wreck wasn't enough, and figured he'd drag Frequency around until a body part came loose. The leather crash suit had been tested as a flight suit for fighter jet pilots, and could withstand a lot of sliding. Ice ran up and down the strip of graveled land before turning hard toward the shore line.

The chain came loose and tossed Freq over the guard rail and down a steep embankment. He felt himself tumbling and crashing into everything that went by. All of a sudden he felt as if he was airborne again, then he hit the water. He was tossed into the river and the currents were not kind. Freq was worn out, and couldn't fight as the mighty river threw him around.

Fire and Ice looked at each other. How would they be able to prove that they had gotten rid of Frequency? Ice searched the ground nearby and found Freq's cell phone, splattered with blood and displaying the number 21.

Fire told Ice, "This will have to do," and they took off to find Mark and John to give them the news.

Webb had just finished working on a customer's car when his phone went off. He saw the code and politely finished the business at hand. Then he rushed for Frequency's house. He jumped in his work truck and was driving it hard when he saw a Black Dodge come up from behind. He knew it was a setup, just like he knew His old truck was no match for the Dodge as he drove it even harder. The car pulled past Webb as guys hung out the windows and started firing shots.

Webb stomped the gas pedal and the old pickup rammed the Dodge from behind. One of the guys fell from the car and hit the ground rolling. Webb started laughing and prepared to ram the Dodge again, until the remaining people in the car rained bullets on his old truck until smoke burst from under the hood.

Webb saw his only outlet and ran the old truck through a huge plate glass window into a sporting goods store. The Dodge tried to follow but the tires burst on the frame of the glass. Webb kept stepping on the gas until the truck wouldn't move anymore. He quickly jumped from the truck and ran further into the store. Three men jumped from the disabled Dodge carrying their weapons. People were running every which way trying to get away. One of the guys saw Webb and started shooting. One of his bullets caught Webb high on the shoulder, and Webb rolled on the wall but kept running. Webb knew he had to get his hands on a weapon. The guys that were chasing him followed him around the corner thinking that he was defenseless. Webb passed a set of bow and arrows, but couldn't use it because of his shoulder. Then he saw a crossbow with some serious tipped arrows, so he grabbed it knowing he had to make the shot count.

Webb saw how he could use the store's ladder system to get the jump on the guys trying to kill him. He climbed atop the highest shelf just behind a bunch of new tires. He saw the guys split up to search for him. One went around the center section, and the other two on each end. Webb could see them all. Two of them had handguns, but the other one had a Bulldog shotgun.

Webb knew he had to take out the guy with the shotgun first. He waited to make sure he had the shot. His shoulder ached like hell, but he wasn't going to let that stop him. He breathed in deeply as he pulled the trigger, and the crossbow responded and released the arrow into the air. The guy never felt a thing as the arrow pierced his skull. He fell to the floor and Webb turned his attention to the other two. He started kicking the tires and that started a chain reaction among the other items on the shelves. The tires rolled off and bounced in every direction hitting one guy in the chest and knocking the other over the paint center. Webb jumped down and ran for the center aisle. One of the guys got up and started shooting, hitting Webb in the leg.

He dove on the floor and slid into the guy with the arrow in his skull as he said, "That's gotta hurt"! Then he grabbed the Bulldog shotgun from the dead man's hands. It was time for him to fuck the remaining two guys up! As he stepped out he saw one of them coming over the center island and he released two shots. The gun reacted violently and he missed. He knew he couldn't make that mistake again. He ran around the other aisle and saw the other guy walking around the scuba gear. Webb jumped out and fired three rounds one hit a scuba tank which burst and threw the guy into the path of the other two rounds. He hit the ground dead.

Then Webb turned to face the last guy who was running down the aisle shooting and screaming. He just kept firing until he was out of bullets. He didn't hit Webb once, but he did manage to shoot up the store. He stopped running and screaming when he realized he was out of ammo. He slid to a stop directly in front of the barrel of the Bulldog shot gun. Webb smiled and pulled the trigger once. The guy lurched back as the bullet sent him sliding down the store aisle. Webb dropped his gun to the floor when another bullet hit him on the right side of the chest. It was the fourth guy, who had fallen from the car during the chase. He was scarred and torn from head to toe, but he was still alive.

He walked over to Webb and said, "You should always look a man in the eye before you kill him."

All of a sudden Webb heard a rush of gas from the scuba gear area. When the third guy was running and shooting he'd accidentally pierced one of the tanks. The tank exploded and came off the stand like a torpedo, hitting the fourth guy dead in the chest. Webb grabbed the Bulldog and pulled the trigger, but it only clicked. The guy got up and went for his gun until he heard a familiar sound. Webb had cocked the shotgun. The fourth guy turned to reason with Webb, but it was much too late.

The last words he heard were, "LOOK AT ME!!"

BDB was just getting back from picking up his new lawn equipment and tractor when he got a call from Webb.

Webb said, "Come get me man, I'm hurt bad!"

BDB told Webb, "Activate your phone's GPS system. I'll get Long Haul be there soon."

Webb told BDB, "Hurry because I think everybody's probably been ambushed."

BDB headed straight for the storage center where they were keeping Long Haul. When he opened the door the alarm sounded. BDB grabbed the door of Long Haul and the alarm shut off automatically.

He started the engine and the truck's display panel came to life. BDB heard CMAX come online, and he remembered that Frequency took CMAX offline to move him from the house to Long Haul. CMAX went through his usual salutations, and then his sensors started making BDB aware of how bad the situation was.

BDB told CMAX, "I've spoken to Webb and he thinks they've all been ambushed. No word yet from Don1, EoW, or Frequency."

CMAX said, "I have the ability to activate their individual GPS locators."

BDB said, "You lead the way and I'll get us there."

First they found Webb. He had limped his way out of the sporting goods store and hid under the bed of a trailer that was being unloaded. BDB drove by the store and saw cops everywhere. He saw Webb's pickup truck inside the store. BDB drove around until according to CMAX they were directly beside Webb. BDB was looking around when he saw Webb's arm hanging down. He threw the truck in park and rushed to pull Webb down.

Webb said, "I'm so glad you made it."

BDB said, "Me too my friend, me too," as he quickly got Webb inside Long Haul.

Then he asked CMAX, "whose next?"

CMAX said, "Don1 is next since he's only about three blocks away." "Okay, that's where we're headed," said BDB.

Don1 was in pain. When he hit the alarm system on his car he heard a tremendous explosion. The last thing he saw was the door of his car flying straight at him. When Don1 came to, he saw BDB looking down at him. BDB was saying something, but it was all muffled. He helped Don1 get into Long Haul then started driving.

Don1 felt like crap! His ribs were sending pain signals up through his skull, he could barely move, and couldn't hear anything. He knew something was wrong when he saw Webb stretched out on the couch with blood coming through his clothes. Don1 was just glad to be in Long Haul because that meant things were going to get better.

BDB asked CMAX, "Who's next?"

CMAX said, "I have EoW moving down toward the warehouse district. I still have no signal from Frequency."

BDB headed straight for the warehouse district. EoW had been beaten badly. He was in somebody's trunk headed for, who knows where? He had been unconscious after somebody hit him on the back of his head. When he came to, they started taking turns using him for a punching bag. EoW knew his ribs were busted and his nose was broken. He knew they had smashed his hand with something. He couldn't move because they had him hog tied. EoW had always realized that there was a higher being in life, so he was okay with dying. He just couldn't fathom being tortured.

He heard some guys talking and saying that they needed to have an old warehouse crate destroyed. The other voice said that there was a $125.00 fee for dumping and destroying. He heard the voices haggle over the price, and EoW was really upset when he realized that these guys were haggling over a price to kill him. If that didn't beat all! EoW began to struggle against his bonds, but to no avail. They had made sure he couldn't break the ties that had him bound.

EoW was lying on his side when he felt whatever he was in start to move again. It felt as if he was being carried. Next he felt it sway back and forth, then go airborne. He felt a jolt as his container slammed to the ground and rolled several times before it finally came to a halt. EoW passed out again.

BDB was riding through the warehouse district and following CMAX's instructions. They rode around to the back of one warehouse where a lot of old crates where being stored and destroyed.

CMAX told BDB, "Go straight for the one marked DO NOT OPEN WITHOUT PERMIT."

BDB took out a crowbar and started prying the box open. There inside was a severely beaten EoW, whose packing carton was waiting to be destroyed. EoW came to long enough to see a familiar face. He smiled but it caused him so much pain that he blacked out again.

BDB had three of the guys in Long Haul, but he still had to find one more.

Frequency was floating down stream in the river. His body had gone numb so he couldn't move to see where he was. Freq knew he needed to get word to the guys of his whereabouts, but he couldn't find his phone. He then remembered that he might have dropped it when he crashed. Freq was desperate, in pain all over his body, and he was floating in the river. He knew that whoever did this wanted him dead. It hit him like a ton of bricks that it had to be Mr. White. He didn't have the courage to do it himself, so he paid someone to do his dirty work for him. The more Frequency thought about it, the more his ambush pointed to the Hudson Brothers.

Frequency got mad as hell the more he thought about it! Then he got worried, He knew that if they came after him, they show nuff would have gone after Webb, Don1, and EoW. The good part is that White knows nothing about the newest member, BDB. And that was a silver lining in his gray cloud. With that very thought, Freq used his right hand to reach into the lining of his helmet and activate the GPS device that he installed just in case he ever got separated from his cell phone. Frequency pushed the button on the back side of the device and saw the little glow of the light. He dropped his arm and relaxed because he knew help was on the way.

BDB had just gotten EoW into Long Haul, when CMAX reported, "I have two signals reported on Frequency.

BDB asked, "Which one should we target?"

CMAX said, "One signal is coming from the cell phone and the other is the emergency device in Frequency's helmet."

BDB made the choice to go to the cell phone. He headed in the direction of the phone. CMAX reported that the signal was moving at a very high rate of speed just six miles ahead. BDB stepped on the gas to see if Frequency was in some kind of trouble. CMAX told BDB to pull over and let whatever it was pass, and then chase it. BDB pulled Long Haul over and waited. Within minutes two motorcycles zoomed by. BDB was about to give chase until CMAX said that Frequency was not on either bike. He pulled up the passing video and neither rider matched Frequency physically.

BDB said, "Hurry up and track that other signal!"

CMAX said, "It's done. It seems the signal is going down stream in the river."

BDB asked, "How far away?"

CMAX said, "If we continue in the direction that we are going we should see him in less than 15 minutes."

BDB told CMAX, "Plot me a course to overtake him," and began to follow that course with purpose and precision.

Frequency was cold and exhausted. He was doing everything he could to stay on his back. He promised himself that he'd buy stock in the company that made the suit that he was wearing. Freq thought he was delusional when he heard the familiar voice of CMAX online.

Frequency said, "Is that you old friend?"

CMAX replied, "It is I Sir."

Freq then asked, "But how?"

CMAX said, "You and the guys gave me a whole new array of technologies with the upgrade."

Freq asked, "Can the guys hear me?"

CMAX said, "Only one can hear you, the rest are in pretty bad shape."   Frequency's heart stopped for a second. Then he asked, "Who made it?"   BDB reported in, "Good to hear your voice my friend."

Frequency came to the realization that BDB would be the saving grace for them all.

BDB told Freq, "We'll rendezvous in exactly five minutes."

Freq said, "Okay, just don't stop talking to me."

Don1 came to and grunted as he tried to move. CMAX addressed him and told him his vitals and the percentages of his life expectancy.

Don1 quipped, "Just what I need, a computer with no sense of humor!" Then he asked CMAX, "What's the status of the rest of the group?"

CMAX said, "All of the crew members are badly hurt. EoW and Webb are the worst so far."

Don1 asked about Frequency Since CMAX hadn't mentioned him.

CMAX said, "He's in the river but we're about to pick him up."

Don1 just fell back in his chair.

BDB stopped Long Haul, got out and started to release the wench. Then he went to the storage area and got the climbing gear. He put on the gear and told CMAX to lower him down to the river.

CMAX told BDB, "Make sure you don't lose your ear piece, because that's the only way I can guide you to Frequency."

BDB said, "I understand," and CMAX started lowering BDB. It was dark outside and BDB could barely see. The under current was strong, but the water's surface was calm. BDB let CMAX use his precision calculations to ensure that he wouldn't miss his friend. CMAX lowered BDB directly into the path of Frequency.

CMAX said, "I'm going to put you in the water now," and dropped BDB directly onto Frequency. BDB grabbed Frequency with a death grip to make sure he wouldn't lose him.

BDB shouted, "I'VE GOT HIM!" CMAX reversed the winch and pulled BDB and Frequency from the river. BDB was just glad to see his friend was still alive. He knew he had to hurry up and find medical help for them all. He felt the land bump his shoulder so he put his legs in position to walk as the wench pulled them to safety. Frequency looked at Long Haul like it was a giant angel. He could barely move so BDB got him into Long Haul before he put up the climbing gear. Then BDB headed for the hospital. Frequency was strong enough to tell BDB not to go to the hospital.

Freq told BDB, "The people who did this to us would finish the jobs if you take us to any hospital in the city."

BDB asked, "Where should I go?"

Frequency said, "I have an old friend who'll know what to do. She runs a rehabilitation center on the outskirts of town. No one would think to look there for us."

BDB asked, "Why?"

"Well because this clinic uses experimental practices of healing. Some of them are archaic, but others are so technologically advanced that the government has it set up like an area 51," Freq said.

BDB said,"You mean like space alien type shit?"

"Something like that my friend," said Frequency.

"Well, all I'd like to know is what stuck on stupid individuals did this to you guys?"

Freq said, "I know who did it. Very soon there will be a time to get even. First we have to heal, then payback will definitely be put on the menu."

BDB just shook his head.

Frequency told CMAX, "Plot a course to Roz Wells."

BDB looked at Frequency and was about to ask a question until he saw that Frequency had passed out.

Chapter 15

U Don't Say

Roz was just getting out of the shower, when her computer acknowledged an incoming transmission. She went to the screen and couldn't believe what she was reading. Frequency was coming in to the facility that he'd made possible. Roz sent a reply and an acknowledgement to allow vocal replies from the computer. The voice she heard next was a shock to her. A man who called himself BDB told her that Frequency and his crew had been hurt badly. Roz knew all too well of Frequency and his crew, what she couldn't figure out was what person would do them harm.

Roz said, "Just follow my instruction to get to the center."

BDB said, "CMAX is online so I'm going by its instructions. Frequency has passed out again from his injuries, but he'd already instructed CMAX to get me to you."

Roz said, "Come straight here, and don't waste any more time."

BDB said, "Lady, if I could fly there I would!" and went full throttle toward the center.

When he arrived, BDB was amazed at how well hidden the center was. It was way on the outskirts of their county and looked as if it was an old farm. He was tripping when the floor of the barn he parked in began to lower him into a garage. When it stopped descending, BDB parked Long Haul and opened the door.

He saw a lady hurrying out to meet him, and she introduced herself as Roz. BDB had to really pay close attention because she talked really fast! She was babbling about something that BDB couldn't figure out. He thought to himself this woman must have been a cheerleader once in high school.

BDB grabbed Roz and said, "Lady slow down!" Then he took her inside Long Haul where the guys were all sprawled about, still bleeding from their wounds Roz was surprised to see them all in such bad shape.

She told BDB; bring them into the clinic immediately!" As he did, Roz pulled out enough surgical tables to hold all of the injured. BDB unloaded each of the guys one by one. He unloaded Frequency last and when he laid him on the table, Frequency came to with a loud groan of pain. Roz ran straight to him and tried to comfort him.

Frequency looked into her eyes and said, "I'm glad to see you."

Roz said, "I promise I'll get you back in shape in no time. Then we'll talk."

Frequency pulled her close and whispered something in her ear. Roz was shocked to hear what he said, but she promised Frequency that she would do it as soon as she got everybody patched up. Roz went immediately to work on Webb to remove the bullets from his body and get his wounds closed up. Next she worked on Don1 and his numerous cracked ribs and bruises. After Don 1, she worked on EoW who was busted up so badly she had him damn near mummified by the time she was finished.

Then she finally got to Frequency, who wasn't as badly injured thanks to his crash suit. But being in the river for so long had him damn near frozen to death, not to mention all of his scrapes and bruises.

Roz was totally worn out when she finished. She went to find BDB to thank him, and found him inside Long Haul going over the tape of the bikes that had passed them earlier. He finally got CMAX to enlarge the footage so he could get a better look at the bike riders and their license plates. One said FIRE and the other said ICE.

BDB had all of the information that he needed. He let CMAX do the rest. The crazy thing about the whole situation was that they were riding around with Frequency's cell phone which has GPS tracking. CMAX had a direct link to them and BDB was ready to put in the work. He was about to go live when Roz called out to him.

He went to see what she wanted and there was Webb, sitting up on the table.

BDB ran over to him and said, "Lie back down."

Webb said, "I'm alright, but those bitches have to pay for what they did to us!"

BDB said, "I'm about to take Long Haul and go handle business!"

Webb laughed but cut it short because it hurt too much. He handed BDB a USB drive and said, "Give this to Roz."

BDB asked, "What's this?"

Webb smiled and said, "It's a way to get even."

BDB smiled and helped Webb lie down. Then he called for Roz and she came in a hurry. He gave her the USB drive which she put it in her computer. The information it contained even amazed Roz because it contained a program that told her how to hook Long Haul to the main computer of the clinic. She followed the instruction, then went inside Long Haul and typed in the proper codes.

CMAX came online and said "Hello Roz."

Roz typed in "Hello," and CMAX told her that voice command was activated and she could just talk.

Roz asked, "What's this program for?"

CMAX said, "This program was created by Frequency to be used only if something should happen to him or any of the other guys."

Roz asked, "What do I need to do?"

CMAX said, "Nothing you have done everything necessary to set Frequency's plan in motion. Now just sit back and watch."

The lab's floor elevator system opened and a Chevrolet SSR came out. Roz was so shocked; she was speechless, as she tried to figure out when and where that car came from. CMAX then told BDB that all of the tools of his industry were inside the car. BDB went to the trunk and opened it up. Inside, he found an arsenal befitting a small army! BDB checked each weapon because he knew what he had to do.

CMAX told BDB, "Get in the vehicle and I'll guide you to the proper destination."

Roz was trying to stop BDB but he was much too strong to stop. He got in the car and followed CMAX's directions. Roz watched him drive away, and then went back to the injured and started working on them.

BDB was driving like a bat out of hell! CMAX had the GPS system on lock and he was giving BDB audible directions as he drove. BDB made up his mind that he was not going to take any prisoners. It would be an all out war when he made these people pay for what they'd done to his friends. BDB started reminiscing about how he used to take on hits for the drug mob. He also thought about how he'd sent many a man to the morgue just for talking smack. Now he had a real purpose! He was going to teach these people that when they mess with his friends, they have to answer to him.

CMAX came online and said, "You're exactly five minutes from your destination."

BDB slowed the SSR down and got himself mentally prepared for battle. Then he pulled over, went to the trunk and pulled out plenty of weapons. He had everything that he used to use and then some. He had his favorite type of weapon, the shotgun. The one that was inside of this truck had a drum on it that held fifty shells. There was a mini gun and a couple of m16s.Then BDB found something that made him laugh.

It was a chrome bat that looked as if it had some kind of gizmo built into it.

BDB asked CMAX, "What does this do?"

CMAX said, "Use it only as a last resort."

BDB said, "Acknowledged," then put his earpiece on and headed for the house that had several motorcycles and cars parked outside.

Mr. White had assembled all of the people who took on his plan, and all of them were trying to collect. Mr. White told everybody that they'd have to wait for the Hudson brothers to approve all payments. He was really paying attention to what Fire and Ice were saying about how they dragged Frequency down the street and into the river. They laughed when he tried to outrun them as they were beating on him. Everybody was laughing and having a good time while waiting on the Hudson brothers. White had plenty of food and drinks, plus there was a good movie on the big screen television.

BDB had all of his weapons locked and loaded, so when he burst through the door retribution began. He kicked the door down and started firing. He pointed and pulled the trigger at everything that moved. Most of the people were totally caught off guard, but White had set it up for the Hudson Brothers to do the same thing. When he saw BDB he took off for the back of the house and jumped through a window.

White hit the ground hard but the fear of being killed kept him moving. He ran to his car, started it up, and sped off. He immediately called the Hudson brothers but couldn't get in touch with them. BDB was still shooting and hitting everything that moved inside White's house.

Fire and Ice knew they'd been setup and decided to fight back. The two women pulled mini Uzi's and started firing at BDB. He quickly jumped behind a table as the rounds peppered the table. BDB dropped the m16s and started using the handguns. He used them till he ran out of bullets. He dropped them to the floor and started using the big shotgun. Fire and Ice knew they had a huge problem when the first shot he fired took out a chunk of the wall beside them. They took out running just as one of the other guys started shooting at BDB, so he turned his attention away from Fire and Ice for a moment.

BDB made short work of the last few guys, and then turned his attention back to Fire and Ice, but they'd already made it to their bikes and started them up. They burned out as fast as they could. BDB ran for the SSR and chased after them, but Fire and Ice rode like demons possessed! When they realized that they were being followed and he was coming fast, they pushed the bikes even harder. The car was still right on their butts. Fire and Ice were trying everything to get away until Ice's bike was hit on the chain sprocket. The bike screeched and veered as Ice tried to control it as much as possible. Just as Ice regained control, the SSR hit the back wheel sending Ice flying through the air. She hit the ground and rolled until she hit the guard rail. BDB then went after Fire who stopped and decided to go back to help Ice. Fire turned the bike around and went straight for Ice. BDB aimed straight for the forks of the bike and fired the shotgun. The bullet hit the fork and shattered it instantly. The impact flipped Fire over the handlebar and onto the pavement. BDB stopped the SSR and went over to Fire, but when he pulled the helmet off he saw the pretty face of a woman. BDB didn't care as he dragged her to the SSR and tied her hands to the rear tow bar. Then he got back into the SSR, drove over to Ice, pulled her helmet off and found another woman. He did the same with her as he did with Fire.

He got back in the SSR and drove to a hidden section of the road. BDB got out and walked along the side of the road, looking for something wet. He scooped up some muddy water and walked back to the SSR. Then he got the ashtray out and gathered up some more water and went over to Fire. When he poured the muddy water into her mouth she came to spitting and coughing.

BDB threw the rest of the water in her face and asked, "Why did you two attack Frequency?"

Fire said, "I'm not talking!"

BDB told Fire, "I want to see what your girlfriend has to say." He went back to the place where he got the muddy water and got some more. BDB followed the same procedure with Ice and achieved the same results.

He told the ladies, "I appreciate your loyalty. I'll be in the car when you're ready to talk." BDB lowered the convertible top and started the SSR. Then he headed back to the house that he'd just shot up. Fire and Ice were being dragged far worse than anything they'd done to Frequency, and they screamed their protests until they had no voices left. .   All the while, BDB kept hollering back, "I can stop as soon as you tell me what I want to know."

Out of nowhere, a car sped up and slammed into the back of the SSR, killing Fire and Ice instantly. When he realized what had happened, BDB turned and fired a shot into the car's windshield. When he was hit in the shoulder by a shot from the car, BDB stomped the gas pedal and the SSR took off. The back bumper was totally ripped from the SSR with Fire and Ice still attached to it. BDB held his arm as he drove like crazy to get away.

The Hudson Brothers had seen BDB dragging Fire and Ice and decided to handle business before the girls could be persuaded to talk. Now, they were after BDB and John was shooting the SSR to pieces! John hit the SSR with every shot, but couldn't hit anything that would stop it.

When he ran out of ammo he got back inside the car and yelled to his brother Mark, "Try to get me closer to him!"

BDB laughed to himself thinking about all of the modifications the guys must have made to the SSR to keep it running like it was under these extreme circumstances. He was feeling invincible so he decided to try something truly crazy. He suddenly spun the car around and headed straight for the car that was shooting at him! The Hudson Brother both hollered as they saw the SSR coming straight at them. BDB stuck the barrel of the shotgun out the driver's side window and started pulling the trigger. The first shot hit the engine of the car and shut it down; the second shot busted the right front tire and axle and sent the car into a rapid rollover.

The brothers braced themselves as the car tumbled over and over, then hurriedly bailed out as soon as the vehicle stopped. John grabbed the M16 from the roof and Mark grabbed a 9mm that they had inside the car. BDB saw the fellows get out with guns and aimed the SSR directly at them. Mark looked at his brother and they opened fire. A couple of the bullets tore through the windshield and hit BDB in the left side of his chest and arm. He grimaced in pain as he released two rounds from his shotgun that found the gas tank of their overturned car, which exploded into flames and sent the brothers flying. Both of them hit the ground hard and appeared to be unconscious.

BDB was in too much pain to go back and make sure they were dead. He had to make it back to RozWell, because he was now in very bad shape himself. BDB started the SSR and headed back to the center as CMAX came online and talked to BDB to keep him going. BDB made it to the center and pulled inside. He told CMAX that he was in bad shape and CMAX told him that he was down to 45% of his life expectancy. BDB tried to laugh, but it hurt too much. He heard the voice of Roz just before he passed out. Roz looked at the car and knew that this man had been in a war.

She shook her head and mumbled to herself, "I sure would hate to see the other guys."

Mr. White was on the phone constantly trying to get in touch with the Hudson Brothers, but neither of them would answer their phone. Finally, Mr. White got a call from Mark saying he needed help badly. White ran the car hard to find him and couldn't believe the damage just one man had caused. Mark and John were beaten up badly, but were able to walk to White's car and told him everything that had happened. Mr. White could only assume that the demise of Frequency had happened due to the story he'd heard from Fire and Ice.

Mark told Mr. White, "John and I took out Fire and Ice and the Dude in the SSR did the rest."

White said, "Yeah I already know about that because I was there when it went down."

John asked, "Why did you run?"

White said, "I wasn't about to fight a gunfight with a knife!"

John then asked, "Do you have any idea who sent that guy?"

White said, "I don't know for sure, but I think it might have something to do with Frequency Hunter."

The Hudson Brothers knew they'd gotten themselves into a real fight this time. They said, "You mean this dude destroyed almost everything in your house in less than an hour? And now we can't go back there because the police are involved."

Mr. White said, "I just pulled some strings to get in touch with a CEO at the bank who'll clean up the mess, but we have to find out who this guy is."

Mr. Wimple had indeed received a call from Mr. White during which. White told him everything that had transpired since he set his vendetta against Frequency Hunter in motion.

Wimple laughed at the story and said, "I need to meet with you and your superior as soon as it can be arranged."

Mr. White asked, "Can you take care of this little matter with the police?"

Wimple said, "It's already been taken care of."

Mr. White asked, "Do I need to come to this meeting alone?"

Wimple told him, "Come alone and make sure you're unarmed. You'll get a phone call with the exact details of the meeting time and place."

White hung up the phone and told the Hudson Brothers what was going on. John and Mark were cool with everything and now had to turn their attention to the big man who had caused them so much trouble earlier that day.

Roz was in a zone of information! CMAX was giving her all of the information that Frequency had compiled on Nanotechnology. Roz was reading it because she couldn't heal the crew as fast as need be. Frequency would regain consciousness periodically, but he still didn't have enough strength to remain conscious for a long period of time. Frequency was pushing Roz to use the nanobytes to help heal the crew.

Roz finally got all of the fellows to sleep and began reading the information on nanotechnology. Roz was amazed at all of the information that Frequency and CMAX had put together, including the following:

Nanotechnology, a Modern Industry

Visualize a scenario, seemingly unrealistic yet personified in the sci-fi classic Fantastic Voyage, molecule-sized machines with the ability to travel through the human bloodstream while repairing clogged arteries. A nano-machinery prototype under development at New York University could prove to be a stepping stone toward this captivating fantasy: injectable, programmable, molecule-sized robots.

Intrigued by the technological advances and break-throughs, Nano-technology became the topic of my research. I have added inserts from various sources throughout the world, which see this technology as the cure of all cures to support my theory. To help with the understanding of "Cure All," is to open your imagination to how the human body cures itself. The immune system, common to all human beings, with proper health and diet fights off infection introduced to the human structure. Its primary goal is total destruction. Now let's add new technology to the immune system. As you have seen on shows like Fantastic Voyage and Star Trek, the doctors never make surgical incisions to rid the body of infections. The body is injected with a type of medicine, nanodes, and a few minutes later the person is healed. I know what you are thinking, "Yeah that's fine and dandy for Star Trek, but how does it relate to me today?" My response is this: Nanotech-nology is no longer science fiction. Well-funded research exists and includes a broad spectrum of hiring "project managers" developing time lines when testing will begin on diseases such as AIDS, cancer, leukemia and even the common cold. As we sit in our homes, a solution to the world's infectious disease problems is being researched and developed. The thought may make you really nervous, microbots.

Waiting for Breakthroughs; April 1996; by Stix; 6 page(s)

"ThatÆs the messiah," confides Edward M. Reifman, D.D.S. The Encino, California, dentist has paid hundreds of dollars to attend a conference to hear about robotic machines with working parts as small as protein molecules. Reifman nods toward K. Eric Drexler, the avatar of nanotechnology. Drexler has just finished explaining to a strange mix of scientists, entrepreneurs and his own acolytes the fact that nanotechnology may arrive at any time within the next three decades. The world, in his view, has not fully grasped the implications of molecular machines that will radically transform the way material goods are produced.

Nanotechnology is the manufacturing of materials and structures with dimensions that measure up to 100 nanometers (billionths of a meter). Its definition applies to a range of disciplines, from conventional synthetic chemistry to techniques that manipulate individual atoms with tiny probe elements. In the vision promulgated by Drexler, current nanoscale fabrication methods could eventually evolve into techniques for making molecular robots or shrunken versions of 19th-century mills. In the course of a few hours, manufacturing systems based on DrexlerÆs nanotechnology could produce anything from a full-sized rocket ship to minute disease-fighting submarines that roam the bloodstream. And, like biological cells, the robots that populate a nanofactory could even replicate themselves. Finished goods in this new era could be had for little more than the cost of their design and of the raw material involved--such as air, beet sugar or an inexpensive hydrocarbon feedstock. The Drexlerian future posits fundamental social changes: nanotechnology could alleviate world hunger, clean the environment, cure cancer, and guarantee Biblical life spans. Here is a press advisory titled $4 Million in Grants to Research Environmental Impact of Nanotechnology.

The EPA has awarded grants to 12 universities to investigate the potential health and environmental impacts of nanomaterials: unusually small man-made particles that are measured in billionths of a meter (nanometers). Nanotechnology allows scientists to work at the molecular level, atom by atom, to create materials and structures with fundamentally new functions and characteristics. Nanotechnology is a promising new field that may lead to great advances in environmental protection. For example, filter systems for drinking or waste water could be designed at the nanoparticle level to remove even the most minuscule of impurities. Nanoscale materials are being used in a wide range of products, such as sunscreens, composites, medical devices and chemical catalysts. As new nanomaterials are manufactured, there is the potential of human and environmental exposure from waste streams or other pathways entering the environment. Currently there is very limited scientific information on the effects of nanomaterials on human health and the environment.

Six of the grants awarded will investigate whether manufactured nanomaterials could have any negative health effects or environment impacts. The other six grants will study the fate and transport of nanomaterials in the environment. The grants were awarded through EPA's Science to Achieve Results (STAR) research grants program.

Now with EPA's addition to a project of global proportions look at mass of resources that will be tapped in the Operation Management industry. Another thought is how many project managers will be hired, with how many timelines. The processes are endless, and to except that now that we have a new entry into the manufacturing process is just utterly exciting. Not only will the project manager have to watch deadlines and calculations, they'll be working on a project that will change the course of history and the ways we survive for many generations to come. More information on the nanotechnology STAR grants and the 12 recipients   is   available   at: http://cfpub.epa.gov/ncer_abstracts/index.cfm/fuseac tion/recipients.display/rfa_id/352

Dr. Nadrian Seeman, NYU professor of chemistry and head of the nano-robot research team, said the device might be used to revolutionize angioplasty -- a procedure that eliminates blood clots with tiny balloon catheters.

"I recall an incident when the balloon exploded while deploying a stent [an instrument that provides support for tubular structures or body cavities]," said Seeman. "If the stent had been expanded by a nano-robot, this type of accident would not occur. Indeed, the stent could have been a nano-robot, itself, one that expanded to its ultimate state based on a simple chemical reaction, rather than air pressure." The only question is whether the small devices will have the muscle to take on their enemies. Scientists and re-searchers have long sought a nano-robot that could work autonomously in the bloodstream, Seeman said. However, he said, "we do not yet know how much force, if any, our device can transmit." Since the tiny device is made of strands of DNA, it is biologically compatible with a living organism.

"If this is to be used for problems such as clogged arteries you may be able to have an advantage by not having to introduce foreign objects," said Leemor Joshua-Tor, a researcher who works with the structural biology of DNA at Cold Spring Harbor Laboratory, on Long Island, New York. The basic anthropoid anatomy of a nano-robot could be just around the corner. "However, as you know, the essence of robots is that they do things not look like things," Seeman said. Within the next decade, scientists say these tiny robots could actually perform tasks. The NYU prototype has two rigid arms that can rotate between fixed positions, a goal the researchers worked eight years to achieve.

"You really can control this using environmental conditions according to how the arms are oriented or twisted in respect to each other," Joshua-Tor said. "It is a little molecular motor and it looks a lot more controllable than anything previously done."

This prototype is the largest and potentially most practical of all nano-machines thus far, Seeman said. It functions much like an elbow, while smaller devices act like finger joints. Unlike other nano-machines, which are built from regular molecules, the NYU scientists used synthetic DNA to build theirs. Seeman has been working with DNA as a building block for almost 30 years, but until now couldn't make the spaghetti-like helices of DNA stiff enough to function as an arm. Exploiting the fact that DNA molecules build themselves, the team created a cube and a truncated octahedron, among other structures, but their branches were too floppy. "It was relatively easy to make the previous versions, but because they were not stiff, we could not demonstrate the motion," Seeman said.

By fusing two Holliday junctions together, the researchers created what Seeman describes as a "four-lane highway." The group then had their rigid structure.

But before we unleash nano-robots inside our arteries, Seeman sees other uses for the invention.

"Most of the applications that I have in mind are analytical procedures, for the measurement of scientific parameters," he said. "I expect nano-devices to be involved intimately in molecular computing." And with all this new technology all the operational management professional will have to use all of their learning abilities to help the scientist with the timelines of getting a project of such massive proportions completed on time. In March of 2003, researchers said the big little science known as nanotechnology could improve medical diagnostics vastly within the next two or three years, Many people think of nanotechnology -- the process of altering or building materials a molecule at a time -- as a way to build microscopic machines. In medicine, it means making tiny particles using either organic or inorganic materials.

If the different kinds of nanotechnology were in a race, biomedicine would be in the lead. The most likely applications will be in biomedicine, not electronics. In computing and electronics, researchers have yet to figure out how to wire particles together, but with biotechnology, no wires are involved, just molecules. Within biomedical nanotechnology, diagnostics will come of age the quickest. In two to three years, there should be something significant in the clinic.

For example, researchers are developing diagnostic tests for cancer and cardiovascular diseases. When a person is sick, markers -- genetic material or proteins -- for the disease appear in body fluids. If blood or urine samples from the sick person are mixed with a solution of synthetic nanostructures, they can be designed to emit light in the presence of specific disease markers.

This kind of test would improve the accuracy of current tests on the average of about 50 percent – a dramatic improvement. Diagnostics now have the capability to look only for one marker at a time, while new tests based on nanotechnology could detect multiple markers simultaneously.

Soon nanotech treatments will follow their diagnostic partners. It will be a medical breakthrough to combine diagnostics with treatment as stated by the researcher of the project. "Treatment will have to come later because it requires regulations, which might take another five to seven years."

The wait and investment could be well worth it. Can you envision a "smart bomb" treatment for cancer? A nanostructure could recognize a cancer cell, bind to it and trigger the release of a therapeutic drug. So far, though, there have not been any breakthroughs but the field is progressing incredibly fast. As stated by Jorge Barrio, professor of molecular medical pharmacology at the University of California, Los Angeles, "Nanotechnology in its many dimensions will be incredibly important in medicine." Barrio's team is working on diagnostic tests for Alzheimer's disease. They are developing non-invasive, in vivo (inside the body) probes to detect brain plaques associated with the disease. He said the key to medical advancements is in understanding nanostructures and how to prevent their formation, as in the case of Alzheimer's plaques. "It's not only intriguing -- it's very relevant," Barrio said. "Everybody knows a parent or relative who has Alzheimer's." Early diagnosis should be tied to hope, Barrio commented. Currently there is no treatment for Alzheimer's. However, he said developing diagnostics based on molecular understanding of the disease also could lead to treatment possibilities.

As of Feb. 18, 2005 – SEMI® announced that NanoForum® 2005, an international conference for leaders in nanotechnology and the semiconductor industry to explore commercialization of nanotech applications, will be Oct. 5-6 at the Marriott, San Jose, Calif. NanoForum is the only global nanotech conference that leverages the technical and manufacturing expertise of semiconductor equipment, materials and service suppliers.

NanoForum 2005 will explore expanding opportunities for nanotechnology in 10 major markets, as well as the latest technological developments for producing nano devices. Markets to be addressed include medical, biotechnology, automotive, consumer, energy, industrial controls, defense, aerospace, information technology and telecommunications. Technology topics include materials, metrology, deposition, surface conditioning, etch, implant, planarization, diffusion and annealing.

"With the participation of nearly 400 delegates from North American, Europe and Asia, NanoForum 2004 launched a global discussion of commercializing nanotech between the semiconductor industry, and investors, entrepreneurs, scientists and government officials. NanoForum 2005 will bring key groups back together to share their expertise and insights and to explore the evolving opportunities and technological developments for nanotech."

Who is SEMI, you may be wondering. SEMI is a global industry association serving companies that develop and provide manufacturing technology, materials and services to make semiconductors, flat panel displays (FPDs), micro-electromechanical systems (MEMS) and related microelectronics. SEMI maintains offices in Austin, Beijing, Brussels, Hsinchu, Moscow, San Jose (Calif.), Seoul, Singapore, Tokyo, Shanghai and Washington, D.C.

Now with all the respect given to FedEx, General Motors, Grocery chains, and department stores, here is a technology that will change the way all of the known businesses operate, and it will use the Operations Management industry in its highest and lowest forms to make deadlines on time. It will reach out and affect all parts of the daily lives of humans throughout the world. Nanotechnology has stepped out of the imagination into today. As a person striving for additional knowledge, the industry of nanotechnology will push me to the limits of imagination. Then it will let me take what I imagine and make it reality. I will make something you can actually use and not just watch on television.

Roz was totally convinced that this was the solution to healing the crew. She went to CMAX and started trying to make changes to the Nanobyte file but she couldn't access it. She knew it would be well protected and thought that maybe Frequency used a code that she would know. Roz was stumped and decided to take a break. She turned on the television and started watching the news.

She had totally forgotten that BDB had activated the voice command in CMAX. She was engrossed in the news and when the news caster made a certain statement about a house fire in the hills, Roz said out loud "U don't Say!" CMAX came to life and acknowledged the command. CMAX integrated all of the center's computers into it, then started manipulating the data and the machines to work in order to make Nanobytes become real and useable.

All of this was happening while Roz was watching television. She did not take notice until CMAX took over the television and told her that nanobyte programming was complete. Roz was floored! She was about to type in a command, but CMAX told her to speak.

Roz asked, "What's happening?"

CMAX told her all of the procedures that he had performed.

Roz then asked, "Is it possible to make a nanobyte?"

CMAX activated the robotic arm to bring her a surgical sheet with five needles on it. CMAX told Roz to inject all of the guys with this injection.

Roz asked, "What is it?" but there was no response from CMAX. She decided to do what she was told. She grabbed the needles and injected each man in his right butt cheek. Neither guy budged when she stuck them so she was able to finish quickly. Roz went back to CMAX and said she had finished the task.

CMAX came back online and said, "Now we wait."

Roz asked, "What did I just do?"

CMAX responded, "You've just injected the guys with nanobyte serum."

Roz was overwhelmed and asked, "What if they have an allergic reaction or something?"

CMAX replied, "You've just injected the guys with the cure of all cures."

Chapter 16

N the Clique

Mr. White was all set for his meeting with Mr. Wimple with everything in place as specified.

When Mr. Wimple arrived to pick up Mr. White he said, "We will address each other by last name only."

Mr. White said, "I understand. "I need to know where we're headed."

Wimple told White, "I don't know either since I'm a passenger in this vehicle just like you. I guess we'll find out our destination together." Wimple fixed himself a drink then fixed one for White. They sat back and enjoyed their ride with some business conversation until the vehicle came to a stop.

The driver opened the door and told them, "Get out and follow me." They walked into a separate area of an old warehouse, then down a dark corridor and around several turns before getting to a huge freezer door. The driver put his hand on the door and a biometric reader scanned his hand. The door made a clanging sound then opened slowly. There was a long table inside with a man sitting at one end. Wimple went in first and sat beside the man at the end of the table. White entered next and as he got closer, he started to recognize the face of the man sitting there.

Judge Warren Hill introduced himself and shook hands with Mr. White. He told him, "I appreciate the information that you gave Wimple."

White asked the Judge, "Do you remember the case of Frequency Hunter?"

The Judge said, "Of course I remember that case. That man was a menace! We were fortunate to have some inside Intel to get him."

White said, "I was the inside Intel, Judge, and now I'm getting ready to do it again only on a much bigger scale."

The Judge sat down and told White, "I have something that might be of interest to you."

White said, "You know if it doesn't pay, I don't play."

The Judge called for one of his guards who came with a briefcase. The Judge opened the case and gave White the information on the battle they had the other night. The Judge said, "I've already cleared up that little matter. My people made it out to be a drug deal gone badly."

White said, "I appreciate that."

Then the Judge threw a manila envelope full of money to White.

He said, "The money is for your services at the bank. How would you like a piece of the action within my organization? I'm not a greedy man, but I expect you to carry your weight."

White thought about it and asked the Judge, "What is it that you need?"

The Judge got up and told White and Wimple to follow him. They walked down another corridor and White could hear someone grunting in pain. He could also hear a woman shouting and screaming then more grunting. The Judge smiled and said, "We're just in time."

The judge opened the door and there before them was a naked man tied to an apparatus that had him locked in a very compromising position. There was a woman behind him thrusting deeply up into him. The man was grunting and trying to scream, but he had a gag in his mouth. The Judge called to Bobbie and the 'woman' turned around, stopped thrusting, and pulled out of the naked man. White then got a good look at the woman called Bobbie and noticed that 'she' was a 'he or at least half of him or was.

The Judge introduced White to Ms. Bobbie. The Judge then asked Ms. Bobbie, "Do you have any information for me?"

Ms. Bobbie reported everything that he had learned so far.

The Judge walked over to the naked man and pulled the gag from his mouth and said, "Mr. Whitaker, you have disappointed me for the last time,"

This had been Whitaker's fate every day for the last week. Bobbie had made him his play toy and there was nothing Whitaker could do about it. Bobbie and his boy toy had raped Whitaker so much and so often, he didn't know what day it was.

The Judge then slapped Whitaker and said, "I have something to show you."

Mr. Whitaker followed the Judge's arm then his hand down to his finger that was pointing to a man the Judge called Mr. White.

The Judge said, "Look at him closely because he's your replacement."

Whitaker started pleading with the Judge but he turned to Ms. Bobbie and told her, "Finish your business with him."

Bobbie nodded and told the Judge, "Give me an hour and then I'll see you at the meet and greet table."

The Judge turned and told Mr. White, "Look at failure and understand that it is not tolerated."

As they walked out of the room Ms. Bobbie resumed her torment of Mr. Whitaker, but this time he would finish. He had a long knife just beside the contraption used to torture her victims and this time it would be used. Bobbie humped until she felt her orgasm come and then he picked up the knife and stabbed his victim with a clean thrust that killed him instantly. Ms. Bobbie stayed inside him until she knew he was dead, and then made several more thrust just for the fun of it. He then withdrew himself and left to get cleaned up for his appearance at the meeting with the organization's leaders.

The Judge sat down and watched as all of his organization's members filed into the room and took their seats. He had Mr. White sit next to him opposite Mr. Wimple. Next came Gay Mack, and then there was an empty seat, where Ms. Bobbie would sit when he finally arrived. As usual he was late. Next there was Madame and beside her in a wheel chair she'd brought

Big Trouble. On the opposite side of the table was a pissed off Benjamin Dover and next to him was Cupcake. The Judge looked at his watch and was about to call the meeting to order when Ms. Bobbie burst into the room with his boy toy in tow and said "HELLO." The Judge showed his feelings by his expression, and then called the meeting to order.

The Judge said, "We've got a lot to discuss and I absolutely will not tolerate any distractions or arguments. First, I want to introduce the newest member of the organization, Mr. White. He'll be taking over for Mr. Whitaker."

The Judge then asked Madame, "How is Big Trouble doing?"

Madame was strong outside, but miserable on the inside. She stood and began to speak. "Big Trouble is paralyzed from the knees up. He has tubes in him to handle his bodily functions. The doctors say that this is a temporary state and that in time he could make a significant comeback. Most of the damage was done by the shots fired by Mr. Whitaker after the fights. The rest happened during his last fight." Madame then said, "I've been by his side day and night ever since. Just the other day a tear fell from his eye, which the doctors said means the healing process has begun."

The Judge was furious as he said, "No expense will be spared to get Big Trouble all the help he needs."

Next the Judge addressed the Elevator Man Ben Dover. "Ben," the Judge said, "I heard you have a problem with one of the members of the organization."

Ben stood up and told the Judge, "I fulfilled my contractual agreement with said member, and ended up getting pissed on for doing it!"

The Judge said, "I don't need to hear any details." The Judge looked at Gay Mack and nodded. Gay Mack produced a briefcase and had Ms. Bobbie's boy toy take it over to the Elevator Man who opened it and found it was filled with cash.

The Judge then spoke directly to Ben and offered him membership in the organization. Ben closed the case and said, "As long as I don't have to work with those two," as he pointed to Ms. Bobbie and Gay Mack, "I accept."

The Judge looked down the table at Wimple and they both nodded.

"Next," said the Judge "is Ms. CupCake." CupCake stood and the Judge addressed her accordingly. He said, "You have disappointed the organization many a time, but for each mistake you managed a good comeback. Once again we're about to have a discussion about an incident at the Galleria."

CupCake apologized to the group for her behavior, and the Judge told her,"Dress appropriately for the next party, because instead of watching you will be a participant." CupCake dropped her head and knew she was in for a long night. But at least she didn't end up like Mr. Whitaker. He wasn't at the meeting at all and that was not a good omen.

The Judge then went over the new order of business and how the money and process would flow. He kept Mr. White in the dark about the pedophile side of the organization and would not include him until after the party was totally set up in their undisclosed location.

Madame asked, "Is it ok if I don't attend?"

Judge told her, 'It's imperative that you and Big Trouble attend. Of course I'll handle all of Big Trouble's requirements for travel." Madame nodded and sat down.

She was in her own little world trying to get some movement out of Big Trouble. As soon as she was away from the group she would resume the therapy that she thought would bring big Trouble back to her.

The Judge then told the group, "We're going to have an induction ceremony for the newest members at the next party in the undisclosed location." The Judge sat down and the Banker, Mr. Wimple stood up.

Mr. Wimple addressed how much money was made and the breakdown in the payouts. He then told the group about the various investments and construction projects the organization had invested in. Mr. Wimple said, "We're now doing business as an entity known as Clique, Inc."

Mr. White said, "So I guess me and Ben can say that we are in the Clique now." All of the members laughed and Mr. Wimple finished up detailing the group on their finances. After Mr. Wimple finished and sat down and the Judge stood up and asked, "Does anyone any issues with anything that was said in the meeting?" No one said anything and so the Judge ended the meeting then left. All of the members went by and shook Mr. White's and Ben Dover's hands. The tension got thick when Ben Dover and the Gay Mack shook hands. You could tell they wanted to break into a fight, but both men knew they would be eradicated as soon as the melee had ended. Gay Mack broke the hand shake and went to his car.

Ms. Bobbie stood in front of him and then grabbed him in an unwanted hug. Bobbie whispered in his ear, "I've had enough fun already so you have nothing to worry about."

Ben just watched as Ms. Bobbie left and got into the same car as the Gay Mack. The car then started up and whisked off. Ben Dover, Mr. Wimple, and Mr. White all walked out of the room together. Cupcake left on her own and the last 2 people that were there were Madame and Big Trouble. Madame was wiping the tears from Big Trouble's eyes. She was going through some serious withdrawal pains. She had not had sex since Big Trouble started to train for the fight. She had been with women, but she needed a man and she was really having issues with that.

Big Trouble was screaming to the top of his lungs, but it was only inside of his mind. He was frozen inside his own world and could not communicate. Big Trouble could see Madame go through all of this pain and he couldn't do anything about it. He tried to move but nothing would move. He tried everything he could and still nothing would move. He tried to move his head but it wouldn't budge. But he could look up. He then tried to move his eyes around and they worked. Big Trouble remembered what the doctors said: that he would regain movement as his body healed. Big

Trouble watched as they pushed him to the van for transport. They got him loaded up and then they were headed back to his home. Madame got into the back of the van and made a phone call. She didn't know it, but Don1 had been waiting for her to make a call. The fact that they hadn't left the building where the meeting was held gave Don1 an exact location to go to and find out some information.

The whole crew was on the mend. Roz had administered the Nanobyte serum and it was working well. According to the test, the healing process should have been much faster. Roz was monitoring Frequency's progress and she was totally baffled. Some of the nanobytes had started the healing process, but they hadn't evolved into a working entity inside his body. Roz was so involved in her research that she did not notice that the guys were all starting to move around. Webb was first, then EoW and then Don1. BDB was awake, but he did not get off the table. Webb's wounds were healing, but they had not healed fully. All of the guys started telling their stories of how they'd been ambushed. They then started making phone calls to ensure that all else was well and their people knew that they were alright. Don1 had his girl on the phone and she was hysterical. He told her everything and that he would be home soon. She was trying to find out where he was and he told her he did not know. He told her to be strong and he would explain everything to her later and then he hung up the phone.

Don1's girlfriend went from concerned girlfriend to FBI agent in a heartbeat! She got on the phone to

Agent Layrock and had them try to use GPS to trace Don1's last call. Layrock used everything in their arsenal but couldn't find anything. He couldn't figure out why there was no information available on his whereabouts.

Of course, CMAX had all of the FBI computers linked in and was blocking that information. CMAX made a note to alert Frequency that Don1 had a direct connect with an FBI agent. All of the other guys were good, and their calls were also being monitored. CMAX ensured that none of the FBI equipment could access their GPS locators until Frequency gave the authorization.

Frequency was just coming to when he was met with the smiling face of one Roz Well. He tried to sit up, but he needed a little assistant from Roz.

He asked, "How long was I out?"

She said, "A while."

Frequency looked at Roz and asked about the crew just as they all walked in. They were moving slowly but at least they were all there. Frequency and the guys all cracked jokes for a few minutes then they got down to business.

Frequency informed them that all of White's crew had been paid back in full. He called out to CMAX and it responded with a cheerful "ACKNOWLEDGED."

Frequency asked CMAX for a full status report and all of the video footage that he had.

CMAX activated a projector that was attached to one of the lab's systems and showed the crew all of the video intelligence that it had acquired. The crew was amazed at what had happened while they'd been incapacitated. They cheered as if they were at a football game when they saw how BDB had handled business with White and his crew. The guys then listened as CMAX reported all of the news coverage and phone calls made to their businesses. Out of all of the guys Don1 took his news the hardest. He was really hurt when he found out that his new girlfriend was definitely an agent for the FBI.

BDB went over and cheered him up by saying, "Look Don you're the first guy I ever met that turned an FBI agent. Think about it, how many guys can say they made an FBI agent break cover for the sake of their feelings for a person? Now that's some Don Juan type stuff, if you ask me."

Don1 started to smile and said, "I did make her do that; I must have done something right." The fellows started to laugh when CMAX came on and told the crew that he had the location where Madame and Big Trouble were. The crew wasn't concerned until CMAX said that the entire group was in the same vicinity. Frequency moved slowly toward Long Haul and all others followed. They all got into Long Haul, but were still too sore to drive. So they made Roz drive them.

Madame finished her phone call then went to Big Trouble's side. Big Trouble wanted to feel the pleasure of his woman, but he couldn't move to tell her. He tried so hard but the only thing that would move was his nose. Madame moved her hand between his legs and unzipped his pants. She tried masturbating Big Trouble, but there was no response. She kept trying until she broke a sweat, then she just stopped and started to cry. She had finally lost it, so she zipped up Big Trouble's pants then made another phone call. This call was to CupCake.

Madame told CupCake, "Bring me a boy and bring him out to the main house." Madame turned to face Big Trouble and told him, "If you can't please me you can at least watch me indulge myself."

Big Trouble was going insane! He couldn't move and now Madame was going to force him to witness her having sex with another man. Big Trouble made a promise to himself that if he was ever able to move again he was going to make her pay.

Roz had finally gotten the crew to the location. The guys were totally upset at Roz's driving. Long Haul had all of this high performance stuff built into it and Roz drove it like it was an old Deuce and a quarter! Upon their arrival everyone went inside except Frequency, Roz, and BDB.

Webb grabbed an EMP pistol and told EoW, "Make sure all three of stay in constant communication at all times. They entered the building and systematically moved from room to room until one of them came upon the dead body of Mr. Whitaker. EoW found him and screamed out the news to the crew. By that time, Don1 had located the equipment room or least, what was left of it. He couldn't believe that in such a small space of time, they hadn't left a trace of anything else that had happened there. Don1 left the equipment room and went to join EoW and see the body. Webb got there ahead of him, and was tripping at the position they'd left the body in. EoW used the camera on his phone to make a video of the area; they uploaded it to CMAX so he could use all of his data gathering tools to ascertain what had happened before they arrived. When Roz saw the footage it nauseated her to the point that she turned vomited. Frequency just observed the live footage and then lay back to relax in his seat.

Webb made a statement that none of the guys could fathom. He said,   "It looks as if the guy was raped then killed."

Don1 said, "We'd better leave before the authorities show up, so they guys went back to Long Haul and drove away. They were all quiet as Roz drove back to the center.

As usual the Feds and the local authorities were way behind the culprits. Agent Layrock couldn't figure out how they stayed ahead of them. He had his crew there making tire prints and casting footprints and looking for anything that would lead them back to those responsible for this latest violent act. They found the dead body, but there was nothing to go on except the fact that he'd been brutally sodomized then stabbed with a huge knife that was still protruding from his body. They had onsite forensics and that came up negative. Layrock was furious he knew he couldn't break the cover of his agents and he knew h he'd have to tell his superiors something!

All of the agents were trying to make some head-way on this case, but their hard work was getting them nowhere. The only one who was showing some consistency was Agent Pain. She was an emotional wreck, because she had fallen in love and she knew she still had to maintain her cover.

Agent Pain called into Layrock and told him that her subject had been injured, but he was alright and recouping in an undisclosed location.

Layrock asked, "Did you try locating him using his phone?"

She replied, "Somehow he has his cellular signal scrambled."

Layrock ended the call and added Don1 to a list of people that he wanted to investigate after he finished this case with Frequency Hunter. He used his laptop and put all of his gathered data into his database of unanswered questions.

Frequency and the crew had made it back to the center. Roz drove a lot faster getting them back and the crew really appreciated it. Frequency had CMAX gather data from all of the computers infected with his worm programs and send all of it to his laptop so he'd have time to come up with a plan to keep ahead of the authorities. Frequency saw the information that Agent Layrock had gathered and he kept it from Don1.

He noted that the Feds got nothing from the crime scene, but then he remembered that they would be taking tread samples from the grounds.

Frequency asked Webb, "Did you put the usual tires on Long Haul?"

Webb said, "The tires came from a repo."

Frequency laughed because he knew this meant that the tires wouldn't come back to haunt them.

Frequency turned his attention to the center's medical monitors and watched as the nanobytes reported his entire crew's healing process. They all were healing, but not at the speed at which he thought they should. Frequency changed the programming within CMAX to troubleshoot the process of the nanobytes and found that their energy level was a lot lower than it was supposed to be. CMAX took over and started working on a solution to help alleviate the problem. Then Frequency pulled the information that he was getting from all of the other computers. The Judge made an entry on his computer that answered a question that none of the crew had been able to. The Judge's name for his organization was Clique and they were setting up some kind of private function.

Frequency knew he was on to something and now he was very interested in where their little party would be. Roz walked in and told the guys they needed to get some rest. They all grumbled as they went back to finish recouping.

Frequency never left Long Haul and Roz was very concerned. She went back into the truck and Frequency was sitting in his chair sleeping. Roz decided to have herself a little intimate fun so she got down between Frequency's legs to see if she could wake him up in a sensual way. As she started with her hand and then her mouth Frequency awoke to see a woman who was indulging herself in a little pleasure. Frequency knew Roz was not one to have time for a relationship because she was totally dedicated to her work at the center. Since he had her in a position where she wanted to have some intimate time, he decided to push it to the limit. Roz didn't expect to be having sex, but before she knew it she was. Frequency had her in a position that made her accept everything that he had to give. Roz enjoyed her moment as she shuddered with excitement. Her body experienced the long awaited orgasm that she had put on a shelf for a very long time. Frequency also achieved an orgasm, but it took all of the strength he had left.

He and Roz slid from the chair to the floor of Long Haul. Roz thought about the possibility of the crew wandering in and seeing her exposed, so she hurriedly pulled on her clothes and went to shower. Frequency pulled his pants up and did the same. He and Roz had never had sex before, but at least now they had that out of the way and would probably do it again. Roz was in the shower and she was mellow. She had always wanted Frequency, but didn't know how to ask him. Now she knew that she would be doing it again soon and maybe for keeps.

Big Trouble was being tortured by the one person he would have never imagined. Madame had Cupcake bring her a new youngster and she was having her way with him in front of Big Trouble. First, she and Cupcake started together and then they brought the youngster in to help them get off. The boy was only fifteen years old. His name was Matt and these women were all over him. He was overwhelmed by the one called Madame cause she couldn't get enough! As fast he would cum she would be giving him a blowjob to get him back inside her again. She finally had another orgasm and collapsed in front of Big Trouble's medical bed.

Matt was confused and worn out. Madame grabbed him up and made him and the other woman leave. Big Trouble knew that his life had changed and he knew at the moment he had no control. He lay in his bed and waited for the torture to continue until he died. Trouble was so mad that he didn't pay attention to the laptop sitting on the table. Madame had used the laptop to contact some of their clients and she forgot to shut it down. Don1 had a copy of everything that went on in real time.

Frequency saw it and decided to help Big Trouble's healing process along by giving him a shot of nano-bytes. Frequency got Don1 to watch what happened to Big Trouble and told them that Roz had a way to help heal him. Don1 and EoW both agreed to do the task of breaking in Big Trouble's house and administering the shot. EoW and

Don1 then asked, "How will we get to Big Trouble, since BDB got the SSR shot all to hell?"

Frequency couldn't turn to Webb cause he was in the same shape as the rest of them, so he came up with the idea of using Roz's car. She had an old minivan which was on its last leg. The fellows cracked jokes about it as they drove off in the minivan. They took their time not because they wanted to, but because the minivan would only go forty-five miles per hour.

It took them 2 hours to get out to the property where they found that Madame had left Big Trouble at home alone. It was perfect for EoW and Don1 because they didn't want to be confronted by Madame. They were able to walk into the house with no problem because Madame had left the door unlocked and hadn't even bothered to set the alarm. They went in and walked around looking for anything that would give them some information. They found nothing new so they decided to administer the shot and get the hell out of there. They made it to the room where Big Trouble was kept, but as they entered the room they were warned that someone was coming into the house by CMAX.

They ran and hid so that they would not get caught. CupCake walked into the house and went directly to Big Trouble's room. She had a bag with her and she sat it down and pulled out a syringe. Big Trouble came to and looked directly at CupCake.

Cupcake shouted "Damn, you had to wake up and make this more difficult than it already is!"

She slapped Big Trouble on the right cheek and asked, "Where do you want to be stuck?" Of course she knew he couldn't answer, so she pointed the needle at his eye first and then down toward his groin.

CupCake told Big Trouble, "Aw it's just a little battery fluid and a bit of mercury from a thermometer."

Don1 heard her and knew they couldn't let her kill him. Don1 moved around quietly in the closet and found a bat. This was just what the doctor would have ordered. He was about to burst out of the closet and attack Cupcake, when the alarm on her car started to go off. CupCake put down the syringe and went outside to see what was going on.

As soon as she left EoW came into the room and switched the syringes. He whispered to Don1 and the two looked at Big Trouble and swore to him that this injection would help him. They ran out of the room and to the back of the house.

CupCake came back in cursing about a damn dog. Big Trouble was totally taken aback that his two newest friends had come to his rescue. CupCake picked up the syringe and stabbed it dead into Big Trouble's heart area. She pushed the plunger down until all of the liquid went inside of Big Trouble. She pulled out the syringe, put it back into the bag, and made a hasty retreat.

Big Trouble just lay there waiting for something miraculous to happen. He didn't know if anything should be hurting and that was a good thing. He tried to move and couldn't so he decided to go to just sleep.

Madame walked into her home expecting to find her lover dead in his bed. She went into the bathroom and took a shower. She walked out of the shower naked and went over to Big Trouble's bed to see if the job had been done. She was totally shocked to feel the grip of Big Trouble's hand around her throat. Madame was gasping and scrambling as she tried to get air into her lungs. She grabbed Big Trouble by the groin and he released his grip. She moved to get away, but he already had a hand full of her hair. He pulled her into the bed with him and slapped her across the back and buttocks. Madame screamed as each blow hurt like hell. She couldn't believe that he was alive and moving!

Big Trouble was just as shocked that he was moving. Every thought that went through his brain energized his body to respond. He tried to speak, but nothing came out, but he didn't care because now at least he could move. He didn't try to move his legs because he was too busy disciplining Madame, who was now screaming at the top of her lungs to no avail.

Big Trouble was still hitting her everywhere he could and she could not get away. He knew he had to buy himself some time, so he decided to do something he'd sworn he would never do. He pulled Madame up by her hair and punched her directly in the back of the head knocking her unconscious. Then he released Madame as she slumped to the floor.

Big Trouble then tried to move his legs, but they didn't move. He then tried to move his waist and he could. Big Trouble felt for the tube in his throat and pulled it out. He vomited fluids everywhere and found it hard to breathe at first. The equipment monitors notified the specialist that the Judge assigned to him to get there ASAP. When he arrived at Big Trouble's house, notified the Judge about everything that had happened.

The Judge told him, "You stay there and make sure nothing happens to him."

The specialist removed all of the special equipment because Big Trouble was now breathing and moving on his own. It was miraculous how much progress Big Trouble had made in a few short hours. The specialist hurriedly drove Big Trouble to the hospital that the Judge specified for further observation and evaluation. He left Madame in the middle of the floor unconscious as the Judge had instructed.

EoW and Don1 made it back to the center with one little problem. They blew the engine on Roz's minivan just as they got there. Roz was very upset, but Frequency promised her that they would replace her beloved van with something much more current and functional. The crew had gotten their heads together trying to find out where the next meeting of the Clique was to be held. They had CMAX pulling together anything that could help them crack the code within the Gathering file.

EoW decided that he would try to hack into the Judge's new encryption computer. Frequency told EoW, "I don't think that's a good idea with everything that's been going on. It might bring more heat down on us."

They decided to go after one of the smaller players in the game. Don1 decided to try CupCake or Madame because they had tried to take out a man who was totally helpless at the time.

Don1 went online and looked into the computers at Big Trouble's house. He found out that the plot to kill Big Trouble had failed thanks to himself and EoW.

Madame was on the phone talking to CupCake. She said, "When I got back to the house, Big Trouble came to and totally whooped my ass! I mean it! What did you give him?" She continued, "Somebody has already come in and taken Big Trouble away from here."

CupCake asked, "What are you going to do now?"

Madame told her, "I've got to find him and try to make up for the stupid mistake I made."

CupCake told her, I "If the Judge finds out that I tried to kill Big Trouble he'd send Ms. Bobbie after me! Right now I do enjoy living."

Madame said, "Girl, I'm with you right now and I don't know what they'll do to me." The two women stayed on the phone talking and stressing about their big mistake and the fear they both felt.

The specialist had Big Trouble hooked up to a couple of monitors and was amazed at the progress he was still making. Big Trouble didn't know what EoW and Don1 had put in that syringe but he was incredibly grateful. He was now able to walk with a walker and he had most of his other body movement back as well. He wasn't able to talk yet, but at least he was able to move on his own. The specialist stayed in constant contact with the Judge, and asked if he could bring in physical therapists to help Big Trouble in his rehab.

The Judge said, "You do whatever you deem necessary to get him back as close to one hundred percent as possible."

Don1 and EoW were overjoyed when they found out that Big Trouble was in a rehab facility getting help. Frequency was working at trying to break the code on the number files, Webb was working on Long Haul, and BDB was working out and trying to get himself back into working shape.

Roz decided to cook a dinner fit for a King and she already had all of the materials there at the center. The fellows had totally forgotten about her until the smell of the food wafted throughout the center and made their empty stomachs growl. They stopped what they were doing and went to the kitchen, where Roz had everything set up and laid out. Roz had all of them sitting down and enjoying the meal in no time. Frequency and his crew hadn't had a meal like that in years, and it showed! They sat, ate, and shared stories with Roz. Frequency even told the guys that he had Roz shoot them up with nanobytes to help speed along their recoveries. All of the crew were surprised and had lots of questions, which Frequency brought CMAX online to answer. They were totally amazed at how CMAX had all of their improving health data right there in front of them.

CMAX told them that the process would speed up once an issue with energy was fixed. BDB was like a kid in a candy store as he learned how the nanobytes would increase the speed of his healing process which had already experienced a 15% increase. BDB then started using CMAX to help him with the information gathered from Mr. Wimple and the Judge. BDB knew he had to be on top of his game to get the Judge and Mr. Wimple online with his landscaping services so that he could gain access to the information that Frequency needed to clear his name.

The specialist sent the Judge all of the information about Big Trouble's improvements. The Judge was amazed at how fast Big Trouble was healing, but now he knew that the big man would be at the meeting in Johnson City. The Judge made all of the necessary arrangements to accommodate the big man. The Judge contacted Mr. Wimple and told him to have a special package for Big Trouble. The Judge wanted to ensure that everybody had a great time in Johnson City so he had the coded information sent out to everyone in the organization and it started out. "5646766-2489" is just a week away. We'll be paying homage to one of our members because of his unfortunate accident. All persons who have received encrypted information please attend and be punctual. there will be no tolerance for tardiness. The Judge sent the information and he knew that all was well now that Big Trouble was back on his feet and soon even he would be back to 100%.

Frequency intercepted the message and it was driving him crazy that he couldn't figure out what it meant! Then as if lightning had struck him, Frequency went and picked up an old telephone. He matched the numbers until he had cracked the code. Frequency jumped up and down as if he'd won the lottery, as all of the crew ran into the room to see what was going on.

Don1 asked, "What does it mean?"

Frequency said, "We're going to Johnson City."

EoW asked, "How the hell did you come up with that?"

Frequency then told them that the Judge just used the numbers on the telephone to mask the location of the meeting place. The crew started to laugh and then they began getting Long Haul ready for their trip to Johnson City.

Chapter 17

Johnson City

Long Haul pulled in to a gas station on the outskirts of town. The crew had traveled through the night to get there without any traffic tie ups. Everybody had taken turns driving. Roz was the caretaker of the crew and she was exhausted. Frequency got out and fueled up for the next leg of the trip. Then he headed toward the signal of the last phone call made by Madame. Frequency had CMAX on full alert and CMAX was monitoring his vital signs to make sure he wasn't overdoing it. CMAX had all of the programs sending information across the secure wireless network that Don1 and EoW had designed. CMAX pulled in the information and had it hard recorded in several different locations just in case something went wrong. Frequency found a trailer park and decided to shut down until morning.

Madame was a mental wreck and she was desperate to do damage control with Big Trouble. But Trouble was recuperating under guard and would not allow her anywhere near him alone. Big Trouble knew that EoW and Don1 had saved his life, but he didn't know what it was that they'd given him. Big Trouble had regained full use of his arms and some of the use of his legs. He was able to walk, but not without a walker.

Big Trouble wanted Madame sexually, but mentally he couldn't get past the fact that she'd turned on him at his weakest moment when he needed her most. He was hurting bad and he could not mask his feelings. He tried to follow the instruction of the specialist but he just couldn't concentrate! He told the specialist to leave him alone for tonight. Then Big Trouble used his walker to get back to his suite, took a shower, and went to bed.

He couldn't sleep and soon he felt someone else climb in his bed. It was Madame and she was not leaving without being with Big Trouble once again. Trouble had the physical strength to stop her, but mentally and emotionally he was too weak to fight her. Madame had a mouth full of what she had longed for, and Big Trouble couldn't resist the pleasure she was giving. He was amazed that his body responded so strongly as Madame indulged herself. She was soon straddling him and fulfilling her own desires to the fullest.

Madame did everything in her power to make Big Trouble acknowledge her, but he didn't say a word. She found herself achieving orgasm after orgasm until she collapsed, totally exhausted. Big Trouble rolled her off of him onto the floor of his suite. He threw the covers off his bed on top of her and went to take another shower. Big Trouble knew in his heart that he was no longer emotionally attached to Madame, so he no longer needed her. He washed all traces of Madame off himself and went and slept on the couch of his suite.

Mr. White had settled down in his suite, and he had CupCake and her girl Kim in the room with him. The Judge gave them to him for his unlimited pleasure while they were in Johnson City. White could indeed say that it had been a pleasure. He was very interested in CupCake, but she was using Kim as a shield. Mr. White decided to play her game for now, but he fully intended to indulge in her pleasures later. White knew just what to do for CupCake. He wanted to make her regret becoming a full blown lesbian.

Mr. White and Kim got out of the shower and saw that CupCake had a very sour look on her face. White let it go and began to get ready for the organization's meeting that was about to start.

CupCake grabbed Kim by the hand and said, "Come with me." CupCake had no choice but to answer to the Judge's call. The Judge had told CupCake that spending time with white was part of her penalty for the bad decision she'd made when she attacked the center's director. That one careless incident brought unwanted attention by the law enforcement community. She had to do it, but she didn't have t like it one bit!

Cupcake got into the car with Kim and headed for the meeting location. Both she and Kim were wearing bathrobes. All of the others were being picked up and driven to the undisclosed location.

Big Trouble was doing something that he had never done for one of the meetings before. He was riding alone. He made sure that the Judge had him and Madame riding in separate vehicles. Big Trouble had on a tailor made suit that he was wearing for the first time. It seemed strange that he owed his life to a couple of guys who'd befriended him when they hooked up a computer system in his house.

Big Trouble walked into the meeting room and everyone inside started to applaud. They were all so proud of him and his comeback from adversity. Big Trouble walked over to the Judge.

The Judge hugged him and said, "I'm so proud of you."

Big Trouble whispered, "I really appreciate everything that you've done for me. I don't know how I would've made it without your help."

The Judge knew that Big Trouble had not fully regained his voice. The Judge got the meeting going and made sure it didn't last too long. After the Banker got all of the financial materials out and handed everybody their bonuses, the Judge brought the business meeting to an end and got the party started.

A bed with Cupcake, Kim and a few under-age teenagers came out into the middle of the floor. All of the people on the bed were naked except for a mask that covered only their eyes. The Judge was the first to indulge in his sick fantasy as he started having sex with a young boy and a girl. Then all of the other members joined in except for Big Trouble and Mr. Wimple. They sat back and indulged in conversation instead.

Big Trouble asked Mr. Wimple, "Can you help me get out of there 'cause I can't stand seeing any more of this."

Mr. Wimple said, "Sure," and helped him get out of there.

Big Trouble looked over his shoulder and the last thing he saw was Madame, CupCake, and a young boy engaged in a threesome. He closed his eyes and walked away from the party and back to his suite.

The party continued without a hitch as they indulged themselves in the young flesh of the captive participants. Ms. Bobbie and Gay Mack lay on top of a couple of teen boys totally exhausted and depleted. The Elevator man had his fill then left the orgy for his own suite. All of the other members left and went to there suite.

CupCake was ordered by the Judge to make sure all of the participants were secured so that they couldn't divulge any information about the night's festivities. CupCake blindfolded all of the participants, led them into a room, tied them to their chairs, gagged each one and then closed the door. The room was actually a container that had been placed on the property. Cupcake had a gigantic hole dug and had the container placed in it. Once the container was in place CupCake had the hole refilled. Then she and Ms. Bobbie murdered every single one of the teenagers who had participated in their orgy. The two then went back to their own suites to join their companions as if nothing out of the ordinary had happened.

CupCake was met by a surprise visitor. Mr. White was already in her suite and he had Kim all tied up.

CupCake asked, "What do you want?"

Mr. White told her, "Come on in and talk business with me."

CupCake had seen the way White had looked at her, and she'd been avoiding him all night. Now he had her exactly where he wanted her, so Cupcake entered the room and closed the door behind her.

Mr. White told her something that caught her attention immediately.

He said, "I'm putting together a little plan to bring your old director to me."

CupCake lit up light a Christmas tree, so White continued, "I know that you're the one who attacked her. You may not know it, but her lover had sworn revenge on whoever committed that act."

CupCake looked of very concerned and asked, "What do I need to do to stop him?"

Mr. White told her, "Submit to me and come under my protection. Oh, you can have the woman once I'm finished with her."

CupCake slowly undressed in front of Mr. White and let him have everything he wanted.

Frequency was watching everything that went down thanks to the cellular taps that EoW and Don1 had put in place. He was making sure that CMAX had all of the visuals saved onto the compromised computer in his probation officer's office. Frequency was just finishing up saving the main file and shutting down for the night when he was informed by Don1 that Doc was in trouble. Frequency froze not saying a word.

EoW came into the room and said, "Webb and BDB are going to shut down the Judge before he gets away."

Frequency found his voice and told EoW, "Tell BDB and Webb not to waste their time because the Judge is already on the move. You all get Roz and Long Haul back to the center."

Don1 and EoW understood exactly what was going to happen and they told Roz that they were leaving immediately. Roz wanted to ask question, but Don1 already had Long Haul on the move.

Roz asked EoW, "Where's Frequency?"

EoW pointed out the window as they pulled away. By then Webb and BDB pulled up in a Chevy Tahoe they'd just bought off a private seller. They paid cash for the vehicle and stocked it with a few of the EMP weapons from Long Haul's stash. Frequency jumped into the vehicle and was immediately handed a couple of EMP pistols. The crew then headed straight for the last cellular transmission that Don1 had intercepted.

Mr. White had the Hudson Brothers en route to him with an extra special package. Frequency was en route to intercept this same package, but White had no idea that Frequency was on to him. When the Hudson Brothers arrived, they pulled the person they'd kidnapped from the back of the car.

Doc had no idea where she was or why she'd been snatched. The men who'd grabbed her at the super-market caught totally off guard She was alone and afraid.

John and Mark were careful not to harm her because they knew it would send Frequency over the edge. They did not want Frequency gunning for them because he wouldn't stop until they'd been annihilated. They knew this for a fact, and they already had enough problems.

Mr. White and his new protégé were waiting to meet them. CupCake was the first to greet Doc and let her know what she was in for. She grabbed Doc by the shoulders and kissed her directly on the lips. Doc's hands were tied behind her back so she couldn't resist.

CupCake pulled away and told Doc, "I wanted to kiss you that night in your home, but I had to leave before we had time to get to know each other."

Doc was furious when she realized the person who brutalized her in her home was standing right in from of her! She brought her knee up quickly and caught CupCake directly in her stomach. The blow sent CupCake to her knees, but she recovered quickly and slapped Doc hard in the face. Mr. White stepped between them and Doc knew that something was very wrong.

White said, "Why don't you call your friend Frequency?"

Doc said, "I no longer deal with him."

White said, "Yeah I know that, but I need to get Frequency's attention."   Doc said, "I can't give you something that I don't have."

Mr. White said, "Since you don't want to help me I guess I'll let my girlfriend finish having fun with you."

Doc dropped her head as CupCake walked over and gave Mr. White a big kiss and said, "I'll make sure you get more of me later."

CupCake grabbed Doc by the hair and pulled her toward the car they had waiting.

Mr. White settled with the Hudson Brothers and said, "Gentlemen, prepare yourselves for war."

The Hudsons knew that they had gotten themselves into a major fiasco and now they'd have fight their way out – probably to the death. They jumped into their vehicle and took off, but all of a sudden their vehicle shutdown. They looked at the car that Mr. White was in and saw that his driver was getting out also. The two immediately got out of the car and went to the trunk for weapons. John grabbed a shotgun and Mark grabbed an M16. The brothers took off running toward a set of nearby buildings. Mr. White went into the car's backseat and pulled a couple of 9mm and told CupCake to follow him. CupCake tried to grab Doc, but White stopped her so she could make it to safety.

White's driver was hit by an EMP round and was knocked unconscious. Frequency was pleased that his invention worked flawlessly. Webb jumped into the car and said, "What's up Doc/"

Doc saw Webb and knew instantly that she was going to be alright. BDB was with Frequency who was trying to catch White and CupCake as they ran to a set of buildings. He sent BDB after the Hudson brothers.

BDB chased after the brothers, who had separated from White and CupCake. They tried to lose BDB but they couldn't, so they gave each other the nod to stand and fight it out. BDB jumped behind a wall as the rounds the Hudson brothers fired hit close to home.

BDB laughed and shouted, "My mother can shoot better than that boys!"　　John said, "Stick your head out and give me another try!"

BDB went around the building and climbed up on a short wall. From there he could see Mark trying to sneak around to where he was. BDB immediately moved to the opposite end of the wall where he could see both brothers. Just as he was about to fire a shot it started to rain. BDB decided to get a little closer to the brothers and his foot slipped. He felt himself falling and braced himself for the impact. He landed on top of Mark Hudson who had just moved around to the end where he was. The two men got to their feet and started brawling. John heard the scuffle and ran to help his brother. He wanted to fire a shot, but couldn't without hitting Mark also. He dropped the shotgun and into the battle. BDB grabbed both men as they fell to the ground. He was able to keep them from getting in any damaging kicks or punches while they fought. The rain was really pouring as a full-fledged thunderstorm raged above them.

BDB hit John in the top of his head then punched Mark in the chin. This bought him time to get to his feet so he could really fight with the brothers. Mark jumped to his feet first and was met with a knee to his stomach and a hard right to his jaw that put him down.

John recovered and hit BDB in the jaw then kicked him in his face. BDB staggered backwards and fell to the ground. John ran to kick BDB but he was caught with a solid kick to his stomach which knocked all the wind out of him. BDB jumped to his feet and hit John with a punch that knocked him to the ground unconscious. BDB grabbed the EMP rifle and went to find Frequency.

Frequency pulled the trigger and the round found its target with pinpoint accuracy. CupCake fell to the ground and was totally incapacitated. White kept running but he wasn't paying attention to where he was going. He ran down between a series of building and ended up in a construction area. He was out of breath when he tripped over a piece of scrap metal and fell to the ground. He dropped his weapons and tried to scramble and get them, but the rain had really started coming down and the ground was muddy. He was just about to grab one of the pistols when Frequency stepped on his hand and kicked him in the face. The kick did not hit solid, because Frequency slipped in the mud. White rolled over and hurriedly got to his feet. The two men started exchanging blows and trying to knock one another down. Mr. White tried to grab Frequency by the throat, but Frequency ducked and hit him in the nuts. White doubled over and Frequency hit him in the back of his head.

Mr. White fell to the ground, grabbed a steel pipe and hit Frequency with it. Frequency groaned in pain as Mr. White hit him again. Frequency rolled so that the pipe would not hit him. He found his own pipe and blocked the next blow from White. Frequency recovered fast and hit White in the chest with the end of the pipe. White rolled, got to his feet, and he and Frequency went at each other like trained swordsmen. They traded some good shots until the two pieces of steel met and the two fought to overpower one another. All of a sudden the pieces of steel were hit by a bolt of lightning that threw both men several feet apart.

BDB was just running up to help Frequency when the lightning struck. He was amazed at how far Frequency was thrown. He got on his phone and told Webb where they were and what happened. All of the crew came online to tell BDB that they saw everything from the building's surveillance camera. Webb had Doc in the Tahoe and they went straight to get BDB and Frequency. Frequency was out cold and his partners were trying to get him to a hospital.

Mr. White was left out on the ground and the Hudson Brothers were just coming to from the beating they took from BDB. Mark and John quickly found White and CupCake. Then the brothers stole a car from the area for a clean getaway. White finally came to, but he was in bad shape.

He told the Hudson brothers, "Break out the heavy artillery and take no prisoners."

Mark said, "It's about time we took the gloves off!" John just smiled.   Frequency came to just long enough to tell BDB to follow CMAX's instructions for plan "F."

BDB called CMAX and said, "Initiate plan F."

CMAX said, "Drive Doc home now and have her notify Don1's girlfriend about what had just happened to her." Then CMAX encrypted a message and left it on Mr. Master's computer for him to see when he came to his office the following morning. Plan F was in full operation.

Doc wanted to tell Frequency something, but he passed out again before she could tell him. Webb and BDB dropped Doc off around the corner from her home.

Doc asked "Is Frequency going to be alright?"

"Sure he will, and when all this is over I'll make sure that you and Frequency have some time alone."

Doc said, "Thanks," as she jumped out of the Tahoe and walked to her house.

BDB and Webb headed straight for the center so they could get Frequency the medical attention he needed.

Doc walked around the corner where her mom's house was ablaze with law enforcement lights. One of the officer's in charge of crowd control would not let her through until another officer recognized her. They immediately pulled her into the house and started interrogating her. Doc told them everything that had happened earlier from her kidnapping, to her meeting with White and Cupcake, and didn't leave out any details. By the time she had finished detailing all that she could remember, the Feds showed up in full force. This was all part of Frequency's plan. He knew that once Doc's story and the details of White's treachery got back to the Judge all hell would be breaking loose!

Agent Layrock and his entire team showed up and basically put the whole block on lockdown. Layrock was still amazed at how much information Frequency and his team had collected, and how they were able to disappear even from them. Mr. Master had just gotten the call and headed straight to his office. He got in and read all of the information that he had received from CMAX then he called Agent Layrock. Layrock told Mr. Mack Master everything that he had and that he needed to get him all of the information on his computer. Mack Master made a CD copy and a jump drive copy of the information. He was about to shut down his computer and leave when an explosion rocked his facility.

The explosion sent Mack Master over his desk and into a wall. Mack Master pulled his service revolver and tried to make it to the stairwell, but rounds of ammo peppered the area all around him so he dropped to the floor and crawled for cover. He knew the building had a safe room built in case of natural disaster, so he headed straight for that room. He dodged bullets and several fires before he made it to the entrance, put in the code to open the heavy door, jumped inside the door and hit the emergency close button as ammo rained all around him. The door slammed shut and then sealed itself as all of the electrical devices inside the room came to life and several surveillance monitors were activated. Mack Master could see the heavily armored team moving about the building shooting anything that moved. They pulled all kinds of computer equipment apart after taking the necessary data receiving devices from them. Another guy went about setting off detonators throughout the facility as they completed their mission.

Mack Master tried to use his cell phone but couldn't pick up a signal in the safe room. He tried to use the secure line system but somehow the intruders had shut that down also. Mack Master saw that there was a computer system that had an active internet connection, and he remembered they had switched to an encrypted voice over IP phone system. He quickly got on the phone to Agent Layrock and was notified that they were having problems of their own.

Agent Layrock could not believe the fire power that these guys had! They were shooting at the Feds with such a heavy barrage of weapons that most of the law enforcement officers were helpless. Layrock barely made it to a car before it was hit with several rounds that peppered the car and hit him in the back of his right shoulder. But Layrock and his crew still managed to get out of there alive with Doc and her family.

Doc was more scared than she'd been in her whole life, and she knew in the back of her mind that this was the doing of that lousy bitch CupCake. Doc just prayed that Frequency would recover quickly so he could put an end to this mess. Agent Layrock had never met Frequency Hunter, but now he owed him a bit of gratitude. He forewarned Layrock about this group and because of it he and his crew were prepared. Agent Layrock stayed in constant contact with his crew.

He found out that even though they took some heavy artillery they all made it out with their lives. The local law enforcement officers didn't fare so well. They sustained heavy casualties and millions of dollars in structural and property damages. Agent Layrock maintained radio silence until he and his team could regroup and assess the damages.

BDB and Webb had gotten Frequency back to the center where Roz was waiting with a stretcher when they pulled up.

EoW told Webb, "Make the Tahoe disappear cause we don't need any more attention."

Don1 was watching the news of the simultaneous attacks on the federal agents and trying to find out if his girlfriend was alright, but the news wasn't specific. Roz and CMAX were working on Frequency's wounds when CMAX set off an alarm like none of the guys had ever heard. Webb had just made it back and ran into the room where all of the crew had gathered. Frequency was convulsing on the stretcher so hard that all of the crew had to hold him. Then Frequency went into cardiac arrest. Roz ran to get a defibrillator, but CMAX had it under control. CMAX sent an electric charge into Frequency that filtered through him into all of them, knocking everyone to the ground except Frequency, who was still on the stretcher.

Roz dropped her defibrillator and ran to check all of the guys who were now unconscious. She was a bit hysterical until CMAX came online and said "ACKNOWLEDGE."

Roz asked CMAX, "What happened?"

CMAX explained to Roz that his Artificial Intelligence had been activated by Frequency and that the mystery of the nanobytes not functioning fully had been solved.

CMAX then told Roz, "Look at the screen to see the before and after effects of what had just happened." She was stunned by the speed at which the nanobytes had multiplied by the thousands and were and were just as quickly fixing all of the crew's injuries. Don1 was the first to regain consciousness, then BDB, Webb, EoW, and finally Frequency himself. All of the guys were confused and dazed as Roz helped them to a seat.

They all asked, "What happened?"

Frequency said, "When I got struck by lightning, that electric shock gave the nanobytes in my body the boost they needed to heal my wounds. Then I used the electrical surge generated by CMAX to boost along the nanobytes in all of you. BDB was the first to notice that the cuts he'd sustained earlier were healing faster and no longer hurt. Webb and the rest of the guys started pulling off bandages and discovered that their wounds were healed and had left no scars. Frequency smiled as the crew started acting like little kids with a new toy.

Frequency then had CMAX explain that the nanobytes are basically a hospital inside of your body. They will help your immune system fight off any unknown unhealthy organism within your body.

Don1 quickly said, "What about unwanted weight gain?"

All of the crew burst into laughter as he showed off what he called his keg.

CMAX came online and said, "I can make adjustments within the nanobytes to help any of you cut down on the foods that produce the majority of your fat cells."

The whole crew was fascinated and told Frequency that he had come up with the cure of all cures.

Frequency told them, "You can't divulge any of the information about the nanobytes or their healing to anyone."

The crew all put their hands together and made a pledge to take this secret to their graves. They asked Roz where the champagne was because it was time to celebrate a brief victory. Roz got the champagne and the crew did a toast the nanobytes.

The Hudson brothers were in a zone of destruction and so far had been unstoppable. They had destroyed countless homes and businesses trying to find Frequency. They knew they had crossed the line by attacking the probation offices trying to find information, but they didn't care. John loved his connection to the army's artillery battery. He had gained access to military weapons and he'd been trained by some of the best mercenaries on how to use them. John then taught his brother Mark and the rest of their gang how to use the army tactics against any target.

He had munitions stashes in several states and he was expanding it by the day. John's ultimate goal was to have a weapons stash in every state in the United States. He was working on his goal with the help of Mr. White and the information gained from Frequency Hunter. Now John Hudson and his brother Mark had to ensure that everything Frequency Hunter had been a part of was totally eradicated. John and Mark met up and had another one of his guys make the weapons that they'd used disappear. The guy had a hook up in a steel manufacturing plant. He would take everything to the plant and drop it into the molten hot steel.

That was a guarantee that none of the weapons could be used against them in the court of law. Mark had a contact in the local law enforcement property room, which circumvented anything that the Brothers wanted back on the street, or made sure that it was disposed of. The brothers kept their contact loyal with plenty of money and damn near anything else he wanted.

The Hudson Brothers took the two vehicles they were driving to the scrap yard and had them destroyed. Once the cars went through the compactor, they were sent over to the steel factory to be melted down. The Hudson Brothers pulled away from the scrap yard in a convertible Saab, and went to the hospital to pick up Mr. White and CupCake. Mr. White was ready to go. He'd seen all the carnage from the Hudson brothers' video and was ready to contact the Judge.

CupCake was sitting in a wheel chair being pushed down a hall by an orderly. She saw Mr. White getting dressed in his room and had the orderly leave her alone to visit her friend. CupCake knocked on the door and waited to be told to come in.

Mr. White said. "Come in," and looked around to see CupCake seated in a wheel chair. He asked, "Are you going to be okay?"

CupCake told him, "There's some swelling near my spinal cord that's got me temporarily paralyzed from the thighs down."

White looked into her eyes and saw how afraid she was. He went over to her and planted a kiss on her lips. CupCake was afraid and now she was not able to walk.

She said, "I guess you're through with me."

He said, "Why do you say that?"

CupCake said, "I can't walk with you; I can't help you if I'm in a wheelchair," and burst into tears.

Mr. White went over to comfort her just as the Hudson Brothers knocked on the door and told Mr. White it was time to go.

Mr. White told CupCake, "Go back to your room and someone will come there to pick you up." CupCake watched as Mr. White struggled to leave his room. He was assisted by Mark Hudson, while John led the way.

They were soon in the Saab, headed out to Mr. White's house. White asked John for his phone and called the Judge. He talked to the Judge as if he had him by the testicles.

Mr. White told the Judge, "I want you to break me off a bigger piece of your organization."

The Judge laughed into the phone and told Mr. White, "You've made a very grave mistake. Why don't you just take a chill pill and enjoy the gift of CupCake."

White politely reminded the Judge, "I've already secured that and now I need for you to contact the

Banker and let him know that all of Cupcake's profits will now come to me."

The Judge said, "I applaud your ambition Mr. White, and I need for you to get rid of another peon for me."

Mr. White said, "I'm listening."

The Judge said, "If you get rid of the Elevator Man I'll double the money you're asking for."

Mr. White said, "Sure, but I need for you to send your specialist to the hospital to get CupCake."

The Judge then asked, "Where do you want her to go?"

White told the Judge, "I want her here with me."

The Judge agreed and said, "As soon as I have confirmation that the Elevator Man is through I'll have CupCake delivered to you without delay.

The Elevator Man was in hog heaven! He had secured all of his business dealings with the Gay Mack and Ms. Bobbie. The Judge let him indulge himself within one of the organization's parties. Now he had all of the cash from the kidnappings and he was able to run his business as it suited him. His day had gone very well and it was time to shut down for the night. He got a call from the Children's Center that the elevator was stuck on the 13th floor.

Benjamin Dover was very superstitious and did not want to take the call. He tried to contact his other two technicians, but they didn't answer. Ben decided to take the job so he went to the center with all of his equipment. He went straight to the guard's station and signed in. The guard called out to another guard to come and escort Ben to the broken elevator. They had to take the stairs and the guard was exhausted when he got to the top. He told Ben that it was his fifth trip up there and he hoped that he could get the damn thing fixed. Ben used his elevator equipment to get the doors open. The car was stuck midway between the 12th and 13th floors. Ben pulled out his climbing equipment and started climbing into the elevator shaft. He climbed to the upper car circuit box and found it had been tripped. Ben reset the breaker then went back outside of the elevator car. He pushed the button and the doors closed then opened.

The elevator car dropped down to the 12th floor and then stopped. The doors opened and the car just stayed there. Ben reopened the doors and started to unhook his climbing gear from inside the elevator shaft. All of a sudden he was snatched into the elevator shaft and banged around the shaft of the elevator like a rag doll. Ben began immediately trying to reach his hook knife so he could cut the harness from around his waist. He struggled to fight against being dragged throughout the upper shaft but he couldn't.

He saw that his line had somehow gotten entangled into the weight of the other elevator car. Ben knew that was impossible and struggled harder to get to his knife. He grabbed the knife and began cutting at his ring strap, which the knife went through quickly. Ben grabbed the ledge of one of the floor doors and pulled himself up. The elevator car came up to just below him and he jumped on top of it and worked the upper door open. He jumped down into the car and found no one inside. Ben relaxed as he pushed the button for the 1st floor. He was looking himself over to assess the damage when suddenly he felt a rope around his neck. The elevator car's weight dropped fully decapitating Ben instantly. The elevator car stopped and the doors opened. One of the Hudson brother's henchmen stepped out onto the 13th floor and disappeared into the stairwell.

Cupcake was as afraid as she had ever been. She knew that her time had ended and it was not going to be easy. She had been blindfolded and dropped off somewhere unknown to her. All of a sudden the blindfold was taken off and there was Mr. White in a white bath robe and holding a glass of champagne. He was standing in front of an enormous whirlpool tub.

White said, "This is the day that you put your past behind you and you start fresh." He gave CupCake a glass and watched her drink the contents down in one gulp. He undressed her and put her into the whirlpool. Then he disrobed and joined her for a relaxing bath that included rehabilitation for her legs and some love making for her heart and head.

Chapter 18

The Banker

Mr. Albe Wimple had made it home and he was so glad to be there. He had already disposed of his encrypted cell phone and he did not turn on the radio to listen to any radio programming. Mr. Wimple pulled into his garage and left all of his luggage in the car. He went into the house and hung his keys in their usual spot, then turned to see his beautiful wife wearing only a diamond choker and black stiletto heels. Lisa Wimple was so happy to see her husband that this was as good a spot as any to have some fun with him. Mr. Wimple indulged his wife's every whim and desire. He found that he just couldn't say no to her The Wimple's enjoyed themselves in the privacy of their home without a care about might be happening around them.

Agent Layrock and his entire crew all had injuries of some sort. He was nursing several bruised ribs and a cut across his forehead, and his other agents had everything from gunshot wounds to a broken collar bone. Layrock and his agents were thankful to still be alive. He made a few phone calls to ensure that his own family was alright. He couldn't take anything for granted with the ruthless bunch that had ambushed them. He opened up his laptop to go over the data from this case that had just become personal.

Agent Layrock logged in and began his research, when he suddenly received an encrypted message that asked, "Are you alright?".

Layrock typed in, "Who is this?" but there was no reply.

Instead, the same message was repeated, "Are you alright?"

Layrock thought for a minute then typed in, "A few bumps and bruises, but I'll live."

The next message told Agent Layrock, "Get your crew back in shape as quickly as possible for the next run in with those guys. You've got to be ready for anything!"

Layrock typed in, "How will we be notified?" but there was no answer.

Agent Layrock immediately ran to one of the other agents and told him what just came across his laptop.

This agent was assigned IT and he told Agent Layrock, "That's impossible! An encrypted message couldn't be received without setting off an alarm on the main server." Layrock tried to show him the information, but it was no longer there. The IT agent then tried to retrieve any transactions from the message, but nothing was there. Agent Layrock grabbed his laptop and went back into his office. He immediately tried to call Mr. Mack Master, but he didn't answer his phone.

The IT agent came into his office and gave Agent Layrock some disturbing news.

"The probation offices were totally destroyed at about the same time we were attacked," he said.

Agent Layrock sat motionless and silent as he remembered that he received a call during the ambush from Mack Master. Layrock had two of his Agents drive him to what was left of the probation offices. The three men made it to the building in no time and found firemen all over making their way through the rubble as they searched for any signs of life.

Agent Layrock asked the fire chief, "Did your guys find a safe of any kind?"

The fire chief replied, "Yes they did and we're awaiting a crane to help remove it from the rubble. The vault fell down into the basement of the building, but it's still intact."

Agent Layrock was shocked, because he knew of no weapon that could render so much damage at one time. Agent Layrock was brought back to reality when the construction class crane was backing into place. Once the vault was hooked to the crane's arm, it was as if a giant had stepped in and plucked the vault from rubble. It swung to the right and sat the giant vault onto solid ground. The firemen frantically worked to get the vault opened. They tried prying, and using a torch to get the door opened, but it was not happening.

Agent Layrock asked, "Can we get power to the vault?"

The fire chief said, "Sure," and they hooked up some jumper cables to the frayed electrical wires hanging from the vault. The crane driver revved up the engine of the big crane and all of a sudden they heard the locks of the vault's door disengage. The door of the vault swung open and there stood Mr. Mr. Mack Master. He looked awful, but at least he was alive. The firemen helped Mr. Mack Master get into the ambulance and Agent Layrock went over to check on him.

McMaster immediately told Agent Layrock what had happened to him, and Agent Layrock told Mr. Mack Master about how he and his agents were also ambushed. Then Mr. Mack Master told Layrock about the firepower this group of guys had used. Layrock told him he knew first-hand about their weapons and how they must have been specially trained to use them so effectively. The ambulance driver then told Layrock that they needed to get Mr. Mack Master to the hospital and Layrock told Mr. Mack Master that he'd be in touch.

The Banker was getting out of the shower when his wife came and told him about the latest news.

Lisa told Albe, "Some federal agents were attacked in two separate incidents by some kind of special assault team. The news said that they were after some kind of files on their computer systems at the two locations, but nothing important was lost."

Mr. Wimple acted as if he wasn't interested, but he knew that the Judge would be up to his eyeballs in litigation if he was involved. He walked over and kissed his wife and told her, "I'm going to get my luggage out of the car."

Lisa told him, "Take your time because it'll be a while before dinner is ready."

Wimple went out to his car and gave the Judge a call from his personal phone.

The Judge was livid and he let the Banker have an earful, "I've been trying to call you for hours and there hasn't been a response!"

Wimple reminded him of the routine that the two of them had agreed upon, and the Judge calmed down. The Judge told Wimple everything that Mr. White had done. Mr. Wimple was so shocked that he didn't see his wife walk up on him. Lisa called out to Mr. Wimple and it startled him. She saw that he was frightened and ran to his side. Wimple dropped the phone and grabbed his wife to gain his footing.

Lisa was now scared that her husband was having a heart attack or something. She kept asking," What's wrong?"

Mr. Wimple said, "I was just startled when you called to me and I slipped. I'm fine." Lisa was hesitant to leave him, but she went back into the house to finish cooking.

Mr. Wimple immediately told the Judge, "We need to meet in a very secure place where we can talk and plan."

The Judge agreed and told Mr. Wimple, "I'll be in the bank in the morning to make some deposits."

Mr. Wimple said, "I'll be looking forward to seeing you."

Wimple hung up the phone and regained his composure. He knew that things were going bad, but he needed to put on a good face for his wife. So he went outside to pick some fresh flowers and he noticed that his flower bed was full of weeds and the grass had not been cut. Mr. Wimple immediately turned to go into the house and asked his wife, "What is happening with our yard?"

Mrs. Wimple turned to her husband and said, "Old man Jones retired all of a sudden and he didn't leave a number or any information to contact him. I didn't want to bother you while you were away on business."

Mr. Wimple calmed down and went and gave his wife a kiss. He then told her, "Don't worry about it, I'll find a replacement in the morning." He pulled out his personal cell phone and decided to call his secretary to have her look for a yard man.

Frequency was on to the Banker and had all of his personal devices tapped and feeding him the information. He notified BDB that the banker was in the market for a new yard man.

BDB told Frequency, "I finally got to the old man who used to do their yard and made him an offer he couldn't refuse."

Frequency asked, "Did you give the old man all of the money?"

BDB said, "Yes and I also told him there would be dire consequences if he showed up again too soon."

Frequency said, "Be at the bank as soon as they open for business tomorrow morning."

BDB said, "I'm on it, and I'll have the trailer with all of my lawn equipment on it to show for good measure."

Frequency hung up the phone and contacted Agent Layrock with another encrypted message. Layrock was running scans for taps within their infrastructure when Frequency's encrypted message came in. The message told Layrock that the bottom of the puzzle was about to fall in place, and the Feds would be able to their thing as soon as all of the pieces were assembled.

Layrock tried to ask a question, but he got an 'End of Transmission' message. Agent Layrock was furious! How was this person getting to them without leaving a trail? Layrock had all of their best IT people working and they couldn't even get close! Layrock shut down his computer and started making phone calls to find out about the medical condition of his team members. He also had to check to ensure that Mr. Mr. Mack Master and the Doc were okay, since they both seemed to be targets of the assault team. He had them moved to a safe house where they could both be under 24-hour guard.

Mr. Mack Master and the Doc were sitting and looking out at the beach when they got a call from Agent Layrock.

He told them, "I don't have proof yet, but we think we're being contacted by Frequency Hunter. He may have somehow infiltrated the group responsible for these ambushes."

Mr. Mack Master then asked, "Is that a good thing?"

Layrock answered with a frustrated, "Hell No! I can't find a piece of Frequency anywhere, and to make matters worse, he's making a mockery of our high class computer network! This Frequency Hunter will have a hell of a lot of explaining to do when we finally catch up to him!"

Doc overheard all of the conversation and decided to butt in.

"Frequency will never show his hand unless somebody close to him is in harm's way. I know it was Frequency who saved me from my attackers today and delivered me back to the house just before the attack."

Agent Layrock said, "Frequency had to be the one who warned me that my agents need to be prepared for another serious attack."

Doc said, "If I was in your shoes I'd get out the heavy guns and be waiting for Frequency to contact me with the next move."

Agent Layrock was silent a moment. Then he asked, "Is there any way you can contact him?"

Doc said, "Honestly the last time I saw Frequency, he didn't look too good. Just for the record, he'll contact me before I could contact him."

Layrock said, "If and when he does contact you, tell him thanks and that we'll be much better prepared next time."

Doc said, "I'll pass the message along if I have the chance."

Layrock ended the call and immediately had a team dispatched to the safe house to watch for any suspicious movement. Their orders said if anyone showed up he was to be contacted immediately.

Frequency had all the information he needed from the Feds so he decided to check on the personal information of the Banker. He found out that the banker came from humble beginnings. He put himself through college and graduated number one in his class. He got his CPA certification on his first try and went straight into business on his own. He met his wife while doing a stint as a tax adjuster and put her through school. They were married as soon as she graduated with a BA in business. The Wimples didn't have any children, but they were able to make money in the tax business. Everything after that seemed to disappear and then reappear when Wimple he became CEO and owner of the largest bank in the region.

Frequency had to get deep into the computer hacking to find out how the Judge and the Banker ended up working together. Mr. Wimple ended up leaving the country to go work for one of the largest money laundering cartels in the south. Wimple testified against a couple of thugs who tried to rape his wife. The cartel was quickly arrested and the leaders disappeared or were found somewhere with their throats slit. Mr. Wimple returned to the states with enough loot to open his own bank and there was the Judge to ensure that there would be no questions asked about how he did it.

Mr. Wimple woke up every morning to a hearty breakfast, and this morning his wife was in the kitchen cooking his favorite morning meal. Wimple got up and went into the kitchen and found his wife wearing nothing but an apron and it reminded him of last night festivities. Wimple walked up behind his wife and started to kiss her neck. Lisa laughed heartily as her husband showered her with affection. She had to remind him that his breakfast would get cold. Mr. Wimple stopped messing with his wife and sat down at the kitchen table to enjoy his breakfast. He and his wife finished their meal and before Mr. Wimple left the house his wife decided to tease him a little before he left for work. Wimple was a stickler for time, but this morning, he barely made it to work on time. He smiled to himself thinking about what his beautiful wife had in store for him once his work day ended. Mr. Wimple was pulling into the bank's parking garage when he saw a humongous truck and trailer filled with the latest lawn equipment.

On the side of it said BDB Professional Lawn Service? Mr. Wimple parked his automobile and got out. He stopped to copy the information off of the truck when the door opened. Wimple swallowed hard as the big man got out of the truck.

BDB asked, "What time does the Bank open and where do you go in?"

Mr. Wimple stood silent but then came to his senses. He said, "I apologize for staring."

BDB said, "No problem, I get that from everybody who walks up on this truck." Wimple laughed and said, "Honestly I was mesmerized by your size and not the truck."

BDB said, "I know, and that was a joke." The two men laughed and Mr. Wimple introduced himself to BDB.

BDB told Mr. Wimple, "I'm about to open an account here and I need some business advice."

Wimple thought about his yard problem and decided to kill two birds with one stone. Wimple said, "I need a good yard man. If you can help me out, I'll personally help you with all your business needs."

BDB said, "You've got yourself a deal," and followed Mr. Wimple into the bank.

The Judge was sitting in Wimple's office and getting more irate by the minute. He was about to give Wimple an earful until BDB stepped into the office directly behind him. The Judge was impressed and let all his irritations disappear with a smile and an introduction.

BDB shook hands with the Judge and introduced himself. Wimple called BDB by his last name, but BDB cut him off by saying, "All my friends call me BDB."

The Judge and Wimple both asked if they could call him that and BDB said sure. Mr. Wimple said, "Have a seat BDB and we'll get you started on the paper work to set up your business."

The Judge sat by listening and putting together a plan to use a fellow like BDB to his best advantage.

Mr. Wimple finished all of the business account setup and told BDB, "You can see my secretary for all of the other things you'll need for your account."

BDB stood and shook hands with Mr. Wimple and then asked, "How soon do you want me to start on your yard?"

Wimple said, "How about I meet you at noon today at my house?"

BDB said, "That would be fine."

Mr. Wimple then told BDB, "I'll call you with the rest of the details."

BDB asked, "Do you have a cell phone with beaming capabilities?"

Mr. Wimple looked at the Judge and both men were clearly confused.

BDB pulled out his phone and showed the two men what he was talking about. The Judge and Mr. Wimple laughed and said they were both still a little old fashioned when it came to cellular technology.

Then the Judge asked, "Would you mind taking a look at my yard too?"

BDB said, "As soon as I'm finished at Mr. Wimple's, he can bring me by your house if that's alright with both of you."

Wimple said, "No problem."

The Judge got up and said, "I'll see you two later this afternoon."

BDB shook hands with the Judge then left to get the rest of his account items from Wimple's secretary.

As soon as BDB left the Judge asked, "Where did you find that monster of a man?"

Mr. Wimple said, "I ran into him on the parking lot. He was just getting out of his truck to come into the bank."

The Judge said, "As soon as you finish with him make sure you come to my house. I think we can use a man of his stature to help control our little problem."

Wimple thought for a second and then asked, "How are you going to explain the extra muscle to the rest of the organization?"

The Judge said, "You let me worry about that while you do everything you can to get on BDB's good side. Our new friend Mr. White already gotten rid of our little up and down fiasco."

Mr. Wimple dropped his head for a moment and then said, "I'll make the necessary financial adjustments."

The Judge said, "The financials should go this way," as he handed Wimple a piece of paper that contained the demands Mr. White had made. Mr.

Wimple was not one to argue with the Judge, so he went to work making sure that all of the Elevator's man financials from within the organization went to White and the Judge. The Judge walked out of Wimple's office and down to his car. He had his driver take him to his office so he could do some work and then meet up with Wimple and BDB later.

Wimple finished up all of his scheduled meetings, and then told his secretary that he'd be out for the rest of the day. He rushed out of the building to ensure that he didn't get cornered by any of his employees, and headed straight for home.

He called his wife and asked, "What was for lunch?" When Lisa told him she wasn't planning anything big, he told her about his chance meeting with the big man that does landscaping. He also told her that they would be meeting at the house at noon.

Lisa said, "Thanks for the early warning. That gives me time to put together a nice lunch for you."

Mr. Wimple said, "Thanks Lisa, and I love you."

Lisa said, Yeah, I know. I'll see you when you come home for lunch." Mr. Wimple hung up the phone and called BDB to tell him how to get to his house.

BDB was already in the area, and was awaiting Mr. Wimple to pass him. BDB drove around and stalled for time, to ensure that he and Wimple arrived exactly as scheduled. Mr. Wimple pulled into his driveway and saw the big truck of BDB pull up to the curb behind him. Mr. Wimple parked the car and got out to meet BDB. The two men shook hands and then Mr. Wimple took BDB in to meet his wife. Wimple was a very jealous man and he judged other men by how they treated his wife.

BDB followed Mr. Wimple into the house and out came his wife. BDB immediately noticed how beautiful his wife was. BDB figured this was a test, so he immediately started talking about the business at hand. Mr. Wimple was very pleased with how BDB handled himself. BDB had passed the test and secured his business with Mr. Wimple.

The Wimples and BDB went out to the yard and BDB explained that he was going to get started on the yard. Mrs. Wimple pointed out something that she wanted and BDB handled each request immediately. Mrs. Wimple saw that BDB worked fast and neatly so she was very impressed.

She told Mr. Wimple, "Can you make sure that BDB does the yard from now on?"

Mr. Wimple was surprised because his wife had never made a decision that quickly.

Mrs. Wimple went into the house and finished making lunch for them, while Mr. Wimple went to his car and left BDB to finish up the yard work. He pulled the car into the garage, and then went to his bedroom to change.

He took off his suit and hung it up to go to the cleaners. Just as he was about to put on a pair of khakis Lisa burst into the closet and knocked him to the floor. She quickly undressed and enjoyed a quick love session with her husband, and then the two of them took a shower together. They had to hurry because they did not want to keep their company waiting.

Mr. Wimple finished dressing first, so he went outside where BDB was just finishing the yard. Wimple watched as BDB cleaned up all of the grass clippings and shavings from the shrubbery. When BDB was finished, the yard looked great! Mrs. Wimple came out and announced that lunch was ready, so all three of them walked to the back yard where they had lunch on the patio.

BDB ate heartily and said, "Thank you Mrs. Wimple for that great lunch."

She took their plates and left them to sit on the patio to discuss business. As soon as Mrs. Wimple was out of earshot, Mr. Wimple got directly to business.

He said, "I'm very impressed with your work and want to know how you'd like to be paid. Do you prefer check, charge, or cash?"

BDB told him, "Neither because I appreciate everything you did to help me setup my business account. This one is on me."

Wimple said, "I can't allow that. Certainly there is some way I can repay you for your services."

BDB told Wimple, "Just put it in my account then."

Wimple smiled and said, "I'll do one better. I'll pay for your business to be able to accept credit cards."

BDB thought for a minute and then asked, "Do you mind riding to this cellular store to look at a new setup that has a credit card scanner incorporated into it?"

Wimple was very interested in seeing how that worked so he agreed. He went to let his wife know that he was going with BDB to get some cellular equipment and then they were headed to the Judge's house. Mrs. Wimple didn't like Judge Hill and Mr. Wimple knew it.

Before Lisa could say anything about it, Mr. Wimple said "The Judge met BDB at the bank and wants him to do his yard too."

Lisa asked, "Why do you call the yard man BDB?"

Mr. Wimple said, "BDB told me that he prefers that his friends call him that."

Lisa laughed and said, "Well I'm glad that we're his friends," as she kissed her husband.

The two men drove off and headed straight for Don1's cell shop. Once they arrived, BDB had the store clerk show him the cellular phone that could handle credit card transactions. The clerk had already been notified by Don1 that BDB would be in to look at the phone and he played his part very well. Wimple purchased everything that BDB needed, and then called his secretary to ensure that all of BDB's transactions would be tied directly to his new business account. While they were there, Mr. Wimple also bought some better phones for himself and his wife. The clerk showed Mr. Wimple how to use some of the features and the rest Mr. Wimple said he would learn on his own. Wimple paid for everything and the two men left the store and headed to the Judge's house.

It didn't take BDB long to get to the Judge's house and he was impressed with all the gated security that the Judge had. Mr. Wimple called the Judge on the phone and the giant wrought iron gates swung open.

BDB drove the truck through the gate and around the bend in the driveway. The Judge walked outside to meet the two men and they all walked together across the large lawn. Wimple showed the Judge his new cell phone and told him that he could now beam information.

The three men laughed and the Judge asked, "Where did you get the phone?"

BDB told the Judge, "My friend owns cellular phone shop with all the latest gizmos and gadgets available."

Wimple told the Judge how friendly and informative the employees at the cell phone shop were.

The Judge said, "I will personally go to your friend's shop to get myself a new phone."

Wimple said, "That's the best idea because the shop has so many phones with so many features to choose from no one could possibly make that decision for you."

The Judge asked BDB: "Now that you've toured the grounds, where do you want to begin?"

The Judge and Mr. Wimple left BDB to his work while they went into the house. After BDB had finished all of the hedge trimming and mowing, he went into the house looking for the Judge and Wimple. BDB turned on his cell phone so CMAX could tell him where to go and what to do. CMAX tapped into the surveillance system of the Judge's house and directed BDB to the Judge's main office. CMAX instructed BDB to plug the USB cable from his cell phone into the Judge's computer. CMAX uploaded a worm program to the computer and told BDB to get out of the Judge's office ASAP. BDB made it out into the main hallway and heard noises coming from one of the rooms. He pushed on the door and peeked inside, where he saw a woman wearing headphones exercising.

BDB moved away from the door when his cell phone started to vibrate and looked at the screen. He could see the Judge and Wimple in the kitchen discussing something. BDB didn't want to get caught in a compromising position so he called out to the Judge. The Judge pushed a button on his desk that activated the intercom system within the house.

He said, "Come to the kitchen, where Mr. Wimple and I are."

BDB found his way to the kitchen and the Judge wrote him a check for the yard work. BDB started to protest, but the Judge insisted so he accepted the check.

The Judge asked, "Could you handle more clientele?"

BDB told him, "Yes sir, as many as you can send my way!"

The Judge made a call to the local golf club. After asking to speak with the manager, he said, "I'm sending a new lawn service up there that all of your members should consider doing business with."

The manager said, "I'll certainly pass that information on to our membership as soon as possible." The Judge hung up the phone and gave BDB a card on which he'd written all of the information BDB would need when he got to the golf club.

BDB and Mr. Wimple got back into BDB's truck and pulled away from the Judges' home. BDB was surprised that he was able to plant the worm on the Judge's computer so easily. Wimple was quiet at first, and then he asked BDB a question that made him stop the truck.

Wimple asked, "Have you ever done something that you ultimately regretted?"

BDB thought for a second then he said, "I've killed before and that's my biggest regret. I never killed anyone unless it was in self-defense or in defense of another person."

Mr. Wimple swore BDB to secrecy then he told BDB everything about how he was forced to work for the Judge. He even told BDB about the orgies with young boys and girls.

Wimple told BDB, "The Judge always makes sure that I'm an accomplice so that I can't go to the cops."

BDB asked, "Why don't you just leave?"

Wimple told BDB, "Once I ran from one bad situation, but found myself in an even worse situation. I don't want to put my wife through that again."

BDB asked, "Why did you choose to tell me all of this?"

Wimple said, "BDB you're the first person ever to come to my house and be genuine. That means a lot to me."

BDB started driving again, and it wasn't long before they were back at Mr. Wimple's house.

BDB told Mr. Wimple, "I have to run to my next appointment now, but you can call me anytime."

BDB pulled off and left Mr. Wimple standing in the doorway of his house. Wimple walked in and was met by his wife.

She asked, "Did BDB accept the job offer?"

Wimple said, "I'm not sure if he accepted the offer or not."

Mrs. Wimple didn't say another word, as her husband walked past her and took a seat on the sofa. She looked at her husband as he sat on the sofa and let his mind wander. She decided against trying to cheer him up and went into their bedroom to watch television.

Frequency had just finished getting some last minute testing done on CMAX, when the transmissions from the Jude's house started coming in. As soon as Frequency was able he made a copy of all the files on the Judge's computer. BDB was pulling into the center to tell Frequency everything that he had witnessed. Frequency was very pleased with what BDB had done so far.

He told him, "It's time to reappear in public."

BDB was confused and so he asked, "How are we going to pull that off?"

Frequency said, "We're coming back by spending the Clique's money. It's all illegally and immorally earned anyway. I've got to go to a meeting with a very powerful woman."

BDB thought it was a date, but Frequency had something else in mind.

Frequency said, "Go gather up all of the crew. We have some shopping to do." BDB rounded up all of the guys while Frequency listened in on one of the Judge's encrypted phones as he talked to Mr. White about Frequency and his crew of friends.

The Judge asked, "Could we trust Rome and the Hudson Brothers if it came down to a Mr. White vs. Frequency Hunter show down?"

White couldn't give the Judge a sure fire answer, so the Judge made the decision for him.

The Judge, "You need to sever ties with anyone that both you and Frequency Hunter know. If Frequency can get to these people with the right amount of information and the right amount of money, he may be able to persuade them to turn on you and the Clique. Think of how much is for us and our organization now that you're a member."   Mr. White, "I have no problems with not contacting the Hudson Brothers or Rome, but they know something about me that could jeopardize my business outside of the Clique."

The Judge said, "I have a very simple solution for that."

Mr. White asked, "What's the solution?"

The Judge answered, "Why don't you ask Mr. Dover?"

The Banker had just finished working on some other money transfers when he received instructions from the Judge to transfer a large sum of money to Mr. White. Wimple knew the last time this kind of money was dispatched the Clique became short one member. Wimple was tired from all of the work he had put in already, but he didn't hesitate on the Judge's request. He wondered what soul was about to be put to rest then quickly he shook off the thought. He moved the money into Mr. White's spending account and did the appropriate paper work to make everything look legit.

Albe Wimple then had a very earth shattering thought: What if this mess came back to haunt him? How would he survive with no cash flow and no business? He thought about his current lifestyle and his beautiful wife. Then he had an even more troubling thought: What if the Judge decided that it was time for him to meet his maker? Wimple couldn't shake the thought so he decided to put aside some readily available cash just in case the Judge ever decided that he knew too much. Wimple opened up all of his accounts and set up withdrawals of cash to be picked up the next time he was leaving work.

Mr. White had finished up all of his morning chores so he went to meet with Mr. Wimple. Mr. White was enjoying the new abundance of cash that membership in the Clique had afforded him. He went out and bought himself a new Porsche Cayenne Roth edition SUV. It was powerfully fast and Mr. White made sure that anyone who challenged him paid dearly. It didn't take him long to make it to the drop spot for the money the Judge and Mr. Wimple had left for him.

White pulled into the old warehouse, parked next to the old office, and walked inside. There was a briefcase on the old desk that was unlocked and full of money. It also contained a cell phone and a note. Mr. White picked up the phone and the note. which read "If you have decided to go through with the plan at hand call the number on the paper and tell the individual on the other end where to go to find the subjects. Mr. White looked at all of the one hundred dollar bills and started dialing. He told the person on the other end how to handle the Hudson Brothers and Rome. He told the subject that he would be leaving town immediately, and didn't wish to be notified when the job was done. White hung up the phone and took all of the money out of the briefcase. He left the note and the phone in the briefcase as he looked around the old warehouse until he found an old gas can with a little gas left in it. He poured the gas over the phone and paper and set it on fire. He hurriedly jumped into the Porsche and headed out of town.

Frequency had heard enough and he was furious at the thought! The rest of his crew came into the room and he told them what he had just heard. EoW and Don1 were both furious and wanted to warn Rome about Mr. White's plan. Frequency knew the Hudson brothers' mother and he couldn't bear the thought of hurting her. Frequency decided to a least warn Rome and the Hudson Brothers of their impending doom.

Frequency said, "I'll take care of the Hudson Brothers, if EoW and Don1 handle Rome."

Roz came into the room and asked, "Are we still going shopping?"

Frequency said, "We sure are just as soon as we return from a little errand."

Roz gave Frequency the report that she had spent the night running. It said the nanobytes in his system had doubled and his healing rate had increased at a phenomenal rate.

Frequency smiled and tried to explain to the crew what that meant. BDB and Webb were confused so Frequency gave them a small demonstration. He took off his shirt and showed them his upper body.

Webb said, "You look fine to me."

BDB asked, "Where are the scars from the attack?"

Webb realized that the nanobytes were healing Frequency from the inside like a damn plastic surgeon. Webb asked Frequency about their nanobytes. Frequency grabbed a stun gun from a nearby table and shot Webb with it. Webb was hurled to the floor and all of the crew ran to help him.

Roz looked at Frequency and shouted, "What in hell are you doing?"

Frequency said, "I just fixed the problem with his nanobytes."

Roz had the guys put Webb on the exam table and ran the scanner over him. Sure enough his nanobytes had double and his recovery rate had increased.

Webb came to and was ready to fight.

Frequency, "Calm down," and Roz explained everything to him.

Webb still didn't get it until EoW said, "It's like Wolverine in the X-Men comic strip, only not as fast."

Webb understood fully and was excited by his new found healing powers.

Neither EoW nor Don1 wanted to be shocked so Frequency said, "I'll get you guys when you least expect it."

BDB was about to sneak away when Frequency said, "I won't get you until further test are run. Go unhook the trailer from your truck and take the signs off of it. Everybody be on standby and have Long Haul ready to roll as soon as I return."

BDB said, "This truck isn't in the best shape and could use some work, but it'll get you where you need to go." BDB explained how to put the truck in four wheel drive. Frequency said, "I'm off to visit the mother of some old friends."

Mr. Wimple made it home and found his wife sitting in her car. He immediately parked his car and ran to see what was wrong. Mrs. Wimple was terrified and wouldn't leave her car. She pointed to a box that was underneath her seat. Wimple looked under the seat and saw a small box with a note attached to it. He pulled the box out of the car and read the note which said, 'Inside this box is something that will change your life forever.'

Mr. Wimple opened the box and started to scream. "No!" He grabbed his wife by the hand and walked her into the house. Wimple sat his wife down and asked her, "Did they harm you in any way?"

Mrs. Wimple said, "It's all on that DVD inside."

Mr. Wimple played the DVD and saw for himself how Ms. Bobbie and Madame toyed around with his wife. They told her that she should tell her husband he to convince the Judge to bring more money back their way instead of to Mr. White. To let Mr. Wimple know that they meant what they said, Ms. Bobbie showed Mrs. Wimple what she was going to get if her husband refused to do what they asked.

Mr. Wimple picked his wife up and took her to the master bedroom where he gently stripped off her clothes. He immediately stripped out of his and took her into the shower. The two of them took a shower together as he tried to help her wash away the memory of what had happened to her.

Afterwards, Mr. Wimple held his wife close and promised her that he would take care of this intrusion immediately. Then Mr. Wimple took all of the clothes he'd taken off his wife to the fireplace and burned them.

He immediately called the Judge and found out the Judge was already aware of the situation. The Judge expressed his displeasure and firmly promised the Banker that he would handle it swiftly and without mercy.

Chapter 19

The Judge

U.S. District Judge Warren Hill had a lot of things going on and he couldn't afford the luxury of excuses from anyone. His personal life was fine, but his professional life was headed to hell in a hand basket! The Judge had to get his Clique back under control and he had to do it immediately. The Banker had entirely too much information on him so he couldn't let him out of his sight, and to top it off, the Banker also had total access to all of the Judge's finances.

The Judge had to very quickly get in touch with the Dark Crew, a pack of mercenaries that he put together to handle his dirty work. The Judge called the leader and gave him instruction about taking out Mr. White's associates Rome and the Hudson Brothers.

The leader asked, "Which one do you want to disappear first?"

The Judge told him, "Take out the Hudson Brothers first because they'll be the most difficult to handle."

The Leader said, "I'll contact you when the deed is done."

The Judge ended that call, and then he dialed Gay Mack. and was very upset when Gay Mack's answering service picked up. He was so intensely upset that he hurled his cell phone to the ground and stomped it. He realized what he had just done and went to his bed-room to get his car keys. He burst into the room and found his woman using a vibrator. She didn't hear him come in until it was too late. The Judge was even angrier and snatched the toy from her and stomped it.

His woman jumped up and pushed him from be-hind and the Judge turned and smacked her hard on the cheek. Lydia fell to the floor and looked up at the Judge, who opened his robe and beckoned for Lydia to come pleasure him. Lydia got to her knees and con-sumed the Judge's manhood. The Judge had taken some male enhancement pills and they had started to work. He let his temper get the best of him and now he was about to take it out on Lydia. The Judge usually would have a younger and smaller woman in his presence, but Lydia would have to do for this moment.

Lydia couldn't understand what was going on with the Judge and decided not to fight him. She knew that the Judge was usually good for a few minutes before he'd be fast asleep. The Judge had a surprise for her this time, and he decided to wait until she'd given him her best. The Judge felt like a new man once Lydia backed away from him exhausted.

The Judge rolled her on her stomach and had his way with her. He performed like he was a twenty one year old man, as he worked out all his anger on Lydia's body, pulled himself out, and left her lying on the floor in a heap. Then he went and took a quick shower, dried himself off, and got dressed.

Lydia slowly got up from the floor, sore from the pounding she had just taken from the Judge. She felt his semen run from her body and knew she'd blacked out from the brutality. The Judge had been brutal before, but it had only lasted a few minutes before he'd collapse into a deep sleep. Lydia slowly walked into the bathroom and prepared herself a hot bath to soak in. She climbed into the tub while the water was running and squeezed in some bubble bath to help her relax.

The Judge totally ignored Lydia and headed straight for the garage. He jumped into his Maserati, pushed the garage door opener, then zoomed out of the garage and headed for the city. The Judge called the Banker, who had just made it to work when his phone rang.

He answered it and the Judge asked, "Where's that cellular shop where you got your new phone?"

Mr. Wimple told him and the Judge said, "I'll be at the bank as soon as I pick up a new phone."

Wimple hung up the phone and called BDB. He said, The Judge is headed to your friend's cellular shop and he'll be needing some assistance."

BDB said, "I'll notify the same clerk that helped you to help the Judge."

Wimple asked, "Can you meet me for lunch?"

BDB could sense that something was very wrong so he said, "Sure, I'll meet you for lunch."

Wimple said, "Meet me in the bank's lobby at noon. We'll leave from there."

Frequency had left the center and was going to a part of town he hadn't been to in years. He knew he could make to his destination with no problem thanks to the two-inch lift on BDB's truck. Frequency drove through the old wooded area to see the Hudson brothers' mother. She still lived in the same neighborhood where they'd grown up.

Frequency got out of the truck and headed for the house. He was met by someone that had worked for Mrs. Hudson for years and was still faithfully employed. Liz was just about to go in the house when she heard a familiar voice and turned to see Frequency standing in front of her.

She told him, "Come and give me a hug!"

Frequency gave Liz a hug and a kiss on her cheek.

Liz invited him in and said, "I'll tell Mrs. Hudson you're there to visit."

Frequency knew the boys hadn't told their mom that they'd been feuding, so he'd have to tell her. He also knew that Mother Hudson was a no-nonsense type of woman who had already put two men in the ground and earned the nickname the Mother Widow.

Mother Hudson came into the room and immediately gave him a big hug. She told him, "I ought to whip your behind for not coming by to see me sooner!"

Frequency looked at Mrs. Hudson and thought this woman still looks good! He told her, "I don't need any of your old boyfriends coming to hunt me down."

She smiled and said, "You're just joining me for lunch and I will not take 'no' for an answer."

Mrs. Hudson told Liz, "Set the table for three so you can join us for lunch." When Liz had everything ready, the three of them sat and ate their meal. Then

Liz and Mrs. Hudson cleared the table, then came back and sat down.

Mrs. Hudson asked Frequency, "What brings you to the old neighborhood?"

Frequency took a deep breath, and then told them everything that had happened between his crew and her sons. He didn't leave out any of the details.

Mrs. Hudson asked, "So what about your loyalty to your lifelong friends?"

Frequency went high tech on her and asked if he could borrow her counter top LCD screen.

Mrs. Hudson said, "Sure as long as you don't take it out of the room."

Frequency connected with CMAX and had CMAX play back all of the video footage they'd captured via Mrs. Hudson LCD panel. She and Liz watched in silence until the footage ended. As soon as the footage ended, Mrs. Hudson was on the phone calling her sons. Neither one of them answered so she sent Liz to get them.

Mark and John shared one of the houses that their mother owned. They had moved girls in with them and had been shacking without telling their mom. Krystal and Nina both had submitted to the brothers and let it be known that they were not going anywhere. Mark had Krystal wear a diamond studded collar that attached to a diamond studded shackle on his right wrist. The two had a platinum chain that connected them. John and Nina had a matching set of diamond hoop earrings that had their names in them. The couples were still sound asleep after a night of intense love-making. The men were so tired that neither of them heard the phone ring when their mom called. Even worse was the fact that when Liz let herself into their house, not even their barking dog notified them that she was inside.

First Liz went to John's room and saw him and some woman naked in his bed. She left that room and went to Mark's room and saw him naked with another woman chained to his wrist. Liz went back into the room where John was and grabbed him by the neck and his right wrist. John moved to grab his pistol under the pillow but he couldn't. He knew that hold was done by only one person, and he didn't dare cross her.

John calmly said, "Liz can I at least put some clothes on?"

Liz let John go and went to Mark's room and did the same to him. The outcome was a little different in Mark's room because he and Krystal didn't take the chain off the collar and wrist shackle. Mark couldn't move and Krystal got choked a little bit.

As soon as Mark realized Liz had a hold of him, he thought something might be wrong with their mother. He jumped up, but then remembered he was still chained to Krystal, so he unhooked the chain and quickly got dressed. Liz left the room and waited for the boys to come out and talk to her. John and Nina were first, and then came Mark and Krystal.

Neither of them had an explanation for not going to see their mom lately and they couldn't tell Liz without hesitating that Krystal and Nina had moved in.

Liz told them, "Get the girls in the car cause we're going to see Mother Hudson." The boys didn't say a word as they rushed the girls into their rooms to get respectfully dressed to meet their mother

Mother Hudson was happy to see Liz pull up with the boys in the car, but she was a little perplexed as to who the women with them were.   Liz   came   in without saying a word. She did laugh out loud as the boys led their girlfriends into their mother's house for the first time.

Mother Hudson and the boys sat down to discuss the matter at hand. John and Mark both nearly pissed their pants when Frequency walked into the room. Frequency had caught them at their weakest moment and John and Mark felt vulnerable to a sneak attack from Frequency if he chose to do so.

Frequency said, "Look guys, I'm just here to warn you not go to war with you."

Mother Hudson said, "Show the boys the footage that you have and then let them hear how easily Mr. White change sides on them."

Mark and John were mad as hell after they watched all the footage that Frequency had.

Mother Hudson told Frequency, "You can leave now and thank you," as she gave him a hug and a kiss on his cheek. Mother Hudson told Frequency in front of her sons, "You have an open door invitation here and you're always welcome." Frequency thanked Mother Hudson and then followed Liz as she walked him to the door.

As soon as Liz opened the front door all hell broke loose as the squad of killers White hired began shooting. It was a miracle that neither Liz nor Frequency was hit as Frequency kicked the door closed and followed Liz back into the living room where everybody else was.

Liz quickly shouted, "We're being shot at!" The Hudson brothers started scurrying for cover. Liz and Mother Hudson went into different rooms and returned with some firepower of their own.

Mother Hudson said, "Liz take the boys to the basement and get them some weapons from my stash."

John laughed as Mark ask, "Where'd you get guns Mom?"

Before she could answer shots started coming through the wall. John and Liz returned from the basement with an assortment of rifles and shotguns, plus plenty of ammo. Everybody grabbed a gun of some kind and found a position within the house to get off some clear shots.

Frequency went back through the kitchen and saw that the men had their vehicles parked back there and on the side of the house. He waited until everybody in the house returned fire then bolted outside to the vehicles. There were only two guys watching the vehicles and Frequency shot one in the foot and the other in the arm. He quickly grabbed their automatic weapons and disabled their vehicles, and then he ran back into the house where John and Mark had been watching.

John said, "Man I thought you had abandoned us."

Frequency said, "No, I just wanted to even up the odds a bit." He handed John and Mark the automatic weapons and asked if they knew how to use them.

Mark and John let their actions answer for them as they went to work dismantling the squad of hired assassins. The last few tried to run off, but Liz and Mother Hudson took care of them. As they finished up they heard a truck crank and take off.

John was about to shoot, but Mother Hudson stopped him and said, Frequency just saved all our lives."

John dropped his weapon and hugged his mother. All of them started gathering items to put away while they waited for the police. Mother Hudson knew they were in a world of legal trouble, so she called the family attorney and explained everything that had just happened. The attorney was shocked to hear the details and told Mother Hudson, "I'm on the job. We'll be ready for whatever charges they bring."

Frequency made it back to the main highway without a hitch. BDB's big truck coughed and sputtered from time to time, but it made it back to the center, where Webb was waiting for him. Frequency told Webb about the ambush. Webb was hyped and ready to go after some vendetta, but Frequency convinced him to hold back until everything was in place.

Webb was still uneasy about it until Frequency told him something that made everything else unimportant. Frequency said, "Now everybody gets to go buy themselves the vehicle of their choice, as long as it's fully loaded."

Webb went and got EoW, Roz, and Don1. He found a note from BDB that said he had gotten a taxi and was having lunch with the banker. Frequency said, "Just pile into BDB's old pickup and I'll take you to the dealerships to get the cars of your choice."

Since Roz was the only woman, she got to pick her vehicle first. She chose a fully loaded "R" class Mercedes. The guys did rock, paper, scissors for who'd be next and EoW won. He chose a fully loaded E500 AMG Mercedes straight off the showroom floor. Webb and Don1 didn't want Mercedes so Frequency paid for two vehicles and left the Mercedes dealership.

Then they went to the Cadillac dealership where Don1 chose a fully loaded DTS Limited off the showroom floor and left instructions to have it customized just for him. Frequency paid for this vehicle and he and Webb headed to the next dealership.

Webb was undecided until he saw a limited edition Chevy 2500 HD and decided that he wanted it, but only if it could be customized just for him. Frequency said, "Dude, get whatever you want and Webb picked out the CHEVY HD that he liked and had it shipped off to his favorite custom shop. Frequency paid the bill and left Webb there to handle the details.

Then Frequency got on the phone with BDB who had just finished his meeting with the banker.

BDB said, "I was just about to hail a cab."

Frequency said, "Do that and meet me at the truck dealership that's just off the interstate loop."

BDB asked, "Why, what's up?"

Frequency said, "Your truck is in dire need of an upgrade so let's take the time to get it done now."

BDB didn't think anything of it and said, "I'll be there shortly."

BDB arrived at the dealership and saw Frequency inside looking at a fine International CXT pickup truck. He was very impressed with the truck and said, "When I get my money right; this is the kind of truck I'm going to buy."

Frequency egged him on by asking, "Would you have the DVD entertainment system in it like this one?"

BDB said the only thing that I'd change about that truck is the name on the title."

The two men laughed and saw the manager of the dealership come out and start putting a temporary tag in the window of the truck.

BDB tapped Frequency on the shoulder and said, "We better move. Looks like somebody beat me to this one."

The manager walked over to Frequency and asked, "Is this the friend we've been waiting on?"

Frequency said, "Yes, the one and only!" and the manager handed BDB some papers to sign.

BDB asked, "What are these for?"

The manager said, "It's the trade in for your truck and the paper to get tags for this CXT."

BDB felt like shouting and started running all around the dealership! He ran back over to Frequency and the manager and hugged them both.

BDB stepped back to regain control and said, "If you don't want your doors damaged, I suggest that you open them up."

The manager said, "I sure will as soon as all of the paperwork is taken care of. True to his word, the manager unlocked the doors and handed BDB the keys to his new truck as soon as they finished the paper work. Then he and Frequency jumped into the CXT and headed for the center.

The Judge had picked up his new cellular phone and was headed home when the banker called with the bad news.

The Banker said, "The hit on Mr. White's friends had gone way bad. All the members of the team had been killed and the other guy has disappeared without a trace!".

The Judge said, "Mr. White will have to handle his own problems."

The Banker said, "No, it's our problem too because the Clique's main account has been hit!"

The Judge was very upset and asked, "Just how in hell did they manage to do that?"

The Banker said, "It wasn't 'them' but just 'him' and he left you a personal message."

The Judge asked, "What did the message say?"

The Banker put the Judge on hold and did a three-way call to listen to the message. The Judge heard a computer generated voice that said, "YOU"VE BEEN FREAKED!"

The Judge started screaming with anger.

The Banker was dumbfounded until the Judge regained his composure and told the Banker, "We've been hacked by Frequency Hunter!"

The Banker was speechless. He had no idea what to do next.

The Judge asked, "how much did he take?"

The banker replied, "All of it.

Agent Layrock was awakened by an early morning phone call. He was ordered to meet with a Federal Judge about a case he was working on. As soon as he could make it to the Judge's office he walked in and saw Probation Officer Mack Master sitting in the room with Judge Warren Hill.

Judge Hill said, "Please sit down. I have evidence that Frequency Hunter is up to his old tricks again."

Mack Master was surprised, but remained quiet.

Agent Layrock spoke up and said, "That's impossible because Frequency Hunter is missing and presumed dead."

The Judge said, "But that can't be. He left me his calling card and took all of my money from my account!"

The Judge played back the message and said, "This has to be him. He is the only one capable of something this big!"

Agent Layrock pulled out his laptop and showed the Judge the footage of the wreckage. He detailed to the Judge all of the information that pointed to Frequency Hunter crashing his motorcycle and being lost in the rushing river.

The Judge was floored and didn't have anything else to say.

Mr. Mack Master spoke up and said, "The night of the accident, Frequency Hunter's home was bombed and set ablaze. The firefighters found pieces of his main computer throughout the rubble."

The Judge asked, "Was a body found?"

Agent Layrock told him,"No."

The Judge told the two men, "You should assume he's alive until you have a body to show for it. Now if you'll be so kind as to leave, I have a meeting with my accountant to try and fix this problem."

Layrock and Mack Master walked out of the Judge's office.

Once they were outside, Mack Master asked Agent Layrock, "Do you really think Frequency Hunter's dead?"

Layrock said, "Hell no, I just said that to get the Judge off my ass. If I'd agreed with the Judge I wouldn't have been able to finish up the case I am working on now. I am determined to catch the persons responsible for the attack on my team and all of the other people involved, including you."

Mack Master said, "I appreciate that, and I hope I'll be there to put the cuffs on the bastards when you catch them."

Layrock promised, "I'll personally guarantee that you have that opportunity when the time comes."

The Judge was so incensed he could barely see straight! He was trying to deal with all of the companies that he owed money without any money. He'd never been in this position and he didn't like it.

Mr. White called and the Judge gave him an earful.

Mr. White told the Judge, "You used your people and they failed miserably. Now you have to fix this mess you've made!"

The Judge said, "I've been hacked and this time, all of my money is missing."

Mr. White laughed and said, "It sounds like you have some kind of rat."

The Judge cut Mr. White's laughter short when he said, "I'm suspending all of the members' payments until my problem is eradicated."   The Judge disconnected that call and placed a call to the Banker. He said, "All members' payments are to be suspended until further notice!"

The Banker didn't ask any questions as he transferred all of the Clique's earnings into the Judge's account.

As soon as the money was in his account, the Judge paid off all his creditors and withdrew a third of what was left. Then the Judge had the all the Clique members contacted with instructions on when and where to meet.

The Judge was in a vicious zone and wanted to make an example out of one of the weaker members of the Clique. He had everybody sitting in their assigned seats, and was walking around the table asking each member questions about their last retreat. The Judge had decided to discipline whichever member could not give him a direct answer. Unfortunately, it was Ms. Bobbie and the Gay Mack, who didn't take the Judge seriously. The Judge hit Ms. Bobbie across the back of the head knocking him into Gay Mack's lap. The Judge then kicked the Gay Mack in the face and pulled out a gold plated Desert Eagle.

The Banker jumped in front of the Judge and made him come back to his senses. The Banker then directed everybody to get back to their places and calm down.

The Banker said, "The Judge has been robbed by a computer hacker." Everybody at the table was shocked to hear that.

The Banker continued, "The hacker also gained access to the Clique's database and historical information."

All of the members were concerned except for Mr. White because he was the newest member and there was nothing in the database that could hurt him.

The Banker turned to Mr. White and said, "It appears that everything you brought to the organization has begun to sour. Frequency Hunter is the man causing all of these problems."

Mr. White turned to the Judge and asked, "What do you want me to do about it?"

The Judge said, "I'm going to handle Frequency Hunter once and for all. I'll let the judicial system make Frequency Hunter disappear and once he's behind bars for the rest of his life, the prison system will handle the rest."

Agent Layrock and his team were back on the case and were putting together a lot of information coming in from an unknown source. Mack Master contacted Agent Layrock and told him, "I haven't been able to find Frequency Hunter anywhere."

Agent Layrock said, "Hold off for now. Don't put out a warrant for his arrest just yet, because I have a hunch that Frequency Hunter will show up in some grandioso fashion and have some answer for a lot of question that the Feds have."

Agent Pain came into the room and gave Layrock some interesting news. "Don1 showed up at his condo in a brand new Cadillac DTS and it's fully loaded."

Layrock asked, "Did you speak to him?"

She said, "No, but I'm going to pop by the condo tonight just to see if he'll be there."

Layrock told her, "Keep me informed."

Mack Master and Agent Layrock went over some new information that Layrock had received from his agents, and then Mack Master left to go visit some other parolees.

Frequency Hunter was on cloud nine! He had administered shock treatments to all of the team members and CMAX reported that all of the member's nanobytes were functioning 100%. Frequency had each member go about their daily routines as their new vehicles were delivered from the various dealerships. Everybody in his crew had brand new vehicles except for him. He decided to wait until after all of the mess he was in was cleared up before he bought himself a new set of wheels. Frequency watched from the center as each member received the keys for their new cars.

He was so happy that he could give them something for just sticking by him in his time of need. Frequency then pulled in the newest information from the Judge and saw that the Judge had a meeting to discuss his latest shortcomings. Frequency saw his old friend Mr. White and laughed at the thought of what the Hudson's and Rome were going to do to him.

Judge Warren Hill was headed to his chamber to get ready for another day of sending lawbreakers to jail. He'd just unlocked his door when one of the clerks approached him and asked if she could speak to him in private. The Judge had strict rules for all of his employees to follow and this particular employee was breaking a rule.

The Judge didn't trust anyone under his jurisdiction to be alone with him. He knew the possible ramifications of an employee making up some kind of false charges against him.

The Judge asked, "What is your full name?"

She said, My name is Melody Walker."

The Judge asked, "What do you need?"

Ms. Walker said, "My 14-year-old daughter is about to appear in your courtroom."

The Judge asked, "Why are you talking to me, because I will stand up for the law at all cost."

Ms. Walker looked at Judge Hill and said, "The Madame told me to talk to you."

The Judge was furious! He would take his anger out on this lady and all others who brought this trash to his bench.

The Judge opened the door to his chamber, then turned to Ms. Walker and said, "You must contact Madame and follow the instructions she gives you. If you are late or miss any details, you will pay dearly."

Then he slammed his chamber door shut and kicked a vase to pieces. The Judge made a call to the Madame and told her what to do for Ms. Melody Walker. He told Madame, "You're damn lucky that Big Trouble is a close associate of mine or your fate would be sealed."

Madame hung up the phone and opened the bottle of gin that was on her table. She poured herself a big glass full and downed it. Madame stripped down to her bra and panties and went to look for Big Trouble. She was horny and had enough of him ignoring her. Big Trouble was just getting out of the shower when Madame burst into the room and jumped on his back. He caught his balance and adjusted his weight to keep from falling.

Madame started swinging like a mad woman and hitting Big Trouble on the top of his head. Big Trouble tried to throw her off but she would not let go. He grabbed her arms to keep her from hitting him and she kneed him in the stomach. Big Trouble took the blow and threw Madame across the floor. She hit the floor hard and didn't move. Big Trouble knew he had hurt her so he ran to her. Madame quickly wrapped her legs around Big Trouble's waist and would not let go. The two scuffled until they found themselves in a passionate embrace naked on the floor.

Judge Hill had before him his last case of the evening. One Ms. Renee Walker was called and the Judge saw Ms. Melody Walker sitting beside her. Renee and Melody were arguing about something and the Judge became angry.

He said, "Both of you shut up. Renee Walker step forward."

Renee stepped forward and the Judge could see that she had a wild streak a mile long. The Judge looked at her record and found himself becoming aroused.

He asked his bailiff, "What are the charges?"

The bailiff said, "Indecent exposure and resisting arrest."

The Judge read her rap sheet and saw that Renee was only fourteen years old and was already out of control. Her mother Melody had lost control long ago and there was no sign of a father figure in her life. The Judge decided that he'd have a little mother -- daughter action very soon.

The Judge said, "Renee Walker I sentence you to a six week boot camp course at The Center for Unreformed Children. While you're there you'll learn the proper way to act and how treat your mother."

Renee yelled "I'm not going anywhere with anyone!"

The Judge had the bailiff to restrain her and lock her in the solitary cell of the courthouse. Her mother stood and was about to say something when the Judge had her arrested for contempt of court. Both of them were handcuffed and taken to the solitary confinement cell in the courthouse.

The Judge loved what he saw in Renee and was ready to feel her young flesh. He was totally gone and had no mind for decency or reasoning, and trouble did not matter. The Judge turned on his surveillance system monitor and saw that the solitary confinement area was not under the full video surveillance system. He licked his lips as he knew that he was about to indulge in some young girl flesh.

The Judge took his pants and underwear off. He grabbed a gavel that he liked to break his first timers in with and some KY jelly. He went down the private fire escape so no one could see him, and found his way into the containment area. There was only one guard on duty. The Judge knew that it took two hours to do rounds for the guard so he waited until the guard came by and entered the code to signal that he was beginning his rounds.

As soon as the door closed the Judge went into the confinement chamber and shut off the lights. Melody screamed and Renee ran to the corner of her cell. The Judge sat still and didn't make a sound. Melody quieted down and Renee starting making fun of her. Renee was cocky and she was making so much noise that she didn't hear the Judge enter her mother's cell and knock her unconscious. The Judge put Melody on the cot in her cell then exited the cell.

Renee walked over to the bars and felt a sharp whack on the side of her head. She fell to the floor and before she could move she felt herself being dragged across the floor. Renee began to struggle but it was too late and the Judge was too strong. Renee screamed as the Judge forced himself into her. Renee fought for a little while but finally collapsed from exhaustion. The Judge indulged himself inside of Renee until he unleashed his desire within her.

He stood up from Renee and found himself wanting more. He had done all he could to her so he turned his fury against her mother. The Judge went into Melody's cell and gave Melody the same treatment that he'd given her daughter. Just as the Judge finished his debauchery, the alarm on his watch went off. The Judge knew he had exactly fifteen minutes before the guard came back.

The Judge took out a cleansing solution and injected it into both victims. He put them on their cots and covered them up as if they were sleeping. The Judge slipped out of the cell and turned on the lights. The door shut behind him as he made it up the stairs and back to his chamber. The Judge hurriedly took a shower and placed all of the items that he had worn in a plastic bag. He made sure that everything was in its proper place and then exited his chamber. No one was in the building and he headed straight for the garage where his car was parked. The Judge got into the Maserati and headed straight to the incinerator. The Judge had his friend who worked there burn the contents of the bag, no questions asked.

The following morning chaos was widespread throughout the courthouse. The news media had found out that a mother and daughter had been sexually assaulted in the courthouse lock up. Judge Hill was home watching the news thinking about his little rendezvous the night before. He was beside himself when heard the news reporter say that there was no evidence found anywhere in the area to lead to a suspect. The Judge got out of his bed and strutted around like a peacock. He took a shower and then prepared himself for his morning activities. The Judge had decided to take the day off, so he put on some leisure clothes and headed for one of the local breakfast restaurants. The Judge let the wind blow all of his past debauchery out of his mind as he headed to get himself a hearty breakfast.

After breakfast the Judge went and played a game of golf at the golf club. He played all eighteen holes and then went and had lunch at a local Italian restaurant called Old Venice. The Judge ordered his food and ate it all and had ordered wine. He finished his meal and gave his waitress his credit card to pay for his meal. The waitress came back with a puzzled look on her face. The Judge saw her and she gave the Judge his receipt. The amount on the receipt was correct, but at the bottom of the receipt it read, "You've Been Freaked!"

Chapter 20

Freak's Masterpiece

Frequency Hunter stood outside where his old house used to be. Everything had been destroyed in the fire except his safe in the basement of the house. The only things he owned now were the items inside Long Haul. He went to the area where the basement stairs would have been and lowered himself using the wench on Long Haul. Frequency had to maneuver around a lot of charred lumber before he found the safe and hooked it to the winch cable.

Frequency climbed back out of the basement on his own, then activated the winch and pulled the safe out of the basement. He opened the safe, gathered all of his important papers, and then called in the damage report to his insurance company.

The insurance agent pulled his account and said, "We've been trying to reach you Mr. Hunter since the fire occurred We've already sent out a representative who confirmed that your house was a total loss, so you've already been cut a check for the appraised value of your home. When would you like to pick it up?"

Frequency was happy about that because the appraisal was three times what he'd paid for it. Frequency really didn't have his mind on his business because.

he was focused on what he was going to do to the people who were responsible for his troubles. Frequency had already notified the Judge and was assembling his own troops to take out the Judge's entire crew. Frequency had all of the information he needed to lock the Judge up for life. He'd really cut up when he hid all of the information on his probation officer's computer.

Frequency got finished with the insurance company and left instructions for them to wire the money directly into his account. Then he contacted Agent Layrock and Mack Master to set up a face to face meeting. Frequency contacted his crew and told them about the meeting with Mack Master and the Feds. EoW, Don1, BDB, and Webb showed up and met with Agent Layrock and Mack Master first.

Frequency watched from a distance as the crew gave the officers the information they had gathered. Agent Layrock was furious! He wanted to go get the Judge immediately, but he knew the Judge was very well connected so he needed to catch him red handed. Mack Master just wanted to see Frequency Hunter and he was persistent in questioning the guys on his whereabouts.

The crew would not budge until both men promised them that Frequency wouldn't be arrested until the case was closed. Agent Layrock guaranteed the crew that Frequency's arrest could wait. Mack Master was 'by the book' and he was being very stubborn.

BDB told Mack Master, "This is your only chance. Frequency could disappear and take pertinent information with him. Then you'll never be able to finish this crime spree case."

Mack Master finally folded and BDB contacted Frequency who soon drove up in Long Haul and shook hands with his crew. He shook hands with Mack Master and Layrock as well before they all stepped inside Long Haul. Once everyone was seated and settled inside, Frequency played back all of the information they had collected. He even showed the Feds how he'd been sending them information that they failed to use properly. Agent Layrock was quite impressed and was thinking outside the box.

Mack Master smacked Frequency on the back and said, "I want to thank you for letting me know that I was about to be attacked."

Both men could clearly see that all of the information led back to one man: Judge Warren Hill.

Judge Hill was livid! Frequency Hunter was alive and well and was toying with him. The Judge called Mr. White and demanded to know everything there was to know about Frequency Hunter.

Mr. White gave the Judge all of the information he had available, and offered his assistance in helping eradicate Mr. Hunter.

The Judge called in another group of his mercenaries and said, "I want Frequency Hunter's head on a platter! I will give $100,000 to the man who takes Frequency Hunter out."

The merc said, "I will make sure that Frequency hunted no more."

Judge Hill then said, "I'll add in an extra $100,000 if you wipe out his entire crew and anyone they have with them!"

The merc said, "I'll take care of everything."

Agent Layrock was rolling hard as he headed for the house where Big Trouble and Madame lived. When he got there the place was abandoned. Somehow they had been notified and were long gone. Layrock then directed federal agents to raid the location that had been given to him by Frequency, and he was able to find a few of the missing teenagers. Layrock made it to CupCake's home just in time to see her and another young lady leaving on motorcycles in a hurry. Layrock gave chase but the motorcycles easily outran his automobile. Layrock was upset until he received a call from Frequency saying he'd patched in the homing signal of CupCake's cell phone to Layrock's phone. Now Agent Layrock could follow CupCake anywhere in the world.

Layrock quickly notified his team and told them to use the GPS in his car to follow him. The team followed instructions exactly and soon converged on a farm way on the outskirts of town. Layrock briefed his team on what he had found. CupCake and her girl had been notified by the Judge that they were coming. He told them that their cover had been blown and that the Banker was missing. The Judge told CupCake to meet him at the farm to receive payment and then disappear with her girl.

Next the Gay Mack and Ms. Bobbie showed up. There was no sign of Big Trouble but the Madame showed up.

Madame said, "Big Trouble disappeared sometime during the night."

The Judge said, "I haven't been able to contact the Banker and the people at the bank said that they haven't heard from him either." The Judge took a call that made him cringe.

The mercs said, "The center where the targets were staying was destroyed, but there were no bodies inside."

The Judge was about to go off, but then the alarm sounded to let him know that it was time to leave. The Judge decided that he no longer needed the services of his Clique members and decided to finish them all off.

The Judge calmly said, "I've enjoyed working with all of you," then he pulled out a gun and started firing. He caught CupCake's girl in the chest with the first shot killing her instantly. The rest of the Clique scattered as the Judge continued shooting up the place.

Agent Layrock and his team heard the shots and decided to move in. The Gay Mack and Ms. Bobbie made it to their vehicles and got weapons of their own. They started to run, but when they saw the Feds coming, they ran back into the building to face the Judge. CupCake and Madame were together but they separated after the Judge chased the Gay Mack and Ms. Bobbie. Madame pulled a Glock 9 out of her purse and decided to fight instead of run. CupCake just hung close to Madame without a word.

The Federal Agents kicked in the door and the Judge hit them from up high. He shot about four agents before they could see where shots were coming from. One of the agents crawled to the side and Madame shot him in the head and took his weapon. CupCake grabbed his side arm and started firing shots up at the Judge. The Judge started laughing maniacally, and was about to take her out when Madame fired shots from the slain officer's weapon.

The Judge quickly moved to another spot and that gave CupCake time to get her own high powered weapon from another slain agent. The Judge saw that he was out numbered so he called for his cavalry. The mercs that he'd hired flew in via helicopter that was outfitted with a minigun. They took out the Federal cars, and then started raining shots onto the building and the surrounding area.

Several of Agent Layrock's men got hit but they continued to fight back as best they could. Layrock heard a high powered rifle shot and saw smoke coming from the helicopter's engine. Next he saw an old Monte Carlo drive up with Mack Master at the wheel. Old Mack made the shot that gave Layrock and his men the break they needed.

Then agent Layrock saw something that he thought was an illusion. It was a humongous truck and it was coming fast! The truck stopped in front of him and he saw BDB at the wheel. In the back of the truck were Frequency, Don1, Agent Pain, and EoW. Webb got out of the truck and handed Layrock and Mack Master an EMP weapon. He briefed them on how it worked and how to use it, and then they all gathered together and went to handle the problem at hand.

The Judge was still inside wreaking havoc on everyone he saw. Madame had just run around a corner and was in his crosshairs when the Gay Mack shot him in his side. The Judge turned quickly and returned fire hitting Gay Mack twice but not killing him. Frequency and all of the men with him ran inside and kept his eyes open for the Judge. He saw CupCake running by and gave chase. The Judge caught sight of him and started firing shots like a madman until he ran out of ammo. Then the mercs came in and told the Judge that the helicopter had been shot down but it was a minor repair.

They gave the Judge more ammo and told him, "You get out and let us take over." The Judge reloaded his weapon and headed for the helicopter.

Ms. Bobbie was moving as quietly as he could until he tripped over something. He looked down and saw the Gay Mack, and he was really messed up. Ms. Bobbie started crying and trying to stop the bleeding.

Gay Mack said, "Don't worry 'bout me. I'll live if you can get me some medical help in time."

Ms. Bobbie said, "Alright, but I will get the Judge for this!!" He gathered his composure and went after the Judge. Ms. Bobbie was going on pure emotion. He was going to make the Judge pay for hurting Gay Mack. He saw an open door and hurriedly made his way to it.

Ms. Bobbie made his way inside and saw no one. He moved around as quietly as possible. Ms. Bobbie went around a corner and got a glimpse of another person, but it was the Madame and she was walking right into a trap. Before Ms. Bobbie could warn her the Judge shot Madame and knocked her to the floor. She dropped her weapon and the Judge ran over and kicked it away from her.

He told her, "Now lie on your stomach," but instead she raised her dress instead and the Judge saw her bulging belly.

He laughed and said, "I didn't know Big Trouble still had it in him," and then there was a shot that caught the Judge in his shoulder. He turned to see who shot him and Madame kicked his feet from under him. He fell to the floor and Ms. Bobbie ran over and hit him in the head with her gun. The Judge lost consciousness and fell to the floor. Ms. Bobbie had him right where she wanted him. The Judge was going to pay for what he'd done to Gay Mack. Ms. Bobbie pulled out a knife and cut the seat of his pants open. She saw an area in the room that would be perfect for what she had in mind.

Agent Layrock and the federal agents were holding their own against the mercs. They were working their magic and slowly took out all the mercs except for five of them. These five pulled back and decided to make a retreat to the helicopter. Layrock remembered that the helicopter had that minigun mounted on it and knew that would be the end of him and his men if the mercs reached it. Layrock decided to let his agent give chase while he went a different way. He made his way around a few corners and thought he heard someone. He followed the sound until he saw a woman run out of a door and go down the hall. Layrock went to the door and heard more noises coming from inside. He stormed in and found a woman with a long knife about to stab someone. Layrock shot the knife out of the woman's hand and she turned around screaming.

Layrock noticed that this 'woman' was having sex with someone and 'she' showed him that 'she' had more to offer than any other woman he'd ever seen. Ms. Bobbie ran toward Agent Layrock and jumped on him. He fired a shot that caught him just to the right of his hard member. Ms. Bobbie doubled up in the air and tumbled to the floor.

Agent Layrock then saw that this thing had fastened someone to a column and was raping him. He went over to the person and started to laugh. It was old Judge Warren Hill himself! "Just what he deserves," thought Layrock. He unfastened the Judge and waited on Mack Master to come and handcuff him. He called to the rest of the agents and asked for a report. The agents had taken out all of the mercs and Frequency's guys had the helicopter on lockdown. Agent Layrock told the men that he had the Judge and that they needed to call in for cleanup.

Frequency chased Cupcake throughout the maze of corridors and down into a tunnel of sorts. He made it to the end of it just in time to see that it was an escape route. Frequency saw that one of the vehicles had already taken off and the occupants were hurt. There was blood spattered all over the ground. Frequency moved around carefully because he knew CupCake was not that far in front of him. Then he heard the engine of a motorcycle start. He ran toward the sound and saw CupCake riding a quad runner out of another part of the escape hatch.

Frequency saw another quad runner in the corner and immediately went to see if it would start. The engine started and Frequency began chasing after CupCake. who had a large lead on him. She knew this guy wouldn't stop chasing her. She still had her weapon and wouldn't hesitate to use it.

Frequency followed the tire tracks to see if he could catch up to CupCake. He was having a hard time until he heard a helicopter overhead. Frequency stopped and pulled out his headset. As soon as he put it on, he heard his crew conversing about how to fly a helicopter.

Don1 was in the driver's seat. He told the others, "I've got lots of hours logged on Microsoft Flight Simulator so that makes me the most qualified person to fly the helicopter."

Frequency interrupted them and said, "Whatever guys, can you go find CupCake on the quad runner up ahead?"

The Helicopter took off and in no time Don1 and the crew had her pinpointed. Frequency rushed ahead and suddenly heard shots fired from the ground and then from the helicopter's minigun.

Frequency asked, "What's going on?"

Webb said, "CupCake is shooting up at us, so I decided to shoot back."

Frequency told Webb, "You can shoot anything you want as long as you leave CupCake to me."

Thanks to his crew Frequency was able to catch up with CupCake who was riding the quad runner hard and hitting jumps and ruts like a pro. What she didn't expect was for her quad runner to lose power all of a sudden. Frequency used the EMP weapon and it worked like a charm. As soon as the round touched the quad runner it shut down. CupCake fell off of the quad runner and hit the ground hard. She immediately grabbed her weapon to fire it, but Frequency had her in his sights. CupCake tried to fire off a round but Frequency took her down. The EMP round knocked her to the ground unconscious. Frequency went over to her and picked up her weapon. By that time BDB, Agent Layrock, and McMaster had shown up.

BDB ran over to his partner and said, "Now you can live."

Frequency handed the weapon to Agent Layrock and put his hands out to be cuffed.

Mack Master said, "There'll be no need for that because I need the guys to take me back to my car." All of the men laughed as the helicopter landed. EoW, Webb, and Don1 came out running and all of them were excited.

Agent Layrock asked, "Will all of you show up to testify in court?"

They said, "We wouldn't miss it for the world!"

Frequency Hunter walked out of the courtroom a free man. The remaining probation time and fines administered to him by Judge Hill were totally waived.

Frequency found out that Madame, Ms. Bobbie, Gay Mack and Mr. White had all escaped. The Banker and his wife were now in the witness protection program. Big Trouble had disappeared into the city's underground, but he stayed in touch with EoW and Don1.

Frequency didn't know what had happened to Roz Well, but he vowed he would find out. The Hudson Brothers chilled out and became backup for Frequency and his crew just in case things ever got out of hand again. Agent Layrock was assigned a new team and had a new partner in Mack Master.

As for Frequency, EoW, Don1, Webb, and BDB. Let's just say, "You've Been Freaked!

Chapter 21

Federal Response Enforcement Against Kid Sex

Agent Layrock walked in his new office and immediately liked what he saw. His desk was shiny and it had a brand new laptop on it. His second in command walked in and was impressed too. Mack Master was a full agent now and was assigned to Layrock's elite team .They went over to inventory their vehicles. They had a helicopter that they commandeered from the mercenaries. Of course, it had been modified with so many new gadgets it was a wonder that it could fly. There were a couple of H2 Hummers, several motorcycles and several high dollar automobiles. There were a couple of command vehicles setup to handle any situation that they might dream up and of course, there were the men to run it.

First there was Don1 the communications specialist. Then there was EoW the computer hardware specialist. Webb was the automobile mechanic specialist, and BDB was their weapons specialist. Frequency was number one agent in control of all them. Frequency was offered the job by the head of the Federal Agents. He was told that they needed his expertise in capturing individuals who harmed children, so Frequency didn't hesitate to take the job. He believed that as long as he did something positive, one day he and

Doc could reconcile their differences and get back together.

Frequency and the crew had CMAX design a name for the team and it came up with F.R.E.A.K.S. which stood for Federal Response Enforcement Against Kid Sex. The guys just cut it short and called themselves Freaks. They all liked it and laughed about it. Agent Layrock went to his office and came back with their first assignment.

Mr. White sat in his new home and looked around his scenic paradise. He had contacted Ms. Bobbie and GayMack in South America. The Two were healing and would be back in business before long. Madame had given birth to twin boys and she was doing fine. The word on the street was that Big Trouble was aware of the children and he was going after them.

Mr. White had cashed out all of his money from the Clique. He had made a considerable amount and was on cloud nine. He had not a care in the world and decided to go out for lunch. He went to a quaint little restaurant and had a Martini and Oysters Rockefeller. White sat and watched one of the patrons at the bar messing with one of the very young patrons at the restaurant. The man was loud, drunk, and out of control. The staff at the restaurant apologized profusely to the young lady who got her food and left.

The man came to the bar and asked for his bill. He gave the bartender his credit card and the bartender went to run the transaction. White finished his last oyster and was about to drink his martini when he saw the bartender come back to the gentleman and give him his receipt.

The man looked really puzzled and said out loud, "What do you mean I've been FREAKED?"

Mr. White damn near choked as he quickly swallowed his Martini and left more than enough money to pay for his bill. White jumped into his car and sped off., wondering when it would be his turn to be freaked.

The End

About
Ronnie D. Johnson

Nickname: RonnRamm

At forty-two, Ronnie D. Johnson has had a many titles added to his name - not all of them good, but the experiences outweigh the persona. He started his career out as a teenager in the US Navy aboard the super carrier John F. Kennedy. After a four year career onboard the ship, he ended his enlistment and return to his home in Memphis, Tn. He started to pursue a career in music while working for ADT Security Company. While working for ADT , Ronnie found a passion for computers and started to develop his skills using technology as his focal point. After leaving ADT, Ronnie acquired a position with the City of Memphis Police Department. Ronnie used his amazing skills of technology and his uncanny knack to finish what he started to propel himself to the upper level of the department that he was assigned to.

After leaving the police dept. Ronnie put together a fictional persona that he made up loosely based on himself. "Frequency Hunter" would be Ronnie's alternate ego with an unlimited potential of growth and depth. Frequency Hunter is a mix between Microsoft (Bill Gates), who he greatly respects with a touch of MacGyver and a Navy Seal. As Ronnie life progressed his quest to bring "Frequency Hunter" to print began. After starting a successful business, working a full time job, plus dealing with the day to day antics of his two gorgeous children (Eboni and Ronnie Jr). Ronnie D. Johnson has brought to print a multitude of stories that will entice your passion to read.